Soul Siphon

Book One of the Vengeance Doctrine
A Novel by James Harrington

Soul Siphon

ISBN: 978-0692608449
First Printing: April 2016
Cover Art:
Jabari Weathers
Editing:
Meghan Harrington
Eric Klingenberg
Copyright © 2016, James Harrington
Illustration © 2016, Jabari Weathers
Printed and Bound in the USA

I

"Nurse, what happened?"

"I don't know, Doctor. He just started convulsing. We were monitoring him after his skin became discolored, and then he flat-lined."

Corban McConnell felt his body slipping away and was powerless to stop it. He tried to scream, but Adramelech would not allow him enough control over his own muscles to do it. He was trapped in a cage in his own mind, one that he could not escape from. All he could do was sit and watch helplessly as the demon destroyed his world.

Corban could feel a burning sensation in his chest where the crucifix that his mother gave him used to reside. It had been removed when he had been committed, but the scar from where it was, remained. When Adramelech possessed him, it felt as though someone had cast the crucifix into a fireplace and allowed it to get red hot before placing it around his neck.

The blessed artifact had kept Adramelech at bay, but it eventually began to cause him pain. The doctors had long since removed it, fearing that he could use the chain to harm himself. It was the final nail in his proverbial coffin.

Corban had been cursed with the demon for almost a year and it had been slowly and painfully gnawing away at him. His stomach was so tight that he had not been able to eat much in months. He was emaciated and covered in scars from head to toe, his face bearing the worst of it. The demon had forced him to abuse himself and those around him in every way physically possible. He had been forced to alienate the ones he cared for the most for their own safety and allow himself to be locked away in a safe room at

Soul Siphon

Mclean Hospital. He spent the last few weeks restrained to a hospital bed while doctors wired him with monitors and probes. His dark brown hair had been shaved down to little more than stubble to prevent him from ripping it out.

He was aware that his mental state was continuing to deteriorate. It would only be a matter of time until Adramelech gained full control and was able to cause his organs to rupture. He was soon transferred to Massachusetts General Hospital to deal with his injuries. He didn't really have the consciousness to care about the difference of scenery. He was too busy fighting the entity within to even acknowledge the new doctors that were looking after him.

Corban wasn't angry at them for his suffering, they were doing their best, but what he was dealing with, no medical science could save him from. There was nothing any mortal could do to stop Adramelech.

"Get me a defibrillator, STAT!"

Corban watched one of the nurses quickly pull a small cart over with a pair of pads resting on top of them. Another nurse began chest compressions while a third pumped oxygen into him with an Ambu bag. The group ignored the sounds of the machines around them as they went to work in a futile attempt to save their patient's life.

Doctor Morgan grabbed the pads and applied them to Corban's chest, "Device charging now..."

The doctor waited a moment for the defibrillator to charge. Corban braced himself as he listened to the high-pitched sound of the electricity powering up as the device came to life. When the indicator on the defibrillator turned red, the doctor returned his attention to Corban, "Everybody, clear!"

The surgical team backed away as the doctor began defibrillation, "200J..."

Soul Siphon

Corban's lifeless body convulsed as the electricity flowed through it. Once the system turned off, the group began CPR again. Every alarm was still sounding off, indicating that he was still flatlined. The monitoring nurse shook her head as she checked Corban for any response, "No pulse."

"What's going on in there?"

Doctor Morgan had been with Corban since he was transferred. He knew that Doctor Morgan had read the report on the events surrounding Corban's transfer and was sure that the whole case had him perplexed. The failed medical treatments which had both therapists and doctors alike baffled were bad enough, but then his psychological report also mentioned an exorcism that had somehow made his condition worse. He didn't know if the doctor was a believer or not but he somehow doubted it.

Adramelech had allowed him to live through each of these experiences while keeping him in a comatose state. He couldn't react, speak, or move but he could see and feel as that was all that the demon would allow. It was as close to Hell as he'd ever been.

Doctor Morgan's voice appeared again as Corban tried to shut everything out, "Again, 200J."

"Everybody, clear!"

It was the same as the previous attempt. Corban's body convulsed but did not respond. He was not coming out of it.

Finally, Doctor Morgan made the call to move him, "No good, get him to OR 2! Page the oncall surgeon."

The lead surgeon, Doctor Teach met Doctor Morgan in the surgical prep room as his team rushed to get Corban ready. He could hear them talking from the next room. Doctor Teach's voice had a detectable level of concern, "Status?"

Soul Siphon

"We've been administering CPR since he flat lined."

"How long?"

"Two minutes."

"All right, once we're in, let's get him on the table."

"Immediately, doctor."

As Corban's bed was wheeled into OR 2, the surgeon immediately went to work, prepping him for surgery. His body began to tremble as even more alarms went off. Doctor Teach knew that he was running out of time, "There's blood coming out of his mouth. He's most likely suffering from internal hemorrhaging. We need to get in there now or we're going to lose him."

Corban fought to regain some control and closed his eyes as he heard the machines nearby begin to beep in alarm. His head turned to the side and his world went completely blank. At that moment, all doubt was banished from his mind. Death was inevitable. *Father… into your hands, I commend my spirit.*

Adramelech cackled in the back of his mind, "He can't save you now, no one can! You are mine and you always will be!"

You can't have my soul, Adramelech. You've destroyed my body, but that's all you'll ever take. You… will lose!

"Small words… even the priest who tried to exorcise me failed and he is a man of faith. You have always been a man of doubt. What do you possibly think you can do now?"

In a desperate attempt to shut the demon out, Corban thought back to his last day with his girlfriend, Janine. He remembered how her long blonde hair blew in the breeze as she stepped out of his jeep. It was a very bittersweet memory.

Soul Siphon

The last few months of their relationship had been rocky. They both went to college in different places which put considerable strain on their relationship. In hindsight, that was probably a good thing for them both. Corban would not need to worry about her as much as she would have an easier time moving on. In his heart, he'd known that their relationship would not have survived more than a few months anyway.

A beep on the wall caused Corban to snap back into reality. He was back on the operating table in Mass General's Division of Trauma. Though not conscious, he was fully aware of what was happening. Adramelech would not allow him to miss a minute of the pain. Even the medications that were being pumped through his body could not keep the demon at bay.

I'm sorry Janine, Corban thought to himself. *I have to break my promise. I can't be there anymore. I hope you have a wonderful life...*

Adramelech cackled in his mind, "That's it, let her go. There is no escape for you now. Let go of all you hold dear and submit."

That's what you think I'm doing? You've spent this much time in my head and you still have no clue.

"What other choice is there? It'll only hurt more by holding onto them."

But it keeps you from winning. Giving up what makes me who I am would be to submit to you.

You already have.

Not yet, just you watch.

Corban knew exactly what he had to do. He dreaded it but knew that Adramelech would never let him be at peace as long as the demon lurked in his mind. As long as the demon was there, he would forever be a slave. He pulled together what little mental fortitude he had left and blocked out Adramelech one last time. He had regained control of his body just long enough to release himself. He had to act quickly as this was the only chance he'd get. *Just one last push.*

Corban appreciated everything that the doctors were doing, but he knew that his body was broken. Even if he wanted to remain, he knew that it was no longer an option. If he didn't vacate, Adramelech would have a chance to regain control.

As Corban braced himself, he could feel the sense of nervousness in his mind. Adramelech reached out to him, "Wait... wait, if you try to cast me out, you'll die too. We've become too intertwined for you to survive."

I know that. I'm not trying to cast you out. I'm denying you your prize.

"You'll lose everything."

No other choice.

"There is always another choice."

Not interested.

"Janine and your mother will be hurt."

I know that...

"Wait, listen to me!"

No, I'm done with having you in my head! The game is over!

Adramelech cried out in panic, "No!"

Go back to Hell!

Corban braced himself for the coming shock to his system. No doubt it was going to be painful, but it couldn't possibly be worse than what he had already experienced. He was spent and nothing that happened now was going to faze him.

At that moment, as the doctor worked, Corban's eyes shot open and a look of distress appeared on his face, startling Doctor Morgan, "Is he sedated?"

Soul Siphon

The anesthesiologist eyed her panels and turned back to the surgeon, "Yes, he's under general anesthesia and everything looks stable on my end. I don't understand, what's happening should not be possible!"

"Increase his dosage."

"I can't, it's at the maximum. If I increase the dosage it could do irreparable damage!"

"Doctor..."

Before the surgeon could continue, Corban smiled at the lights above him. He was unable to speak with the tube down his throat, but he still managed to smile widely. *The game is over, Adramelech! You've lost, now go back to Hell!*

At that moment, Corban's eyes closed forever. His body went pale. As his world blurred out, he could hear the screams of the scanners hooked up to his body, trying to find any sign of life. It sounded as though they were in a panic.

The surgical team went frantic as they went to work in an attempt to save his life. Yet even amidst the chaos, Corban was able to take solace in the fact that he had won. He had denied Adramelech his prize but would now face the consequences for doing so.

An hour later, it was all over. The surgical team had done everything that they could, but his body was not responding. Doctor Teach lowered his eyes as he was finally forced to admit defeat, "He's gone."

As the group backed away from Corban's body, Doctor Teach checked the clock on the wall, "Note the time of death, 8:53 PM."

Doctor Morgan looked over the mess of equipment and blood, "All right, let's get cleaned up here... I've got some bad news to deliver."

The surgical team had lost patients before. It was something that came with the job, but it never got easier. There was nothing more they could do. As the nurses went to work clearing out the equipment, the surgeon braced himself to give Corban's loved ones the bad news. As a high-risk surgeon, he'd had to deliver this news before, and it was always the part of the job that he hated the most.

As they cleaned up, the anesthesiologist had a perplexed look on her face, "How could he have come out of that?"

Doctor Teach didn't have an answer for her. He'd never seen anything like that before, "I have no idea. I can't explain it, but he almost looked like he'd just won a fight."

"Whatever it was... he actually seemed happy about it."

Doctor Morgan left the OR, got cleaned up and headed out to the waiting room where Corban's mother had been sitting with Janine for hours, waiting for news. It was late and the lights in the waiting room were dim. The lighting mixed with the plain colors of the walls provided anyone in the room a rather calm feeling. The dim light also provided the perfect vale for a pair of dark figures that stood in the corner, one male, and one female. Both were paying close attention to the scene that was about to unfold with Corban's family. The male figure studied the facial expressions of Corban's mother and Janine while the female one appeared to be completely disinterested. She preferred to hang back, leaning on the wall.

The quiet was quickly interrupted when doors to the OR slowly parted and the two doctors appeared at the entrance. The figures watched intently as Corban's mother stood up with Janine holding her by the arm,

Soul Siphon

"Well Doctor, did everything go okay? How is he? When can we see him?"

An apologetic look appeared on Doctor Morgan's face as he shook his head, "I'm sorry…"

Corban's mother went completely pale, "What? What are… no…"

Doctor Teach hesitantly took over, "I'm afraid he didn't survive the procedure."

The older woman looked away as tears streamed down her cheek, "Oh God… please not him. No… my baby…"

Janine's eyes filled with tears, "No it can't be true! He's stronger than that… don't you dare tell me he's gone."

Doctor Morgan opened his mouth to speak, knowing that nothing he could say would make this easier, but Janine cut him off, "Don't you dare… he can't be gone! It's not true!"

Janine buried her head in her hands and sobbed as Corban's mother looked up at Doctor Teach, tears continuing to flow from her eyes, "What happened?"

"I'm afraid we don't really know, we were working to repair the hemorrhage and he was responding really well but then he suddenly regained consciousness. He looked up with a big smile on his face and then became lifeless. We have no idea how it happened. Our instruments were finely tuned before the procedure and our anesthesiologist double checked just to make sure. All attempts to resuscitate him failed. It's like he didn't want to be brought back."

The female figure stepped forward and studied Corban's mother. Though she still looked pale and was about to get sick, a small feeling of relief comforted her as she realized what had happened. She was barely able to speak and her words were little more than a whisper, but everyone was able to hear her, "He beat it... it cost him his life, but he freed himself of that... thing inside of him."

Doctor Teach rubbed his hands together gently as spoke to Corban's mother, "I'm really sorry that everything turned out this way. We do have on-sight counselors that are trained to help your loss... I could arrange for one to come by if you'd like to speak with them?"

Grief counselors. The female figure thought to herself. *As if they'd do any good here.*

"Mary, watch the younger woman." The male figure said quietly to the female. "She'd known Corban since childhood and loved him for almost that long. Their relationship may have been on the rocks, but she still cared deeply for him."

Mary moved closer, while careful to remain in the shadows, "Why all this interest in her, Mike?"

"I'll explain later, for now, she's our best bet to learn more about Corban."

From her vantage point, Mary could see Janine's face. Though in pain herself, Janine was doing the best she could to comfort Corban's mother and remain strong. She hugged the older woman and rubbed her arms, knowing that as bad as she felt, his mother had lost the last of her family.

Mary watched as Janine turned to the doctor. She was about to say something when Corban's mother finally fought through her own pain and spoke up, "Did he suffer?"

It looked like Doctor Morgan was doing the best he could to sound certain, but the quiver in his voice made his words harder to believe, "No, I don't believe so. He was heavily sedated, so it's unlikely that he felt anything. As for the rest... well his suffering is over now."

"He doesn't know that," Mary scoffed. "How could he?"

"Shh!" Mike scolded, trying to listen in.

Mary noticed a smile appear on his face as Corban's mother collapsed back into Janine's arms, "There was a lot of fight in that one. A lot of fight... this is very interesting."

"It's not every mortal human that can stand up to a demon as fierce as Adramelech," Mary agreed. "Still, I think this is a really bad idea. He's a possession victim. You remember what's happened every other time, yeah?"

"This time will be different, I can feel it. Yes, I think he'll do nicely."

"You really came out of nowhere after four months of hiding to show me this? Did I really have to be here?"

"Yes. You've been with me the longest. I want your opinion."

"Is that really what you want, or do you just want to hear me agree with you?"

"When has that ever happened?"

"Rarely."

"So?"

Mary sighed, she knew that he was going to do whatever he wanted regardless of what she said, but at least she could voice her concerns, "He's defiant, yeah? Short-sighted, and extremely jovial with the people around him. Those aren't the qualities we need. Not to mention his powers could be dangerous! We have no idea what he'll become!"

"I seem to recall thinking the same thing about you when I first pieced you back together, but you assured me that you wouldn't disappoint, and in over a hundred years, you never have."

"That's different."

Soul Siphon

"Is it really?"

Mary did not respond. She lowered her eyes and returned to her corner, defeated. Nothing she said was going to change Mike's mind.

Mike's smile widened as he turned his attention back to Corban's family, "Yes… Yes, I think he'll do perfectly."

II

St. Bridget's in Framingham was bustling with activity in preparation for Corban's funeral. His casket sat in the middle of the center aisle of the large stone church. Friends and family came by to pay their respects.

It was a solemn occasion, but Janine and his mother had done their best to try to spruce things up as much as possible, knowing that Corban would have wanted that. The procession proceeded into the church with the priest at the end. The priest stopped in front of the casket, whispered a quick prayer over Corban, and then proceeded to the podium. He thanked everyone in attendance before delivering the opening blessing.

Mike and Mary hid in the shadows at the back of the Church. Mike kept his eyes locked on the crucifix above the altar. He felt as though he were facing down an old friend he hadn't seen in years.

Mary followed his gaze with concern, "You seem uncomfortable, yeah?"

"Do I?"

"You kind of have a look of death on your face."

"Well, it is a funeral."

The expression on Mary's face told him that she wasn't buying it, "Uh huh..."

Mike ignored her. He was too focused on the people in the church, particularly Corban's girlfriend and mother to bother with Mary's interrogation. He could sense their thoughts and feelings. After briefly scanning the room, he became particularly interested in Janine's.

The smell of burning incense was sharp in Janine's nose as she listened to the priest give his sermon, "It is truly a tragic occasion when one so young is taken. When there are still chapters to be written and stories that will never be told..."

Mike watched as Janine turned away and tried to block out the words. He could see that this was torture for her. At several points, she looked towards the exit as though feeling the urge to flee the church, especially when the melodic psalms played. She bit her lip and bore the grief.

Mike didn't even need to sense what she was thinking, her body language was telling him exactly what he needed to know; *a celebration of life? Is that what they say a funeral is supposed to be? If that's the case, why are we focusing on the tragedy of his death? Why aren't we talking about all the great things he did?*

He watched as she looked at all the blotchy red faces and wet eyes. *Look at all of these people. They should hear about what he was like in life and more than just a eulogy!*

Mike smiled from the back of the room, "There's a lot of disdain for the time-honored order of things in that one."

"Which one?"

"Our subject's girlfriend."

"You were just as focused on her in the hospital. Why are you so interested in her?"

"You can tell a lot about people by the company they keep, especially the ones they're close to. Our subject spent a lot of time with that girl. It merits examination."

Mary shrugged, "If you say so."

Mike pointed at Janine she closed her eyes sat down, "Look at her. She wants to cry out, to let someone in the church know the pain she felt, but it isn't possible now. Pain is such a difficult emotion to describe. They all feel the same way, yet I doubt any of them would understand."

It wasn't a lengthy ceremony, which is exactly how Corban would have wanted it. The priest gave a fairly typical sermon about hope and remembering that Corban was going to a better place. It was a nice sentiment, though Janine wasn't sure she believed it after what she'd seen him live through.

As the mass concluded, the priest came in to deliver the final blessing before dismissing the precession. Unlike most funerals, Corban wasn't to be taken out by pallbearers. Instead, the undertaker would transport his body out to the facility where he would be cremated.

As preparations were made for transport, the funeral procession moved to John Harvard's for a little impromptu celebration of his life. As preparations were being made, Janine sat next to his casket, alone. She didn't want to leave him alone.

"You should be out with your friends at the party."

Janine looked up to see Corban's mother smiling at her through bloodshot eyes, "I know… I just didn't want him to be alone…"

Mrs. McConnell sat down next to Janine and put her arm around her, "He's in a better place now and I'm sure he's at peace."

Janine frowned, "I know."

"Go on, I'll stay with him."

Mike followed Corban's body as it was taken to a crematory. He remained in the shadows as it was moved to a back room and transferred into a special box to undergo the process of cremation. The room was kept dark and quiet while the preparations outside were made.

Once the caretakers left the room, Mike stepped out of the shadows and slowly circled the box for a moment, "This is not a fitting end for someone such as yourself. No, I would have you accomplish more before you go to your rest."

He opened the lid of the box and looked in at Corban's face. Corban was pale and his skin looked rubbery, but there was an air of peace about his features. Mike almost regretted disturbing him as he placed his right hand on Corban's forehead and went to work.

Mike breathed deeply for a moment and focused as he spoke in little more than a whisper, "Expergisci…"

A sharp pain flowed through Corban's body as his soul was forced to return to its previous dwelling. His heart began pumping blood through his veins. His skin, which had gone pale from a large amount of blood loss, returned to its normal color. However, his hair grew back to its original length and slowly faded from dark brown to white. It almost seemed like his skin drew the color out of his hair. As the color spread to his chest, his lungs animated, he slowly began to breathe, and his consciousness returned. His eyes shot open, revealing complete darkness where his pupils used to be. It was as though his eyes had been replaced by black marbles. There was no life in them at all.

Corban slowly began to sit up. His eyes fully opened and he began to scan the room to figure out what had happened, "What… wh…"

Mike placed his hand on Corban's shoulder, trying to slow him down a little, "Easy now, easy my boy. Your body is in a mild state of shock. I know it's unsettling, but it will pass. You'll be okay."

Soul Siphon

Corban's breathing increased as though he were incredibly stressed out. Whatever was happening, clearly wasn't supposed to be. He looked at Mike accusingly, "What have you done to me?"

"Given you back that which was wrongfully taken from you."

"You mean you…"

Mike nodded, "Yes, I've brought you back from the land of the dead."

Corban climbed out of the box that he'd been placed in, and awkwardly stumbled as his feet struggled to remember how to walk. He looked around the room with his newly regenerated eyes, searching for a mirror. He found one resting on a nearby table and picked it up. Like all else in the room, it was sterile and lacking in detail, but it suited his needs.

Corban's eyes widened as he barely recognized the figure looking back at him. He was more demon than human now. His hair and eyes were nothing like they had been. He dropped the mirror and grabbed Mike by the collar of his shirt, forcing him to the light, "Who are you, an ally of Adramelech?"

"No, not at all. Quite the opposite in fact."

"Why did you bring me back? Why couldn't you let me remain at peace? What… what gives you the right? You have to put me back!"

"Calm down."

"No, you don't understand! He'll find me now!"

Mike appeared mildly irritated, as though he'd been through this exact scene several times. Like Corban, he had white hair, but it was matched by a white beard. He walked with a limp and kept a cane at his side that black with white ivory at the top that had been carved into the head of a cherub.

He spoke with an almost grandfatherly tone that was calm and reassuring, "The world still needs you,

Corban. Don't worry about Adramelech. His powers will soon be infinitesimal compared to yours. He won't be able to find you. I promise."

"My powers?"

"Yes, it'll take time for you to realize and figure out how to wield them but when you do…"

Corban's hands found their way to his temples. He was struggling to come to terms with what was going on. The memories of what happened at the hospital came flooding back. However, there were no memories after that. His mind was totally blank.

Anger overtook his senses. He grabbed a scalpel off the table next to him, gripped Mike's collar even tighter, and pressed the sharp end against his throat, "Who are you?"

Mike moved his lips, about to answer when Corban felt a sudden blunt sensation on the back of his head. He became aware of another person in the room with them just as his world went black.

Mary lowered her dagger as she gave Mike a scornful stare, "I told you this was a bad idea, Mike! You're risking all of our lives here."

"It matters not," Mike replied. "He'll come around just like you did, Ripper."

"How many times do I have to ask you to stop calling me that?"

"Oh yes, excuse me, Mary."

Mike pushed Corban on to her shoulder, "Well would you mind carrying him?"

Mary grimaced, "As if you're going to give me a choice? The mighty general, now having someone else do his work."

"Oh stop. You know I can't blow my cover if I'm to remain here, at least not now when we're so exposed."

"Yeah, yeah, so you keep saying. I think you're just being lazy... fine... let's go."

"Cor...ban..." A dark voice called out to him.

Corban found himself in a dark void as chills flowed down his spine, "What... where are you?"

"Not far now."

"What do you want?"

The voice became a growl as it responded, "You."

Corban's eyes shot opened and he gasped for air. The back of his head throbbed with a pulsing pain from where he'd been hit. His vision was blurred and it took him a moment to adjust. All he knew was that he was indoors. There was not a light on anywhere in the room that would reveal any more detail than that. It was slightly chilly but well within tolerance.

Corban rubbed his head as his eyes compensated for the darkness. *What happened... where am I?*

Corban's eyes widened as he remembered his encounter with the mysterious figures. He sucked down a few deep breaths and pressed his hand against his chest. To his terror, his heart was beating. He was alive and he shouldn't be *No...*

His eyes were unable to completely compensate, yet somehow Corban was able to find his way to the door. The ground was smooth tile and was cold against his bare feet as he stumbled forward. He was dressed in a pair of black sweatpants and a t-shirt, the origins of which were a mystery, but it was not important at that moment. He gently leaned himself against the wall next to the door, scared to death of what might be waiting for him on the other side. There was no handle; it appeared to be a sliding door that was wedged shut.

Soul Siphon

Corban put his shoulder into it and pushed. He was careful not to apply too much force as he didn't want to make any noise that could alert his captors to his presence. The door immediately gave way and slid slowly open.

A ray of light appeared on the other side which grew thicker as the door slid open. Whatever horrors awaited Corban were about to reveal themselves. On the other side, he heard voices accompanied by the sound of light-hearted laughter. Oddly, one of the voices sounded like that of a child, "I'm telling you, it was a long pass down the field! If you add the incline and decline, the pass was a hundred yards!"

Another sounded foreign but Corban couldn't put his finger on where, "Sounds like you're worried about zem."

"No way, we're not even playing the Packers this year!"

"You could always catch zem in ze Superbowl. Vat zen?"

"Then we'll still kick their asses! Their quarterback has been playing like crap recently. I'm not worried about it!"

Corban released his breath and felt his stomach unclench. These didn't sound like what he'd expect to hear from hardened criminals. He pushed the door open the rest of the way and stumbled into the next room, a little more confident that he wasn't in any danger.

Corban found himself in a large living room. It was completely windowless and its furnishings were very Spartan. The room was reminiscent of a basement man-cave that Corban had seen at one of his friend's houses. There were only a few places to sit, a single TV off to one side, and a few pieces of equipment that looked like what you'd find at a local gym or dojo, including wooden weapons used for sparring. He guessed this was used for training of some kind.

Then he saw them, four normal looking people sitting around talking. They were all dressed in dark clothing much like his own. Their outfits were either all black or black and an almost navy blue. If he'd see someone dressed like that out on the street, he wouldn't have thought twice about it. For the most part, they were normal street clothes. However, having them all dressed so similarly almost made them look like a team or… or a gang.

Chills traveled down Corban's spine as the possibilities hit him. Had he just fallen in with some group of criminal thugs? What did they want of him? Were these people conscripted the same way he was?

He listened in to their conversation as he slowly moved towards them, careful not to make himself known before he was ready. He positioned his feet carefully to make sure that no noise was made as he moved closer. He wanted to hear more about them before making the decision to either join them or to try to make a break for the door.

One of the four members of the group was a child of no more than 7 or 8 years old. His hair was black and, like Corban's, so were his eyes. His skin was somewhat darker, possibly of southern European origin and he had a devious smile on his face. There was something odd about this child. His physical features were young but the look on his face and the way he spoke was indicative of someone much older, "No, dumbass. The one I got last week was the first to actually put up a decent fight. That bastard withered a lot slower than any of my others. It was like he had more life energy than he should have and forced it against me!"

Soul Siphon

The tallest man, a burly fellow with a foreign accent that was as thick as his graying beard stood next to Johnny. Though he only appeared to be about ten to fifteen years older than Corban, his hair was an iron gray. His physique was somewhat of an enigma; his rolled-up sleeves revealed tight, well-toned muscles in his arms that were offset by a fairly large gut.

Corban noticed a black and gold patch on his arm that looked like something either a police officer or a soldier would wear. Was this guy ex-military? His sharp features and the scar over his eye told the story of someone who had seen more than his fair share of action, but Corban couldn't be certain.

He smiled as he looked at the child, "Johnny is losing touch, I think. Maybe Johnny need more practice?"

"Oh fuck off Vlad, like you'd have done any better? What happened to your…"

"Ahem!" A voice cut in from the side of the room.

The hair on the back of Corban's neck stood up and chills shot down his spine when he realized that he'd been caught. There was a dark figure over in the opposite corner that had been watching him since he entered the room, "Am I the only one who noticed that our guest has finally decided to join us?"

Corban froze. He had not even noticed that she was there. How could he have? She was little more than a black on black shadow against the wall. *Oh shit!*

Even after discovering that she was there, she was impossible to see until she moved. The lack of lighting where she stood cloaked every feature except the curvature of her form. She was little more than a black figure, but as she moved, the nearby light shined on her features. She was slender with extremely fair

Soul Siphon

skin and bright red hair that was long enough to reach below her shoulder blades and was brushed back to stay out of her face. She had very light freckles that seemed to congregate on her cheekbones and nose just below her eyes. Despite her scowl, the edges of her lips were curved in a way that she almost always had a slight smile on her face. When her lips curled, they caused a small fold in the philtrum under her nose. She was strikingly pretty, even with a disgusted look on her face.

She was as unconventional in her appearance as women came. It was something that Corban found attractive, but he was careful to keep his staring brief, certain that it would piss her off. He got the feeling that being on her bad side would not be good for his health.

As the mystery woman got to her feet, she made no sound on the floor. The expression on her face became nearly emotionless, but the level of scorn in her sapphire eyes was so potent that it was almost tangible.

She circled Corban like a shark circling its prey before striking, "Thought you could get the jump on us, yeah? Thought someone wouldn't notice you standing there?"

Corban was surprised by her brogue. She was Irish, probably from the southern area. She walked slowly over to him as the other guys turned their attention away from what they had been doing.

Corban froze up, unsure how to respond, "No... I just... well, I didn't know what to expect. I thought it was a good idea..."

"... to size us up, yeah?"

"N... no, I mean... what I mean is..."

The woman scoffed and turned away as another voice from behind spoke up, "That's enough, Mary. You've had your fun."

The old man that he had met the first time appeared at the door. Unlike the others, this man was dressed in all white. He smiled as he spoke, "Don't mind Mary, she's always been abrasive like that."

Corban backed away defensively, "You? Why have you brought me here? What do you want? Who are you people?"

An inundated look appeared on Johnny's face, "Lots of questions from this one."

"Vas Johnny any different ven he joined team?" Vlad asked.

The man approached Corban with a slight limp, smiled, and opened his hands as a gesture that he intended Corban no harm, "Allow me to introduce myself. My name is Michael. I am the leader of this group."

Corban nodded but remained in a defensive stance, "My… my name..."

"I must have hit him harder than I thought," Mary said as she returned to her seat over in the far corner. "His name is Corban McConnell."

She turned and looked at him, "Welcome to your new existence. Hopefully, it'll be as productive and fulfilling as your old one.... as long as you stay out of the way."

"What does that mean?"

Vlad approached him and mustered up as warm a smile as he could manage, "Mary means zat ve all have new identities for ourselves in our new lives. Ve're not the people ve vere."

"New lives… what?"

"Only the people here will know you by your true identity," Mike replied. "I'm sorry to say this, but

Soul Siphon

you were brought back for a purpose. Your life as you knew it is a thing of history now. As far as the world is concerned, Corban McConnell has been cremated and is long gone. His life will enter the history of time. You will now have a new purpose."

Corban's breathing rapidly increased as he processed what Mike was telling him, "No... that can't be true, it can't be! You're telling me that I was brought back from the dead? That now I'm expected to just forget about everyone I know and love? Are you kidding me?"

"I'm afraid not. What's the last thing that you remember?"

Corban thought for a moment. The last thing he remembered was the demon screaming in his ear as his body died on the operating room table and then waking up in the crematorium. His breathing quivered as he responded, "Adramelech... He had control over me. He's been in my head for months. I was trying to fight him off and... and..."

"And you shut down your autonomic functions to prevent him from being able to take over your body or claim your soul as a prize."

"That's incredible! None of the others were able to do that!" Johnny chimed in.

"Others?"

Michael smiled nervously and spoke quickly, seemingly trying to avoid the question, "Corban, meet Johnny."

Corban turned to the boy who had an impressed look on his face, "Hey there, kid."

"Kid?" Johnny said in an angry tone. "Man, who the fuck you calling a kid?"

"Vait... possession victim?" Vlad cut in. "Mike brought a possession victim here? You've gone crazy, no?"

Soul Siphon

Corban looked at him with confusion, "What's wrong?"

"Michael did not tell you, did he?"

The final member of the team stepped forward, out of the kitchen and spoke up from behind Corban's back, "When he brings you back, you gain powers based on how you were killed."

Corban hadn't seen her until now. She had been working on something in the next room over, listening in as the others introduced themselves. She stepped forward, barely making a sound on the floor as she walked.

This woman was extremely thin, Asian, and fairly short but had an athletic build about her. Her long black hair had brown highlights and was done up in a bun on the back of her head. Like Vlad and Mary, her accent made it clear that she was not from the area. Michael had most likely brought her over from the Far East.

Michael turned and extended a hand to her, beckoning her from the kitchen, "Thank you Lihua, I was just about to get to that."

Corban felt his face heat up. He was frustrated and ready to explode. It didn't help that everyone was only giving him half-answers, "Look, can someone please tell me what the fuck is going on here? I don't know where I am or why I'm here! Someone give me a straight answer, or I'm leaving!"

The way Mary's lips curled made Corban think that she was about to strike him, "And this is the guy Mike had to come out of 4 months of hiding to bring us. –Where you gonna go exactly? Who you gonna go see? Everyone thinks you're dead."

Chills traveled down Corban's spine that contrasted the heat in his cheeks. He was about to

Soul Siphon

respond, but Mary didn't seem interested and cut him off, "He brought you back to join our team."

Corban looked over at her as she pulled out a curved dagger and began sharpening it on a small stone nearby, "What team?"

"This team, we're a sort of group fighting for justice," Mike replied.

"What like a fucking superhero team? Do you guys all prance around in red spandex?"

Johnny smirked, "No not exactly."

"Like I said, start talking... or I'm leaving."

Mary shook her head and looked away as Mike continued, "Okay... well, the long and short of it is that I've collected these poor souls from all over the planet at different points in time. They're here because their desire for justice and vengeance was higher than most."

He turned and looked at Vlad, "This is Vladimir Pietrov. He joins us from Siberia when the whole area was under the oppressive heel of Josef Stalin."

"I vas member of KGB back zen, stationed at remote outpost vere I learned about secret experiments on alien life."

Corban raised his left eyebrow, not buying a word of Vlad's story, "Alien life?"

"Vat, you sink Roswell vas the only place veird sings happen? Mother Russia vas visited at least three years before."

"Yes, and Russia also put a man on the moon in fucking 1930, despite not having a single rocket capable of making the trip," Johnny chimed in.

"Zat vas just movie, yes? Zis is truth! I find out about vat zay vere doing and vas silenced."

"Silenced?" Corban asked.

"Ya, I vas on ze vay home fere much deserved vacation. I vas killed by sniper's bullet. Sere vas no reason for silencing me. I vas a patriot. I vould never do anything to harm country of birth."

Vlad walked over to a safe that was nailed to the back wall and pulled out an old bolt action rifle. It was fairly scuffed and definitely old. He caressed the rifle like he would have a lover, "Good old Mosin Nagant 91/30, nothing like Russian ingenuity! Thanks to zis old girl, I got back at Cossacks!"

Michael stepped forward, "Vladimir now has the ability to manipulate bullets and other metal projectiles, or would-be projectiles. He also has the eyesight of an eagle."

"Ya, I can make bullet go anyvere I vant now! I can shoot it and make it go anyvere! Zis Mosin already had better range than most American rifles, but now I can make it go even furzer!"

"Okay… what does that have to do with me?" Corban asked.

"He may be strong-willed, but he is certainly not the brightest of bulbs, is he?" Lihua chuckled.

Corban looked at her in anger, causing the smile to drop from her face, "My sincerest apologies… Allow me to explain; each of us has gained powers based on how we died. Vlad was shot, so now he can manipulate bullets, Johnny was starved to death by his stepmother, so now he makes anything he touches wither away and die."

Johnny smiled as he held up an apple, only for it to quickly go bad and turn to ash in his hand, "My stepmom hated me. My dad didn't see her bad side until after he married her and it was too late. She was a real bitch. She only cared about herself and what she could get out of people. She hated me because I was an obstacle to her sucking my father completely dry. After my father died, she didn't want to take care of

Soul Siphon

me, so she locked me in the basement until I starved to death."

That caught Corban off guard. He didn't think that he could feel sympathy for such an obnoxious individual, "My God, that's horrible!"

"Fuck yeah it was, but I got back at that bitch! Mike brought me back and once I realized what my powers were, I went after her. I made her wither to dust... slowly and enjoyed every scream, every plea for mercy, and every death grunt. When I was done, I spread her worthless remains in the sewer of that cheap dive of a strip club where she'd been working."

"Zat vas twenty-five years ago, no?" Vlad replied.

"Twenty-five years?" Corban asked.

"Ve don't age either, since ve're not really alive. I vas born August 12, 1925. Do I look like 90 year old?"

"Look, sound... smell!" Johnny replied snidely.

Lihua ignored them as she continued, "I was born in 1960 in China. When I was seventeen, I was raped by a street gang in southern Hong Kong. Not long after, I discovered that I was pregnant. When my father found out, he accused me of being a whore and threw me out of my home. Because he was a prominent person in the town, I was shunned."

Lihua clenched a fist as she spoke, "I suffered a miscarriage and died on the streets not long after from internal hemorrhaging. No one helped me. People walked by and looked at me like I was some disease-ridden yaojing."

"Yaojing?" Corban asked?

"Imp... demon if you will."

Corban didn't know what to say to that. These people had suffered truly horrible crimes that had resulted in the violent and painful ending of their lives.

How could he relate to these people? In his mind, he couldn't. Even commiserating with these people would be difficult. He appeared to be very uncomfortable and out of place as he replied, "Um... I'm sorry."

"Don't be, I am not looking for sympathy," Lihua replied calmly. "It happened and I cannot change that, but I took care of it. I took care of them."

"You killed the people who hurt you?"

"Almost every one of them... including my father. They all died for what they had done. Only one managed to escape my wrath."

"So one's still out there?"

Lihua frowned. It was clear that she didn't want to volunteer any more information, "Perhaps this story is best suited for another time."

"So..." Corban said slowly, being very cautious with his words. "What's your power then? You were assaulted and died on the street so..."

"I can lure anyone to me. My body produces different pheromones depending on my target. They become instantly fixated on me and once I draw them in, they are susceptible to my suggestions... including suggestions of suicide."

Corban nervously took a step back, "That so? Remind me never to piss you off."

"Do not worry," Lihua replied with a faint chuckle, "it does not seem to work on my comrades here, and believe me I have tried. So I doubt that I could harm you... at least when it comes to my powers."

At that point, Corban turned to Mary, "What about you, Mary? What's your story?"

"None of your fucking business is what it is, yeah?" Mary replied sternly, still not looking at him.

"I'm sorry?"

Mike smirked, "Yes… she doesn't open up much about her past. Only a few people really know what happened to her. If she wants you to know, I'm sure she'll eventually tell you.

"It's useless for us to dwell on the lives we have departed from. We're not those people anymore. They no longer exist," Mary hissed.

"Departed?" Corban asked in a shocked tone. "If you think that I'm just going to pretend that the people I care about don't exist anymore, you're out of your fucking mind! I'm not doing anything until I see them. I need to let them know that I'm okay!"

Lihua sighed, "That is impossible. You cannot go home again. The life you led is no longer your purpose. Your family believes that you are dead, and they will not even recognize you now. If you go..."

"To hell with that!" Corban replied, cutting her off. "I'm not fucking staying here and you can't make me! I didn't ask you to bring me back and you can't force me to stay here! I don't know what's going on and none of this makes any sense. I'm leaving!"

"Corban this is extremely ill-advised, please see reason. You can not…"

"Let him go," Mary replied. "Let's see if that Janine girl even recognizes him. –Go, see what happens!"

Corban pushed past Mike and Vlad, heading for the door. He stopped and gave Mary a quick nod before disappearing outside, "Thanks."

A frustrated look came over Lihua as he vanished from sight, "You know Mary, a little more tact from you might not have been uncalled for."

"Think so?"

"I do, Corban seems to have come from a loving family with many friends. You can call him a spoiled kid for that if you must, but he is being asked to give up a lot more than we ever were. You might try to remember that."

"Whatever."

Lihua rolled her eyes and went back to her room, fed up with Mary's attitude for the day. Vlad and Johnny turned to Mike, "Should ve go after him?"

Mike shook his head, "He has to find his own way. You know that."

Mary leaned back but kept her eyes fixed on the door. Her thoughts dwelled on her own past for a few moments. After contemplating Lihua's words, she released the air from her lungs and walked out of the room, "Oh fuck it."

III

Corban wandered out into the street. He was breathing irregularly and his chest hurt almost as much as his head did. He had no clue what had just happened, but he didn't care. The only thing he knew was that he had to go somewhere safe. He needed to go home.

The cool night air caressed his face as he tried to get his bearings. The building that he'd run from was an old warehouse. It was a large, unremarkable stone building that looked like it had been built during the last century and had been updated with two gray rolling steel doors. That didn't give him any clues. He turned onto a larger road with a sign on it. "Fay Street? Where the heck am I?"

At that moment, he saw a large signing hanging off the brick building across the street. It was in the shape of a coat of arms, painted green with gold lettering and a border, "J.J. Foley's… I'm in Southie? Oh great… of all places to be in the middle of the night with no car!"

Corban had been to J.J. Foley's before with a group of friends during the summer break. It was a favorite hangout for people who lived in the area, as well as students from nearby universities. Corban knew the area but being out there after everything had closed with no cell phone was a major problem.

At that moment, a loud roar was unleashed from an unseen source behind him. Corban whirled to see what was going on. A black Dodge Charger appeared out of the night and pulled up behind him. He didn't see where it came from and only noticed it when the lights turned on.

The sleek black car stopped next to Corban as the passenger side window rolled down, revealing an

Soul Siphon

annoyed looking Mary on the inside. The engine hummed as she beckoned to him, "Get in, I'll take you home."

Corban took a step back, "Get lost, I don't want your help!"

"All right, fine. Good luck getting around the streets of Southie at this time of night, yeah?"

As she was about to speed away, Corban embraced the reality of his situation; he wasn't getting anywhere on his own. He had no money and everyone thought that he was dead. Having no other choice, he stepped forward, and raised his hand, "Wait... all right, you win."

Corban opened the door and cautiously slipped onto the soft leather seats. He closed the door behind himself, quickly fastened his seatbelt, and turned to Mary, "Thanks."

"Whatever just keep quiet, yeah?"

Corban sat back as she revved the engine. The car was sleek, even on the inside. There was a large touch panel console in the middle with a map on it, and even the door handles lit up a gentle blue color. Where could she have gotten something this hot?

"So where does this Janine girl live?"

"Huh?"

Mary sighed as she sat back, maintaining the annoyed expression, "That's where you were going, wasn't it, to your girlfriend?"

"Well... yeah... but how did...?"

"So where does she live?" Mary interrupted, clearly disinterested in what he had to say.

Corban hesitated. Did he want to tell her? Giving her the address of someone he cared about could provide her with a hostage later if he refused to join them.

Soul Siphon

Mary picked up on his hesitation, "Look I don't care whether you join us or not. If you take off, I'm not going to hunt you or her down later. We're the good guys, yeah?"

Corban wasn't convinced. Mary released an impatient breath, "All right. either tell me where she lives or get the fuck out of my car and find your own way there."

"Weston, I can show you the way once we get out there."

"Weston it is then."

Mary hit the gas, causing the engine to roar, and the car took off down the road. The massive engine blazed like nothing he'd ever heard before. Buildings that had appeared clearly a second ago were now nothing more than blurs in the window.

A slight sense of panic came over Corban as the car whipped around each corner, heading for the highway, "Whoa, don't you think you ought to slow down in the middle of the city?"

"No."

"Well… this isn't really safe."

"I didn't ask your opinion."

"… All right."

Corban pressed himself against the seat as the charger turned onto Berkley Street and then quickly turned onto Commonwealth Avenue. Much to Corban's relief, they made it to Route 20 without incident, which they stayed on for a few minutes. It was lucky for them that it was so late at night, otherwise, there might have been traffic on the road.

Corban looked out the passenger window at the Charles River. He still hadn't come to terms with what was going on, and the roaring engine wasn't helping to break the awkward silence, "So we didn't really get an introduction earlier…"

No response.

"I'm Corban McConnell."

"I know."

"Well, I don't really know your name."

"Mike told you, Mary."

"That's it, just Mary? No last name, surname, family name... house name?"

"Nope."

"I somehow doubt that."

She didn't appear to care, "Not my problem."

"Oh come on…"

Mary remained silent for a few moments, her eyes fixated on the road. Corban watched her and waited for a response. Seeing that he wasn't going to accept her answer, she finally released a deep sigh and responded, "Fine, if it will shut you up. Depending on whom you ask my name is Marie Jeanette Kelly or Mary Jane Kelly."

"Whom I ask?"

"Different people call me different things depending on where you are," Mary replied.

"Which do you prefer?"

"Neither, just Mary."

"You seem pretty standoffish about your name. Are you famous or something?"

Mary hesitated for a moment, obviously reluctant to answer. A faintly sinister smile appeared on Corban's face as he spoke, "What, did you die on the Titanic or something and your power is having an icy personality?"

Mary clenched the wheel, keeping her fist in check. It looked like she was ready to strike him. Finally, she looked over with a serious expression in her eyes, "That's where this conversation ends."

Corban immediately turned his attention back to the window, afraid that she'd kick him out if he pressed her for any more information. His attempt to lighten the mood had failed and he wasn't even sure she'd say anything else if he asked, "Sorry."

"You should be."

Corban decided to keep quiet. He didn't want to push any more buttons. All he could do now was wait until they arrived in Weston.

Corban arrived at Janine's house about 20 minutes later. Relief poured over him as the uncomfortable trip came to an end. He stared motionless at the house out his window for a few moments.

Mary looked over at him, waiting impatiently to see what he'd do, "Are you going?"

"Yeah, thanks for the ride."

Mary didn't respond as Corban opened the door and climbed out. The moment he closed the door, the charger sped away into the night. It disappeared as quickly as it came. *Strange girl...*

Corban found himself alone in the darkness. He was filled with a sudden sense of dread as he slowly approached her home. It was as though a horrible specter waited for him on the other side of the door. His chest felt tight and he was having trouble breathing as a scene that was once comforting and even exciting to him had become something ominous and he did not like it.

His apprehension disappeared when a beautiful blonde girl opened the door and exited the house. A voice called after her, "Don't be home from the McConnell's too late!"

"Don't worry Mom, I just want to check on Mrs. McConnell, then I'll be back!"

Corban watched as she proceeded down the driveway to her car. Nothing looked out of the ordinary until she noticed a dark figure standing at the end of her driveway. She took a cautious step backward and a look of apprehension appeared on her face. Though the figure had made no threatening moves, something about it gave off a dark aura, "C… can I help you?"

Corban took a step closer to her, "Janine, it's me, I'm… I'm back!"

Janine's eyes narrowed as a chill traveled down her spine, "C... Corban?"

"Yes."

The darkness veiled Corban's face. He was too far away from the lights of the house for her to see him, "It sounds like you, but… Come closer, I can't see you."

As Corban stepped into the light, a look of sheer terror came over Janine's face. She gasped and stepped back, "What… you're not Corban! Who or what are you?"

"Huh? It is me, Corban!"

"Stay back, you're not Corban! Stop saying that!"

Corban became confused. Why was Janine acting like this? He held out his hand as though begging her to see him, "Janine, what are you talking about, it's me! Can't you tell?"

"No," Janine shrieked as tears flowed down her cheeks, "Corban is dead. I saw his body! I wish he were still alive, I really do, but he's not. You are not him, you may sound similar, but you look nothing like him. I don't know whose joke this is, but it's not funny. Whoever put you up to this can go to Hell! It's unbelievably cruel!"

"Janine…"

"Go away!" She screamed.

Soul Siphon

Corban shook his head, "I told you that I'd come back for you, that we'd see each other after the fall semester. I drove you home in my red jeep, remember? You loved the color…"

"Stalker!" She interrupted in an accusing tone. "Get out of here now, I'm calling the police!"

Without another word, Janine turned and ran into the house. Corban knew Janine's father, if she felt threatened, he would soon face the man's wrath. Given that he had access to firearms, Corban felt it best to beat a hasty retreat.

He ran back down the driveway as quickly as he could, but as he moved, his mind filled with questions; what exactly had just happened, why did she not recognize him, and more urgently, where was he going to go now? If he went to his mother's house, he'd probably experience the same reaction.

The moment he hit the street, he heard the familiar sound of a large engine. Once again, the charger appeared out of the darkness and the passenger door opened, "Get in."

"Why'd you come back?"

"I never left."

Corban nodded and jumped into the passenger seat. The car sped away before he even had the chance to completely close the door. He struggled to get himself settled as Mary picked up speed. Once he was settled, he slammed his fist on the side console and rubbed his forehead with his left hand.

"Satisfied?" Mary asked.

"Why didn't she recognize me?"

"Have you looked at yourself in the mirror lately? You're still you, but to any normal person, you can barely pass as a human. Your loved ones are not going to recognize you anymore. They're not supposed to. We can go out in public, but the people we used to know will now see us as though we were strangers."

Corban lowered his eyes, "I don't want this..."

"None of us do, it's not like we chose it, but the alternative is to return to our graves."

"I can't live like this... my family doesn't even know who I am. I... I'm alone."

Mary gave Corban a look of scorn like someone would give a bratty younger sibling. He could tell that she wanted to say something when he looked into her eyes. However, when she saw the look on his face, her features softened. Her scorn was replaced by a combination of annoyance and sympathy. She hesitantly placed a gentle hand on Corban's shoulder, "Look... okay, I know it's no comfort, but it does get easier as time goes on and you're not alone. Mike, Lihua, Johnny, Vlad... and I are all in this with you. We're a team, yeah?"

"But why... why would she act like that? She's usually more reasonable. I don't get it."

"Grief can do weird things. You probably startled her... like I startled Joe..."

"Joe?" Corban asked in surprise.

Mary lowered her eyes, "Yeah, he was a guy I was seeing for a while."

"Oh, I'm sorry. The same thing happened to you?"

"Yes."

At that moment, Corban put it together, "You were trying to spare me the pain that you went through, weren't you?"

Mary fell silent.

"Well thank you for trying at least," Corban replied.

Mary's face tightened up, "I didn't want you being exposed. We live in secret, in the shadows. If you got caught by the wrong people, it could be a problem for the rest of us, yeah?"

A faint smile appeared on Corban's face as a feeling of warmth entered his heart. He didn't believe the given explanation of her uncharacteristic act of compassion. The fact that she tried at all made him feel slightly better, "Well... thank you anyway."

Silence.

Corban could feel his face heat up as tears entered his eyes. The evidence was nearly irrefutable now. The life he knew was truly over now, "If I were to go see my mother, I take it that she would react the same way?"

"Probably..."

Corban wiped his eyes and sat back, breathing heavily, "So what now?"

"I'm taking you back unless there's anyone else you want to terrify?"

"I... I have to go check on her at least."

"Your mother?"

"Yes."

"You're serious, you didn't learn your lesson already?"

"I did... but I still have to make sure she's okay."

"I shouldn't do this."

"Please?" He asked in a pleading tone.

Mary sighed, "Ugh fine, but this is the last stop. After this, we're going back, yeah?"

"Deal."

"Wonderful, now where does she live?"

"Sudbury. I'll show you the way."

"All right."

Corban directed Mary to his mother's house. It was a large home at the end of a cul-de-sac. The

Soul Siphon

driveway was lit up by small solar-powered lights on either side.

Mary pulled up at the end of the driveway and shut off the lights. Corban opened his door, stepped out and stood at the end of the driveway. He looked up at the house but did not move.

Mary put the car in park, shut off the engine and got out. Corban could feel her looking at him, waiting for him to make any kind of move. She waited a few minutes before walking around the car and standing next to him on the other side, "Nice house."

"Yeah, it was."

"You going?"

"I don't know..."

"Well, you better make up your mind before someone sees us."

"You're right."

Corban took a step forward, then another, and another. Each step sent an icy chill down his spine. A shrill voice in the back of his head screamed at him to back away.

To his surprise, Mary stayed with him, "You're coming?"

"You look like you're either going to fall over or do something really stupid. So yes I am."

"Fair enough," Corban said, feeling oddly comforted by Mary's presence.

Corban got within fifty feet of the house before he froze in place. From where he was standing, the large bay window provided him an excellent view of the living room. Everything appeared to be illuminated by a lit fireplace on the far corner.

Shadows danced about the room as Corban and Mary peered into the large window. His mother was sitting on the small loveseat in front of the fireplace. Seated next to him was a man with short, graying hair and a cleanly shaven face. She had all but collapsed into his arms and was clearly crying.

Corban then saw his urn sitting on the coffee table in front of them. He went cold with shock as a tear escaped his left eye. Mary flanked him, standing less than a foot back from where he was. Her breaths became visible in the cool night air as she waited for Corban to come to terms with what he was seeing, "Who's the guy?"

Corban shrugged, "Jeremy, my mom's boyfriend. They've been seeing each other for a little while now, but I never thought it was serious."

"Maybe it got serious while you were possessed?"

"I doubt it."

"Could it be that it was serious and your mother just wasn't ready to tell you?"

"You think?"

"Did you tell your mother the moment you and Janine got serious?"

"No..."

Corban stared for a few more minutes. His skin broke out in goosebumps as his body temperature decreased, but he didn't care. The urge to burst into his house and announce that he was still alive was unbearable. More than anything he wanted to be back in that warm house one more time, but he knew what would happen if he did. Most likely it'd just be a repeat of what happened with Janine.

Mary kept her eyes focused on him. He could feel her eyes drilling into him but remained motionless. He still didn't know what to do.

"Are you going in?" Mary asked impatiently.

Corban didn't respond. He continued staring for a few more minutes. He could not take his eyes off of his mother as he thought back over his life. His feet felt like they were numb. He wasn't sure if it was from the cold or his own sadness. It was an odd feeling; he was the one that was technically dead, but he mourned the living, knowing that he no longer belonged amongst them.

He finally turned to Mary, "No."

"Are you sure?"

"What's the point?"

Mary shrugged, "There isn't one really. I was just asking."

"I needed to make sure that my mom was okay... at least she's not suffering alone."

"She won't be the same, but eventually she'll be okay. That's how it goes."

"Thanks."

"Yup."

"So... back to Southie?"

"Are you finally ready?"

"No, but I don't have another choice. I have nowhere else to go."

"If it makes you feel any better, I know the feeling."

Corban appreciated her effort, but he was a mere shell of himself. His family and friends were moving on with their lives while he was trapped in a sort of limbo. He was completely numb as Mary led him back, "It doesn't."

"Oh well."

Mary got back behind the wheel of the car and waited for Corban to get in. He opened the door and was about to climb into the passenger's seat when he stopped and took one last look at the house, "Goodbye."

Without another word, Corban got back in the car and leaned on the door as he rubbed his forehead. Mary looked over at him and saw the look on his face.

Soul Siphon

He was already missing his family and friends, and despairing that his life as he knew it was over. A partial look of sympathy was all she could offer as she spoke, "Listen, for what it's worth I really am sorry that you have to go through this."

Corban looked over at her with tear-soaked eyes, "So what's your story?"

"My story?"

"Well... it seems like we'll be seeing a lot of each other. You know my backstory, but I don't know anything about you other than your name."

Mary sighed, "You really want to hear this?"

"Yes I do, if for no other reason than to change the subject and get my mind off of my own problems, please?"

"Fine... but this conversation never happened as far as the rest of the team is concerned, yeah? You repeat this to anyone and I will rip your tongue out."

"Agreed."

"All right let me ask you then, have you ever heard my name before, perhaps in a movie or history book?"

Corban thought back to his classroom lessons and readings. He dug through his memories but found nothing, "Maybe in a comic book... and Mary Jane is another name for weed but not from a history book."

Mary sneered in disgusted as her lips revealed part of her story, "Does the name Whitechapel mean anything to you?"

Corban thought carefully for a moment, "Whitechapel..."

The name sounded familiar but Corban couldn't place it, "Isn't that a fast food restaurant?"

Mary rolled her eyes as she clenched the wheel, "Yeah... sure. It's a fast food restaurant... whatever."

"What?"

Soul Siphon

"Nothing."

Corban frowned. He couldn't be certain, but he thought he heard Mary whisper the word 'idiot' under her breath, "No, come on. I want to hear this."

"Fine... I lived in a London gutter back in the 1880s along with the rest of the poor and destitute."

He studied Mary's face carefully. What was she trying to tell him? Was she from that time period? Her appearance was that of a normal 25-year-old girl. Curiosity with a hint of suspicion overtook his senses, "How old are you?"

"It's bad manners to ask a lady her age."

"If you were a lady, I wouldn't have asked."

A partial grin appeared on the right side of Mary's lips, "Nice..."

She sucked down a deep breath. Her lips quivered and she appeared to be in pain as she responded, "I was born in 1863 in Limerick, Ireland. I moved around Great Britain a bit after my husband died and then I moved to France. I really didn't like it there so I went back to England and spent time moving from place to place working as... well, I..."

Corban's eyes narrowed, "Go on."

"I guess it was what you would call an escort. I worked in a London brothel."

"You were a prostitute?"

Intense anger washed over her face. It appeared as though she had taken what he had said as a personal attack or accusation, "I did what I had to in order to survive and it was only enough to feed and shelter myself! I was not like one of those disgusting toothless street urchins that would have taken your money and left you with syphilis!"

"Okay," Corban responded, trying carefully not to offend her. "Sorry, I wasn't accusing you... I mean..."

Mary pressed herself back into her seat, "I know the negative stigma that comes with prostitution, but let me ask you this; when's the last time you had sex?"

"Um..."

"Before you tell me that it's none of my business, or that it's too personal, just remember that you opened this can of worms."

"A few days before I was possessed."

"And how often were you doing it before that?"

"Fairly often."

"Then you've had more in your 25 years of life than I have in the last hundred. So you tell me who the whore is."

"I never said you were a whore."

Mary bit her lower lip and gripped the wheel as she calmed down, "Anyway... I lived there until 1888 when..."

She paused for a moment. Corban noticed that her eye was twitching. He shifted uncomfortably in his seat, afraid of what was coming next, "It's all right if you don't want to..."

"I was murdered in my own home."

"What?"

"A guy broke it, slit my throat, and... left me for dead, all right?"

That touched a nerve, and Corban was certain that there was more to the story than he was being told, but he wasn't about to press her for more info. Just by looking at her, he could tell that she was a nudge away from exploding and decided not to press for any more details, "All right."

Corban waited a few moments before saying anything else, "Was that when Mike found you?"

Mary once again kept her eyes on the road. A pained look came over her face. Her face began to flare red as she responded, "Yeah..."

Soul Siphon

"Can you tell me... what is Mike anyway?"

Mary smiled, "You heard of Saint Michael, yeah?"

"What?" Corban asked in a shocked tone. "You mean the angel, Michael?"

"Archangel," Mary corrected, "and the general of the angelic armies."

"So we're working for angels now... I don't get it."

"I'm not surprised. Angels are forbidden from directly interfering with human society. They can't stop people from being killed and they can't enforce any notion of justice... but we can."

"Why not?"

"Who knows... something about disrupting the order of reality or some bullshit."

"So Michael brought us back in order to do his dirty work?" Corban asked.

"Essentially, yes. We act as sort of a loophole. He gave us our chance to get revenge on those who wronged us. We were allowed to right the previous wrongs from our own lives and prevent those people from hurting anyone else. We'd be allowed to return to the world we knew, the only catch is that we'd have to serve as Michael's enforcers. I thought it was a fair trade."

"I see," Corban replied.

"So what are your powers?"

"You've seen them."

"When?"

"Or rather you haven't seen them. That's how they work."

"What the hell are you talking about?"

"I was murdered by a man who hid in the shadows," Mary replied. "He struck quickly, quietly, and very methodically. My powers reflect that. I can

Soul Siphon

veil myself and go unnoticed by my victims. I also have inhuman speed and can make quick clean cuts faster than any butcher or surgeon, even with a dull blade."

"So you can move really fast."

"Yup."

"How fast?"

Mary's smile became a devious grin. She stopped the car on the deserted road, put it in park, and unbuckled her seatbelt. The moment Corban blinked, she was gone. He didn't see or hear her open or close the door. His eyes darted back and forth as he looked for her, but she was nowhere to be found. She had instantly vanished.

"Over here!"

Startled, Corban jumped and jerked his head to the right. Mary was kneeling down next to the open passenger door. Somehow, she'd gotten out of the car, run to the other side and opened it without him noticing. Again Corban blinked and when his eyes reopened, she was gone and his door was closed again.

"Can't keep up?"

Corban turned to see that she was once again behind the wheel of the car. The devious grin never left her face. She clearly enjoyed showing off, "Impressive, yeah?"

"Yeah, I'd say so," Corban replied. "No one can see you coming and you move at super-human speeds... that's pretty much the makings of a perfect assassin."

"I like to think so." She replied confidently.

The look on Corban's face didn't go away as the car drove through Watertown, "So Vlad has the power to affect projectiles and can see great distances because he was sniped, Lihua has the powers of a femme fatale because of the events surrounding her

Soul Siphon

death, Johnny can make people wither and die because... well that's how he died, and you have the superhuman abilities that allow you to kill as effectively as you were. What about me though? I wasn't murdered. I shut myself down to prevent a demon from taking over, what's my power?"

"That's the thing, we don't know... and that worries us."

"Why?"

A hesitant look appeared on Mary's face, "I... should probably let Mike explain."

Corban frowned, unsure about Mike's intentions, "I think I'd rather hear it from you."

"Why?"

"I don't really know or trust Mike."

"But you trust me?"

"More than him."

"Why?" Mary asked in surprise.

"You're very blunt and you've been honest with me so far."

"I could have lied."

"Did you?"

"No…"

"Okay then?"

Mary sighed, "All right, but don't get mad at me later."

"I promise."

"Right well, as a rule, Michael has stayed clear of possession victims for a while now because of the powers they may gain."

"What do you mean?"

Mary sucked in a deep breath and closed her eyes, "You're not the first possession victim to be part of the team. Mike tried numerous times before we convinced him to stop. The powers they gained often led them to madness. Some gained demonic powers

Soul Siphon

that corrupted them, some were able to steal spirit energy which made them too powerful, and others were able to jump from one body to the next."

"What happened to them?"

Mary looked like she had tears in her eyes as she spoke, "I don't want to talk about it. Just trust me, it didn't end well. Mike will need to fill you in on the rest."

Something about Mary's response made Corban's blood run cold. "I see... so then why was I brought back?"

"Because of what you did to Adramelech. You fought back and won. We've never seen anyone do that with such a powerful demon."

"So Mike thinks that I can control those powers where others failed?"

"Exactly, which would have some obvious advantages, but we'll need to keep a close eye on you until we're sure. You've got a long road ahead of you and your training will not be easy... or free of danger."

"How so?"

"No," Mary replied sternly, "I've already told you too much. Drop it. Mike will fill you in on the rest."

"All right..." Corban replied defensively.

He knew that he had to change the subject and was still having trouble believing that Mary was who she claimed to be. He was sitting next to someone who physically was no older than 25, yet she spoke like someone who had lived much longer. Could she really be over 150 years old? "So it seems like everyone else here is from the 1900s. You're the only one that's over a hundred years old, why is that?"

"There were others who were older than me, but over time, they grew weary of this eternal darkness. They had become tired of all the killing and opted instead to return to their graves and rejoin their loved ones. When I was brought back, the team had been out of existence for decades. For the longest time, I was the only one."

"So if we don't want to do this, we have the option to go back to being dead?"

"Yes," Mary replied. "We're not slaves here. Many decide very quickly that they don't want to be killers, others watch their families move on and live their lives without them. The emotional strain eventually becomes too much to handle and they move on. It's just how this goes sometimes."

"What about you?"

Mary shrugged, "I don't really remember my parents anymore. I was on my own at a young age. My husband wasn't exactly a prize, and... Well, let's just say that the prospect of moving on for me isn't one I look forward to. I found this existence much more fulfilling."

An appreciative smile formed on the right side of Corban's lips, "Thank you for sticking around."

Mary's face remained emotionless as she spoke, "When Joe turned me away, I was alone. There was no one there to help me make any sense of what happened and Mike wasn't much help. I recognized the look in your eyes when you first began to grasp the horror of what was happening to you. I don't like the idea of anyone having to go through what I did. It was too cruel."

Corban stared out the front windshield but didn't respond. He didn't know what to say to that and remained silent as Mary glanced over a few times. She seemed almost disappointed by his lack of response, "Just don't make a habit of running off like that, yeah? It's dangerous and I'm not going to keep chasing you down. I have better things to do with me time."

Soul Siphon

"Where would I run to at this point?"

Soul Siphon

IV

The charger finally arrived back in South Boston. It was late, but neither Mary nor Corban were tired. Mary pushed a button on top of the middle console, activating the garage door on the warehouse in front of them. The door made a loud metallic clanking sound as it rolled up into its compartment.

The car pulled in next to a motorcycle and a large red van. The metal garage door slammed shut behind them with a loud crash. Mary put the car in park and opened the door, "Welcome back, yeah?"

"Right…"

Corban turned to Mary once again as he got out of the car and looked around. Mary beckoned to the door, "Ready to go inside?"

"Sure."

Mary led Corban through the door to the lounge where the group was working out. Johnny was in the middle of sprinting and looked up when he saw them enter the room, "Welcome back, Ripper."

Mary flashed Johnny an angry look, "I swear if you don't stop calling me that…"

"What?" Johnny said in a daring tone. "What could you possibly do to me that hasn't already been done? Come on, I want to hear this."

Mary snorted and turned to her other teammates, "Look who I found out wandering the streets."

Lihua was hanging by her knees off of a bar that was attached to the ceiling. Her eyes snapped open at the sound of Mary's voice. It appeared as though their return had snapped her out of a transic state. She let go and did a flip in the air so that she landed on her feet, "You went after him, Mary? That is not like you at all."

Soul Siphon

"Whatever, I just didn't want him doing something stupid and exposing us, yeah?"

"Uh huh..."

Mary flashed Lihua an annoyed look as she headed to her corner, grumbling something under her breath. Lihua smiled as she turned back to Corban, "Looks like you have made your first friend here... interesting choice. So I take it that you have realized that you cannot go back and can now accept the reality of your situation?"

"Mostly, I'm still not clear on what we do here. I know we each have powers and we work to bring justice to the world, I'm just not clear on the how or our overall goals. Is it just revenge or something more?"

"Come, I will show you."

Corban followed Lihua closely. She took him to a small outlining in the wall. Lihua touched a panel on the right side of the outline, which beeped softly and turned green. The door immediately opened, allowing Corban and Lihua inside.

The air in the next room was chilly and very sterile. It felt like a night out on Boston harbor in late spring; cool, damp but manageable. The moment Corban stepped through the door, there was a loud mechanical sound as though something was coming to life.

The recessed halogen lights in the ceiling immediately came on. They were directed to shine on the walls, which helped to reveal what was mounted there. Corban found himself in the middle of a small arsenal.

He could not believe his eyes. On one wall were large rifles, machine guns, a rocket launcher with a selection of different rockets, and an extensive collection of swords. The other side had a selection of handguns, knives, and grenades. The guns ranged from small caliber revolvers to Uzis that could go full auto.

Corban looked around, impressed, "Quite the collection you guys have going on here. Where'd you get this stuff?"

"We have collected it over the years, mostly from our targets. They do not need them by the time we are done, so why not?"

"Aren't you afraid that some of these have been used in crimes and could be traced?"

"No," Lihua replied. "The room is wired with a special plasma explosive. Do not ask me where we got it. Should this place ever be discovered, the explosive can be remotely detonated. The heat would destroy everything in this room."

"And everything in a two-mile radius!"

"Unlikely. The room is reinforced concrete. It would withstand the brunt of the explosion."

Lihua moved to the back wall as the lights came on. This wall had an unusual mounting of ancient swords and other hand weapons. It looked like a museum display when compared to the modern weapons on the other two.

Lihua picked up a short Japanese sword and ran her finger along the blade until it bled, "This kodachi is over six hundred years old, yet it still retains its sharpness. It is a very rare weapon indeed, but it still has its uses as most weapons do. It took years to assemble such a collection. In time, you will be able to choose which weapons you prefer when we go out to accomplish our mission. Or you can choose what you want to use for our specific missions."

"Our missions?"

"Yes," Lihua replied, "we are a secret society of sorts. Mike assembled us to help him dole out justice on those who have committed the worst of sins.

Soul Siphon

Murder, rape, molestation, abuse, serious theft, terrorism, all of these and more are the crimes we hunt. We track down those with evil intent and neutralize them."

Corban had a suspicious look on his face, "By neutralize, I assume you mean kill?"

"Aren't you the sharp one?" Mary asked as she appeared behind them.

Corban was about to utter a retort when Lihua cut him off, "It is just her way, you will get used to it."

Johnny came over and joined them as well, "Yeah, but she seems to have already warmed to you. It took me months to get her to even say a single word to me. Even then, it was mostly swearing or her telling me to get lost... or worse."

"Good to know."

"So..." A voice chimed in from behind. "It's time for us to figure out what powers you possess."

Corban turned to see Mike standing behind him, "Fine by me, Saint Michael."

A surprised grin formed on Mike's lips, "Oh so it would appear that Mary took it upon herself to tell you everything?"

Corban didn't respond. He didn't want to throw Mary under the bus, but it appeared that his silence was all the answer Mike needed, "Well at least now you know what we're all about."

"Yeah... I do..."

"And, what do you think?"

"Honestly, I'm not really sure that I know what to think."

Mary crossed her arms as she spoke, "Corban, are you daft? He's asking if you intend to stick around. Are you going to join us, or return to the land of the dead? It's not a difficult question, yeah?"

Soul Siphon

Corban scoffed at Mary as responded. How could she honestly say that? "Choosing whether to remain or die isn't a difficult question? Since when?"

Mary rolled her eyes and turned away as Lihua chuckled, "Be that as it may, you still must decide."

Corban looked at the four of them waiting intently, "We're going after bad people?"

"Yes," Lihua replied.

"We stop them so that they can never harm anyone else?"

"In the best way possible," Johnny replied.

Corban looked at them for another moment. This was to be his new life, fighting with a group of undead warriors that were hell bent on revenge for what had been done to them. *Well... could have been worse I suppose.*

"Are you in?" Johnny asked.

Corban turned to Michael, "Adramelech?"

"After you threw him out, he was in a weakened state," Michael replied. "Most demons that have been weakened that badly have to go back to Hell for some time in the pit to recharge."

Corban's heart sank. More than anything, he wanted a chance to take on the demon on equal ground. How long would he have to wait?

Michael smiled, "Oh don't worry, he won't stay there. They never do. You messed with one demon that has been around for several generations. I'll see to it that you get your shot at him. You have my word on that."

"I'll hold you to it."

Lihua's eyes brightened up, "So you are in then?"

"Yeah, I'm in."

Johnny clapped as Vlad joined them, "Velcome to ze family, boy."

Soul Siphon

"Thanks, Vlad."

Mary turned and retreated to her corner now that the question had been resolved. Corban couldn't be certain, but he'd sworn that he'd seen her smile as she turned away. It was pretty much the first time he'd seen anything resembling happiness from her. It was a refreshing change.

Mike smiled at Corban as he beckoned him to the next room, "Come, we need to resolve the issue of your powers."

"Sounds good."

Mike put his left hand on Corban's back and led him into the next room. Lihua followed closely behind them. She appeared to be concerned about something, though Corban couldn't tell what.

The moment they were out of earshot, Mike began talking to Corban, "She's a fascinating woman, isn't she?"

"Who, Lihua?"

"Well yes, but that's not who I was talking about at all."

"Oh... Mary."

"I saw the way you were looking at her," Mike said in an almost suspicious tone.

"She's... different. She comes off as cold and uncaring but..."

"She's not," Mike cut in. "She's shut herself down in many ways so as not to have to deal with the horrors of her past. It was the only way that she could cope with what she faced. I doubt any of us could have done any better. However, under that cold exterior, the Mary that was there before what happened is still there. It's just a question of getting to know her."

"I know. I think I met that person tonight."

"You're lucky, few ever do."

Corban smiled, "I'll keep that in mind."

Soul Siphon

Corban winced as the pungent stench overwhelmed his sense of smell. His nose flared as tears to form in his eyes. He began to wonder if this was some sort of test of endurance.

As the initial shock died down, he studied the small room that they were standing in. There wasn't much to see, a small window that allowed a mere sliver of moonlight to illuminate the room. Other than that, the only notable quality was the rank smell of mold, "What are we doing here?"

Mike raised his cane and brought it down hard. A loud noise emanated from the floor like ripples in the water when the cane struck, "It's time for us to discover your powers."

At that moment, there was a noise at the door. Vlad and Johnny appeared, dragging a brown sack behind them that appeared to be moving. Corban eyed it suspiciously as the two of them dropped it in front of him and spilled its contents on the floor.

A man fell out. He was cut and bruised but otherwise unharmed. He looked up at Corban, "What the fuck is going on here? Where am I? Who the hell are you?"

Surprised, Corban looked over at Mike, "What is this about?"

Mike beckoned towards the man, "This man is responsible for multiple rapes throughout the city. He preys on women who are out and alone. He has an established pattern but alters it every few years and has never been caught."

A nervous look came over the man's features. He wasn't very tall but he was muscular. He had a shaven head which was a stark contrast to his hairy arms. The man spoke through quivering lips, "Hey man, I don't know what the old guy is talking about. He's fucking crazy!"

Mike stood behind Corban and whispered in his ear, "Focus… draw on your internal energy and let it do as it will."

Corban knew what Mike wanted him to do, but taking a life was a lot to ask. Even so, he didn't want to appear weak, "I… I don't know…"

"Do not show him mercy," Mike whispered. "This man has done more damage than you could know. He's responsible for ruined lives, leaving women as psychological shells, and even a death. All of this to satisfy his animal lust. He can't be rehabilitated. I think you know this."

Corban was conflicted as the man struggled against his the ropes that tied his hands. This went against what he had been taught as a child about right and wrong, but what Mike was saying did make sense, "I…"

"Still not convinced?" Mike asked, grasping his cane, "Then behold."

Mike raised his cane and tapped Corban on the forehead with the cherub figure. At that moment, the image of a cute young girl appeared in his mind. Mike spoke in an angered tone, "Tammie Nicholson, she's fourteen. She was found on the street violated and near dead. The poor girl was only fourteen."

Tears formed in Corban's eyes, "Ugh… no…"

"No?" Mike asked, "All right then, how about this one?"

Another face appeared in his mind. This one had dark brown hair and a cynical look on her face. Corban gasped when the image of the woman appeared, he knew her, "Danielle?"

"I'm afraid so," Mike replied. "You went to High School with her, didn't you? She was a friend of yours and Janine's."

"She set us up."

Soul Siphon

"Shall I tell you what he did to her?" Mike asked.

"No... stop!"

Mike's tone became almost a whisper, "He caught her when she was on her way to the T station. He pulled her into an alley and tore her clothes."

Corban covered his forehead with his right hand, as though trying to hide the beads of sweat that were forming, "No..."

Mike's words were relentless, "He beat on her pretty badly, had his fun, and then when he was done he left her there, a bloody mess! You can't imagine..."

"Michael!" Lihua shouted with a shocked expression. "That is enough!"

It was too late. The damage had been done and the floodgates that held back Corban's anger were now open. He screamed, "No!"

His eyes widened and became red. His hands glowed blue and his world went dark. He hadn't felt so alive in a long time, but it wasn't a positive feeling. This was more like the testosterone surge that he felt when Janine's ex-boyfriend showed up during one of their dates. He looked down at the man that they had placed in front of him and clenched his jaw, "You... monster!"

Corban balled a fist and drove it right into the man's chest. There was a bright flash of light and a scream from Corban's victim. When the light disappeared, the man's body fell lifelessly to the ground, an empty shell of what it had once been.

Corban was standing next to him, staring transfixed at the white orb he held in his hand. At that moment, he could hear Mary's voice from across the room, "No... not again..."

Before anyone could react, Corban pressed on each side of the orb with his fingers and crushed it in

Soul Siphon

his hand. The sound of shattering glass echoed through the room as the ball ceased to exist, leaving free-floating energy behind. It hovered over the remains for a few moments before it quickly flowed and swirled around Corban's body. His skin began to glow as it absorbed the energy.

A sense of euphoria overwhelmed Corban's senses. It was a sudden rush of energy as though his adrenaline had gone into overdrive. The charge was quickly becoming more than he could control, but he did not care. It was unlike anything that he'd ever experienced before.

Corban looked down at his hands every few moments they became a transparent yellow color that glowed for a few seconds before returning to normal. It was like looking through a yellow stained glass window, "Wow… this is…. This is amazing! I've never felt power like this before… never…"

Mike rushed to Corban's side as urgency set in, "Corban, listen to me, do as I command and release this energy right now!"

Corban didn't respond and continued to stare transfixed at his hands, "Can this even be real? It's like an intense rush!"

Mike placed his right hand on Corban's heart and closed his eyes, "Release it!"

At that moment, Corban thrust out his right arm, allowing a bright beam of energy to escape his hand. The beam lasted only a moment before dissipating. Corban looked completely disheveled after it disappeared struggled to keep his balance.

It was at this moment that Corban saw the man's victims. He felt their pain, their screams, and the suffering that they all experienced at the hands of the monster Corban had just killed. Then he saw Danielle's face cross through his mind. He closed his eyes, trying to avoid seeing what he was about to, but the image was in his mind and there was no way to avoid it.

Corban had to watch as his friend's clothes were ripped away. He heard her whimpering and felt her pain. Being forced to watch one of his close friends go through this was too much. It tormented his mind to the point of fracture, "Enough, stop it!"

He thrust his right hand forward and sent another energy blast flying from his fingers. The white beam struck the far wall and disintegrated it, exposing the internal wiring and insulation. He collapsed on his knees, worn out and emotionally drained. The rush of energy did not make him feel any better. The dark reality of what he had seen had left him empty.

Mike reached down and patted Corban's back, "Well done Corban."

"Well done," Corban repeated in an angry tone. "Well done?"

Corban jumped back to his feet, "You son of a bitch, why didn't you warn me?"

Mike stared back at him looking confused, "What are you talking about?"

"I saw them!" Corban replied. "Tammy, Danielle… and all the other ones… I saw them all! The memories of what happened to them are now stuck in my head. Their pain, screams, sorrow… I can't get it out! Why didn't you tell me?"

"Corban, I didn't know."

"I can't do this… I can't…"

Corban threw his head back and screamed as he released even more energy, "Enough!"

Everyone watched as the beams shot through the air. Though bright, they were not powerful enough to do any damage other than a few slight burns on the

Soul Siphon

walls. The energy was out of control and took Corban a few extra minutes to get his emotions back in check.

The energy beams slowly dissipated as his breathing became more rhythmic. The entire room was moving as he slouched forward. No matter how hard he tried, he struggled to regain his balance.

Mike took a cautious step towards him in case he fell, "Feel better?"

"Yeah… the pain is more manageable now…"

Mike placed his hands on Corban's cheeks and held his head so they were looking each other in the eyes, "It's okay, my boy. That was a good attempt. At least we know what we're dealing with. You've taken your first step. The other steps, we'll take with you."

Corban felt ill. His stomach felt as though someone had just punched him, "I don't know. I feel so tired. I…"

Corban let out a deep sigh and fell to the side. He felt drained and couldn't keep himself stable. Thankfully Vlad was right there to catch him. He put his arm around Corban and slowly led him out of the room, "Zat vas unexpected to say ze least. I sink it's time for our young friend to rest."

Corban's face was pale and it was pretty clear that he was still in a state of shock as Johnny and Vlad dragged him away. Johnny moved slowly as he held Corban by the legs, "Fuck man…"

The moment they were gone, Mary turned to confront Mike with an outraged glare, "You're fucking daft, yeah? You knew this was going to happen!"

"I don't know what you're talking about."

"I beg your pardon," Lihua said, mirroring Mary's accusing stare, "but I cannot believe that to be true."

Mary's eyes pierced accusingly into Mike as she spoke, "You've awakened a soul siphon. You know what happens to them. They're too dangerous to be kept around. This one also seems to carry the memories of the people he kills. So if he's not driven mad by his powers, the memories he receives will pick up the slack! That spells trouble no matter which way you spin it, yeah?"

"This is bad, very bad!" Lihua added. "Mike, he has to be put back, it is not safe. We cannot go through this again. We were barely able to stop the last one!"

"There will be no putting him back," Mike replied calmly. "We'll work with him, make him understand his powers, and make sure that the previous mistakes are not repeated."

"That won't work and you know it!" Mary said in an accusing tone. "You'll teach him to absorb souls and then set him loose against our enemies. Eventually, he'll learn to harness the power of each soul and when he does…"

"When he does, they will empower him," Lihua added.

A brief appreciative smile appeared on the right side of Mary's lips as she looked at Lihua. The two never agreed on much. In fact, too often Mary suspected the Lihua was trying to be combative, but for now at least they were on the side, "Yeah and he'll continue to gain more and more power over time. He won't be able to stop. It'll be like an addiction and it will eventually take over."

Mary clenched her jaw as she continued, "If he's allowed to do this unchecked, he'll eventually surpass us all in terms of power. Not long after that, he'll be so powerful that he'll become a God. You know this, you've seen it before!"

Soul Siphon

"Blasphemy!" Mike replied. "We won't let it get that far. I'll work with him."

"Why?" Mary demanded. "What is so important about him?"

"He's different from the others, I can feel it."

"How so?"

Mike gripped his cane as he responded, "You were there. You saw what he did. No one else we've encountered has ever been able to push back that much against a demon. This wasn't just any demon either, we're talking about Adramelech. If he can do that, what else can he do? He can resist Adramelech. I don't think it's too much of a stretch to think that he might have a better chance than the previous soul siphons."

"It is a big stretch!" Mary insisted. "Just because he had the momentary strength to shut himself down when Adramelech had him, doesn't mean that he's any less susceptible to the power that he can manifest."

"Fine," Lihua replied. "We will wait and see on this one. However, until that time, we will need to keep him under watch."

Well, that was short-lived. Mary thought to herself as it appeared that Lihua was switching sides. She was about to respond, but Mike cut her off before she could, "I agree. So, I'll leave you to it."

He then turned to Mary, "Make sure you keep an eye on him if that's what you think is necessary. Do your best to keep him out of trouble."

"Me?" Mary asked, in surprise.

"Yes, I've noticed that you two have developed a rapport of sorts."

"We haven't, just because he talks to me whether I want him to or not doesn't mean we're becoming all friendly, yeah?"

Soul Siphon

"Well be that as it may, for reasons I can't quite understand, he seems to trust you more than anyone else at the moment."

"I don't care."

The look on his face told Mary that Mike was becoming annoyed with her protests, "Mary..."

Mary sighed as she turned away, "No, this is not a good idea!"

"I agree," Lihua replied, "but it looks like we are stuck with him for now and he seems to trust you."

"No, I don't want any part of this! You are meddling with powers that no one should be, human or otherwise. It always falls to me to put them back. I'm done with that and I don't want this. Find someone else!"

"Where would we be if we only did the things we wanted to do?"

Mary twisted her lips but said nothing. Her defiance was met by a sigh from Mike, "All right look, he's here and we need him. I'm not putting him back in his grave, so you can either help him or watch him fail. It's on you now."

Defeated, Mary sighed and slowly headed for the living room, "... Fine!"

She paused for a moment after reaching the door. A tear formed in her eye as it seemed like she wasn't getting through to anyone. Angered, she turned back one last time to give Mike one last piece of her mind, "How much more tragedy will it take, Mike? How much more before you're convinced that attempting to wield demonic powers is a bad idea? You had better hope you're right about this because if you're wrong, his blood will be on your hands, not mine! If this just turns out to be a repeat of the last time... if I have to execute another one, then I'm done with you. I'd rather go back to my grave than have to endure this."

Shocked looks appeared on both Lihua's and Mike's faces as neither of them expected to hear Mary say that. She had been dedicated to the job with no signs of letting up, but she'd had enough of having to clean up Mike's mess. This would be the end of it for her.

Mike knew that there was nothing he could say that would change her mind, so he agreed, "All right Mary. If you feel that strongly about it. We'd better make sure he doesn't end up like the others. We'll work with him to make sure that this time will be different."

"I wish I could believe that... I really do," Mary replied sadly as she left the room unwilling to tolerate any more naive words from her companions.

Soul Siphon

V

Corban woke up to find himself in a comfortable bed next to the window in a college-dorm-sized room. It was a very spartan room with only a closet, bed, desk and chair for furnishings. The private bathroom appeared to be the one and only luxury that he had been afforded. It was a minimalist setup that gave him the essentials that he would need to get by. *So this is my life now huh...?*

Corban looked down at his hands. A blue wave of energy flowed from his fingertips to his elbows and then disappeared under his shirt. His breathing became labored as he slowly remembered what had happened. Did he really kill that man? Was what Mike said about what he'd done actually true? Was what he was told about Mike actually true? It was all hard to believe. Mike didn't fit what he'd been told about Saint Michael at all. This guy seemed like a frail old man with an ax to grind. It was impossible for him to wrap his mind around all of this.

Without warning, the memories began to resurface. His mind began pounding as the images began to overwhelm him and another pulse of energy flowed down his body. He saw everything that had happened to Danielle pass before his eyes once more. Except that something was different this time. It wasn't Danielle's face he saw, it was Mary's. He shook his head hard, struggling to keep the images out.

It wasn't working. The memories continued to flow, causing him to throw back his head and scream, "Get out!"

Unexpectedly, this seemed to do the trick. Corban gasped as he found himself alone in his room with the images and cries of the man's victims no longer echoing in his mind. He leaned back against the

Soul Siphon

wall, covered in sweat and let out a deep sigh, "I can't do this… It's too much…"

Corban's body screamed for a shower. He was sweaty and his joints ached, but he was in no mood for it. His room felt like a cage that he desperately needed to escape from. He stood up from his bed and headed for the door, not knowing where to go.

Using great care, Corban quietly stepped out of the room, not knowing what time it was. It appeared as though the main corridor was set up as a dormitory with residence rooms on either side. Each door had the name of its occupant on it. The tiled floor reminded him of a hospital or school. He walked to the end of the hallway where a brushed steel elevator door was waiting for him.

Where did he want to go? The number on the door said '3.' Did he want to go down and leave the building, or maybe get to the roof and get a better idea of his surroundings. *Go outside in Southie when it's dark... uh huh... You already tried that once.*

Corban pressed 'up' and waited for the door to open. On the other side of the door, he could hear the faint grinding and squeaking of old mechanical equipment as the elevator obeyed his command. An old world chime sounded as the door opened. He stepped inside and pressed the 'R' button. *Let's hope that means 'roof.'*

The elevator doors closed and Corban felt the small compartment begin to slide upward. The chime went off one more time before the door opened and Corban found himself in a small room with a doorway, which he assumed led outside. Except for the light coming from under the door and the elevator, there was nothing illuminating his way.

The door was solid steel with a push bar locking mechanism. Corban pushed on the bar and the door slowly opened. There was a blast of cool air as he stumbled out onto the roof. He was greeted by a very dark sky that was illuminated by the city. It was a familiar sight that was comforting in its own way.

Even at night, Boston was a city full of activity, but this was closer to the morning hours. Judging by the number of cars on the road and the sun slowly creeping up over the horizon, this was most likely the early morning between 5 or 6 AM.

Corban caught the wall just as his legs gave out. It was only 3 feet in height, but it was enough to support him. His insides were twisted and turned in knots. His stomach churned and ached as though it were doing circles. All of this was made worse by his head spinning as he looked out on the city. Unable to control himself any longer, he leaned over the edge and vomited.

Drained of his energy, Corban leaned against the northern wall and rested his elbows on top. He looked out on the city, breathing heavily. His thoughts dwelled on Janine and his mother. They were out there somewhere at this very moment, believing that he was dead and there was nothing he could do about it.

It was too painful to think about the Janine, so he tried thinking about his mother, but it wasn't much better. She would soon be moving on as well. His relationship with her was yet another aspect of his life that the demon had stolen from him.

Corban lowered his eyes, barely able to keep himself together. He would have been willing to do anything to get back what he'd lost, no matter what it cost him. His heart ached, knowing that it was no longer possible. As things were now, he would most likely outlive them, Janine's children, and her grandchildren. He understood why so many of his predecessors decided to return to their graves after

Soul Siphon

seeing their families. Some people were simply incapable of living without their loved ones and he wasn't certain that he was an exception.

Corban rubbed his forehead, almost wishing that it would make his painful thoughts disappear. *How long will I be able to hold out? The idea of returning to my grave doesn't seem like such a bad prospect now, but I've already signed on here. Maybe I should stick around, at the very least until I get a shot at Adramelech, but I don't know if I can last that long. This is going to be bad.*

"Fighting your demons?"

Corban looked up to see Mary standing behind him. He was happy to have company but at the same time he didn't appreciate being spied on, "How long have you been hiding back there?"

"I'm always here. This is my hangout, yeah? I don't like the small cells we're supposed to sleep in. They bring back bad memories and are usually too hot and cramped."

"I can understand that I guess…"

"So what demon were you fighting?"

"I already fought the demon, remember? That's how I wound up here in the first place."

"You fought the one that invaded your body, not the ones you created yourself."

"Is there a point to this?"

Mary shrugged, "Not really, you just look like you shouldn't be alone right now."

He turned back and looked at the city, "So you're here to keep me company then?"

"Nope. Like I said, you're invading my space, yeah? If you don't want company, then leave. If anything, I'm just tolerating your presence because you're new. Just please don't jump off the roof, yeah? The mess would be a pain in the ass to clean up."

Soul Siphon

"What commit suicide?"

Mary smirked, "It wouldn't be suicide. It would hurt like hell and probably take months to heal, but you wouldn't die."

"Of course not."

"Look, I'm not a fucking therapist, yeah? I don't know what will help you and I doubt I could even provide it if I did."

"I killed that man!" Corban cut in. "God... I never thought I'd live to do something like that. What's worse, I'm stuck with his memories! If I'd known..."

"You did what you had to do, what you're here to do. You saw what he did to those women, yeah? Could you imagine what would happen if he were allowed to continue roaming the streets? You did everyone a favor."

Corban didn't know how to respond, so he kept quiet.

"I know it's no consolation, but it does get easier."

"I don't want it to."

"No one does, but that's how it goes. It's a terrible thing we do, but it is necessary, yeah?"

"Necessary..," Corban repeated, feeling like he was about to throw up again.

"Look if you want to talk about it…"

"What do you want from me?"

Mary was caught off guard by his question, "Me? Nothing."

"Then why do you keep bothering me? Are you enjoying watching me go through all of this? You didn't seem to like the idea of me being brought on board in the first place so what's the deal? Why are you being nice all of a sudden?"

Soul Siphon

Outrage lit up Mary's eyes like gasoline poured on a fire, "Enjoying this? Is that what you think? You know what, fuck you! This is what I get for trying to help? Go ahead and jump for all I care. See what happens. I'm not the one who brought you back nor am I the one responsible for you being here. If this is how you're going to be, then go back to your grave and fuck it for all I care."

With that, Mary turned her back on Corban and stormed away, "I knew this would wind up biting me in the ass!"

Feeling guilty for taking out his mood on Mary, Corban called after her, "Mary, wait..."

A heavy metal door being slammed was the only response he received. In a fit of anger and frustration, he punched the wall with his right fist, "I'm sorry..."

After an hour of sitting alone, the sun began to appear on the horizon. Corban got up, brushed himself off, and went inside to see if anyone else was up yet. He hoped that he would be able to try to apologize to Mary if she'd even listen. He hadn't straightened everything out in his mind, but it didn't seem like being alone on the roof was going to change that.

The look Mary had given him sent chills down Corban's spine. He knew she'd probably try to dismember him for even trying to talk to her, what else could he do? She was the only one who had really made an effort to reach out on a personal level and he owed her that much.

Corban walked out of the elevator, into the dining room, and was greeted by the group sitting down to breakfast. On the opposite side of the room was a small hallway that made up the galley-style kitchen where it sounded like someone was hard at work.

Soul Siphon

Lihua turned and smiled when she saw him, "Corban, come join us. Johnny is very poor company."

Corban sat down next to Lihua at the table and leaned on his right arm, "Where's everyone else?"

Lihua looked around and shrugged, "Mike rarely joins us unless he has a target for us to go after, I have not seen Ripper, and Vlad is cooking."

Johnny leaned over with a snarky look, "Eat sparingly; Vlad likes to make dishes that his mother made him… or rather his variation of them. I don't know if Russian food is normally like this, but the way Vlad cooks it, the food is definitely not for a weak stomach."

At that moment, Vlad appeared from the kitchen, "For zavtrak today, I make mother's specialty; kasha vith tvorog, and butterbrots! My favorite!"

"Oh, God..," Johnny moaned softly as he sat back.

Corban smiled nervously, "Bad?"

"Just hold your nose and chew quickly."

Though Lihua also looked like she was about to get sick, she smiled and politely nodded at Vlad, "You are very gracious in offering to cook for us today. Thank you… it smells… edible?"

"Ass kisser," Johnny whispered.

The food had a very strong odor, but it looked like any other breakfast; toast, ham, some sort of oatmeal, and eggs on the side. It all looked like it had been well-cooked. Corban figured that Johnny was once again giving Vlad a hard time and spooned some of the oatmeal into his mouth.

A sharp flavor stung his tongue and throat, causing his eyes to water. He immediately reached for the tomato juice and downed a glass. He wasn't sure what Vlad used for spices, but he definitely used way too much.

Soul Siphon

As Corban quickly wiped the tears from his eyes, trying not to insult Vlad, Johnny smirked, "I warned you, man."

Corban looked over at Vlad and forced a smile, "It's very good."

A triumphant look appeared on Vlad's face, "Ah, Corban have good taste, no? It not taste like poison? I vill cook more often then."

Johnny shook his head as he whispered, "Well that's a good way to get yourself on a diet."

Lihua chuckled as she slowly ate, taking small bites to avoid getting the full impact of Vlad's cooking. To Corban's horror, Vlad sat down and started spooning large amounts of the food into his mouth. After his first helping, Vlad let out a low burp, "Mmmm good food from ze motherland!"

I guess it's not so bad if you grew up eating it. Corban thought to himself.

Johnny looked over at Corban, "So how are you feeling after your first kill?"

Corban frowned, "Drained and sick. Honestly, I couldn't sleep at all last night."

"That is to be expected," Lihua replied, placing a comforting hand on his shoulder. "We did not anticipate that you would retain the memories of your victims, but it will get easier as time goes on."

"So I've been told."

Vlad smiled, "I remember my first kill during ze var. Zer vas blood and entrails everyvere. I remember private standing next to me getting sick. Vomit vas everyvere in seconds. Corban did much better, yes?"

"I agree," Lihua replied. "Especially after finding out what you can do. You handled yourself quite admirably."

"What, you mean rip the soul out of an unsuspecting victim?" Corban asked.

Soul Siphon

"Exactly, that is a power no one else here has. It is a rare talent."

"But it didn't feel right. That man had no trial, no chance to explain his side of things, he wasn't given due process. I just killed him. How is that justice?"

"I understand how you feel," Lihua replied, "but consider what would have happened if he had been brought to justice. The laws of man are flawed and usually based off of ancient mythology and values, or the whims of a select few. Consider, what would have happened had he been brought to justice. Either the prosecutor may not be competent, or the evidence could be tampered with. What if witnesses were not reliable or the judge had a political agenda?"

"I know but..."

"Even if everything proceeded perfectly, his victims would have to face him in court. They would have to suffer under his gaze while an overpaid lawyer attempted to make them relive the entire incident. They would be picked apart, called liars, or people who were emotionally unstable. It would be an unnecessary mess. Even if they got a conviction, he would be out on the streets in twenty years. How is that justice for the people who had to suffer through it? How is it justice when too many people are too afraid to report it because of that?"

"I suppose it's not justice... but still..."

"Corban, in my country the government would never have brought the men who attacked me to trial," Lihua continued. "The police looked the other way because of their status."

"Yes," Vlad added, "and in my case, ze assassination vas government sanctioned. Who vould be brought to justice for me?"

Soul Siphon

Johnny dropped his fork on the table, "And in my case, my stepmom was going for an insanity defense that looked like it was going to fly. She'd drummed up all sorts of child abuse claims that I'm certain she was never the victim of... and the fuckheads on the jury were eating it up."

Lihua placed her hand on Corban's arm, "I know it is a bit of a shock the first time around, but even if he had been brought to justice, the law would not keep him behind bars forever. Eventually, he would most likely be released to wreak havoc again in a misguided spirit of rehabilitation. His former victims would always live in fear and there would soon be more of them. What you did, prevented such a tragedy. You made sure that he would never hurt another person ever again. Take solace in that."

"I guess I see your point," Corban replied.

"Good," Vlad replied, "not forgetting zat ve have Mike to tell us who is good and who is not. He is able to see zis from his place in ze clouds."

Their words did help mend Corban's conscience somewhat, but he was still a little off after that first kill and the discovery of his powers. He looked around the room at the various weapons hanging from the walls, "So how often are we called on to perform an assassination?"

"Usually once or twice a night," Johnny replied. "We go out after dark."

"Makes sense."

At that moment, a disembodied voice entered the room, causing Corban to jump, "Friends, join me in the next room. I believe it is time for us to finalize welcoming our new friend."

Johnny wiped his face and stood up. "Mike calls... we're saved..."

Soul Siphon

Corban followed the little boy as they all made their way into the next room. Mary entered from the doorway on the opposite side and stood in her normal corner. Corban tried to catch her eye, but she pointedly looked away. The rest of the group stood around the middle of the room near the couches.

Once they were all settled, there was a flash of light and a figure with wings appeared in front of them. The aura was so bright that it caused Corban to flinch. It almost seemed like the aura was shaping itself into a person. As the light finally began to dim, he recognized Mike standing in front of him.

Once the aura disappeared, Mike looked at Corban, "Well my boy, how are you feeling?"

"Fine..."

"Excellent. I know the first burst of energy drained you pretty badly," Mike replied. "Don't worry, it happens to everyone."

"I figured."

The look on Mike's face was that of a grandfatherly old man. He placed a hand on Corban's shoulder and gave it a pat, "Good man."

Mike turned away from him and looked at the rest of the group, "Are we ready?"

Lihua looked at her friends before replying as though looking for their approval. When none of them spoke, she returned her attention to Mike, "We are."

"Very good," Mike replied. "Who will stand in sponsorship of Corban's membership to our brotherhood? Who will stand with him on the field of battle?"

Corban hoped that Mary would step forward. She had a look on her face like she wanted to react but didn't move. She continued to stare at the group, not meeting his gaze when he turned to look at her.

Vlad stepped forward, "I vill accept zat responsibility and stand as sponsor. Corban is of good character. I sink he make good addition, yes?"

"Any objections?" Mike asked.

Lihua shook her head, "Just our previously stated concerns regarding his powers. We do need to be vigilant in his training. Beyond that, I agree with Vlad."

Everyone at that point turned and looked at Mary, who remained in the darkness. Mike spoke up, "Mary, do you wish to add anything?"

"Would it matter if I did?"

"It would."

"Yeah, bullshit. I don't want to add anything, so just get on with it."

"Very well then, let us come together," Mike replied.

The group joined hands, with the exception of Mary. They each looked back and forward between Mike and Corban as Mike began speaking, "Friends, we are gathered here to welcome a new member into our ranks. He is young and has much to learn, but I am confident that with the help and support of his fellows here, he will do just fine. His life will not be an easy one. He will be asked to give up all that he's known in his mortal life. He will be asked to abandon certain human tendencies that may get in the way of his job. It will be difficult and, at times, seem nearly impossible, but in the end, he should come to understand that what we do here, we do for the good of all. Embrace him as your brother."

They released their hands but remained standing in the circle. Mike beckoned to Corban, the warm smile never leaving his face, "Come forward my boy, stand at the center of the circle."

Corban stepped forward and looked at the group that surrounded him curiously. Mike's eyes turned black and he spoke in a low voice, "It is time to recite the Doctrine of Vengeance."

Lihua stepped forward, "We are those, steadfast in our fight. We are those who will never take part in the workings of the world, except to eliminate the machinations of evil. We take no wealth, posterity, or reward of any kind for our actions and will fade into the shadows as quickly as we appeared. We are fire, we are mist, and we are that which does not last but will always be there."

Lihua lowered her head and stepped back as Vlad replaced her, "Ours is burden not all can carry. Ve live vith memories of pain, suffering, and hopelessness. Ve seek to re-trap zat vich Pandora set loose so long ago."

Next up was Johnny, "Some would call us vigilantes, lawless thugs and worse, but there is fulfillment to be found in what we do. There are those who would judge us as villainous... let them. What we do here, we do for the good of all. We are beyond reproach, beyond being judged, and we answer to one call and only one."

To Corban's surprise, Mary stepped forward before anyone else could speak. Her eyes immediately locked with Corban's, "Those who have ears and are willing, let them hear. The only ones who need fear us are those in possession of an evil soul, those wicked creatures that would prey on the weak and the innocent. We invite them to run and hide for as long as they can, but know that they will be hunted down and returned into fires of Hell from whence they came. That is our purpose, and that is our place... Caretakers to the world of light... judgment to the world of darkness. We are vengeance."

Soul Siphon

Mike turned to Corban, "My friend, you have heard the oath that everyone here has taken. You know that we are called to this duty by divine law. However, this duty cannot be assigned. It cannot be forced on someone who is unwilling. It has to be your choice, and it must come from your heart. Think carefully about your decision. What we ask of you cannot be accomplished by the faint of heart. It will tear at you both physically and mentally, but in the end, it will enable you to protect the innocent. What say you?"

Chills ran down Corban's spine. He didn't know what to say. This was the first time he'd heard of any oath, so he wasn't sure if they were just looking for a yes or no. Were they waiting for him to give a long-winded speech about why he should be accepted as a member? His life had changed so quickly that he had barely even had time to think, but he knew that he had to give them some kind of answer, "I... um..."

His mind raced, trying to find the right words. Then he remembered how much he had suffered during his possession and the creature that took everything from him, "Adramelech is still out there. As long as he exists and remains unchecked, no one will ever be safe. He will do the same thing to someone else that he did to me. I can't let that happen. I pledge myself to this group. I will help you hunt these creatures down."

"That'll do, my boy," Mike said happily. "– Friends, let us welcome our newest member, Corban McConnell."

Everyone clapped except for Mary. After a few handshakes and pats on the back, Vlad turned and headed for the kitchen, "I make something appropriate for celebration, yes? Ve have cake later."

"Just as long as you don't put any more of that spice in it," Johnny said, calling after him. "If I spend any more time on the toilet, my ass will have a permanent ring."

"No, no, I not put spice in cake, just on Johnny's slice, yes?"

"Yeah, thanks Vlad thanks a lot, buddy!"

"Johnny is most velcome."

Johnny turned back to the group, "Well, perhaps Corban should begin practicing his moves. —You know any martial arts, buddy?"

"Yeah actually," Corban replied. "I've studied judo before."

"Judo huh?" Johnny said in an unimpressed tone. "Well at least that's a good place to start."

Corban turned to Mike, "So it looks like we've got a lot of work ahead of us. When do we begin?"

VI

Corban's body was sore after the rigorous exercises that the group had put him through. Johnny and Lihua had taken it upon themselves to train Corban in normal combat, without the use of his powers. Vlad busied himself in the kitchen preparing the next meal and a celebratory cake for Corban. However, Mary was nowhere to be found. She disappeared almost immediately after the reading of the Vengeance Doctrine.

As the sun went down, Corban made his way to the shower. He knew that he needed one desperately and it was long overdue. He'd missed taking one the previous day, and the heavy workout added another layer of filth that he would need to scrub off.

As he entered his room, Corban found four sets of clothes folded and waiting for him on the bed, including underwear. Everything matched; it was all either black with navy blue designs or highlights going down the sides. It all looked very similar to what the rest of the team wore, which was something he lamented. He had never liked the idea blending in, but as he had no money and no other clothes, what choice did he have?

A small note was attached to the first shirt,

"Dear Corban,

Welcome to the fight! Can't wait to see you in action! We hope you'll enjoy your new home.

From,
All of us."

Soul Siphon

Corban smiled as he stripped out of his old clothes, stepped into the bathroom and turned on the shower. The bathroom was an oddly large one for such a small room. The shower was a large, black and white checker tiled, alcove with a wall and door of glass that created the shower. Towels and soap had already been provided and were waiting on the soup dish that protruded from the wall.

Corban felt like he was in a hotel as he turned the shower on. If nothing else, at least they had gone out of their way to make the showers a little more luxurious than the rest of the living quarters. He thought it was kind of an interesting choice, given the nature of his other living arrangements, but who was he to judge? Hot steam surrounded him as he washed himself down. The aches and pains were relaxed away by the hot water, allowing him to un-tense his muscles which helped make the healing considerably easier.

After savoring the first moment that he'd felt alive in days, Corban turned the water off and grabbed one of the soft towels. He quickly dried himself and changed into one of the t-shirts and a soft pair of sweatpants that he intended to use as pajama pants.

He paused for a moment to look himself in the mirror. This was the first time that he'd looked at himself since Mike had let him see what he'd become. Now he was able to inspect the differences more closely. His hair was a silvery white, his eyes were as black as cobalt, and his skin had almost no pigment. He was human, but barely passable. He now understood why Janine hadn't recognized him. His heart sank as he remembered what Mary had told him. He really wasn't the same person anymore.

After a few minutes, he turned away from the mirror and left the bathroom. He opened the window to get some fresh air and looked out on the city that he

Soul Siphon

called home. It was quickly getting dark and was also perfect weather, not too hot or cold. Any warm sunlight was accented with a cool breeze.

In New England, such weather only came around in mid-spring and mid-fall, and only for a few weeks. Corban welcomed it as he was most comfortable in those conditions. He'd always hoped to find someplace to live where the weather was like that year round, but he doubted that such a place existed.

He shrugged off his thoughts and lay down to go to sleep. The bed was unexpectedly comfortable, but he still wasn't certain how much sleep he would get. His mind was still racing with everything that had happened.

"Cor... ban..."

Corban once again found himself in the dark void, "Who are you, stop invading my mind!"

"Get used to it."

"I don't think so. Who are you?"

"You know who I am."

A few hours went by as Corban slept. He remained asleep until the loud sound of a fire alarm going off sent a shockwave from his back up to his eyes. They shot open and darted about the room as he sat up. He immediately rolled out of bed and got to his feet. *A fire, here? Give me a break...*

He left the room and ran down the hallway. The doors to each of the other rooms were wide open. He quickly went about checking them to make sure that everyone was up and out, though he doubted that anyone could have slept through such a racket. As expected, they were all empty. The team was most likely already waiting for him downstairs. *I must have slept through part of the alarm...*

Soul Siphon

Corban turned, ran to the stairwell, and made his way down to the first floor. He was about to run out the front door when he noticed that the rest of the group was assembled in the main hall, unfazed by the alarm. He looked at them oddly. The mood was casual, as though this was something that happened all the time.

He approached Johnny, trying to figure out what was going on, "That's not a fire alarm, is it?"

Johnny laughed, "Nope, this is Mike's way of getting our attention... pretty effective, isn't it?"

Corban sat down on one of the couches next to Lihua and across from Vlad and Johnny. Mary stood next to their couch and waited in silence for Mike to appear. Like the others, she was not reacting to the horrible noise.

Corban turned and shouted to Lihua as he took his seat, "Is this some kind of assignment?"

"Most likely. Mike usually only summons us this way if we have a job to do."

At that moment, the alarm went silent and Mike entered the room, "Everyone, we don't have much time to talk if we're to get this one. You need to get out to Castle Island, now."

Corban rubbed his eyes and looked at the small clock on the wall, "At eleven o'clock?"

"Evil doesn't only take place at decent hours, yeah?" Mary replied in a dark tone.

"Target?" Vlad asked.

Mike went over the specifics as they all listened in, "There's gang activity going on there. These people have already caused a lot of harm. They are guilty of drug trafficking, rape, spreading fear and violence through their communities, and assault. They cannot be allowed to continue their reign of terror. These guys must not be left unchecked."

Soul Siphon

"They will not," Lihua said in a confident tone.

"Good. —What do you think Corban, ready to give your powers a field test?"

Corban was unsure of himself. He was still sore from his workout earlier that day and he was exhausted. This didn't seem like the best time for him to cut his teeth, "Mike, I can barely move... I haven't gotten much sleep over the last few nights."

"You think evil is going to wait for you to be ready? Kinda stupid, yeah?" Mary cut in again.

Corban flashed her an angry look, "All right then, I guess I don't have a choice but to be ready."

"Good," Mike said. "I have every confidence in your abilities. I'm certain that you won't let us down. Now get moving!"

The group turned and headed for the armory. Lihua grabbed a pair of small machetes and a Glock pistol, Johnny grabbed a smaller knife and a revolver that fit his small hand, and Mary pulled a pair of the kodachi short swords from the wall that Lihua had been admiring earlier. She strapped them to her belt before grabbing a pair of daggers and attaching them to her hips.

"No gun?" Corban asked, surprised.

Mary looked at him as though he had just asked the dumbest possible question he could have, "What for?"

Corban shrugged. It was a stupid question. She could outmaneuver and probably outrun a bullet, and her blades were more likely to guarantee her a kill than a single bullet fired at rapid speeds. What would she need a gun for?

Corban watched her fasten a sheathed bowie knife to her leg. As she stood up, he got a full view of the curvature of her hips. He'd been too preoccupied to notice before, but now he could see her very clearly.

Soul Siphon

He unknowingly gazed at her figure a little longer than he should have.

Mary noticed and flashed him a dirty look, "Need help with something?"

Corban immediately snapped out of it, "Huh, oh… no nothing!"

He avoided Mary's scornful eyes and turned to see Vlad loading his old rifle. He looked up at Corban with a grin, "All the protection I need, yes?"

Johnny rolled his eyes, "That's just because you do everything from a distance. You don't get into the thick of the fight. I still think you should consider taking a knife for fuck's sake! That antique can only do so much!"

Vlad laughed, "I do not need to get in the middle of giant brawl, yes? Too much energy wasted and bigger chance of evidence being found with little man running around like chicken without head."

"Uh huh," Johnny replied. "We'll just see who gets more of them."

"Loser buys drinks at J.J.'s?"

"You're on!" Johnny said with a smirk. "Let's just hope our targets have some decent cash on them!"

Lihua grimaced as she tried to ignore Vlad and Johnny as they continued arguing. She turned to Corban and held out a holstered gun, "Here, a Smith and Wesson M&P45. That should do for now."

Corban looked at it oddly, "I've... never fired a gun before."

"You and most of the rest of the people who live in this state," Mary replied.

Corban smirked, "As apparently you don't either."

"Care to test that theory?"

Lihua ignored Mary as she returned her attention to Corban, "I figured as much. It is a good solid gun to

Soul Siphon

start out with. You will do fine and most likely will
not even need it."

Lihua then turned to the group, "Everyone ready
to kick some ass?"

"Always!" Johnny shouted.

"All right then, let us get out there."

Corban looked at Lihua oddly, "How?"

He got no reply. His new friends were as
motionless as statues. They each looked like they were
in deep concentration. To his surprise, Mary suddenly
began moving at incredible speeds and almost
instantly disappeared. Lihua grabbed Johnny and Vlad,
and vanished in the blink of an eye.

Corban found himself alone in the room. Then
he felt a hand on his shoulder. He turned to see Mike
with an embarrassed look on his face, "Oh sorry, I
forgot that you can't transport yourself there. That's an
ability you may or may not get when you start taking
on demons. Sorry about that, but when you've been
around for a couple billion years, you start to run out
of room in your memory."

"Um... okay?"

"We'll worry about that later. For now, let's get
you out there. I'll remind Lihua to make sure you get
home safely"

Before Corban knew what was happening, his
eyes began to blur. He blinked several times to clear
his vision and when it finally did, he found himself in
the parking lot at Fort Independence. It was almost
pitch black there, most of the street lamps had been
turned off, and the gate had long since been closed to
prevent anyone from parking there.

Corban hadn't been there since he was a child.
He used to go on the 4th of July to see the USS
Constitution get turned around and exchange cannon
fire with the fort. Many a happy afternoon as a child

was spent there, but at this moment, the fortress was a massive black wall in the darkness that gave off an ominous feeling. Even the playground off to the right looked menacing in the dark.

Corban turned and looked at Mike, "What the..."

Mike smiled, "I don't know how she got it, but Lihua has the ability to teleport and Mary has super speed as part of her power. Depending on your abilities, you may be able to emulate either. We just don't know yet and Lihua can only teleport those she can touch."

"Okay," Corban replied.

"All right everyone, fan out," Lihua called out from behind.

Mike immediately disappeared, leaving Corban at the mercy of his teammates. He grabbed the pistol off of his belt and pointed it into the darkness. Lihua touched his arm, "No my friend, use that only if you need it. The gun should not be your first line of defense."

"Too messy?"

"And too much evidence. We want to leave behind as minimal a trace as possible. That is how we work."

Corban immediately put the gun away. Lihua tapped his hand gently, "Stay close to me, we will show you what to do."

At that moment, Mary appeared next to them, "They're on the other side."

The group split up. Lihua took Corban while Mary followed close behind. Johnny and Vlad went around the other side of the old fortress, closer to the docks.

The groups made their way around to the other side. The sound of distressed voices grew in the distance as they moved. Corban's ears perked up and he turned in the direction that the sound was coming from. It was difficult to tell with the waves breaking against the stone jetty, but it sounded like they were coming from near the flagpole on the far side.

"Where's the money, Nick? You're way overdue. I told you to have the rest today."

"Look, I already paid you what I could. I don't know what more you want. Business has been slow and your interest alone is killing me. You're asking for twice what I owed."

When they cleared the fort, Corban saw a gang of ten people standing around one man. Their leader was holding an old baseball bat. He turned and smiled at his friends as Nick visibly quaked, "Nick, come on man, haven't we been good to you? You came to us, remember? We didn't know you. When you took our money, you agreed to pay it back. It's that simple."

Nick's voice trembled as he spoke, "I know Terry, but like I said, business has been slow and with the interest you charge, it's next to impossible to pay it off. I already gave you everything you were owed in full, but..."

"Hey man, you agreed to the terms. You also know what happens if you don't pay. You've only got yourself to blame here and you know that. So there really isn't much else to say."

Nick backed away, "No... You can't. Come on man..."

"Sorry," Terry said with a wide smile on his face, "time's up."

Terry brought the bat up over his head and was about to bring it down on Nick when suddenly a large laceration appeared on his throat. Terry gasped and fell backward. Blood pooled around his body as he lay on the ground, surrendering to the death throes.

Soul Siphon

The man next to him immediately turned on a flashlight and looked around while screaming, "What the fuck?"

At that moment, it looked as though the back of his head had exploded. The man fell to his side, motionless. Even at such a great distance, Corban could hear the hearty laughter that was undoubtedly coming from Vlad. *This is their idea of stealthy?*

The other gang members spread out. The few that had flashlights turned them on and scanned the area as each armed themselves with guns, knives, or whatever else they brought with them. They breathed heavily as they searched for whom or whatever had killed their brethren.

The tallest gangster pressed his flashlight against his gun as he searched the darkness. His hands shook as he moved and his aiming became erratic. He continued to spin around and look behind him out of sheer terror that someone might be there. He looked like a character in a bad teenage horror movie as continued searching.

An inhuman scream pierced Corban's eardrums as Johnny appeared in front of him. Before the gangster could react, the creature put its hands on his face and dug in with its nails. The gangster screamed as his body began to age and decay at an accelerated rate. It was as though someone had sped up in his body.

After a few seconds, the screaming stopped and the gangster's remains collapsed on the ground. His bones immediately turned to dust on impact. Johnny stood over him smiling.

"Good kill, Johnny," Lihua whispered. "Let us see who is next."

One of the other gangsters ran from the group and attempted to escape via the Head Island

Soul Siphon

Causeway. He looked behind him to see his panicked comrades begin opening fire in random directions in the hopes of scaring off or score a lucky hit on whatever attacked them. He picked up speed, thinking that he was safe, but when he returned his attention to where he was going, Lihua appeared in front of him with a seductive look on her face, "Going somewhere, handsome?"

The gangster stopped dead in his tracks, "Shit's going down back on Castle Island... what are you doing out here so late?"

Lihua smiled, "Are you worried about me?"

The gangster looked almost hypnotized, "I um... yeah... I guess..."

"Aw, that is sweet. I bet you are a real tough guy, huh? Good and strong?"

She walked up and touched his cheek. Her eyes turned bright yellow as she looked at him. The gangster was powerless, "Yes... I am very tough and strong."

"I bet that you would like to prove that to me, huh?"

"Yes."

"Great, I bet that you are so tough that you could swim really far!"

"Yes..."

"Well prove it then."

"How... ma'am?"

"Oh, I do not know… swim to Portugal?"

"Yes... ma'am... of course…"

Lihua stepped aside, allowing him to jump off of the bridge, "I will be waiting for you to get back, sweetie."

She watched him fight the current and swim out into the harbor before turning her attention back to the group, "Happy trails!"

Soul Siphon

The moment that he disappeared from view, Lihua shook her head and smirked as she turned back to the action. Corban couldn't believe her power. Was that man even aware of what had happened to him, or did he think it was his own will?

After only a few minutes of fighting, gangsters were almost completely gone. The few that were left scattered and ran back around to the opposite side of the fortress. One of them, a tall white man, thought that he was getting away when he felt a sudden pressure on his back and a pair of arms wrap around him.

A moment later, a knife that was covered in blood appeared at his throat, "Going somewhere?"

Mary had managed to sneak up on the gangster and was preventing him from escaping. The gangster cried out, "Let me go, bitch!"

"Let me go, bitch...?" Mary repeated slowly. "Do you really think that's going get you freed?"

The sound of Mary's voice was pure rage mixed with euphoria. She was agitated, but clearly enjoyed what she was doing, "You boys are real pieces of work, yeah?"

A click in Mary's ear broke her attention. *Oh shit...*

One of the other gangsters was pointing a gun at her head, "You're dead!"

Corban jumped into action at the sight of the gunman. Before Mary could react, a pair of glowing fists appeared behind the gangster who had threatened her. He froze in place as one of the fists sank into his back. His skin flashed white for a brief moment before the light flowed from his body into the fist and became a glowing orb.

The gangster went limp and fell to the ground as the orb moved away from his body. Mary watched as

Soul Siphon

the small ball of light illuminated the face of her savior, "What are you doing here Corban?"

"You got careless." He replied. "I thought I'd help you out. I didn't want to see you get shot."

Mary tensed her arm and pulled the blade across the other gangster's throat As the skin separated under the blade she was holding, blood poured from the wound and the gangster fell to the ground dead. With him out of the way, Mary pointed her blade at Corban. Her face bore a threatening look as she spoke, "I don't want or need your help, nct now, not ever. Remember that."

"All right…" Corban replied, sensing that he had somehow offended her.

She promptly turned and headed back to the parking lot where they first arrived, leaving Corban where he was standing. The rest of the team had finished off the last of the thugs and were waiting for them. Corban remained a safe distance behind her as he followed.

Lihua saw them coming, "All set? I think we got the last of them."

Corban looked back at Fort Independence, "Well... what about that guy they were attacking? Did anyone see where Nick went?"

Vlad nodded, "I see him bolt and run ze moment ze fun started."

"Coward," Mary said as she walked away from the group.

"Oh come on," Johnny replied, "what could the guy do? He was one person against ten well-armed thugs. What was he going to do? He'd probably be dead right now if it wasn't for us."

Mary ignored them and kept walking, "We're done here, yeah? Let's go home."

Soul Siphon

Lihua looked at her companions, "Johnny, Vlad, I will take you two first and then I will come back for Corban. –Just stay put okay? I promise I will be right back."

Corban rolled his eyes, "Great... why couldn't my powers have given me the ability to fly?"

At that moment, Corban's body felt weightless. His feet levitated off the ground and he hovered above the rest of the group. A nervous look appeared on his face, "What the hell?"

Lihua's eyes widened, "You can fly!"

"How... how am I doing this?"

"Focus your mind, think of the warehouse in Southie. That is how my powers work. See if you can get there."

Corban did as he was told. He closed his eyes and did his best to shut out everything that was going on around him. He thought of the warehouse and his room back in South Boston. At that moment, the world stretched around him, wind blasted his skin, and he began to move at incredible speeds. His eyes stung and were difficult to keep open as he moved.

As the world blew by, Corban blinked a few times in an attempt to force his eyes open. He succeeded just in time to see what look like bricks in the haze that was his field of vision. He knew what it was and did everything to try to stop. He was able to slow himself down, but not stop. He waved his arms and legs in every direction imaginable, but it made little difference. The bricks became bigger and bigger until they took up his entire field of vision, "Oh shit!"

Corban closed his eyes as his body slammed into the wall. His arms and legs were outstretched, and the wind was knocked out of him. He wheezed as his lungs fought to take in air and he collapsed on the ground.

Soul Siphon

The loud thud of the impact made Mary jump. She had just arrived herself and was standing near the door, about to go in. At seeing Corban's cartoon-like impact she began to laugh hysterically, "What the hell? How the hell did you get back here faster than me?"

Corban shook it off and stood up. It took a moment for his body to adjust and he almost fell over more than once as he stumbled in Mary's direction, "I guess I can fly?"

"Your landing needs work, yeah?"

Corban rubbed his aching forehead, trying to clear out the cobwebs, "Yes, thank you Captain Obvious!"

Mary continued to laugh like it was the funniest thing she'd seen in years when Mike appeared at the door, "So it looks like we don't need to worry about you getting around after all. We should, however, teach you how to land properly. I have experience with flying so I can help you with that."

Corban looked over at Mary who was now struggling to quiet down, "Are you done?"

"If only I had a camera," Mary replied as she finally stopped laughing. "The YouTube hits would have been through the roof."

Mary opened the door to the warehouse, allowing the group to proceed inside. She turned on the lights to see that Lihua and the other two had just arrived themselves. Lihua looked over at Corban, "Oh good, you made it back okay. Happy landings?"

Corban rolled his eyes as Mary burst out laughing again. It was as though Lihua's words opened a floodgate that Mary had fought hard to close, but had once again broken loose. Now there was no stopping it.

Soul Siphon

Mary wiped her eyes as she struggled to speak, "You might say that!"

VII

The next morning, Corban opened his eyes and was greeted with the sight of Mike standing over him. His eyes opened to see Mike looking down at him smiling, "Time to get up!"

Corban was still achy from the injuries he'd suffered as the result of his abrupt landing. He wanted to protest, but he knew it was pointless. *You know what he'll say; 'Evil is not going to wait for you to be ready.'*

"I don't suppose I have time for a shower?"

"No point."

"How's that?"

"You'll just need another one when you get back."

Corban rolled his eyes, "Of course…"

He sat up and pulled the black pants on that he had been wearing the night before. He then quickly ran his fingers through his hair before standing up and looking at Mike, "All right Mike, what's going on that you need me up at…"

He looked over at his clock, "Four fucking thirty in the morning… good God man, what the hell?"

"Sorry," Mike replied. "We need you to be able to fly and land without breaking any bones or you won't be much good to us."

"And this is the only time we could do this?"

"It's best if no one sees us."

Corban didn't buy his explanation, but wasn't awake enough to argue, "All right."

Mike beckoned Corban out of his room, guided him down the hallway into the elevator, and up to the roof. Corban walked to the edge and sucked in a breath air before turning around, "All right so what are we…"

His sentence trailed off when he saw that the man standing behind him no longer held a cane. Now instead of being dressed in a nice white suit, he was wearing what looked like battle armor. The most striking difference was the massive wings on his back.

Corban's jaw fell open. To see a Celestial being in all its glory was something his mind was not prepared for. He struggled not to stare at Mike beckoned to Corban, "Ready?"

Corban shrugged, "Not really?"

"Just do what you did before."

Corban looked out on the city. *What is the worst thing that could happen? Am I going to slam myself into another building or something? All right…*

"Fly…"

Corban's body responded by lifting him off of the ground. Mike nodded in approval. A quick push from his wings rendered him airborne. His wings fluttered gracefully in the wind as he hovered just above Corban, "Now let's try something easy… take us back to Castle Island."

"I don't really feel like slamming into those massive stone walls."

"No pain, no gain."

Corban rolled his eyes, "Yeah I've heard that one before."

He pictured Fort Independence in his mind, but tried to focus on the harbor surrounding it instead. If it came right down to it, he'd rather crash down in cold water than smash himself against stone. His powers responded the exact same way they had before.

His eyes blurred as it felt like not only the world, but space itself was passing him by. However, this time he could actually see where he was going. He focused hard on the water, but it didn't change the

Soul Siphon

outcome. He was helplessly careening towards the building.

At that moment, Mike appeared in front of him, attempting to block his path. Corban tried to stop, but found that he was unable to. He slammed into Mike who in turn slammed into the fortress wall.

They both fell to the ground. Corban wheezed from the impact and lay on the ground for a moment trying to regain his composure. Mike looked extremely irritated as he got back to his feet, "I'm getting way too old for this…"

Corban stood up, "See? I can't control it."

"With more practice, you will. You need more time."

Corban wasn't convinced and gave Mike an annoyed look. Mike waved his hand as though to dismiss Corban's expression as he spoke, "All right, let's try something different. We need to go somewhere a bit more controlled. Somewhere a little more open, but with walls that will act as boundaries. Hmm…"

After pondering the idea for a few moments, Mike spoke up, "Let's try this, Fenway Park."

"Fenway, are you crazy?"

"What do you mean?"

"You do know that the park has a ton of security right? It most likely has video cameras and guards all over the place!"

"True, but I wouldn't worry about it. Let's just say I can do things to electronic equipment that would make it difficult for them to detect us."

"Dare I ask?"

"Wouldn't tell you even if you did."

Apparently having no other choice, Corban got ready to go, "Fly."

As he lifted off of the grass, Mike called to him, "Picture the field, not the stadium. Try to land at the center of the diamond."

"Sure."

Corban did as he was told and pictured the field. The world blurred yet again as he picked up speed. In less than a second, he saw Fenway Park in his field of vision. He kept his mind focused on the diamond as he flew over the outfield wall, known as the Green Monster. His descent was too rapid to control and while he successfully landed right behind the pitcher's mound, he bounced off the ground like a skipping stone thrown into a pond.

Corban finally stopped deep in left field by the Green Monster. Mike landed right next to him, "You need to learn to control your descent or this is just going to keep happening!"

He looked up into Mike's eyes. Mike had an annoyed look on his face as he reached down to help Corban up. Corban was frustrated, but he got up, ready to try again.

Mike smirked, "Look, at least you didn't hit the wall this time. Come on, let's try again. Head back to Castle Island."

Corban got to his feet again and deeply exhaled, "Fly."

Corban shot through the sky and was determined to pin the landing this time. He didn't want to crash into the fortress, so he tried to aim for the land behind it. Unfortunately, Corban underestimated his speed. He missed the fort completely and plowed into the harbor behind it.

Mike appeared on the shore nearby and sighed, "Oh boy, this is going to be tedious.'

Soul Siphon

The second day of training didn't go any better than the first. Mike was struggling t help Corban with his landings, but wasn't making much progress, "All right we're clearly not getting anywhere with the landing, so let's take a break from that and try something else."

Corban released a deep breath as he spoke, "What would that be exactly?"

"A game of tag!" Mike replied. "You're it!"

Corban didn't get a chance to react. Mike spread his wings and disappeared in a flash. Corban looked up at the sky like a big brother would when he found out his younger sibling had cheated at a game, "What the hell?"

Not wanting to fall behind, Corban pictured Mike in his mind, "All right…"

The image of the Grand Canyon appeared in his mind. Corban smiled, "Gotcha! –Fly"

He immediately shot up into the sky and began flying west, towards the horizon. He picked up speed until everything became a blur around him. He put his fist forward like a superhero flying through the sky. As he outstretched his arm, he began to pick up speed.

An odd sensation entered Corban's body as he shot forward. He instinctively moved his arm slightly to the side. His body slowly altered its direction to follow. *So this is how I steer?*

This came as a relief to Corban as having the ability to steer himself where he wanted to go was far preferable to just being hurdled where ever he wanted to go. *All right, let's see how this works!*

Corban lowered his fist, which decreased his altitude. He found himself rocketing over Lake Huron. He lowered himself a little more until he was a mere few feet above the water. The wake of his speed parted the water underneath him, causing waves to form.

To Corban, this was an amazing feeling. He spread his arms to either side, which steadied him and kept him going straight. He flew above the waves until he approached the shores of Michigan.

As Corban neared the beach, he returned his fist to the forward position and raised it to bring himself higher in the air. Once he was high enough to not attract attention, he thrust it forward and rocketed off towards the Grand Canyon. The wind whipped over his body as he traveled.

Mike was hovering over one of the stony cliffs when he heard what sounded like a rocket engine in close proximity. He looked up to see Corban bearing down on him. *Not bad kid, but you're going to have to be faster than that.*

Corban saw Mike for barely a second before he disappeared. *Damn it!*

He focused his mind again and discovered that Mike was hovering over a massive citadel that was surrounded by trees with a long stretching wall on either side, "Oh, you have got to be kidding me!"

Corban focused his thoughts on the Great Wall of China and picked up speed. He flew faster and faster through the air until all of existence disappeared and what looked like a tunnel took its place. This was a new phenomenon, but if it would get him there faster, he didn't mind.

Seconds passed before the unusual vortex disappeared and was replaced by trees and a blue sky. He slowed his descent as the Great Wall came into view. Mike was hovering over it, smiling. *You're getting better, but you're not there yet!*

Mike disappeared again. Corban could feel his body beginning to tire. *This is fucking ridiculous!*

He focused again, this time he found Mike in Seattle, hovering over the space needle. His body

Soul Siphon

rocketed back to the East. He was determined to catch Mike this time, but something wasn't right. He was beginning to feel drained and began to lose control of his flying.

A second later, Corban found himself charging out of control towards the Space Needle. He was unable to stop or redirect himself. Nothing appeared to be working anymore. *Oh shit!*

In less than a second, Corban smashed into one of the pylons of the Space Needle. His world immediately went black. As he lost consciousness, he heard a loud crack and a crashing sound. *"Oh... shit..."*

Corban woke up a few hours later in his bed. Mike and Mary looked down at him with annoyed expressions. His head felt like it was about to explode as he sat up. It took a moment for his mind to turn on, but within seconds, he remembered what happened, "Oh, God…"

"Yeah I'd say so," Mike replied. "Congratulations. You managed to take out the Space Needle."

"What?" Corban asked in a panic as his eyes widened.

The look on Corban's face made Mike chuckle, "Oh relax. I repaired the damage you did and wiped the memory of anyone who was nearby. It's as though nothing happened."

"I… I don't understand… I was keeping up when…"

"Yes, you ran out of energy," Mike said, completing his sentence in a calm voice. "You need to be mindful of that. Until you master your powers, you have a finite amount of energy that you can use for flying."

Soul Siphon

As the Sun poked through the window, Mike turned for the door, "Rest up, we'll try again tonight."

"Joy…"

Mike turned and left the room, leaving Corban to deal with Mary's scornful looks. He lay back, trying to quell his headache, "Whatever you want to say, say it."

"Say what? There's nothing for me to say to you, yeah? I told Mike that you'd do more damage than good and I was right. The thing I could say right now would be an 'I told you so' to Mike. Sadly he doesn't feel the need to listen to me."

"I suppose keeping that thug from blowing your brains out was notwithstanding?"

Mary scoffed, "Get some rest, and try not to get anyone killed, yeah?"

"Whatever…"

The next day, Corban chased after Mike once again. This time he made it to the Space Needle, but Mike wasn't there. He had traveled to Niagara Falls just before Corban had arrived.

That's it. Corban thought to himself. *There has to be another way!*

Corban thought about his options for a moment. He really only had a few open to him. He could continue to chase Mike until he caused another catastrophe somewhere, or he could try to predict where Mike would go next. Quitting was also an option, but he got the feeling that Mike wouldn't let him do that.

If only there was a way that he could travel through time. Corban smiled, knowing that this wasn't possible, but the more and more he thought about it, the more various ideas came to him. He couldn't go back in time, but what about moving so fast that he stopped time, or rather it would appear that time stopped. He thought back to one of his science classes as he tried to figure out his next move. *The speed of light? Is that even possible?*

Corban's new idea presented more of a problem than just reaching that speed. Could he figure out where Mike was going fast enough to get there first and could he do it safely? *It's worth a shot...*

As before, Corban arrived where he was supposed to be. He approached the massive Horseshoe Waterfall where Mike was hovering. This was it. He picked up speed and charged towards Mike, going faster and faster.

Mike went wide-eyed and quickly darted out of the way before Corban got close and then disappeared, heading for his next destination. This was Corban's chance. He began his ascension as he picked up speed. The plan was to climb until he was high over the clouds and then make his way to his target.

The plan didn't quite go as he'd hoped and he wound up much higher in the sky than he had intended. Below him, he could see the clouds and the land above him, were stars and a dark void. His eyes darted back and forth as he continued to pick up speed. *Am I in orbit? How am I able to breathe and how am I not freezing to death?*

These were questions for another time. Corban quickly focused on Mike's next destination as he continued to pick up speed. This time, Mike was heading to Paris. He would wait for Corban over the Eiffel Tower. *Gotcha!*

Corban had less than a second. His entire body ached as he picked up more and more speed. The tunnel that had appeared last time wrapped around him again, but this time it stopped and began spiraling in the opposite direction. He didn't know what this meant, but he took it as a good sign that he was doing something right.

Mike arrived at the Eiffel Tower and hovered high enough above it that he would not be seen by any tourists. Oddly enough, he had lost sight of Corban as he moved. Out of breath, he huffed as his eyes scanned the horizon, "Now where could that boy have gone to?"

"Right behind you!"

Mike jumped as he turned, "Where did you come from? I didn't detect you incoming!"

"That's because I was already here."

"What?"

"I saw where you were going and I beat you here. Granted I had to do a couple of hundred laps around the tower to slow down, but I still had more than enough time."

"How…?"

"I began picking up speed as I approached Niagara Falls. I knew I didn't have much time, so I sacrificed any chance of catching you at the waterfall to get you at your next target. Then when I sensed that you were moving to the Eiffel Tower, I picked up enough speed to get here before you."

A bewildered look appeared on Mike's face, "But that's impossible unless…"

Then it hit Mike, "… unless you traveled faster than the speed of light."

"Bingo!" Corban said triumphantly.

Mike rubbed his forehead, "Corban, I have to ask you not to do that again."

"What, why?"

"What you did was essentially a form of time travel. You broke the speed of light and thus was able to travel fast enough to stop time in its tracks. Doing things like that can be very dangerous."

Soul Siphon

Corban let out a deep, disappointed sigh. Mike smiled at him warmly, "You did well my boy. Clearly, your powers are far beyond what I thought. Just please do not do that again."

Corban sighed, "I understand."

"Come on boy, you're probably drained after that one. Let's go home and get you some rest. We'll go back to landings tonight."

"Okay…"

/

Corban woke up after 12 hours of resting. The last few days had put an intense strain on his body. He relished what little time he got to relax, even if it meant alienating everyone around him for a while.

Corban wished he could have gone to J.J. Foley's with Johnny and Vlad, or debated philosophy and politics with Lihua, or even tried to get back on Mary's good side, but he knew that he to train. He didn't want to let them down when they needed him, so it was worth the sacrifice. Even so, he still felt quite alone at a time when he would have preferred to be with friends.

As night fell, Mike appeared to take him out to Castle Island to begin his work on landing again, "Come on Corban, you know the drill."

"Yeah, yeah…"

Corban met Mike outside. He was still tired, but Mike didn't seem to care. He needed Corban ready to go, "All right, let's fly to Castle Island and try having you land there."

"Fine."

Corban took off and headed for Fort Independence at top speeds. He tried using his newfound ability to direct himself where to go to try to stop, but found that he was unable to slow down enough to make it work. The result was the same as

Soul Siphon

before, he slammed into the side of the fort, albeit a little softer than usual.

Mike showed up on the scene a moment later with an extremely annoyed look on his face, "You must learn to control it. Now try again, head to Fenway!"

Oh man, this is going to be fun…

Corban flew hard and as before, crash-landed in the outfield at the ballpark. Mike visibly began to lose his patience with Corban, "No good, again! We'll do this all night if we have to!"

Corban flew back and forth between Fenway Park and Castle Island. The result was the same each time. He'd take off, pick up speed, and then either slam into the fort wall, land in the water, or crash land in the outfield at Fenway. He was getting an impressive collection of bruises and was starting to get agitated.

On his final lap of the night, Corban was aching all over. He was barely able to hold himself in the air and decided that it was time to teach Mike a lesson. He'd had enough for the night and needed to rest. As he picked up speed, his thoughts focused on Mike instead of the ballpark.

He came crashing out of the sky at the unsuspecting angel. Mike didn't have enough time to move as Corban crashed right on top of him. Visibly annoyed, Mike got to his feet and brushed himself off, "That's it, Corban. I don't know what more to do. I get that you can't be perfect after three days, but I would expect to see some improvement."

"Some improvement?" Corban shot back in an angry voice. "I got thrust into the middle of this. I didn't ask for any of it. I've literally had no time to cope with everything, and all you've done is watch me crash and criticize! Where are the pointers you are supposed to give me on how to land?"

Mike looked into Corban's eyes. Corban could tell that he was clearly just as frustrated, but didn't care. He was going to stand his ground no matter what Mike said.

To his surprise, Mike nodded and backed off, "You're right... okay. Look, take the next day off. We'll resume lessons after you've had a chance to heal up. Try to relax and picture how you want to land. See if it helps, okay?"

Corban took in a deep breath and calmed himself down, "Look, I'm sorry..."

"No, I know," Mike replied, cutting him off. "You're right; we have been pushing you very hard lately. It's okay, take the day and try to relax. No more practice or missions until you've had a chance to heal up."

"Okay, yeah that sounds good."

Mike turned and looked south, "Go home, we'll talk later."

Corban nodded and took off. A second later, he landed outside of the old warehouse with a massive thud and rolled down the sidewalk on Faye Street. He was banged up, but at least he didn't strike the building this time.

It was fairly early in the morning when Corban arrived, but he could hear the sound of people stirring inside. He was completely miserable having failed to figure out how to land. It had been the same thing for the past few days; he arrived back at the warehouse with bumps and bruises everywhere and today would be no different. His only comfort was that, with the exception of Mary, the group had taken him in as one of them.

Soul Siphon

Corban proceeded to the kitchen to see what everyone was doing. As usual, the group was sitting around the dining room table waiting for whatever horror Vlad was planning on subjecting them to. The looks on Johnny's and Lihua's faces were a pretty good indicator that they were prepared for the worst. The food never seemed to bother Mary, though she didn't eat much.

Lihua looked up at Corban, "How was flying with Mike?"

"Stimulating…"

"That fun huh?" Johnny asked.

Mary didn't say anything. After a few minutes, she got up from the table and headed up to the roof. Corban smiled at her as she walked by, "Not staying for breakfast?"

Mary froze in place for a moment, but didn't say anything. She released a sigh, brushed past him, and left the room. Corban sat down and leaned on his right arm, "What the hell is her problem?"

"Mary has been known to hold grudges," Lihua replied.

"No kidding…"

"But…" Lihua said hesitantly, "I do not think that this is what is going on here."

"What do you mean?"

"From what little Mary actually says to me, she opened up to you. She actually let herself be… her version of open because she saw something of herself in you. Like you, she lost people that she cared about when she died. That is something that most of us cannot relate to. None of us had families or friends that we had cared enough about to miss. She did, and so do you. In you, at least from my perspective, it seemed like she had found a kindred spirit, or at least someone she could commiserate with."

Soul Siphon

"And I fucked it up when I was mean to her, is that it?"

Lihua looked at Corban sympathetically, "I hate to say it, but yes. Mary is very selective of whom she spends her time with, and I mean selective to the point where she is often isolated. I cannot imagine a more lonely existence. You yelling at her when she was making an effort to help, regardless of your reasoning, probably cut her deeper than you know."

Corban rubbed his forehead with his right hand, "Great…"

"Do not think too much about it," Lihua replied with a comforting smile. "She will come around eventually. You can apologize when she does."

"And hope she doesn't rip your arm out of its socket," Johnny added.

"That too."

The rest of the day was uneventful. The group spent their time either working out or watching TV. Corban was tempted to go up to the roof, but his mind kept telling him that it was best to let Mary have her space for now. He instead spent his time arguing football stats with Johnny.

As the day came to a close, Lihua called in an early night and headed to her room. Johnny sat back in his chair and looked over at Vlad, "J.J.'s?"

"Sounds good!"

Vlad turned to Corban and beckoned to him, "Going out for drinks, you coming?"

Corban wanted to go with them, but decided against it, "Thanks guys, but I'm still a little tender. I think I'm going to lick my wounds a little longer. Rain check?"

"All right, ve'll hold you to it though," Vlad replied.

Soul Siphon

"It's probably best we ease you into it anyway," Johnny added, "Vlad here has been known to drink more than is supposed to be humanly possible and usually has a hard time getting home."

"As if you should talk!" Vlad snapped. "You drink as much as I do!"

"Yeah, but do you see me get that drunk?"

"Ve'll see tonight! Whoever gets drunker pays for the booze tonight!"

Corban laughed as the two friends stood up and headed for the door, "Have fun guys."

He watched as Vlad and Johnny headed off to the bar singing in Russian. He smirked as he wondered how Johnny managed to successfully get into a bar in the first place. It would be something he'd need to ask Johnny about later, but at that moment, he had to take care of himself.

Corban went up to his room, showered, and cleaned himself up. He went through his top drawer until he found a pair of sweatpants that suited him. The moment he was presentable, Mike appeared in his doorway, "Corban."

Corban looked up at him, "Yeah?"

"Sorry to bother you."

Corban studied his features for a moment, "Uh oh, you look like you just got some bad news."

"Your perception is accurate. We received another mission, this time out to Chicago."

"I thought you said no mission today?" Corban asked.

"I did and it seemed like you guys were having fun, but this one was important. I wanted to give you enough time to adjust and bond with the other members of our team, so Mary insisted that she could handle it."

Soul Siphon

Corban's eyes widened, "You sent her out alone?"

"Yeah I did and she's in trouble. She was a bit overconfident this time around."

"Stupid... Why would you send her out alone?"

"Like I said, she insisted that she could handle it."

Corban felt his face begin to heat up. He wanted to rip into Mike, but now was not the time, "Where is she?"

"An old abandoned garage off of South Pulaski Road."

Corban's hands shook, ready to rip Mike's head off, "Are you nuts? From what I read a while back, that's one of the worst neighborhoods in Chicago! You really sent her there alone?"

He didn't wait for Mike to respond. Instead, he turned and ran to the open window at the end of the hallway. Without thinking, he pictured the city of Chicago and his idea of what one of the worst areas would look like. His powers levitated him off the ground as he jumped out of the second-floor window and rocketed him out of the city. *Sending her out on her own like this, what an idiot! I know she's tough, but that was just stupid!*

Soul Siphon

VIII

Corban arrived in Chicago within minutes, faster than any fighter jet. He hovered over the city for a few moments before he found the area that he was looking for. Unwilling to let a single moment go to waste, he dove down towards the street he was looking for and scanned the area for the abandoned garage.

It didn't take him long to find it. The area was covered in garbage, extremely unkempt, and evidently not being used. He set down in his typical rough landing as quickly as he could. After taking a moment to recover, he stood up, brushed himself off, and immediately heard sounds of violence coming from inside.

Corban ran as fast as he could and barged through the door. What he found inside was total chaos. There was a group of roughly twenty people trying to fight off a dark shadow. Though it was little more than a blur, the reddish top gave away its identity. It was Mary.

She danced around two gunshots before decapitating her assailant and moving on to the next one. This gangster was a tall black man with cropped hair. He swung at her with a club, but was unable to connect. As he brought his club back around, a spike appeared under his shirt on his chest. He had been stabbed from behind. Blood poured from his lips as quickly as the life force fled his body.

Mary withdrew her blades before moving on. Her next target was an Asian man dressed all in black with fairly long hair. Corban noticed that, while the other thugs panicked, this one remained calm and studied her moves and fighting style. He almost seemed like a professional fighter as he watched and waited.

Soul Siphon

"Nick, watch out!" One of the other thugs called out.

Mary dodged around a few more pot shots that were fired in her direction. They weren't a threat, but dodging them forced her to take her attention off of her target and this slowed her down.

Nick calmly brushed a strand of black hair from his face as he continued to stare at Mary. The moment that she moved towards him, he moved out of the way and prepared to counter her attack. Before she could strike, he pulled a knife in anticipation of her movements. Using impressive speeds of his own, he was able to dodge her attacks and land two hits with his own blade, "Not this time!"

Mary yelped in pain as she tumbled across the room. She had been cut badly on the cheek and stabbed clean through her left hip. She pressed her hand against it and dropped to one knee.

Two of the remaining gangsters grabbed her, one by each arm. These two looked Italian. They were extremely tall with dark hair and a slight tan.

Nick pointed at Mary as he spoke, "Phil, Ian, get her up!"

Phil and Ian did as they were told and dragged her up on her feet. Her wounds bled out as she was violently thrust upwards. Her eyes pierced into Nick as he stood in front of her, holding a bloody knife. He took a menacing step forward, "Time to pay for what you did, bitch!"

"You can't kill me," Mary replied in a low voice.

"Oh don't worry. I'm not going to kill you. I'm just going to carve your eyes out of their sockets!"

Nick took another step towards her, grabbed her hood, and pulled it back with such force that her neck ripped the collar of her shirt wide open. The moment

Soul Siphon

he let go, her shirt fell back into place, partially exposing her chest while Ian, the man on her right, grabbed her hair and held her head back. Nick's eyes widened in surprise, "Well well, what have we here?"

"She's not bad boss, maybe we should make her a working girl. At least then she'd be worth something."

Nick laughed, "If I thought for a moment that we could make that happen, I'd be all for it, but this one doesn't look like she'd be susceptible enough. I'm with you; it's a shame to waste something so fine…"

Nick ran the flat side of his knife down her cheek as he spoke. The fire in Mary's eyes was a good indicator of the ticking time bomb within. As the blade reached her chin, she spat into Nick's eye.

Nick backed away slightly and wiped his eye as he continued, "… but it's not worth the trouble."

Mary clenched her jaw, showing her teeth as Nick brought the knife up to her right eye. She braced herself for what was to come. Her face remained emotionless as the knife drew closer. She sucked in one last breath, but kept her eyes wide open in defiance.

Nick held his breath as the blade reached within a millimeter of her eye, "Lights out."

"Ugh!"

He pulled the knife away and whirled around to see who had made that noise. He barely grazed Mary's cheek as he turned, "What was that?"

Every eye in the place darted around trying to see where the sound had come from. It was dark inside the building as there were no functioning lights, but the group could still tell that something was amiss. It felt like there was another presence in the room with them.

Soul Siphon

"Where's Mark?" One of the gangsters called out.

"Wasn't he with you?"

"Yeah, he was right here a second ag... ACK!"

The voice went silent. Nick's breath began to quiver, "Tom? Tom are you okay?"

Silence.

"Tom!"

A few moments passed as the gang continued to scan the area for any sign of life. Nick quickly began barking out orders, "There's another one here. Fan out and find him! Make sure his remains can't be identified when you're done!"

"You got it, boss."

At that moment, another blood-curdling scream could be heard from the other side of the garage

Another henchman cried out in the darkness, "Get him, fucking get him "

Nick's henchmen were getting cut to ribbons all around him. The sound of gunfire could be heard all about the room. He quickly turned back to Mary, intent on quickly blinding her before having his people get out of there.

Corban appeared in front of him with a menacing stare. The world around them seemed to have frozen. The gunfire and screaming sounded distant and muffled and the two men holding Mary looked frozen in time. They were as still as statues, completely unaware of Corban's presence.

Nick took a step back, "Who the fuck are you?"

Corban didn't respond. He didn't see any need to as he quickly knocked the knife out of Nick's hand and grabbed both sides of his head. Corban then focused his mind, pressing as hard as he could, "Give me your soul!"

Soul Siphon

Nick screamed in agony as Corban ripped the soul right out of his head. He remained standing long enough for Corban to rip a white orb from his chest. The orb rotated in Corban's hand for a moment before he crushed it as Nick collapsed on the ground.

Corban felt the flow of energy and saw the mob's victims. They were not only guilty of pretty much everything from murder, stealing, rape, and corruption, but also something far more malevolent.

Corban clenched his jaw, "You monsters..."

The images passed through Corban's mind for less than a second. It was all the time he needed to process the information. He then came back to reality to deal with the scene. Time was of the essence and Mary was too badly injured to keep fighting. All he could do was get her out of there as quickly as possible and leave the gang for another day.

Panicked shots fired in their direction as Corban approached the two men that were holding Mary. He felt his face heat up as he stepped towards them, "I saw what you do... slave traders. Not only do you abduct people who don't pay, but you also force them into submission by various means. You condition your victims... subject them to all kinds of evils in order to break them..."

Before either one had a chance to react, Mary broke free of Phil's grasp and punched him in the face, breaking his nose. Corban grabbed Ian's face and pulled his soul out of his body, "Is that what you had planned for Mary?"

As Mary was released from their grip, she dropped to her hands and knees, still injured and bleeding. She looked up at Corban, clearly surprised to see him, "What are you doing here?"

Soul Siphon

"You're dealing with twenty well-armed gang thugs and you thought you could handle this on your own? Very stupid move!"

Corban pushed away from Mary and helped her knock out two more gangsters that came at them with clubs. He then grabbed Mary and backed her out the door as quickly as he could while dodging gunfire, "I'd say this mission is a failure."

Mary shook her head, "I'm fine!"

"Stop being stubborn."

"I said I'm fine!"

"Bullshit, you can't even stand!"

Before Mary could protest any further, Corban picked her up and floated out of the garage. Mary tried to kick free, "We need to finish here! This scum needs to pay!"

"Not going to happen today."

"Put me down...!"

"You're going to get yourself killed!"

"I can't die."

"Not from bullets or knives, but what about stupidity?"

Corban ignored Mary's protests and rocketed off into the sky like he had before. He brought himself up above the clouds as high as he could while still being able to hold on to Mary. The stars above and the city lights below complimented each other as Corban glided through the night sky.

Mary stopped protesting and trying to get out of Corban's arms, which was good because he wasn't listening anyway. Her eyes instead seemed focused on the view around her. Blood dripped from her face and hip, but it looked like she was ignoring it.

Corban was relieved that he got her out of there. He knew that she would heal up very quickly, but in a fight, those minutes might as well have been days.

Mary flashed Corban an annoyed look, "I didn't know there were going to be this many. Mike's Intel was a little off this time, yeah?"

Corban's eyes narrowed, "Does this happen often?"

"Never."

"Very odd."

Corban's abrupt touch down at their hideout interrupted his thoughts. He crash-landed again, but was able to keep her from hitting the ground. Mary gripped his arm tightly. He looked down at her in concern, "You okay?"

"Yes, though I'm lucky to still be alive with the way you fly!"

"Doesn't matter, you can't die anyway, remember?"

Corban quickly brought her inside, over to the couch. She fought out of his arms and sat sulking while he ran into the kitchen, "Wait there."

He sifted through the largest cabinet, making a lot of noise as plates and metal pots were shifted around on the shelves. *Damn it, where is it?*

He could hear Mary's annoyed voice from the next room, "What the hell are you doing now?"

Corban looked back, annoyed, "What does it look like I'm doing? I'm trying to find the damn first aid kit. I know it's here."

"It's not necessary, hero."

"Yeah so you say, but then again you also said that you could still fight! –Ah, here it is!"

Corban pulled a white box out of the cabinet and brought it out to the living room. He set it down on the couch next to Mary and opened it. Inside, he grabbed a piece of gauze and some hydrogen peroxide. He poured some on the gauze and moved towards her hip.

Soul Siphon

Mary rolled her eyes and slipped a thumb down the waist of her cargo pants. She then pulled the left side down enough for Corban to see her wound. To his surprise, the cut was gone. All that was left was some dried blood and a red mark on her milky white skin. His eyes narrowed as he noticed the last line of tattooed lettering right above her hip. He decided to ask her about it later and turned his attention to her face. His fingers quickly brushed her red hair out of the way to look at her cheek. The cut there was also gone.

Mary turned her head slightly to the side with an annoyed look, "See? Nothing to worry about, yeah?"

Corban sighed, "I guess I underestimated our healing abilities."

"Clearly."

Corban packed up the case and returned it to the kitchen, "So I'm curious, what happens if we lose a limb or, Heaven forbid, our head?"

A brief silence was the only response that Corban would get. He closed the cabinet and went back out to the living room to see what was going on. To his annoyance, Mary was gone.

Frustrated, Corban sighed as his arms dropped to his sides, "Oh God damn it!"

Corban slammed his fist on the doorway, just about ready to just give up. *This is getting me nowhere. She clearly doesn't want anything to do with me, so why do I keep trying?*

Corban proceeded to the elevator and headed to the dorms. The elevator beeped and let him off on his floor. He pulled out his set of keys and opened the door to his room.

Frustrated, he flopped down on his bed and closed his eyes, but he wasn't tired. He immediately reopened them and lay in his room staring at the ceiling restlessly. He sat up and looked out the window at the nighttime cityscape for a few minutes.

As he watched the lights in the buildings flicker on and off at different times, he remembered the night that he'd talked to Mary on the roof. Then the memory of Mary's angry face appeared in his mind. Granted he had been in rough shape as he tried to cope with the direction his life had taken, but Mary had been the one who tried to reach out to him, despite her cold exterior. *Maybe just one last try. She'll probably either blow me off or let me have it, but at least my conscience will be satisfied then.*

The elevator door slid open a few minutes later and Corban made his way outside. He stopped and took a deep breath of air as the breeze passed over his skin. He stepped out on to the open roof and slowly looked around.

Mary was nowhere to be seen. Was she not up there? Corban sat down in the same place he had previously and waited. If she wasn't already there watching him, he was certain that she'd appear at some point.

His thoughts began to dwell on everything that had happened. Should he try to reach out to his family again? He didn't even give his mother a chance, but given how Janine reacted, he doubted that she would be any different. No, to them, he was now a stranger and it was unlikely that anything would ever change that.

At the very least, this would give Janine the chance to move on and meet someone at her own school. Trying again to reach out to her wasn't worth the stress it would subject her to. Their relationship had been all but done, so there really wasn't any point.

"You're invading my space again, hero!"

Soul Siphon

Corban turned to see Mary looking at him. The anger in her eyes appeared to have been slightly tempered. Judging by the look on her face, she was more annoyed than angry.

Corban looked at her apologetically, "Sorry?"

"You should be, what are you doing here? Come to bitch me out again, yeah?"

"No... I..."

"Then what, why are you bothering me?"

Corban sighed, "I came to apologize for what I said. I was bent out of shape over what happened, and honestly, I'm still not sure that I'm ready for all of this."

"You're not; you have no idea what you're doing. You have very little control over your powers and they drain you way too quickly. The mental strain put on you by the memories of your victims can't be healthy for your mind, and who knows where all of this will lead!"

"I know all this," Corban admitted. "I'm not here to argue with you. You were trying to be nice and I was mean to you. You didn't deserve that, and I'm sorry for it. I don't want this to be the way things are between us. I'm sorry, okay?"

Her fists were clenched at her side and the look on her face had not softened. It didn't seem like he was getting through to her at all, "Okay, I'll leave you alone then. I don't want to upset you any more than I have."

Corban got up and walked past Mary, heading for the elevator, "Have a good night."

Mary's features slowly softened and she let out a deep, irritated, sigh as she spoke, "Hero, wait..."

Corban stopped in his tracks and turned back to her, "Yes?"

Mary brushed a few strands of hair out of her face that had been caught by the wind. A pained look appeared on her face, "You saved my ass earlier and I didn't really thank you for it... we're even, yeah? You don't have to leave if you don't want to."

Corban smiled, "All right. If you're sure, I'll hang around for a while."

Corban walked back over to the edge and knelt down, looking out at the city. Mary stood completely stiff for a moment. She seemed unsure of herself as though a decision to kneel down next to him could somehow be painful. He waited to see what she'd do. Was she going to join him or keep him at arm's length?

Corban didn't say anything. He didn't even look at her and kept his eyes on Boston. He hoped that she would make the first move, but she seemed hesitant. After a few tense moments, he felt her body gently brush against his as she sat down next to him. Relief poured over him as he let out a breath that he hadn't realized he was holding

She finally released her muscles and knelt down next to Corban. He glanced over at her before looking back out at the city. She followed his gaze as she hesitantly spoke, "How are you handling your new surroundings? Vlad's cooking hasn't done any permanent damage, yeah?"

"No it hasn't," Corban chuckled. "Can't complain much... unless you mean our living situation. Our rooms are a little bare, except for the bathroom, holy shit!"

"They are really nice. Definitely a stark contrast from where we sleep, yeah?"

"I know, weird huh?"

"Don't look at me, I didn't design the place."

Soul Siphon

"Well it was a logical assumption," Corban replied jokingly. "Especially given that you're most likely older than this building."

"You watch yourself, little man!" Mary shot back.

"Little man? I'm at least a foot taller than you!"

"True," Mary admitted, "but there are at least a hundred different ways I could dismember you right now, yeah?"

The look in her eyes told Corban that she was not kidding, "Okay point taken. Please don't kill me."

"Haha, I'll think about it."

Corban was happy to see that she was smiling. She was actually quite a bit prettier when her face wasn't twisted into a scowl. It was like her whole face brightened up.

Mary looked back at the door, then at Corban, "You died at 21, right?"

"Very funny, I'm 22 and I'm... or rather I was in my last year of college..."

"Good enough."

Mary ran back to one of the air conditioning vents and pulled out an odd looking green bottle. The label had all but worn off and the glass looked ancient. She the wiped dust off as she brought it over to Corban, "Want a drink? You look like you need one. I've seen that distant stare before."

"Yes!" Corban admitted, gratefully.

Mary bit down on the cork and pulled it out. She spit it into her hand and took a quick swig of the bottle's contents. Her eyes closed as she lowered the bottle and allowed the liquid to slide down her throat, "Good, very smooth."

She then handed the bottle to Corban. He held it up under his nose and examined the contents. A strong scent of licorice filled his nostrils, "What is this?"

Soul Siphon

"Absinthe."

"Absinthe?" He asked. "What was this something that people commonly drank back in your time?"

"Depended on the person I guess. I kept a couple of cases from my time in France. That's one of the last bottles."

Corban looked at it oddly, "How old is this?"

Mary shrugged, "A hundred thirty years old, give or take? I lost count. It's good quality though and it cost me quite a bit."

"Imagine what it'd be worth now," Corban said as he tilted the bottle back.

The green liquid slid into his mouth where it overwhelmed his senses. The strong flavors and sharpness of the alcohol were like a kick to the teeth. Surprisingly though, it went down very smoothly. Corban blinked a few times and cleared his throat, "Very nice."

"Your first time drinking absinthe?" Mary asked.

Corban took another swig and was certain that he would shortly lose his voice. Mary chuckled as she watched his face begin to turn red, "Well don't like it too much. I only have a few bottles left and the stuff ain't cheap."

As Mary sat down next to Corban, her shirt rode up slightly, revealing the tattoo again. It was too dark for him to make out the words, but the handwriting appeared to be a very fancy form of cursive, "What does that say?"

"Huh?"

Corban pointed to her exposed side, "The tattoo, what's the quote?"

Soul Siphon

Mary lifted the left side of her sweatshirt so that he could get a better look. The lettering extended from her left elbow to her hip,

"With Ate by his side come hot from Hell,
Shall in these confines with a monarch's voice,
Cry 'Havoc,' and let slip the dogs of war;
That this foul deed shall smell above the earth."

Corban had heard part of it before, but didn't know where it was from, "A quote about revenge, huh?"

"Yup, right out of William Shakespeare's Julius Caesar."

"That's actually kind of cool. You got that after Mike brought you back?"

"Yup, among others."

"Others?"

Mary took another sip of absinthe before pulling her sweatshirt all the way off, leaving her in a black lace undershirt. She then proceeded to lift it up as she turned away from Corban so that he could see her back, "This is my favorite."

On Mary's back was a massive cross that ran from shoulder to shoulder, and from her neck, all the way down to the small of her back. The body of the cross was decorated with Celtic ties running through it. A large, detailed heart was situated at the intersection of the beams. The vertical body of the cross appeared to be stained in blood while the horizontal beams each had a vicious-looking dragon perched on them. The dragons' wings were spread in such a way that it gave off the illusion that they were actually on Mary's back. The claws of the dragons dug into the cross as though attempting to rip it apart.

Mary looked over her shoulder as Corban's eyes scanned her back. He was very impressed by the artwork. Clearly whoever did it, took their time, "Sweet paint job."

"I have one more on my leg, but you're not seeing that."

Corban laughed, "Understood."

The two sat silently for a few moments as they sipped from the bottle. Corban had a question in the back of his head that he wanted to ask Mary, but wasn't sure what would happen if he did.

"Go ahead."

"What?" Corban asked, surprised.

"You look like you want to ask me something. Go ahead."

"All right..," Corban replied hesitantly. "You spend so much time alone and keep yourself isolated from your friends. I don't understand why. Do you not like us?"

"No, it's not that."

"Okay, then what?"

Mary grabbed the bottle and took a long drink before speaking again, "It's because I couldn't stop him."

"Who?"

"The man who killed me."

"You said he snuck up on you."

"He did, but he also killed other women."

Corban's eyes narrowed, "How many?"

"I don't have the exact number, but there were quite a few."

"Jeez, who was he, Jack the Ripper?" Corban asked in an almost whimsical tone.

Mary's jaw quivered slightly as she looked into Corban's eyes. His features stiffened when he realized that he'd touched a nerve. He half expected her to explode as she replied, "Yeah."

A chill traveled down Corban's spine and sent tremors to his hands. Had he just heard her right? Had she really been killed by Jack the Ripper? "Wait, are you serious?"

She clenched the bottle tightly and looked away, "Yup, I'm what they euphemistically called the last of 'The Canonical Five;' Polly Nichols, Annie Chapman, Elizabeth Stride, Catherine Eddowes, and myself. We were all the victims of a madman. I knew the others, not well, but I knew them. They may not have been the most upstanding of people, but they didn't deserve what happened."

"I'm sorry…" Corban said in as sympathetic a tone as he could manage.

"I don't remember much from the murder… but I do remember that I was in pain… a lot of pain. I still remember the terror I felt as I was being ripped apart, but nothing else. I consider that merciful."

"I can definitely see why. So what happened after that?"

Mary shrugged, "Mike found me. He got to me before the undertakers could bury what was left. He removed me from that lousy wooden box and moved me to his hideout. That's when he started working to rebuild me."

"Rebuild you?"

"You know what he did, yeah? The methods he used?"

"Well some of them. It wasn't exactly a flattering description, but…"

"I don't want to go into the details, but needless to say it took Mike a while."

Corban felt sick. He couldn't believe what he'd just heard, "I'm really sorry."

Soul Siphon

Mary shook her head, "Ancient history, yeah?"

"But that doesn't explain why you isolate yourself."

Mary took another drink and wiped her lips before saying anything, "I didn't get to kill him. After I was brought back, I had no idea who he was. The room was so dark that I never saw his face. So instead I spent my time taking down other people who were hurting the girls that were out on the street. Jack the Ripper wasn't the only threat we faced out there. I spent my first few years protecting the girls from the thugs roughing them up for protection money. I did my best to keep them safe, that was all I could do. Then I found out that there were more people hurt by him... ones that I could have prevented."

"You can't blame yourself for that!"

"Can't I? Had I been able to stop him... maybe they would have survived."

Corban fell silent. He didn't know what to say to that. She was blaming herself for something that clearly wasn't her fault and had been for years.

Mary took another drink before passing the bottle to Corban, "Look, I don't want to talk about this anymore. Can we talk about something more pleasant?"

"I was about to suggest the same thing," Corban replied before choking down another shot of Absinthe. "So tell me about your life. What is there to know about Mary Kelly that the history books don't tell us?"

Mary grabbed the bottled swallowed a little more before she spoke, "There really isn't much more to me. I was born in Limerick, Ireland. My father was an ironworker town. It was a modest life, but an honest one."

"Any brothers or sisters, or just you?"

"Heh, I used to tell people that I had 7 brothers and one sister, but it was just one of each. I was the middle child."

"Why would you do that?"

Mary shrugged, "It was usually a good way to get rid of men that I didn't want to deal with. Prospective suitors tend to shy away when you've got a whole gang of brothers ready to beat them up."

"Okay..," Corban replied.

"My older brother Johnto was a member of the 2nd Battalion Scots Guards, stationed in Ireland. I always looked up to him. My sister, Lilly, was always a little wild one. Running around like there was a barn on fire."

"Sounds like a wonderful life. What happened?"

Mary frowned, "I was married off at 16. It didn't last long. He was killed in an accident a few years later, at which point my life went downhill fast. I was left with almost nothing and thus started working in the brothels."

Corban hung on every word as she told her story. She was actually turning out to be somewhat easy-going and seemed to be enjoying herself, "Haha, so he tried to rough up one of my friends at the boarding house because she wouldn't pay attention to him. So the moment he laid a hand on her, I sucker punched the lousy ass right in the nose!"

"Whoa, what did he do?" Corban asked through his own drunken haze.

"My friends thought he was going to beat the shit out of me, but the fat bastard fell backward and walked away holding his bloody nose."

"Oh, no way!"

Mary laughed, "This was a guy who loved to throw his weight around and act all tough, but one

Soul Siphon

good blow to the nose and he runs away like a whiney little bitch. Not even worth my time, yeah?"

"Heh, doesn't sound like it! What kind of ass would pick on a woman half his size?"

"Well, I was a lot bulkier back then too. Had to be pretty but tough at the same time, yeah?"

"You were fat?"

"No, not really, stout is more like it. It was more muscle than anything. I didn't slim down until about 70 years ago."

"Tough girl!" Corban said in a playful tone.

"Yeah well, the people on the East End certainly thought so. They called me Black Mary after that and I earned the reputation of being quarrelsome. You believe that shit, yeah?"

"Yeah, I could totally see that."

Mary gave him a friendly shove, "Well say what you want, but there weren't many people who wanted to mess with me after that."

Corban frowned, "But it was such a dismal existence. I couldn't even imagine…"

Mary shrugged, "It wasn't as bad as all that, hero! We did all right, and we got by on our own. Don't get me wrong it was tough, but those of us that were able to survive did all right."

"I guess so," Corban replied.

Corban and Mary finished the bottle and gave up talking. Mary's cheeks were almost as red as her hair. She remained quiet for a moment as she watched Corban.

Mary appeared to be getting uncomfortable as the two sat against the wall staring at each other. The silence was becoming awkward and Corban was desperately trying to find a way to break it. Relief came when, out of nowhere, Mary jumped to her feet and started singing.

Soul Siphon

To Corban's surprise, she was actually quite talented and could hold a tune even while completely wasted,

"With me arms around her waist, she slyly hinted
marriage,
When to the door in dreadful haste came Captain
Kelly's carriage,
Her looks told me full well, and they were not
bewitchin'
That she wished I'd get to hell, or somewhere from the
kitchen.
Sing too-ra-loo-ra-lie, singing too-ra-loo-ra-laddie
Sing too-ra-loo-ra-lie, singing too-ra-loo-ra-laddie.

She flew up off my knees, five full feet up or higher
And o'er head and heels threw me slap into the fire
My new Repealer's coat that I bought from Mr.
Mitchell
With a thirty-shilling note went to blazes in the
kitchen.

Sing too-ra-loo-ra-lie, singing too-ra-loo-ra-laddie
Sing too-ra-loo-ra-lie, singing too-ra-loo-ra-laddie.

... Just as the clock struck six we sat down to the table,
She handed tea and cakes and I ate what I was able,
I had cakes with punch and tea till me side had got a
stitch in,
And the time passed away with our courtin' in the
kitchen.
Sing too-ra-loo-ra-lie, singing too-ra-loo-ra-laddie,
Sing too-ra-loo-ra-lie, singing too-ra-loo-ra-laddie.
A too-ra-loo-ra-lie, and a too-ra-loo-ra-laddie!
A too-ra-loo-ra-lie, and a too-ra-loo-ra-laddie!
Woohoo!"

Soul Siphon

Corban laughed as she fell back into a seated position with his arm around her. She had a wide grin and a sparkle in her eyes that was accentuated by her rosy cheeks, "Okay, your turn!"

"Huh?"

"I sang one, now it's your turn!"

"Um... I didn't know this was a sing-off!"

"Well, now you do! Come on, entertain me! Your name's McConnell, so I know you've got some Irish in you."

"Ugh... all right..."

Corban was only part Irish, but he was cultured enough to know a few old-world tunes. His mother had all but insisted that he learn the culture and customs of his heritage. He remained silent for a moment, trying to think of a good song.

A gust of wind caught a few strands of Mary's hair and reminded him of a song his mother sang to him as a child. He turned slightly to face Mary as he began singing,

"The moon was bright, the night was clear,
No breeze came over the sea,
When Mary left her Highland home,
And wandered forth with me,
The flowers be-decked the mountainside,
And fragrance filled the vale,
But by far the sweetest flower there,
Was the rose of Allendale,

Oh, the rose of Allendale,
Sweet rose of Allendale,
By far the sweetest flower there,
Was the rose of Allendale"

Soul Siphon

Mary's eyes looked like they were tearing up as Corban's voice carried through the darkness. She listened intently as he continued singing the old song. She'd heard this song before, but it never held as much meaning to her as it did then.

"And when my fever'd lips were parched,
On Afric's burning sands,
She whispered hopes of happiness,
And tales of distant lands,
My life has been a wilderness,
Unblessed by fortune's wheel,
Had fate not linked my love to hers,
The rose of Allendale,

Oh, sweet rose of Allendale,
Sweet rose of Allendale,
Had fate not linked my love to hers,
The rose of Allendale"

Another smile stretched across Mary's face. This time, it wasn't one of drunken euphoria or just happiness, it was a look of content. She quickly wiped her eyes before any tears could fall, "Damn you for singing that song, hero. It's not even Irish… but… it does bring back memories. I haven't heard anyone sing it in years."

Her eyes closed as they surrendered a single tear. Corban placed his hand on her left cheek, wiping it dry. She bit the right side of her lower lip as she leaned into his palm and clasped his arm with her left hand. A deep breath escaped her lips in a way that it seemed like she had been holding it.

It was at this moment that Corban realized just how badly Mary was still being haunted by her past. Even after all those years, her own demons had never left her. She didn't feel like she was up to the task of protecting those she cared for, after her failure with Jack the Ripper, so instead, she kept her distance. That realization weighed heavily on him as he gently brushed a few strands of red hair from her face. Her blue eyes glistened in the faint light of the city as she looked at him.

Corban wanted to say something, anything, to help quell her guilt, "Look, about what happened, I…"

Before Corban could get the words out, Mary pushed herself against him. Her lips connected with his while her hand found its way to the back of his neck. She gripped him tightly, making it impossible to pull away.

Corban didn't expect this, quite the opposite in fact. He had taken a gamble just putting his arm around her. Part of him had feared that she would rip it off, but when she leaned into him, that fear appeared to be unfounded.

You know it's unlikely she's going to remember any of this tomorrow, right? Corban thought to himself. *I guess we'll just wait and see where it goes. Hopefully some good will come of this.*

Mary released Corban's neck, allowing him to pull back slightly. The heavy scent of absinthe was still prevalent on her lips. She opened her eyes and looked up into Corban's. Her features were completely glossed over and he wasn't much better off.

He stared at her for a few moments. Her red hair flowed in the gentle breeze as she sat back. Her eyes, though pained, were very telling of how she was feeling. Her stare was that of an innocent child, waiting for her parents to say something. The bags under her eyes were getting darker as the night slipped by. Tired, she finally broke her gaze and struggled to her feet, "I think it's time to turn in, yeah?"

Soul Siphon

She looked down at Corban and stretched out her hand to him, "Walk me to my room?"

Corban got to his feet and took her hand, "I'd be happy to."

The two of them stumbled to the elevator. As their feet struggled to hold them up, Corban stumbled over and would have fallen had Mary not been there to catch him. Mary laughed faintly, "Wow, you need to learn to hold booze a little better! You're not doing so well."

"Look who's talking! You're what, 150 years old and you can't hold your shit any better than me?" Corban shot back.

"I'm also half your size, yeah?"

"... yeah, yeah..."

The two guided each other into the elevator, which was open and waiting for them. They were stumbling and tripping over each other, laughing hysterically. Neither thought much of it as they stepped inside the elevator and, without actually pushing the buttons, headed for the dorms. The ride down was quiet and mercifully short.

The moment the elevator door opened, Mary stumbled out laughing loudly. Corban thanked his lucky stars that Vlad and Johnny were so plastered from earlier that they probably would not be roused by the noise. Lihua, on the other hand, would most likely not be very happy with them.

Corban guided Mary down the hall trying desperately to quiet her, "Come on Mary, shhh! Let's get you to bed."

"You seem pretty anxious, hero. You know you've got zero chance in Hell of joining me?"

"The thought never crossed my mind."

"You're full of shit, yeah?"

It wasn't working. Mary was still being loud and obnoxious and it was obvious that he wasn't going to change that. This was at least one area where the history books had been accurate. She was known for getting drunk and singing loudly.

As Corban walked past the first door on the right, it slowly opened. An angry looking Lihua glared at them, "Do you two have any idea what time…"

Her voice trailed off when she realized that it wasn't Vlad and Johnny. She stared at Corban for a moment, "Well now, this I do not see very often."

An angry look appeared on Mary's face, "Hey, you want to start something right now? You got a problem? Corban and me, we worked everything out, yeah? We're like best buddies now!"

"Is that so?" Lihua asked whimsically. "Well, I am glad to hear it."

Corban rolled his eyes and pushed Mary forward, "Okay, you're drunk, time for bed. –Sorry Lihua, I tried to keep her quiet."

"Keep me quiet? Better men than you have tried, yeah?"

Lihua rolled her eyes and turned away. Corban couldn't be certain, but he thought he heard her whisper, "He is a goner."

Finally, they arrived at Mary's room. Corban opened the door and guided her inside. The moment she was close to her bed, she reached down and pulled her shirt up over her head. Corban's eyes widened and he quickly turned away.

"What, you've never seen a girl in a bra before, hero?" Mary asked in an annoyed tone.

"Uh yeah, I had a girlfriend for years before coming here, remember?"

"Then why are you being so hypersensitive? Not as big a fan of girls as you let on?"

Soul Siphon

Corban's eyes widened. To him, it was more of an accusation than a question, "Of course I am!"

"So what's the problem?"

"You're drunk."

"Well... you're dumb, tomorrow I won't be drunk anymore, yeah?"

"Wow good one... now I know you're 150."

"Oh screw you."

Corban could hear some tussling behind him but refused to turn to see what Mary was doing. When the noise stopped, Mary sighed. "Okay, you can turn around now, hero."

Corban turned around to see her safely under the blanket. She moved until she was resting on her side and flashed him an annoyed look, "Satisfied?"

"Hey, I've always been told that I'm an old-fashioned gentleman. I kind of like that reputation."

"Uh huh," Mary replied. "You know, I knew a lot of 'old fashioned gentlemen' back in London and let me tell you, they weren't so gentlemanly out of view of the public, quite the opposite in fact."

"Oh well... you're safely in bed now. I best get back to mine."

"You can stay for a little while. You don't have to leave just yet."

"Yes I do, you're drunk and you need your rest."

"Fine... your loss!"

As Corban turned to leave, Mary called out to him, "Corban!"

He turned back and looked at her. She smiled faintly as she closed her eyes, "Thank you."

Soul Siphon

IX

Corban didn't get up until noon the next day. He rolled out of bed and hit the floor with a loud thud. "Ow!"

His head throbbed as he slowly got to his knees, attempting to keep his balance. He swayed back and forth as he got to his feet and stumbled into the bathroom. Struggling to make his eyes focus, Corban reached for the handle to turn on the shower. He hoped that a blast of cold water would bring him out of it.

The water splashed down over his face as the shower came to life. It was as cold as ice, but refreshing none-the-less. As chills ran down his body, Corban stretched out his arms, "Yeow!"

The stretching made the chills travel even faster. It looked like the shower was doing the trick. Corban was a lot less disoriented as he opened the shower door and grabbed a towel. Unfortunately for him, the haze and lack of coordination gave way to a massive headache.

Corban grabbed another set of clothes and threw them on, not caring whether or not they matched. The mixed smell of absinthe and sweat was still prevalent throughout the room. He decided to go get some food in the hopes of killing his awful hangover.

The moment he stumbled into the dining area, he saw Vlad and Johnny sitting at the table. Both of them were in just as bad a shape as he was. They both looked pale, their eyes fluttered, and they both looked like they were going to pass out.

Lihua came out of the kitchen with water and aspirin and set it down on the table. She then turned and looked at Corban. There was a devious grin on her face as she spoke in an obnoxiously loud voice, "Well good morning!"

Soul Siphon

Corban rubbed his forehead, "Oh fuck... please keep your voice down... What did I do to deserve that?"

"I do not know, Mr. McConnell. Perhaps waking me up at 3 in the morning might have something to do with it?"

Corban groaned, "That was Mary. I was trying to keep her quiet."

"Really, does that effort include singing 'The Rose of Allendale' to her on the roof?"

Both Johnny and Vlad looked up in surprise. Vlad nearly spilled his morning coffee when he heard Lihua drop the bomb on the events of the previous evening. He didn't know the song, but from the sound of things, it was clearly sung with romantic intent.

A shocked and slightly embarrassed expression appeared on Corban's face, "You heard that?"

"I did," Lihua replied in a tone that would befit a braggart. "Interesting choice of songs to sing for a redhead named Mary."

Johnny sat back in disbelief, "Corban man... you putting the moves on Ripper?"

"No!" Corban replied adamantly. "It's not like that! I was trying..."

"Corban not fooling me." The old Russian cut in. "I see how Corban looks at Ripper. Is same look Johnny gives blonde girl at Glass Slipper, except less perverted."

Lihua and Corban looked over at Johnny, waiting for him to defend himself. Johnny shrugged, "I'm short, I'm ugly, I look like I'm a child, I have to wear a hood to pass as a human, and I'm undead. What do you think the chances are of me ever seeing a girl naked any other way? Get the fuck off my back!"

Lihua shook her head, "Really?"

Soul Siphon

"Hey don't think for a moment that I go alone. Vlad is right there with me."

Everyone's attention turned back to Vlad, who had a smug grin on his face, "I keep Johnny out of trouble, yes?"

Corban sighed and turned back to Lihua, "Look, I'm not trying to pull anything. Unlike Johnny, I'm not trying to get into anyone's pants…"

Johnny rolled his eyes as Corban continued, "I'm certainly not trying to hurt her. She was just the first one to reach out to me when I came here. She shared her stories with me and well… we just connected."

Lihua laughed, "Relax Corban, I am just making fun at your expense. I think it is great that she has found someone to confide in and judging by her drunken ramblings she has become protective of you."

Vlad smiled, "She likes you, yes?"

"You think so?"

"I definitely think so," Lihua replied.

"Think so about what?" A voice chimed in as another person entered the room.

The surprise caused everyone to flinch at the sound of Mary's voice. They all stiffened up as though they were a group of recruits that had been visited by an officer in the military. They were all nervous about exactly how much she'd heard. The inquisitive look on her face wasn't much of an indicator either way, "You were all talking pretty loud. Is there something I should know about?"

"No."

"Nothing comes to mind."

"Nah."

"Umm… I'm thinking no."

Soul Siphon

The look on Mary's face indicated quite clearly that she didn't believe a word they said, "Uh huh... right well, Corban, can I talk to you for a moment?"

"Uh sure," Corban said nervously.

Though he had his back turned, he was certain that Johnny was smiling and making some sort of obscene gesture. He didn't have to see it to know that it happened. He followed Mary out into the hallway, anxiously waiting to hear what she wanted to say. Once they were out of earshot, she turned and looked into his eyes, "I just wanted to say thanks."

"For?"

"Well again for showing up in Chicago when you did," she replied, "but more so for reaching out to me last night. I know I didn't make it easy on you."

"Well I admit there were a few moments that I was worried about being dismembered, but honestly, you're all right Mary."

"You're not so bad either, yeah?"

Mary forced a smile and beckoned him back to the kitchen, "Come on Hero, let's get back before people start talking."

"Yeah, about that..."

"Mm?"

"... Did that mean anything last night?"

"Did what mean anything?" She asked in a worried tone. "Did something happen last night that I should be remembering right now?"

Corban's heart sank. *God damned absinthe!*

"Is something wrong?" Mary asked.

"No, it's nothing. Never mind."

Corban turned and walked away, leaving Mary standing alone with a puzzled look on her face. He walked past the kitchen and over to the elevator. The moment he pressed the button, the door opened and he returned to his room.

Soul Siphon

Once he was behind a closed door, Corban flopped down on his bed, "What was I thinking? I should have known better than to believe that was anything more than the booze. She wasn't going to instantly go from hating my guts to liking me!"

As Corban became lost in his own thoughts, a knock came at the door. He returned to reality for a few moments, sat up, and yelled, "What?"

He didn't mean for it to come out that way, but his frustration for the better of him. The door opened and Mike poked his head in, "Sorry, if I'm disturbing you, I can always come back, my boy."

Corban rubbed his forehead, "No it's okay. I guess I just got lost in the moment."

"You're upset about what happened with Mary."

"There you go again," Corban said with a detectable level of annoyance. "How do you do that? How the hell do you always know what's going on?"

"Have you forgotten who I am?"

"I guess not, Saint Michael."

"Then you already know the answer."

"Fine, whatever," Corban replied. "I really don't want to talk about it."

"All right. That's not exactly healthy, but if you're sure."

Corban sighed, "Did you need something?"

"As a matter of fact, yes. We're going to continue to work on your landings tonight. I think I might have a solution to make you land properly."

"I'm not in the mood."

Mike frowned, "I don't recall asking. You're doing this if you plan to continue fighting."

"Fine."

"Good," Mike replied. "See you downstairs at nightfall. Until then get some rest."

Soul Siphon

Mike turned to leave, but paused to give Corban one last thought, "You know Corban, just because she doesn't remember the connection you two made, doesn't mean it's undone. Mary doesn't break out the absinthe for just anyone. Think about that."

A partial smiled appeared on Corban's face, "Thanks."

"You're welcome, my boy."

Without another word, Mike vanished, leaving Corban alone with his thoughts. He decided that he needed to clear his head and went up to the roof. The empty bottle of absinthe was still sitting where they'd left it. *Damn you...*

Corban stayed up on the roof for most of the afternoon. He understood why Mary liked it up there so much. It was quiet and it gave her a nice view of the city. It was the perfect place to gain some reflection on life if someone needed a place to center themselves.

"Hope I am not interrupting…"

Corban turned to see his portly Russian friend coming up behind him, "Not at all, tovarisch. I'm just watching the city light up."

Vlad leaned on the wall next to him, "I know zis sight vell. It reminds me of the ze days ven I vas defending ze city of Stalingrad from ze Nazis. I never forgot that."

"You fought in the war?"

"Of course, all young Russian men did, and many women too!"

"What was it like?"

Vlad frowned, "It vas hell. Imagine zis city so beloved to you ground to near dust. Imagine your friends reduced nearly to skeletons. Is not something you vant to go through. No von should ever have to go through zat, but ve did vat ve had to do."

"My grandfather fought on the side of the allies. I know how it is."

"So Corban, tell me about yourself. Mike says Corban fought off powerful demon to join our ranks."

Corban laughed, "I don't know about all that and I didn't know about your ranks up until now, but let's see… I was born here in the city. I used to go to the Boston Commons as a child, so I know the area pretty well. Then my family moved out of Boston into the suburbs."

"Did you miss living in ze city?"

"Oh, more than you know. I love it here. I always promised myself that I'd move back after college."

"Vell now you protect it like I protected my city."

"If only, the bravery of the men who fought during the Battle of Stalingrad was unmatched. You had it bad. If you stood your ground, you were killed, starved, or frozen to death. If you ran, you were shot as traitors. I doubt I could live up to that."

"Kind vords," Vlad replied, "but Corban should know zat ve vere scared shitless ze entire time. Ze buildings provided no protection and vere as hazards to us. Ze bombs vere going off all around us and it vas freezing."

"Well to be honest I felt the same way when I was fighting off the demon. I knew that I was about to die, but it was the only way to make sure that everyone would be protected."

"Corban sacrificed himself, zere can be no greater form of nobility."

"I just did what I had to do."

"As do ve all, comrade. As do ve all."

Soul Siphon

As the sun began to set, Corban sighed, "Well tovarisch, it's back to the runway for more landing practice."

"Aye, it vould seem zat vay."

"Wish me luck."

"I not sink you need it, but good luck anyway."

The two parted ways as Corban made his way back down to the living room. Mike was there waiting for him as expected. He smiled when Corban appeared, "Ready to go?"

"No."

"Good, let's get to it."

Mike patted Corban on the back and walked him out front. Corban rolled his eyes, "So what's this new plan you have to get me to land properly?"

"You'll see."

The moment they were outside the building, Mike spread his wings, "Meet me at Fenway."

"Okay."

Mike disappeared as Corban began to levitate and took off into the clouds. The cool breeze caressed his skin as he moved through the air and made his way into the clouds above the city. He always considered this the calm before the storm as he came in for the landing at Fenway.

Just as before, he crash-landed, but this time was able to keep from rolling halfway down the field. He was a little banged up, but it wasn't as bad as before. He stood up and brushed himself off before looking for Mike.

To his surprise, not only was Mike there, but Mary was present as well, "Mary, why are you here?"

"I don't know. Mike asked me to come here. I'm as much in the dark as you, yeah?"

Corban shrugged and turned to Mike, "What's this about?"

Mike tapped on Mary's shoulder. Her skin became a blue aura for a moment before returning to normal, "I've immobilized her and taken away her immortality."

Mary looked down and tried to move her legs, but they would not respond, "Mike, what the fuck?"

Corban glared at Mike, "What the hell are you doing?"

Mike shrugged, "We've tried every other way I could think of. I'm hoping that a little motivation will work."

"Motivation?"

"Yup," Mike replied. "You're to fly to Castle Island and then back here. You are then to land in front of Mary without crashing."

Corban could not believe what he was being asked to do, "Are you crazy? At the speeds I travel, the impact could kill her!"

Mary glared at Mike, "All these years we've known each other and you're going to pull this shit? Seriously Mike, if you weren't an angel, I'd be kicking your ass right now!"

"Sorry to push it this far, but Corban, you're not going to be much good to the team if you can't land without getting hurt. If you accomplish this landing, I'll restore her immortality and her powers. If not, then she'll be forced to remain like this."

Corban looked at Mary, "What do you think?"

"It looks like you don't have a choice, Hero. If you kill me though, the moment I become a ghost, you're the first one I'm coming after, yeah?"

"I'll do the best I can."

He then turned to Mike, "You and I are going to have a long talk about this after I'm done, make no mistake."

Soul Siphon

Mike didn't respond and Corban didn't bother waiting for him to. He took off into the clouds, blasted off above the city, and dove down towards Castle Island. Without touching down, he did a slingshot maneuver around the fortress before heading back over to Fenway Park.

Corban began his descent into the green ballpark. He struggled to slow down as he approached the field. He folded his legs up underneath himself and put out his arms. He focused on Mary's feet and the ground in front of her as he pressed his mind to slow his descent.

The green grass of the field came into view. Corban focused his eyes on his target. This was it. He either landed perfectly, or he risked hurting Mary. He sucked in a deep breath and held it for a few moments as he extended his arms as far as he could.

A second later, Corban felt the grass against his hands and knees. His wrists and ankles hurt, but he had successfully landed. He looked up at Mary, who had a relieved look on her face.

"I did it!" Corban shouted.

"Well done," Mike replied.

Corban jumped back into the air, "All right, I did it!"

He shot over to Castle Island and repeated the previous steps. He was able to bring himself down within a few feet of the wall and land without issue. *Yes!*

He took off again and headed back to Fenway, once again landing in front of Mary. The look on her face was pure relief, "I'm happy for you. –Now Mike, he did what he was supposed to, yeah? Unlock my fucking feet and give me back my powers!"

"I'm a man of my word. You are released. Your power has been restored."

Soul Siphon

Corban walked back to confront Mike with Mary on his heels. There were a few things that didn't make sense, but they were starting to come together, "Tell me something Mike, how often do you error on your Intel about our potential targets?"

"It's very rare."

"In fact, it never happens," Mary added.

Mike looked at Corban oddly, "What are you saying?"

Corban's gaze never left Mike, "I'm saying that I think you set that up. I'm saying that I think you knew that the gangsters in Chicago were more than Mary could handle alone."

"So I knowingly sent Mary into a dangerous situation she couldn't handle?" Mike scoffed. "Come now, you can't be serious. Why would I do that?"

Mary's eyes narrowed as her jaw fell open, "It makes sense. You then sent him after me in order to break the ice, thereby giving him something to fight for. You knew if it worked that you could use me as bait!"

"You're thinking way too much into this," Mike said defensively. "However, even if I did, look what came of it. You two were at each other's throats. How were you ever going to trust one another? You needed to come together if you were ever to work as a team and you have."

"And it's just a coincidence that I became bait to force Corban to learn how to land properly?"

"It was nothing so malicious. It worked, didn't it?"

An angry look appeared on Mary's face, "The next time you want to pull something like that, risk your own damn life, yeah?"

Soul Siphon

"You think I actually put you in any danger?" Mike asked. "What I did was a mere light show. I never took your immortality away, just your mobility."

Mary turned away and took off running, headed back to Southie, leaving Corban to deal with Mike on his own. Corban glared at the old angel, "Whether you actually put her in danger or not at this point is immaterial now since everything worked out, but the next time you try to use my personal relationships against me like that, don't expect me to remain as part of the team. That is not how this is going to work if you want to keep me around."

Mike sighed, "I'm sorry you feel that way, my boy. I felt it necessary and relevant to your training. Do you think Adramelech or any other demon would hesitate to use someone you care about against you?"

"I'll worry about that when it comes. I don't need to be reminded of it."

"As you wish."

The next morning, Corban came down for breakfast. He had a dismal look on his face. Nothing appeared to be going his way and he was not happy about it.

Lihua was sitting at the table waiting for whatever horror Vlad was about to unleash on them. She smiled warmly when Corban entered the room, "Joining us for breakfast, Corban? Vlad is trying his hand at a Spanish dish. I believe he called it 'juevos rancheros.' Are you feeling adventurous?"

"El Paso," Corban replied.

"Well, I see being banged around by Mike has not affected your wit."

Corban sat down at the table opposite Lihua and rubbed his head with his hands. Lihua leaned forward, "Trouble with Ripper?"

Soul Siphon

"No, nothing so complicated."

"Okay, care to clue me in?"

"You already know most of it. Just the shit with Mary and my training."

"But I thought that you nailed your landing last night and I heard you beat Mike in a game of tag?" Lihua asked.

"All true," Corban replied, "but none of that has anything to do with being a soul siphon."

Lihua sat back thoughtfully, "Ah I see. That is true. We cannot exactly roundup test subjects for you."

"There has to be some way."

A scratching noise on the floor interrupted their conversation. Lihua turned and saw a small field mouse running across the floor, "Ugh… we get these nasty little things in here from time to time."

Lihua looked at the mouse oddly for a moment. She seemed like she was focused on it. The mouse stopped dead in its tracks and stared at her. She pointed at the ceiling with the index finger on her left hand. The mouse promptly sat back on its hind haunches with its front paws in the air.

She then made it dance around in a circle, showing off for Corban. He watched in amazement, "Wait, our powers work on animals too?"

"Mine does."

"Maybe mine does too," Corban replied as he reached for the mouse.

He placed his right index finger on the mouse's chest and focused his energy. Lihua watched as he pulled a tiny orb from the mouse before it fell over, lifeless. He balanced the orb on his fingertip before crushing it with his thumb, "Better than dying in a mousetrap."

"I guess it does work huh?"

Soul Siphon

Vlad came out of the kitchen and saw the mouse on the floor, "Corban should not play vith mouse! Is not sanitary! No eating until Corban clean up!"

"Not really hungry anyway."

Corban looked over at Lihua, "Can you help me gather up some more mice?"

"Mice, rats, whatever you need."

The days continued to get colder as Corban gathered vermin from the area to help strengthen his powers. He practiced draining each of them very quickly. It wasn't much, but each successful drain brought him closer to his goal. He was slowly beginning to feel more power building up in his soul.

It finally looked like things were looking up for Corban. His relationship with Mary had improved, at least now she was talking to him. However, he was giving her a wide birth, still sore over what happened on the roof. He wanted to talk to her and tell her about it, but things were still fairly tender between them.

A week went by as Corban continued to work on his powers. Mike sent them on small-time hits and assassinations during that time, but never after any major targets. Corban got the feeling that Mike didn't think that he was ready to take on anything major. He understood that Mike was trying to protect him, but he was becoming restless and resentful.

Corban found himself up on the roof more often than not. It was a space he often had to share with either Mary or Lihua, but they tended to leave each other alone. For them, this was a time for personal reflection and they didn't want to be bothered. He was fine with that as he'd been trying to avoid Mary anyway.

One night in late September, Corban leaned against the frost-covered wall, sulking. He wasn't sure what Mike would have in store for them, but he doubted that it would be anything difficult.

"Lovely night, yeah?"

Corban sighed, "What's up, Mary? You need something?"

"Just thought maybe we could talk."

"What about?"

Before she could answer, every alarm in the building went off. They both came to life and immediately made their way back to the living room. The rest of the team was already present when they arrived. Corban sat down next to Vlad and refused to look Mary in the eye. Mary sat down across from him and did her best to pretend not to notice.

Mike quickly entered the room, "All right everyone, let's get down to business. Hope you're all ready to go."

"Always, yeah?" Mary replied. "What's the mission?"

"You're going to New York City this time."

Vlad smiled, "Ze Big Apple! Vats going on zere zis time?"

"It's another mob boss," Mike replied. "He's stirring up trouble.

"Every time we take one down, another seems to pop up. This is turning into a vicious cycle. How long before we have to wreck half the city?" Lihua sighed.

Mary crossed her legs and pulled a dagger from her belt, "Such is the way of the world, yeah?"

"That's right," Mike replied. "Unfortunately, we may never be done with these people. If all we can do is weaken them, then that's exactly what we're going to do."

"Where's the target?" Corban asked.

"There's a little-known club in the Brownsville area of New York City. The place was kind of a

Soul Siphon

speakeasy during prohibition, but the illegal activity there never ceased. They call the place Rosie's. No one really goes there except for gangsters, thugs, and people on the take."

"Corrupt city officials..," Lihua clarified.

"Exactly."

"Are we cleaning house?"

Mike shrugged, "No one who goes there doesn't have a checkered past, and everyone who goes there, goes there for reasons that are illegal and sinful. Use your judgment. Anyone who attacks you though is fair game."

Johnny stood up smiling, "All right, I'm liking this one!"

"Yes, I thought you might," Mike replied.

"So who's the primary target?" Mary asked.

Mike placed a picture on the table. It was a portrait of a chubby man with greasy skin. His hair was a thick, dark brown mat on his head, "This is your target, Matt Trembly."

"Charming, yeah?"

Corban studied the picture. He didn't look like the typical mob boss. The movies had always portrayed them as well-kempt, well-mannered, cultured Italians. This guy looked like a complete sleaze that would kill a person for looking at him the wrong way.

Mary stood up and threw the dagger right into the middle of the picture. It struck the photo and pinned it to the table. Corban smiled, "Right between the eyes, good shot."

"He's as good as dead," Mary said in a stoic tone.

Lihua stood up and turned to the armory, "The more time we waste, the less orderly this mission will be. We should move out."

Soul Siphon

"Let's see who gets there first Corban, yeah?" Mary said in a daring tone.

"Loser buys drinks?" Corban asked.

"All right Hero, you have a bet."

Corban levitated off the ground while Mary took a runner's stance. When she was ready, she looked over at Lihua, "You want to give us the signal?"

"Do not get carried away, kids," Lihua replied.

After a second of waiting, she waved her hand, "Go!"

Corban and Mary burst through the door, heading in different directions. Mary turned down the street while Corban shot straight up into the clouds. As soon as he was high enough over the buildings, Corban focused on New York City and thought of the name 'Brownsville.'

His body instantly jerked forward and sent him rocketing through the clouds. A wide grin appeared on his face as he flew over the cityscape and did a ring around the Hancock Tower. Using the inertia he'd built up, he shot out over Boston Harbor and flew next to a large, blue and white, Boeing 747 that had just taken off from Logan Airport.

A young boy looked out the window and saw him flying nearby. Corban looked at the child and waved before diving downward and heading southwest to New York. The child's bright blue eyes widened as he waved back. He then turned to his mother and pointing out the window, "Mommy, mommy, I just saw an angel on the wing!"

His mother smiled, "Wow, an angel huh? Was she pretty?"

"No mommy, it was a boy angel!"

Corban continued flying through the clouds until the larger city came into view. He slowed down and began to descend towards the ground. It didn't take

Soul Siphon

long for him to touch down in the small alley which was a back entrance to Rosie's. He was just in time to see Mary standing off to the side, smiling, "I win, yeah?"

"Yeah, I figured. I did a slight detour around the Hancock tower," Corban said as he brushed his hair back.

"Uh huh... so you're saying you let me win?"

"Not really," Corban replied. "I just really don't mind buying drinks for you."

Mary checked him with her shoulder in a playful manner as the rest of the team appeared. Lihua stepped away from Johnny and Vlad, "You forgot your guns."

Mary shook her head, "No thanks, they just weigh me down. I like my blades better."

Lihua turned to Corban, "Then you are taking them."

"All right," Corban replied.

He attached the two pistols to his belt, the Glock on his left and the M&P on his right, "You realize that I'm probably not going to use these either, right?"

"You are still new," Lihua replied. "If nothing else, it makes me feel better that you have them. At least that way, I know that I do not have to keep an eye on you."

"Well... fair enough, then I'll keep them close."

"Thank you for humoring me."

A loud bang caused the two of them jump. Mary had already kicked in the door and was standing in the entryway. She turned back to face the startled looks on the faces of her four teammates, "Oh I'm sorry, were you two finished?"

Corban followed her through the broken doorway. They proceeded down a dirty hallway into the small club. It was little more than a basement room with tables set up and a bar against the wall. The floor was shiny and very sticky like it had not been mopped in years. The pungent stench of sour beer made Corban's eyes water.

The bartender, a dark-skinned man with a slick ponytail, eyed the group suspiciously as they made their way into the room, but made no aggressive move. He had one hand under the bar, presumably holding a gun of some kind. His face was emotionless, but he never took his eyes off them.

Vlad kept back in the hallway, unable to conceal his old rifle, while Johnny and Lihua took their positions on either side of the room, ready for the attack. The look on Mary's face was stone cold indifference. Corban moved slightly to the side, allowing her a full view of the scene around them.

The two assassins proceeded to the large round booth that was bolted to the floor at the back of the room. A small group occupied the table; five men and three women. The men were dressed in business casual attire; button down collared shirts and dress pants while the women were wearing rather revealing dresses. Their attire and the makeup they wore gave Corban a feeling that these were most likely paid escorts. A fat man that resembled the picture Mike had given them was seated in the middle of the booth with a woman on each arm.

"Let the women and the bartender go, everyone else is ripe for the reaping," Corban replied in a low, monotone, voice.

Mary looked at him oddly, "How can you be sure they're innocent?"

At that moment, his eyes flickered red, "I can't explain it. I just know."

"More powers you gained, most likely."

"I know, it's weird. Why aren't my powers as specific as yours?"

Soul Siphon

"Maybe because yours are demonic. Whatever they can do, you can also. You may have no limit, yeah?"

Matt Trembly kicked back in his seat as his lieutenant gave him their latest business reports. Matt listened intently and responded in a gruff voice, "All right... I think we're going to need to go see our friends down at the docks for..."

Matt's eyes widened when he saw Mary walking towards him. His pupils dilated at the sight of this slender woman in black with shiny red hair. He sat back and looked at her with a welcoming smile, "Well hello there. What brings such a beautiful rose to this establishment? Can I do something for you?"

Mary grimaced as Matt looked her over. Corban was about to step in front of her to block his view, but she placed her hand on his side, signaling him to say in place. "He's mine..."

She didn't need to say it. The look in her eyes was enough for Corban, "Go for it."

Matt's eyes narrowed as his hand disappeared under the table. The smile on his face slowly faded, "Did you say something sweetie?"

Mary's eyes were full of malice as she watched Matt squirm. Her lips curled to reveal her white teeth. She spoke in a tone that was reminiscent of the hiss of a snake threatening its prey, "Matt Tremblay, yeah?"

"Who wants to know?"

"Hell's gates have opened. They are waiting for you."

Reacting to her words, the man closest to Mary stood up and reached for his gun. Corban stepped between them and planted his hand on the man's chest, "You're mine!"

The group watched in horror as the man's body began to glow blue and a white orb appeared out of his

Soul Siphon

chest. Corban crushed the orb and absorbed its power as the henchman fell to the ground. He smiled as the power flowed through his body. *Oh yeah, I could get used to this!*

The mobster's memories entered his mind, but they weren't as dark as his previous victim and were more than manageable. He was able to shake it off very quickly and was clearly becoming desensitized to the pain. Either that or the justification that they would never hurt anyone else was helping to make it more manageable.

Matt looked back and forth in a panic, looking for a way out, "Light em up boys, we'll see who goes to Hell first!"

The three other men sitting at the booth pulled their guns and began firing indiscriminately. This caused the entire bar to erupt in chaos. Some people ran for the exits while others drew their weapons.

Lihua made her way around the room, enticing the people with guns to begin opening fire on each other while Johnny attacked the people heading for the exits. Vlad blocked the back exist and began shooting at anyone who came too close.

Johnny ran over to the bar, which had been abandoned and grabbed a bottle of peppermint schnapps. He picked up the bottle and took a sip before throwing it against the locked door that a few of the barflies were trying to escape through. The bottle shattered, spilling its contents down the door.

He then grabbed a cloth and stuffed it into a nearby bottle of vodka before lighting it on fire. He threw that bottle against the door as well. This time, as the bottle shattered, the entire door was immediately draped in flame.

Corban heard Vlad sigh from across the room, "Vaste of perfectly good wotka!"

Soul Siphon

The last three men stood between Mary and Matt. Corban flanked Mary, ready to strike again whenever she made her move, "I take the two on the left, you get the guy on the right and Matt?"

"Sounds good."

Corban didn't even get a chance to take a step. The chest of the henchman on the far right exploded with blood. He fell to the ground lifeless. A second later, the second henchmen on the right's head jerked backward with blood pouring from his skull.

Corban beckoned to Mary as Matt took the moment of confusion to bolt and run to the door, "Go get him, I'll take care of this last thug. –Hey Vlad, next time leave some for us, will you?"

Mary smiled and ran after Matt. Corban turned to the last henchman and took a step forward. The henchman was breathing heavily and shaking as he fired his gun.

Corban moved his head to the side, dodging the bullet. The henchman tried three more times. The first shot grazed his shoulder, while the other two hit his right arm. Blood dripped from the wounds, but he ignored them. Oddly, the pain wasn't as bad as he thought it would be. He wasn't sure if it was because of his newfound immortality or not, but it wasn't important.

Corban grabbed the man by the throat, forcing him to drop his gun. He then looked his victim in the eyes with a menacing stare. His voice was almost demonic as he spoke, "Give me your soul!"

Sheer terror appeared on the man's face as he watched Corban's hands begin to glow. Without another word, Corban reached into his chest and grabbed the white orb. The man fell to the ground without even having a chance to scream. The orb turned to dust as Corban held it in his hand. The rush of energy was an unbelievably exhilarating feeling, "This will never get old."

Corban turned back to the hallway where Vlad had taken position as two more men with guns fell to the ground dead right in front of him, "Stop trying to win your bets with Johnny at my expense!"

Mary ran after the mob boss. Ordinarily, she could have easily caught him in less than a second, but she preferred to toy with this one. She didn't particularly care for the lust-filled look he gave her when they first met or the images that came as a result. This cat and mouse game was her way of thanking him for the flashback into her own past.

After watching the sweat pour off of the man's head as he ran for his life, Mary ran full speed at him. Matt felt intense pressure on his back as though he was tackled by a lineman. He fell to the ground and turned on his back. To his horror, Mary was looking down at him menacingly. She was as a hawk bearing down on its prey.

An evil smile stretched across her lips as she spoke, "What's the matter hun, didn't you know that all roses have thorns... especially Irish ones, yeah?"

Matt raised his hands defensively, "W...wait... please...!"

"Begging for your life?" Mary asked.

"Why are you doing this? What did I do to you?"

"You haven't done anything to me, but how many others have you sent to their deaths? How many begged you to spare them? Did you show them any mercy? Did their cries move you in any way or did you wash your hands of them? Do their cries still haunt you or have you turned a deaf ear to them?"

Soul Siphon

Matt's skin broke out in beads of sweat as he tried to respond, "I… you don't understand…"

"Don't I? Come on now. I've been doing this for over a hundred years."

"Please, hear me out."

"I've already heard it, many times, yeah? The liars, the adulterers, the murderers, and the rapists, this is always the way it goes."

"Please… listen… ack!"

Mary slashed him across the throat with the kodachi in her right hand. The cut was clean and almost to the bone. Blood splattered on Mary's face as she slowly backed away, "Sorry, no time."

As Mary wiped her blade on her sleeve, she heard a slight whimper behind her. One of the young women that had been sitting with Matt in the booth was hiding behind the door. Her dress was torn and she was shaking. Her blonde hair was a mess and tears streamed down her cheeks. She could not have been more than nineteen years old.

As Mary approached, she cried out, "Please, don't kill me! I don't know anything. He just hired me for the evening. I don't have anything else to do with him!"

Mary stopped in her tracks as an uncharacteristic look of sympathy appeared on her face, "You're a call girl, yeah?"

"Yes, that's all I am, I swear! Please let me go!"

"Did he pay you yet?"

"Yeah, look if you let me go you can have it!"

Mary shook her head, "Keep it. You didn't see what happened here. You understand, yeah?"

The girl nodded obediently, "Yes, of course. Not a word to anyone."

"Right, then get out of here and find yourself a new line of work. Trust me, you'll live longer."

Soul Siphon

"I will." The woman said in relief. "Thank you... thank you so much!"

The girl got up and ran out the door, leaving the chaotic scene behind her. Mary frowned as she watched the girl run. *Nice to see how little changes with the passage of time...*

The exhilaration Corban felt lasted less than a second. He knew that there were still more wicked people there that needed to be cleansed and quickly turned to see who was left. That was when he noticed another figure dressed all in black in the middle of the room. Whomever or whatever it was, was wearing a black mask that concealed its face. It was clearly not one of his team, nor was it one of the gangsters.

A cold feeling ran down Corban's spine. He hadn't felt fear this intense since he fought Adramelech for control of his soul. There was no doubt in his mind that this was no ordinary person. This was something far more powerful. The amount of power radiating from the creature lead Corban to one inescapable conclusion; Adramelech had returned.

Corban stepped forward. His hands shook with anticipation as his eyes turned red, "Adramelech... you don't know how long I've been waiting for this..."

To his surprise, the creature pulled a medieval-looking sword from under its robe. It said nothing as it began brandishing the blade. Corban could sense anger from the creature and quickly drew his two handguns, "You're dead mother fucker!"

The creature charged at him with its sword out in front. Corban used his power, did a somersault over the creature, turned, and opened fire with both pistols. He had a feeling that it wouldn't do any good, but he had to try.

Soul Siphon

The creature moved with a speed that would have rivaled Mary's. It quickly either dodged or blocked the gunshots with its sword. It then charged at Corban again. A feeling of trepidation came over him as he fought. It quickly became apparent that he stood no chance of defeating this demon. *Ah shit man, you've really stepped in it now.*

Mike sat in silent meditation in the lounge of the South Boston warehouse that the team used as its residence. He'd been monitoring his team's progress and had so far been pleased with the results. They had nearly wiped everyone in the bar out.

As he was about to call the mission a success, a cold chill entered the air and the image of the cloaked figure entered his mind. His skin went pale and a simultaneous expression anger and concern came over his features, "No..."

Corban tried again to hit the creature with a bullet, but again he missed and now his guns were out of ammo. As the triggers clicked, Corban grimaced and dropped the guns.

Once more, the creature lunged at him with its sword out. Corban moved just enough to dodge around the blade but stayed close enough to put his left hand on the creature. The moment he made contact, his hand burned. His whole body felt like it had been jolted by electricity and he was paralyzed.

Memories of pain, loneliness, and darkness entered Corban's mind. He saw medieval Europe in flames and then an endless flow of blood. It was followed by intense sorrow and longing that seemingly never ended.

The creature winced in pain from the shock of Corban's touch. The sword in its hand burst into

Soul Siphon

flames as the creature brought it to bear against Corban, severing his hand at the wrist. Corban cried out and fell to his knees, holding his arm.

The flame from the sword had cauterized most of the wound, but some blood still escaped. The cut was so perfectly clean that no mortal weapon could have made it. Pain shot from the cut and spread throughout Corban's body.

Corban knew that the rest of the team heard him, but wasn't sure that they should be able to get to him in time. The creature stood over Corban and raised its sword over him. Corban closed his eyes. Whatever this creature was, he knew that it had the power to end him once and for all. There was no escaping this reality; he was about to die.

He lay on the ground completely immobilized, waiting for the final cut. He expected a stabbing pain, but none came. He opened his eyes to see Mary standing over him. The creature's sword had impacted on her dagger. The look in Mary's eyes was sheer hatred as she stared the creature down.

Her eyes burned as they looked at the hooded face standing in front of them. It was a look of sheer rage like nothing Corban had ever seen before, "You ready for a real fight, yeah?"

The two combatants separated and circled each other while Vlad and Lihua pulled Corban away from the fight. Vlad patted him on the shoulder, "Take it easy, Corban, the hand can be reattached, and won't hurt for very long."

Corban fought through the pain and watched desperately as Mary's blades created sparks as they ran across her opponents. Her teeth were clenched as she fought. She lunged at the creature with both blades out in front. The creature turned to the side and

Soul Siphon

upended its own blade, causing Mary's attack to be deflected.

Mary landed on her left and smiled, "Not bad."

She was a skilled fighter, but her technique was very basic. This became very apparent to Corban as yet another vicious attack was blocked by the creature, which then moved almost daintily out of the way, "Disappointing... surely you can do better?"

The creature fought with a finesse that Corban had never seen before. Its movements were so fluidic that the creature almost appeared to be dancing as it attacked. These were the moves of a true master that had been training their entire life. The creature twirled its sword in a way that almost made it look like the blade was an extension of its arm.

Mary backed away slowly as the creature began its next strike. The sword it wielded twirled above its head like the blades of a helicopter on full power. Corban watched as Mary focused on the blade until she was able to follow it with her eyes, waiting for the right moment to strike.

He held his breath each time Mary had to absorb an attack. Mary crossed her blades and dropped to one knee, catching the creature's sword in the process. Mary separated her blades as though she were opening a pair of scissors, driving the creature back. She then dropped to her hands and performed a spin kick which knocked the creature off balance. It stammered backward, momentarily dazed

Mary quickly pushed herself back to her feet as the creature stumbled. It had been surprised, but quickly regained its composure. The two adversaries stood face to face once again. Mary glared at the creature, not willing to back down. The standoff seemed to last for an eternity as the creature tried to figure out a way around Mary.

Soul Siphon

After assessing its situation, the creature pointed a gloved finger at Mary and spoke in a whisper, "I'll be seeing you again very soon."

A faintly devious smiled appeared on Mary's face as the creature disappeared into a black cloud of fog, "I can't wait."

A momentary sense of relief entered Corban's heart. It was a short-lived sensation that quickly ended when a second round of searing pain shot through his arm. He cried out in pain, causing Mary to quickly turn, "Ah shit... My arm... it fucking kills!"

Vlad grabbed his arm and tried to hold him in place. The bleeding from his arm had stopped thanks to their accelerated healing. However, his hand would never heal properly unless his left hand was reattached soon. He needed help, quickly.

Mary grabbed his severed hand off the ground before turning to the group, "Get him up, will you? I'll take him and meet you back at the base."

"What are you going to do?" Johnny asked.

Mary looked at his hand, "Whatever I can to fix this. He needs help, yeah? Otherwise, he'll lose the hand forever."

Lihua helped Corban to his feet and helped put his arm on Mary's shoulder, "You must hurry. He is in extreme pain. I can feel it."

"I know," Mary replied in a frustrated tone. "Get out of my way. I need to get moving. I'll see you all at home."

Lihua backed away as Mary held onto Corban as tightly as she could. In less than a second, Mary and Corban were nothing more than a blur. The world passed by their eyes at unbelievable speeds. It was a similar sensation as when Corban flew, except this one involved a lot of twists and turns.

Soul Siphon

Mary knew that she had to move quickly if she was to save the hand, "Hold on Corban, we'll be back before you know it. You'll be good as new in no time, yeah?"

Soul Siphon

X

Though the trip took less than five minutes, to Mary, it felt like an eternity. Corban's arm must have felt like it was on fire. She'd experienced dismemberment before and knew how painful it could be.

Mary got Corban inside and brought him over to the elevator. She leaned him on the wall and turned to the kitchen, "Can you stay on your feet, hero?"

Corban was covered in sweat and shaking. He closed his eyes and clenched his muscles, desperately trying to keep his balance, "Sure, no problem…"

"Good," Mary replied. "I'll be right back."

She ran into the kitchen and grabbed the first aid kit. She returned to Corban's side in time to catch him. He had been leaning on the wall but was slowing beginning to fall to the side. His strength was failing him quickly and he was unable to hold himself up.

Mary had made it back just in time to keep him from hitting the floor, "Come on, let's get you somewhere safe."

"Where?"

Mary pressed the elevator button, "My room, I have everything I need to fix this there."

"Really?"

"What, you think this is the first severed limb I've seen in the last hundred years? I've sewn on hands and feet that were in a lot worse shape than this, yeah? Take it easy, we'll have you patched up in no time."

Corban closed his eyes. Mary saw him beginning to nod off and shook him awake, "No, no. No sleep for you, yeah? Your body is still in shock, you need to stay with me for now."

Soul Siphon

Corban nodded as they got on the elevator and headed up to the dormitory, "I'll do my best... it just fucking kills..."

"I know it does."

Mary pushed the doors in a vain effort to open them faster as the elevator reached their floor. They stepped out and made their way to Mary's room. She quickly unlocked the door and guided Corban to the bed, "Okay, lay back and try to relax. Just stay awake, yeah?"

Corban sighed and tried to relax as Mary gathered together everything that she'd need to sew the hand back on. She grabbed a small box from under her bed as well as a brown bottle. She opened the box and pulled out a small needle and some black thread.

Corban's eyes dilated when he saw them. His breathing became more rapid as he spoke, "What is that?"

"Sutures," Mary replied. "Your hand needs to be reattached. It'll heal quickly once it's together."

Corban forced his eyes to remain open, "I don't understand. Your gashes healed up within minutes. Why hasn't this?"

"It has," Mary replied, "somewhat. You're not gushing blood anymore, but this is much more severe."

"I don't get it. I kind of assumed I'd grow a new hand or something."

Mary looked into Corban's eyes as though scolding him for stupidity, "And a new head if that got chopped off? You're being stupid, yeah? Just shut up and relax."

Corban began to breathe heavily as Mary finished threading the needle. When she saw the look on his face, she softened her expression and reached over to the drawer on her desk. She pulled out a small orange bottle and opened it, "Here…"

"What is it?"

"Ibuprofen, 800mg," Mary replied. "It won't do much, but it's better than nothing. Just take it, yeah?"

Corban took the large white pill, "Thanks…"

"All right, are you ready?"

"Do I have a choice?"

"No"

"Then get it over with."

"Okay," Mary replied. "Here we go. Stay still and this will go a lot quicker."

Corban tensed his muscles as Mary carefully made the first incision into his wrist. She was trying to be gentle, but there was no way to stop the pain. This was going to be torture and no amount of tenderness was going to make a difference.

Corban's toes curled and he bit his lower lip. Every few minutes, his body was forced to absorb more and more. His breathing became even more labored as Mary worked.

Mary noticed the stress that was being put on Corban's body, so she began to work faster, hoping she could stave off him falling unconscious until she was done. Blood dripped out of each incision she made and his muscles tensed each time she ran the thread through. She knew that the Ibuprofen wasn't doing him any good, but at the moment, that was the best she could do. She had no time to run up to the roof and grab a bottle of absinthe. It pained her that she couldn't do anything to stop the pain, but she knew that she had to keep working.

Mary made incision after incision and pulled the thread through. Blood dripped out of each cut as she pulled the stitching tight. Corban winced each time she pulled.

Soul Siphon

Relief finally came when she sewed the last stitch. His hand was sutured to his wrist all the way around. She quickly tied off the last bit of thread and tightened the stitching so that it would stay in place. Once she was done, she gave it a quick kiss before carefully placing it on the bed to grab more equipment, "Do not move!"

Corban's body was shaking as though he were in his death throes. Mary knew that he was succumbing to the agony and had to work quickly. He could no longer absorb any additional pain. Immortal or not, his body was still human and still had limitations. He would need to rest soon, but Mary had to finish her work first. She pulled the scabbard of her largest dagger off of her belt and put it on his wrist. She then grabbed a roll of gauze out of the first aid kit and began to wrap the wound.

After the first layer of gauze was applied, she opened the brown bottle and took a sip of its contents, "Good bourbon..."

Corban looked at her oddly as she lowered the bottle from her lips. Her eyes met his and she shrugged, "What, it's medicinal!"

"Sure..."

"Oh shut up."

Mary allowed the alcohol to drip onto the gauze and soak it. The fabric thickened slightly as it became saturated. Corban's arm tensed up, trying to maintain the composure that was quickly failing. Mary saw him move and held his arm down, "Easy, easy, try not to move. I know it hurts hero, but if you move you could undo all of my hard work and I'm not re-stitching this for you. It's a lot of work, yeah?"

Corban lay back, doing the best he could to follow her instructions. Mary finished the dressing and rested his arm on the pillow, "Okay the dagger's scabbard should serve as a brace, but it won't take much abuse so I wouldn't move much."

"Thank you..."

Mary smiled, "Don't thank me yet. This is going to be a long and painful night for you. I doubt that you'll get much sleep."

"Then I should probably get back to my room."

"Like hell! You think I'm trusting you not to roll on top of this? You're staying here tonight, yeah?"

Corban closed his eyes and slammed his good fist on the bed, "Great fucking day this has turned out to be. First I get a major letdown, then dismemberment... then I let the team down. It's insult made injury, made insult all over again! What's next?"

"Major letdown?" Mary asked in a confused tone.

"Yeah."

"From?"

"You!"

Mary wasn't expecting that response, "Me, what the hell did I do other than play nurse for you?"

Corban let out another sigh, "You forgot about what happened the other night."

"What up on the roof?"

"Yeah."

Mary shrugged, "I remember us talking as we drank. I thought it was a fun time. What's your issue?"

"That's all you remember. You forgot everything else apparently."

Mary was becoming annoyed. She understood that Corban was in pain, but he was being completely unappreciative of the care she'd given him, "Okay, then tell me! I asked you earlier and you blew me off! So please, tell me what's bothering you. That way maybe we can get past it? I mean seriously..."

"We kissed!" Corban blurted out.

Soul Siphon

Mary fell silent as Corban spoke, "You started singing Courtin' In The Kitchen when you were really drunk and I responded by singing…"

"… The Rose of Allendale."

Corban's head turned quickly to look at her, "What?"

"You've got some charm about you, hero," Mary said in a low voice, "You chose a nice song, even if it wasn't Irish. It was really sweet."

"But then…"

"Yeah Corban, I lied to you and I'm sorry. I remember everything. I wasn't that drunk. Even if I was, I doubt that's something I could forget, yeah?"

"Why though, you actually seemed happy. Why shut that out, why shut me out?" Corban demanded.

Mary's eyes filled with tears as she spoke, "Polly, Annie, Elizabeth, Catherine and whoever else he killed. I knew them… I couldn't stop him. They all died."

"What does that have to do with me?"

"Everything."

"Bullshit."

Mary turned and looked straight into Corban's eyes. The blue fire was intensely vibrant as she spoke to him, "I couldn't protect them. I can't protect anyone. I couldn't even avenge them. All I can do is kill after the fact. If I can't protect them, I can't protect you. When my head finally cleared and I realized what had happened, I hoped that you were drunk enough to forget, but…"

Mary watched as Corban struggled to sit up and make his face level with hers. She grabbed his wrist to hold it together. He used the wall next to the bed to support himself, "Mary, you don't have to protect me. I can take care of myself."

Soul Siphon

Mary's frustration was becoming more and more difficult for her to fight back. She steadied her breathing, but her voice still quivered as she spoke, "You don't think so, yeah? Look what happened here!"

"Up until now, things have been fine. Whatever we fought today was not human."

"Exactly!" Mary replied, almost shouting. "Corban, since you joined us, your goal has always been to find and kill Adramelech! He's been around since time immemorial, yeah? If you think what we faced today was bad, just wait until the day comes that you find him... I..."

Corban leaned back against the wall and raised his hand to Mary's cheek just in time to catch a tear. He forced a smile with the little energy he had left, "Maybe my priorities have changed."

"I wish I could believe that."

"Stop."

"Hmm?"

Corban wiped another tear from her eye and brushed back another strand of red hair, "Stop coming up with excuses, stop running."

"I'm not running!" She shot back.

"Yeah, you are! You're afraid of making connections. That's why you spend so much time alone. You were hostile to me when we first met because you wanted me to stay at arm's length, but you screwed that up by having a heart. No more pushing me away."

Mary shook her head, "Corban..."

Corban sacrificed the last ounces of his strength to push himself forward. Their lips connected before she could say another word. Mary didn't know what to think. It wasn't the same tender kiss as the night

Soul Siphon

before, but given Corban's condition, it was the best he could do.

She ran her right hand up his back to his neck and held on tenderly, trying not to hurt him. Her heart raced for the first time in many years. She was still worried about him, still not sure that he was willing to give up on Adramelech for her, but at that moment, she didn't care. She'd have to sort that out another time.

The kiss only lasted a moment before Corban's strength finally gave out. The pain was too much. He collapsed on the soft bed. Mary held his arm together as she guided his head to the pillow. He was unconscious, though probably not for long given the amount of pain he was living through.

"Corban, you're an idiot, yeah?"

She watched him for a few moments as his body relaxed into an agonized sleep, "... But I guess this makes you my idiot."

Mary quickly got up and went into the bathroom. She stripped out of her clothing down to her underwear, pulled off her bra and put on a nightshirt. Cotton always made her skin itch when she slept, so instead, she chose a purple silk top with black lace trim. She quickly brushed her teeth and went back out to Corban. *He says one word or gets the wrong idea, I'll rip the other arm off myself.*

Mary climbed into bed next to Corban and turned on her side so that she was facing him. She placed her hand on his healing wrist and rested her head on his shoulder. She hoped that it would keep him from moving too much.

Was momentarily roused by Mary slipping in next to him, "Mary?"

"Shh…" Mary replied. "You may not think you need to be protected, but right now I'm taking care of

Soul Siphon

you. No questions or comments, yeah? Just try to relax. I know it hurts, but do the best you can."

A deep breath escaped his lungs and his eyes fluttered and closed. He had clearly given up and once again slipped out of consciousness. Mary adjusted herself so that she wasn't putting too much weight on his shoulder. She kissed him on the cheek and whispered in his ear, "I'm here… sleep…"

Mary laid back and watched Corban for a few minutes before she herself grew tired. Her eyes slowly closed and she fell asleep next to him. It was the first peaceful night's rest she'd had in recent memory. She gently stroked Corban's arm as she lay in bed with him.

For reasons Mary couldn't explain, her chest felt tight. She had trouble breathing and her body quivered when she touched him. *What the hell are you doing, girl? You know what this boy is and what he can do. You know what's most likely going to happen. Are you really willing to take this chance? It's been so long, but still...*

Mary sighed as she laid back and fell asleep.

⚔

"Corban..."

"You again, don't think that I don't know who you are, Adramelech!"

"Indeed, if that is what you think."

"What?"

"She won't be able to protect you from me. No one will."

"I don't need protection. I beat you once."

"You will.... soon... you will..."

Corban woke up several times as sharp pains flowed to his wrist. Thankfully, Mary was a light sleeper and was there to comfort him whenever it happened. There were a few close calls, but she was able to coax him back to sleep before he did any damage to the healing tissue.

Around 3:30 AM, Corban's eyes shot open, he clenched his working fist and sucked down a deep breath. It was as though he was struggling to take down enough air to satiate his lungs. His whole body was working overtime and was making sure that he knew it.

Mary's eyes shot open as her ears picked up the commotion, "Corban, what's wrong?"

Corban was wide-eyed. The pain had become intense, "It hurts... it really hurts... ugh!"

Mary grabbed the bottle of bourbon and held it up to his lips, "Drink."

Corban looked at her oddly. There was an apologetic expression on her face as she spoke, "I don't have anything else that will help. This isn't a fucking hospital."

Corban chugged down as much as he could tolerate. Tears formed in his eyes as the alcohol did battle with his pain. It took a few minutes, but he slowly began to calm down. His breathing slowed and he closed his eyes.

Mary rubbed his chest, "It's okay, the hand is healing, it's just going to take more time."

"He's coming for me..."

Mary looked at him oddly, "What, who?"

"I'm not certain. A void keeps coming to me when I'm asleep. It says that it's not far away and makes me wake up."

"It's probably just a dream."

"I don't think so... Something's coming, I just know it..."

"Well when it does, we'll kick its ass, yeah?"

Corban didn't look convinced. Mary looked into his eyes and smiled at him warmly, "Trust me, we've dealt with all types of evil creatures before. We can handle whatever this is."

"Okay... I trust you."

"Good, now try to go back to sleep."

"I can't promise that."

At that moment, Corban heard Mary take a few deep breaths. He opened his eyes and looked down at her oddly as she began singing,

"Over in Killarney, many years ago
Me Mither sang a song to me in tones so sweet and low,
Just a simple little ditty, in her good ould Irish way,
And I'd give the world if she could sing that song to me this day.

Too-ra-loo-ra-loo-ral,
Too-ra-loo-ra-li,
Too-ra-loo-ra-loo-ral,
Hush now don't you cry!
Too-ra-loo-ra-loo-ral,
Too-ra-loo-ra-li,
Too-ra-loo-ra-loo-ral,
That's an Irish lullaby."

"Mary?"

"Mm?"

"Isn't that song from after your time?"

"Shut up and go to sleep or I'll stop."

"Shutting up."

Corban immediately closed his eyes as Mary continued,

"Oft, in dreams I wander to that cot again,
I feel her arms a huggin' me As when she held me then.

Soul Siphon

And I hear her voice a hummin' to me as in days of
yore,
When she used to rock me fast asleep outside the cabin
door.

Too-ra-loo-ra-loo-ral,
Too-ra-loo-ra-li,
Too-ra-loo-ra-loo-ral,
Hush now don't you cry!
Too-ra-loo-ra-loo-ral,
Too-ra-loo-ra-li,
Too-ra-loo-ra-loo-ral,
That's an Irish lullaby..."

The soft sound of snoring made Mary stop
singing. She opened her eyes and looked at Corban.
He was at peace and finally letting his body heal. She
smiled as she watched him. *I guess I'm not as bad as I
thought, yeah?*

Corban slept through the rest of the night,
regaining consciousness only once or twice more for a
few seconds. Mary was right there, ready to hold his
arm down if needed, but he seemed to be doing okay
on his own. By the time he regained full
consciousness, the morning was almost over. The
clock Mary kept on the side table said 11:30 AM. His
injuries had drained him to the point of collapse and
his body had devoted all of its energy to repairing the
damage. He gently brought his wrist to his face.
Miraculously, his hand was working again. He had full
control over his fingers and wrist movements. It was
still tender, but it seemed to be healing up okay in the
makeshift cast.

Corban turned his attention to the red-haired
beauty sleeping next to him who had cared for him so
well. She rested comfortably on his left shoulder. Her

Soul Siphon

hand moved to his chest after he moved his damaged wrist. His other arm was wrapped around her, but his hand rested on the mattress. *Thank you for taking care of me last night.*

Being careful not to wake her, he moved his hand to her back. The lace top she was wearing was very silky below her shoulder blades. He affectionately rubbed her back for a few moments as he watched the peaceful expression on her face. *Does she always sleep like this?*

As he gently continued to rub her back, his hand accidentally slid a little lower than he had intended, where he made a startling discovery; she wasn't wearing any pajama bottoms. He could feel her legs on his, but he'd assumed that she was wearing shorts. He gently felt down a little further. *Nope, no shorts, just lace underwear... is she trying to tell me something?*

"Corban?"

A sudden jolt traveled down his spine as his eyes focused on her face. She was wide awake and staring at him. There was a hint of concern in her eyes.

An appreciative look appeared on Corban's face as he spoke, "Yes?"

"How's your wrist?"

"Still sore, but it's feeling better. Thank you."

Mary nodded, "You like having both wrists attached, yeah?"

"Um… yes?"

"I figured," Mary replied. "So I'll give you this one chance to get your hand off my ass before I rip the other one off."

Corban's hand immediately pulled away from her body. "That's better. Didn't your mother ever teach you that it's rude to put your hands on someone without their permission?"

Soul Siphon

Corban's eyes narrowed as he responded, "Didn't yours ever teach you about sending the wrong signals? You're the one lying on top of me, half-naked!"

"My room, my bed, my comfort. If you don't like it, you can leave."

"No, that's okay, I'm good."

"That's what I thought."

Corban smiled, "Thank you for everything, I mean that. Maybe you're not as much of a hardass as you try so hard to make yourself out to be."

"Oh no trust me, I am."

"And I'm the exception to that rule?"

"I haven't decided yet."

Corban chuckled, "Okay..."

Mary slowly started to move away as she decided that it was time to get up, "Let me see that wrist."

Corban held it up to her and moved the fingers. She nodded in approval, "Good. Now let's take a look at the stitching."

She quickly undid the brace and saw that the separation was now little more than a red line. The stitching was still intact, but it was becoming loose and beginning to fall out, "Great, this should heal up just fine. Take it easy with using it for a while. The bone and tissue are probably still weak."

"No problem."

As he sat up, Mary crinkled her nose, "You smell! Better go take a shower, yeah?"

Corban sighed and got out of bed, "Fine."

Mary watched him stand up and head for the bathroom. She pointed to the door when she saw where he was going, "In your own bathroom!"

Corban stopped and turned to the door, "Oh... right. See you downstairs."

Soul Siphon

Mary smiled as she lay back in bed. Once he was out of the room, she hugged her pillow and closed her eyes. She didn't want to get up any more than she wanted to throw him out, but she was hungry and needed to get herself clean. No doubt the rest of the team was already worried about Corban. He would need to make an appearance before they came asking.

Mary finally pulled herself out of bed and headed for the bathroom. After closing the door, she pulled off her nightshirt and underwear. After closely inspecting herself, she leaned into the mirror to look at her eyes. The bags from a few nights earlier had disappeared. The previous night's sleep had done her some good. Part of her hoped that there would be a repeat soon, but it was at that point that her head filled with doubt. *He hasn't been with us that long. Has it been enough time to get over someone or am I going to be a rebound?*

She pictured Janine's face from the night she saw her and twisted her lips. *Oh, screw it! You're acting like a school girl trying to compete over a guy. Get a hold of yourself. You're not that pathetic, girl!*

Mary turned away from the mirror and jumped into the shower. The fact that Corban had burrowed his way into her head was becoming an annoyance. She knew that she'd probably be safer if she went across the hall and told him off. *Safer from heartbreak or sadness maybe, but would I be better off?*

The warm water caressed her pale, freckled, skin and soothed the aches and pains that she'd been too busy to tend to before. She needed this. She was filthy and probably didn't smell much better than Corban. This was her release as it was not only an opportunity to cleanse her body, but it had also become her ritual for cleansing her soul of what had gone on the previous day.

When she finally finished, she got out and wrapped herself in a towel before brushing her teeth and putting some new underwear on. She fished through her drawers for something more presentable to wear. Her usual choice was a pair of black cargo pants and a tight gray or black top. Anything to offset her pale skin and make her not stand out much, but she decided to change it up for once. Her eyes caught sight of a pair of leather pants. She grabbed them and pulled them on before grabbing a black lace top and a red over shirt. It wasn't the most functional thing in the world if she got into a fight, but it suited her needs. She quickly attached the belt with her daggers to her pants.

Once she was done getting dressed, she quickly brushed her hair and got ready to go downstairs. A quick look in the mirror revealed that she was more presentable now and was ready to join the group. *I can only imagine what Johnny and Vlad are going to say... girl, could you be any more obvious?*

At that moment, she heard the door across the hallway close. Her eyes perked up as she ran to her own door. Carefully and quietly, she opened it and peaked out. Corban had cleaned up and was wearing another black outfit. He was closing up and about to head downstairs.

Mary opened her door widely and confronted him, "Going somewhere?"

Corban turned and looked at her, "Yeah I was about to head downstairs. I'm hungry."

He noticed how she was dressed and gave her a nod of approval, "Wow... you look... different."

Mary's lips twisted as she looked at him. She was clearly unsure about what he meant by 'different.'

He noticed it and quickly tried to reword his response, "No, it looks good on you. You don't look like a stone cold assassin you look… human. I like it."

"I can be human and a stone cold assassin at the same time, yeah?"

"Yeah, actually I'm quite positive of that."

"Well," she said casually, "how's your hand?"

Corban raised it in front of their faces and twirled the fingers and wrist, "Much better, thanks to you. The stitches fell out in the shower, and all that's left is this red ring. It barely even stings anymore."

"Good. That ring should disappear in another hour or so."

At that moment, the two fell silent. They looked at each other nervously, each waiting for the other to say something. The awkward silence irritated Mary to no end, but she didn't know what to do about it. *Jeez Mary, what the hell is wrong with you? You've fought demons, wicked souls, and all kinds of evil, but Corban stops you in your tracks? Snap out of it, girl!*

"So…" Corban said, desperately trying to break the silence, "are you hungry?"

"A little."

"Do you want to go out for lunch?"

"Out?" Mary asked, surprised. "You mean out in public?"

"Why not, Vlad and Johnny get away with it."

"Yeah, but they go out late in the evening."

"True… okay, well dinner then?"

"Sure."

"All right," Corban replied. "Well let's go see what everyone's doing right now. No doubt they're worried."

"Yeah I know, they're probably planning to charge up here if we make them wait much longer."

Soul Siphon

As Corban turned to head for the elevator, a mischievous look appeared on Mary's face. She grabbed him by the shoulder, forced him against the wall and planted her lips on his. The air in her lungs was once again sucked out as she pressed his body into the wall with her own.

When she released him and opened her eyes, she saw that Corban had been completely caught off guard. Mary watched him struggle to regain his composure, "Just thought you should know... I didn't forget everything we talked about."

She took two steps back, winked at him, and turned back to the elevator, glancing back every few minutes. Corban's eyes narrowed as a grin stretched across his face. Mary looked down at her bare feet, deep in thought, "So what are we going to do?"

"Huh?"

"Well after everything that's happened, I assumed you wanted those two kisses to mean something. Was I wrong?"

"No, but I mean... damn it, you've been sending me mixed signals since day one!"

Mary chuckled, "Such as?"

"Oh I don't know, curling up next to me in bed in a pretty sexy outfit and then threatening to rip my hand off if I touched you again."

"You had your hand on my ass, yeah? I didn't have a problem with your hand on my back."

"See, that's what I'm talking about it."

Mary sighed, "Don't take it the wrong way, hero. I know dating today is a tad different then it was in my time, but please understand that it's been over a hundred years since I felt a... an affectionate touch. This is kind of new territory for me."

Corban's jaw nearly hit the ground, "A hundred years? How did..."

Soul Siphon

"No questions, yeah?" She replied. "I've been preoccupied with other things."

"So what does all this mean then?"

"I guess we'll just have to find out. I mean, we live right next door to each other, so let's just take our time, yeah?"

"I see."

Mary frowned, "You sound disappointed."

"No, no I'm not! Believe me, I'm actually relieved. I was beginning to think that you were just messing with me."

"Nah," she replied, "trust me, if I wanted to mess with you, your head would be spinning right now. Lihua's not the only one who knows how to mesmerize people."

"I believe it."

The door to the elevator slid open, allowing Corban and Mary to enter. As the door closed, taking them to the main hall, Mary looked up at Corban, "By the way, that kiss stays where it was for now, yeah?"

"Don't want anyone else knowing?"

"Do you, really?"

"Um… I'm pretty sure they already know."

"Wonderful, all I need is to put up with more flak from them."

"You'll manage."

"Yeah, yeah…"

The elevator doors opened on the main floor. Corban stepped out first, followed closely by Mary. Her right hand collided with his left, sending chills down her spine as they walked.

As they entered the kitchen, Mary and Corban were greeted by a group of worried friends. Lihua's eyes widened when she looked up from her sandwich to see Corban and Mary walking in, "Corban, you are awake! Are you all right? How is your hand?"

Soul Siphon

Vlad and Johnny turned and looked up at them. Corban showed them his wrist, "Nothing more than a little red scar. Thanks to Mary."

"Ripper put you back together huh?" Johnny asked in a sly voice.

"If I can put someone together, I can take someone else apart, yeah?" Mary said in a dark voice while cracking her knuckles.

"Point taken."

Vlad grabbed Corban's wrist and carefully inspected it, "Surgeon Mary did good job, no? Zese injuries often take much longer to heal."

"That they do." A voice chimed in from behind.

Everyone turned to see Mike enter the room. A look of rage entered Mary's eyes. She moved in front of Corban and glared at Mike, "You, how could you send us out into that? Corban was badly hurt and it could have been a lot worse! You're all-seeing, yeah? Why didn't you tell us about that creature? Was another one of your sick plots or something?"

Mike grimaced as he took a step back, "Calm down, my child. If I'd known that it was going to be there, I never would have sent you, I swear. That creature was far too powerful for you."

Lihua stood up and placed a hand on Mary's shoulder, "Perhaps we should hear him out before you try to kill him?"

Mary grimaced and hesitantly released him, "Fine, start talking."

Mike sat down at the table as Lihua returned to her seat. Corban sat down next to him while Mary began pacing around the room. The angel sighed as he began to speak, "Okay like I said, I had no idea that this creature was going to be there. I knew that it was lurking the streets, but I had no idea it would show up. I didn't even think it was interested in what we've

Soul Siphon

been doing. I've been trying to track it for some time but have been unsuccessful. It seemed like it was looking for something, but I was unable to figure out what. Even so, it seemed disinterested in us."

"Why did you not warn us sooner?" Lihua asked.

"I didn't want to trouble you with knowledge of something that you couldn't defeat. It's responsible for a lot of suffering. You're not ready to face it yet. You've seen how powerful it is."

He looked over at Mary as he continued, "I didn't want anyone attempting to go after it alone either."

The look on Corban's face made Mary's blood run cold, "Is it Adramelech?"

"If it's not, it certainly is on the same level with him. This creature torments souls just as easily as he does. It's powerful and extremely passive."

"So we're dealing with the real McCoy then? An actual demon?" Johnny asked.

"I can't be certain," Mike responded. "The evidence does suggest that, given that it's been able to avoid my detection up until now."

"You should have told us about this when the creature first appeared on the planet," Mary hissed. "You should have given some sort of a heads up about it before one of us got badly hurt. We're not expendable, yeah?"

"No, no you're not. Maybe you're right. Maybe I should have said something. However, I made a decision and I stand by what I did. I couldn't have you going after this creature before you were ready and that encounter justified my concern."

"When will we be ready?" Corban asked.

"Yeah seriously," Johnny added. "You've had us going after street thugs and gangsters. It's been a

Soul Siphon

while since we've had a good presidential assassination in one of the genocidal third world countries."

Mike lowered his eyes, "I don't know, my children. I just don't. I didn't want you going against anything too powerful until Corban was ready. –I witnessed what happened when you tried to use your power. It deflected you and you're the most powerful member of this group. This thing may actually have the ability to kill you. I won't risk any of you going against it or anything like it until I'm confident that you can beat it."

"Corban's power is still so raw though," Lihua said. "He needs more training, especially if he plans to hunt down Adramelech."

Corban looked down at his hand, "I wouldn't worry about that so much. It's no longer my priority. If the day comes when I need to confront him, that's fine, but I'm not going hunting for him."

A partial grin appeared on Mary's face as he looked up at her. Lihua noticed it and smiled widely, "I take it that there has been a cessation of hostilities… and possibly a treaty signed?"

"What?" Johnny asked.

"It means zat Corban and Mary on good terms now… or is it more zen zat?"

Mary glared at Vlad for a moment but quickly turned away as her cheeks began to burn. Johnny immediately took the opportunity to embarrass her, "Oh man, she's got it bad. I've never seen Ripper get this way before."

"Johnny, I swear to God, I will tear your arm out of your socket."

"Okay, okay…" Mike interrupted. "Look, I don't like the idea of any of you going out without some kind of protection against that thing, so I'm

Soul Siphon

going to give you a weapon to combat the creature and at least buy you enough time to get away should it appear in your path again."

At that moment, five iron collars appeared on the table. Each of them had strange writings running the length of each collar. Corban picked up the one that was closest to him, "What are these?"

"Binding collars," Mike replied. "Special blessings have been performed on them. If one is placed around the neck of a demon, it will temporarily drain their powers and bind them in mortal form."

Vlad picked his up as well, "I never seen zis writing before. Vat is it?"

"Enochian," Mike replied, "the language of the angels."

Lihua's eyes narrowed as she looked at hers, "So we are to get these around the neck of the creature that attacked us, then what?"

"I don't think you can kill it," Mike replied. "You're certainly welcomed to try at that point. Whatever it is, it must not remain amongst the people of this plain of existence, but if it's not possible, then use its vulnerability as a chance to escape. Keep these with you at all times. If you come across it, you restrain it, and then you get out of there… understand?"

"Fine," Mary replied as she picked one up.

Corban grabbed one as well and stood up, "All right then! I should really get training. I can't very well kill this creature without my powers being stronger now can I?"

"No you can't," Mike replied as he stood up. "Let's go up to the roof, since you seem to favor that area, come… and let's see if we can make your powers a little more manageable."

"Awesome, it's about time."

Soul Siphon

"Oh don't say that," Mike said daringly. "This is going to be a slow process. It will be painful and straining. You will need to rest after each session. Steel yourself Corban, the journey ahead is long and arduous."

"I'm ready," Corban replied. "I can handle anything you can throw at me."

"Foolish words… you have no idea what lies ahead. Overconfidence can easily lead you to ruin," Mike said in a dark voice.

His eyes began to turn black and his face twisted into a scowl that made Corban's blood run cold. Even Mary backed away from the table slightly, "Listen to me, my boy. Do not enter into this blindly. The trials for the type of power you seek have driven many beings of old to insanity. Be confident, but also be humble. Remember my words; they'll help you get through this."

Mary placed her right hand on Corban's shoulder and whispered into his ear, "If they don't I'll be here. I'm not letting you do this alone."

Mike looked at her oddly, "What was that?"

"I'm going through this with him."

"I don't understand."

An annoyed look came over Mary's face, "You said to make sure that history doesn't repeat itself, so that's what I'm trying to do. I will be there during the training to make sure that you don't push it too far. He needs to know what he's up against. I will be there."

Mike rolled his eyes, "If you must…"

"Just tell me what I have to do," Corban said softly.

"You're not ready. Meditate today. Clear your mind of expectations and past images. Anything you hold on to can and will be used against you."

Soul Siphon

Corban nodded and was about to turn and walk away when he noticed that Mary was staring at menacingly at Mike. The expression on his face indicated that he picked up on her feelings and decided to confront her, "Mary, you and I have known each other for many years now. Speak your mind."

Mary sighed, "Mike, I know what you're planning. It's cruel. I don't want you pushing this too far."

Mike studied Mary's face carefully, "Then what do you propose we do about it?"

Every eye in the place focused on Mary. She tightened up her expression and turned away, "I'm training with Corban. I don't care if you don't like it and I don't care if it slows things down. We're doing this my way."

"Corban?"

Corban smiled and shook his head, "Don't look at me. I gave up arguing with Mary a while ago. It wasn't good for my health."

Mike nodded, "Smart. —All right, Ripper. If it means that much to you, I'll allow you to partake in the training. If things go beyond your liking, you may intervene. Will that be sufficient?"

"For now."

XI

Corban went up to the roof where he sat down in an open area and closed his eyes. The sounds of the city caressed his ears as gently as the cool air did his skin. He liked where he was now despite everything. Hopefully, at the very least, it was earning him some points with the people upstairs.

"You're invading my space, yet again."

Corban opened his eyes, "Sorry."

"I can leave if I'm disturbing you."

"You're not, you rarely do."

"All right."

Mary sat down next to Corban, "You like it up here, yeah?"

"It's tranquil. When I'm up here it's like…"

"… Everything that's bothering you, all the voices screaming at you about your problems, is suddenly silenced."

Corban turned and looked at her, "Exactly."

They sat quietly for a few minutes. The peace and serenity was a welcome change from their normally violent lives. It wasn't something that would last long, however, as Mary lowered her eyes and bit down on her lip.

Corban knew that this usually meant that something was bothering her, though she would never reveal what it was voluntarily, "What's wrong?"

"I know I said that I'd be there with you… but… do you really have to go through with this? You told me you were done chasing Adramelech."

"You're having second thoughts?"

"Yeah, kind of… Are you really sure that this is the smart move?"

"I am," Corban insisted. "I'm not going after him, but whatever this thing is, we need to stop it."

Soul Siphon

Mary lowered her eyes, "At any cost?"

"No, of course not."

"Then where does it end?"

Corban sighed, "Look Mary, just say it. What's scaring you about this? I'm just taking some precautions to make sure that if we meet up with it again, we'll be ready."

"Is that all you think it is?"

Corban looked over at her inquisitively, "You know something, don't you?"

The look on his face gave Mary a feeling that he didn't understand, "You're not the first victim of possession that we've tried to add to our ranks. There were a few others, yeah? You also aren't the first soul siphon either."

"So I've heard, what happened to them exactly? I'd heard that they became too powerful and had to be put back?" Corban asked.

Mary looked behind her and then back into Corban's eyes, "I'm not supposed to tell you this..."

"Please? I can't really prepare for what's to come if I don't know."

She didn't want to tell him, but she knew that he had to know the full truth, "Your powers are unstable, just like there's. You don't know how to wield them, just like they didn't. Corban... I'm worried about you. I really am... Your powers could do you more harm than good. Demonic energy was never meant to be used by non-demons, nor was it ever intended to be used for good."

Before she could say anything else, Corban grabbed her and kissed her deeply. She kept her eyes open and locked on his. When he finally released her, a smile spread across his face, "Look, it'll be okay."

Mary shook her head, "Corban..."

"Trust me, it'll be okay."

Soul Siphon

"Of course it will be." A third voice chimed in.

Mary closed her eyes, realizing that she'd been caught. Mike walked over to them with an annoyed look on his face, "Thank you, Mary. Though I thought I made it clear that he wasn't to be told about this yet. We need Corban to be able to focus. If you fill his mind with worry and doubt, it will only hamper him!"

Mary stood up and shook her head, "If you think I'm going to let you put a weapon in his hand that you can't take away later without letting him know the risks, you're out of your mind. Like I said, we're doing this my way."

"Why are you so concerned?" Mike asked slyly, as though he didn't already know the answer. "You didn't seem to care about the others all that much when they were training. Why do you care so much now?"

Mary glared at him menacingly, "I did care! We didn't know then what we do now. Lisa was my friend! Do you seriously think I didn't care about what happened when she died?"

Corban looked at her oddly, "Lisa?"

Mike quickly changed the subject, "A story for another time, but we still need to train you. Mary, are you going to be a problem here?"

Corban stood up and looked at her to respond. Mary bit her lip, unable to say what was really on her mind. She lowered her eyes, "I…"

Corban slid his hand into hers. She looked up at him, clearly worried about what could happen. He smiled at her, trying to let her know that he understood.

A grin formed on Mike's lips, "It's okay, Ripper. I know what's going on here. I know you're worried about what's going to happen."

Soul Siphon

Mary clenched her jaw and balled a fist with her free hand, "I warned you about calling me that, yeah? I hate that nickname!"

"All right, Mary," Mike replied, "I apologize. So what would you like us to do then? If I send you out against that creature again, the same thing if not worse could happen. Next time, it may not be his hand that get's sliced off. If that creature is what we all believe it to be, Corban is the only one who can fight it. What would you have us do?"

Corban looked at Mary, "He has a point. We can't let that thing run amok unchecked. If this is what it takes..."

"Corban..." Mary replied softly, "I just want you to know what you're risking here. I don't want to see you get hurt unnecessarily."

Corban lowered his eyes, "Mary, it's my decision. I won't risk anyone else getting hurt by whatever that monster is. If my power is what can end it, then I have to be ready."

Mary felt her face heat up and turned away, "I... I don't agree with your decision. I know you're doing it for the right reasons, but I don't like it."

Mary's chest clenched as she thought of the other soul siphons, "I think I need to get out of here for a while. I need some time to think."

"Mary, come on."

"No... Like I said, I know you're doing this for the right reason, and I respect you for it, but I need to think things over. I need to get out."

She turned and stormed back to the elevator. Corban called after, "Mary, I thought you wanted to be here for this."

"I do."

"Well, we do need to start soon."

Soul Siphon

"You need to center yourself. Keep meditating. I'll be back soon, I promise."

Without another word, Mary disappeared. Corban closed his eyes and sighed, "Great..."

"Don't worry," Mike replied. "She'll come around, she always does. Let her blow off some steam."

Corban bit his lower lip before responding, "I don't know, apparently it's been a while since she's been close to anyone."

"She's just frustrated."

"I hope so."

Mary was so conflicted; she didn't even know who she was mad at. Mike was the first person to come to mind for forcing this whole thing on them. He chose to bring Corban back, knowing what could happen. How could someone live as long as he had yet not learn from history? Next was Mary herself. Who was she to criticize Mike for not learning from history when she was developing a bond with the very person she wanted no part of? Finally, there was Corban. He'd just promised her that he was done chasing Adramelech, but now he was adamant that he be trained on how to defeat the creature.

Mary decided that she was mad at all of them, pretty much just mad at the world in general. She didn't like the feeling, but she didn't know what to do about it, or who to talk to. Besides Corban, Lihua was her next choice, but she had no experience in situations like this so her opinion really wouldn't help much.

Having no other choice, she headed downstairs to her charger. She decided that she needed to go out and get some air. If she was going to figure this whole thing out, she first needed to clear her head. The plush seats of the car were no comfort to her. She pressed the control to open the garage before inserting the key in the ignition. The healthy sound of the engine filled the air as she rolled out of the garage and down Faye Street.

The car turned onto Harrison Avenue and began to pick up speed as it headed west. She rolled down the window as she began to drive, but where was she going to go? She needed an outside opinion but didn't know who to turn to.

At that moment, the face of someone familiar popped into Mary's head. It was crazy, but that was the norm her life had become. With a destination chosen, she pumped the gas to pick up speed.

Mary could not believe that she was actually considering this. Would she get any information or just wind up causing trouble? Mike wouldn't approve of what she was planning on doing, but she didn't care. All she knew was that she needed to talk to someone, and only one person out there would have the perspective that she needed.

Forty-five minutes passed as she drove out of the city. She passed into a less industrial setting and turned off the main road. A large sign on the road to her right read, "Welcome to Weston."

Mary turned onto a side road and stopped in front of a nearby house. She closed her eyes sighed, "I've lost my mind."

She got out of the car and walked up to the front door. It was a small house for such a wealthy neighborhood, but it was kept up well. The grass was cut and the cobblestone path looked custom. The house was brown with an off-white trim. The front stoop had a small, but welcoming awning.

Mary was extremely uncomfortable as she rang the bell. *You know this is insane right? She doesn't know you...*

Luck appeared to be on Mary's side when a dark-haired woman opened the door. She looked out at Mary with a kindly stare, "Hi, can I help you?"

"Mrs. McConnell?"

"Yes?"

"Um... hi, my name's Mary. I... um... well, I was in the neighborhood and just wanted to stop by..."

"Oh, you must be one of Corban's friends." The woman said as her bright blue eyes parked up."

A relieved look appeared on Mary's face as the woman had just given her an opening, "Yes! I was in the area and just wanted to stop by."

"Oh well, that's certainly very thoughtful of you. Won't you come in?"

An uncomfortable look appeared on Mary's face. This was further than she thought she'd get, "Oh... well yes, thank you."

The woman smiled as she stood aside and allowed Mary to pass through the doorway. Mary quickly found herself in a small hallway that she assumed led to the kitchen at the back of the house. The living room was to her immediate right, but she was more focused on the pictures on the wall to her left.

Corban's mother had lined the wall with pictures of her son. One, in particular, caught Mary's attention. It was a picture of him from back in High School. He was wearing a white uniform that had a black number on one side and a soccer ball with the words 'Lincoln-Sudbury' over it. He was standing with his arm around a blonde girl while holding a trophy.

Corban's mother stood proudly next to Mary as she inspected the picture, "My handsome boy. That

Soul Siphon

was his senior year in High School. He was a varsity soccer player. Got himself a partial scholarship to play at UNH."

Mary listened to his mother ramble on about her son, as any good mother would. When she finally finished, she turned and directed Mary to the living room, "Would you like to come sit down?"

"Sure, thanks."

Mary gently sat down in a small chair off to the side off to the side while Corban's mother sat on the love seat next to her, "So forgive me, but how do you know Corban?"

Oh shit! Mary thought to herself. She hadn't gotten that far into the thought. She'd been so bent out of shape that she'd neglected to come up with a cover story for herself, "Oh... well... from College. I was part of the group that he hung out with. We came down to Boston once or twice and he showed us around the city."

Corban's mother chuckled, "That's typical Corban. He always loved his city. So then you must have been one of the groups that spent the night in the basement last year."

"Yes ma'am," Mary lied.

Mrs. McConnell's eyes narrowed, "Odd, you'd think I'd remember him bringing a pretty girl home, especially one from Ireland."

A chill traveled down her spine as she struggled to come up with a cover, "Oh well... my hair was a lot shorter back then and I admittedly didn't talk much, yeah?"

"That must be it."

Mrs. McConnell turned to a small white tea set that she had arranged on the coffee table, "I was just sitting down to some tea, would you care for some?"

"Thank you."

Soul Siphon

Mrs. McConnell handed her a cup, "Sugar?"

"Thanks, no."

Mrs. McConnell sat back, "So what brings you down here?"

Mary shrugged, "I came down to do some shopping in Boston. I took a slight detour and thought that since I was out in this area, I'd stop by. Corban... well, he was talking about how he was worried about you when he was in college."

"Worried about me?"

"Yeah... he said that he felt bad leaving you alone in this house since his father was gone."

"That was my Corban. He always worried about everyone else first. I was actually worried that he wouldn't go away to college because of that. I think he always pictured me as being all alone here by myself."

"That sounds pretty selfless."

Mrs. McConnell laughed, "Well that's who he was. He was always a friendly boy who wasn't happy if anyone he knew was hurt or unhappy. It didn't matter what was going on, he'd always try to find a way to resolve their problem."

"Even if it meant sacrificing what he wanted?"

"Oh yes. Going away to college was something that he always wanted. He'd talked about it since High School. He was excited about the prospect of being on his own for the first time in his life. It wasn't until reality hit that he'd be leaving me alone that he started having second thoughts."

Mary looked at her oddly as she continued, "Corban's friends used to call him a complete boy scout. He never put himself first. Any time he had a decision to make, he put the people he cared about first."

"So if he ever had to make a decision that could put himself in danger..."

Soul Siphon

"He'd take the risk if it meant that someone else would be safe." Mrs. McConnell said. "I knew him well enough to tell you that. I can't tell you how many times he put his friends first, even when it really wasn't necessary."

"I see."

"Why do you ask?"

Mary shrugged, "Corban was just a good friend to me back in College. There was this guy giving us a hard time and he kind of stepped in. I was actually afraid that he was going to get hurt, but he didn't seem to care."

"Yup, that's him."

Mary looked away from Corban's mother. She was still talking about him like he was alive. *If only she knew the truth…*

This was how Corban was. He was a selfless individual who would do anything to protect the people that he cared about. In her heart, Mary knew that, but she needed to hear someone else say it. His mother had now confirmed what she had thought all along; he wasn't training to break his promise and go after Adramelech, he was doing it to stop the creature should it ever come after them. He was doing it to protect his friends and to protect her.

Mary's heart ached with that realization and she regretted running out on him the way she did. Mrs. Corban put her cup down and folded her hands in front of her, "So Mary, tell me about yourself. How long have you been in the U.S.?"

Mary took a second to compile her thoughts and get her story straight, "Well I was born in Limerick Ireland. I left there at a young age and eventually came here to the U.S. to go to school. I guess I never felt like going back."

Soul Siphon

Mary's eyes wandered the room as she spoke. Her eyes caught sight of a picture of a small baby, "Is that Corban?"

Corban's mother picked up the photo, "Oh yes. This was taken after he was born. He was my little miracle baby."

Mary noticed a weird mark on the baby's hip. It was too small to make out, but it almost looked like writing, "That's an odd birthmark."

"Yes, I know. The weird thing is that he didn't seem to have it there when the doctors took him."

"Took him?" Mary asked confused.

"Yes. I'll never forget it... He wasn't crying when I gave birth. They said that he was still-born. They quickly took him out of the room, but the prognosis wasn't looking good."

Mary was shocked, "He was still-born?"

"At first, but then they brought him back a few minutes later and he was perfectly healthy."

"That seems rather odd. Did they tell you what had happened?"

"Not really. I asked questions, but they said that he just started breathing. They couldn't explain it and there was no medical reason for it."

Her story sent chills down Mary's spine. She began to worry that perhaps there were more sinister forces at work in Corban's life, though she couldn't be certain. She needed to look into it further when she got back. It might be nothing, but it still bothered her.

She quickly finished up her tea before getting to her feet, "Well thank you for the tea, but I do really need to be going."

"So soon?"

"Sorry," Mary replied. "I only had a little while before I had to get going. I've got a long way home."

Soul Siphon

"Well okay, it was very nice meeting you. If you're ever in the area again, feel free to stop by."

Mary smiled, "I will… and thank you… from the bottom of my heart… thank you."

Mrs. McConnell looked at her oddly for a moment, but Mary didn't give her a chance to question her. Mary headed out the door and back down to her car. She was desperate to get out of there before things became weirder. She had the information that she needed as well as a new mystery to solve and it was time to go home.

As the charger pulled away from Corban's house, Mary sat back and let out a deep sigh, releasing the tension in her chest. *There is something weird going on here.*

⚔

"No, no, Corban, you're doing it wrong. Now focus and try again!"

Corban focused his mind and placed his hand on Mike's shoulder. He attempted to draw some of Mike's power but was once again hit by the same electric charge that he received from the creature. He was thrown off his feet and landed on his side, "Look, I'm as focused as I can possibly be. I don't know what more you want!"

More of Mike's memories filled his mind. Images of war from long ago and of the creation of the world shot past his eyes. There was so much to take in that it overwhelmed his senses.

Corban cringed. His mind ached like it never had before. He wasn't sure how much more of this strain his mind could take before it snapped. Mike's memories were just too powerful.

Corban and Mike had been at it for hours. He had bumps, bruises, and minor burns all over. He was sweating buckets and extremely tired. After the last hit, he wasn't sure how he was able to keep getting up.

Mike was not convinced, "You say that and I'm sure that you believe it, but I can sense that your emotions are conflicted. You can't use the full potential of the powers I gave you if your mind is elsewhere."

"I'm focused damn it! This is as focused as I can be right now!"

"You're lying," Mike replied. "What is it, what's wrong, my boy?"

Corban wasn't lying. At least he thought that he wasn't. He was trying as hard as he could, but his concerns for Mary were still lingering in the back of his mind. Could that be the lack of focus that Mike was talking about? There wasn't another explanation.

Corban sighed, "I don't want to talk about it."

"Mary?"

"What part of 'I don't want to talk about it,' did you not get?"

"The part where I know when people are bullshitting me?"

Corban was taken aback at hearing an angel swear. It made him pause for a moment. However, it didn't change the fact that he was still waiting for Corban to respond.

"Yes… It's Mary all right?" Corban finally admitted. "Are you happy now? Anything else you want to drag out of my personal life?"

Mike nodded, signaling that he understood, "She's afraid to lose you, though I doubt she'd ever admit it."

"But why, I'm not going anywhere."

"Look, I won't lie to you, my boy. There is risk involved here. If you gain too much power too quickly, it can corrupt you. The human brain wasn't designed to handle that kind of power nor was that power ever meant for you. You're mortal, and while someday your race may have more supernatural abilities, it takes a long time for you to evolve both physically and mentally to be able to do it."

"So how do I prevent becoming corrupted?" Corban asked.

"I'm trying to help you do just that. Hold on to reality. Remember the people and things that matter the most to you. If you can keep their images solid in your head, there's a good chance that you can beat it."

"A good chance."

"Well, it's never a certain thing. Mary was right to worry about the danger involved, but it all comes down to how strong your own mental fortitude is."

"Can I ask you something?"

"Shoot," Mike replied.

"If you knew that I'd be given this power and you knew how dangerous it would be, why did you wake me? It seems like a pretty huge risk. Why would you want someone on the team that wields unstable demonic power?"

Mike sighed, "I've been searching for you for years. The strength to be able to withstand a demon's attack is a rare thing to see. You took on one of the more powerful demons in existence and held on to your sanity for long enough to end your own life and prevent him from taking your soul. When I saw that, I was hoping that you'd be the right person for the job..."

"What another vengeance-seeker?"

"No."

Corban looked confused, "Then what?"

"You're destined for a much higher calling, Corban. I was hoping that you could withstand the corruption of power."

Soul Siphon

"But why, why is it so important?"

"What if I told you that, because of my superior's decree, I've been forced to watch innocent people suffer at the hands of demons who don't follow those rules? What if I told you that I'm tired of seeing such things and not being able to do anything about them?"

"I'd say that sounds frustrating."

"Try it for a few million years and see what happens to your sanity, my boy."

"No, I'm good."

"Exactly," Mike replied. "As an angel, I can intervene on some level, but only if I'm called upon by human beings, and even then I can't make direct contact or even be seen. Most people don't even know I'm there, which greatly reduces what I can do."

"So I'm to act where you can't?"

"Pretty much," Mike said with a smile. "You are my loophole. You're not just another member of the team. You, my boy, are a demon hunter. Unlike the rest of the group, you have a power that can take on demons. You can drain their energy. When you're ready, if you can maintain your sanity, you should be able to rip a demon out of a person."

"So if we're going after the evil you can't, why are we going after these insignificant targets?"

"What?"

"We've gone after small, local, targets. Why aren't we going after terrorist cells and world leaders who commit genocide in these third world countries?"

"Well for starters, you're not ready. I'm not going to send you after high profile targets when you can barely handle absorbing the energy you absorb already. You have no combat skills, no training with weapons, nothing. It'll be some time before I feel comfortable enough to send you after terrorist cells."

Mike lowered his eyes as he continued, "In some cases though, we can't go after them."

"Why not?"

"If you see someone get stabbed by a knife, do you immediately pull it out, or do you leave it in until you get to the hospital?"

"Leave it in?"

"That's right, because pulling it out might do more harm than good. Well, it's the same with some of these rogue leaders. Look at Iraq. When your nation removed their leader, they installed a weak government that was unable to stand on its own feet. The result was a power vacuum that allowed people who were far worse take over."

Mike sighed as he continued, "Sometimes evil is necessary to prevent even worse evil. Unfortunately, I have to look at the big picture. There are some really sadistic people that I would love to send you guys to take out, but if I were to do so, the people who would take over would be just as bad or worse. We're in the business of preventing tragedy, not causing more. We do the best we can, but often the greater good isn't the one that's the most visible."

"It's starting to make sense now."

"Good, but we're not going to get anywhere tonight. Your mind isn't here. Go get some rest."

"Probably a good idea. I'm sorry Mike."

"Don't be, just go. We'll get back to this later."

Corban turned and walked towards the elevator. He opened the door and was about to proceed inside when he heard Mike behind him, "And Corban… talk to Mary, settle this. She may be mad, but I think you'll be able to get through to her. You won't be much good to anyone if your mind is conflicted like this."

"If she'll listen," Corban replied.

Soul Siphon

The door slammed behind Corban as he headed to the elevator. He had aches and pains everywhere as he returned to the dorms to rest. The elevator doors opened, allowing Corban to exit. Within a few moments, he found himself standing between his room and Mary's. His joints screamed at him to go to his own room and get some rest. He was tempted to obey them but instead knocked on Mary's door, knowing that his issues with her were more urgent. She didn't respond. He tried again but got nothing.

"She is not in there."

Corban looked up, "Then where is she, Lihua?"

"This I do not know," Lihua replied. "She left a few hours ago. She looked like she was about to cry. I think she was really upset by what has happened with that creature and what now has to happen as the result."

"Great and she didn't say anything?"

"I was actually going to ask you where she might have gone. In the years I have known her, it is rare to see her get this bent out of shape."

"No idea, I just think she's frustrated with me."

"Why?"

Corban could feel his legs giving out. He leaned on the wall for support, "I need to sit down. Come inside and I'll tell you."

"All right."

Lihua followed Corban into his room. She sat down on the chair next to her bed and brushed the black hair out of her face, "Mike has been working you that hard huh?"

"Yeah, you might say that."

"So what is this all about? What happened that made Ripper so angry at you… again?"

"Well, you know how I have siphoning power?" Corban asked.

"Yes, you can pull the soul straight out of a mortal body. I am familiar with it."

"… and I can steal a demons power as well."

Lihua's eyes narrowed as she looked at Corban, "So you have perfected your powers then?"

"No, Mike is working with me to enhance them and hopefully control them, but Mary doesn't like that."

"Well that makes sense," Lihua replied. "She has seen what happens when soul siphons become corrupted. Up until now, it has only bothered her because of the threat they pose… but with you…"

"Yeah, I know. Listen…"

Lihua shook her head, "Don't bother, it is none of my business. Just know that you are risking more than just your own life here. You are risking the wrath and the heart of someone who cares for you very much, someone who reached out to you when she did not have to and went against her better judgment to befriend you. It is a terrible, awful thing to waste what you have now. It is something for you to consider."

Corban sighed, "Yeah…"

Lihua turned to leave the room as Corban went to take a shower. The door closed behind her as she headed to her own room. She didn't get more than a step before she noticed that Mary's door was open. She immediately walked over to Mary's room and peeked in, "Ripper, are you there?"

"Go away."

"What is the matter?"

"I get the feeling you already know, yeah? You've always been annoying good at snooping around in matters that don't involve you."

Lihua opened the door, "Corban's training has you all knotted up, I take it?"

"I don't know… I… I don't know!"

Soul Siphon

Lihua sat down on the bed next to her, "Ripper… Mary, we have known each other for more than thirty-five years. In that time, I have never known you to get this bent out of shape. You hate the name Ripper, you get annoyed whenever anyone looks at you in a lustful way, but you have never acted like this."

"I know," Mary replied. "This sucks! It's driving me crazy. I haven't even known him that long, but he's managed to bore his way into my head! Now he's planning on doing something incredibly stupid!"

"You love him."

"I haven't even known him that long!"

"Evil does not wait until it is convenient and neither does love."

"How would you know?"

Lihua gave her a serious look, indicating to Mary that she had gone too far. Mary lowered her eyes, "Sorry, I didn't mean that. It's just driving me crazy. He's on this mad quest for power after he told me that he was done chasing Adramelech!"

"He is not," Lihua replied. "He is doing it for all of us."

"What?"

"He saw you fight," Lihua said. "He knew you could have been badly hurt. In his mind, this is the only way we can defeat that creature and any more that may come our way. He knows the risks, but he wants to protect us, especially you."

Mary lowered her eyes, "I don't want this. I don't want this burden on my shoulders. I can't protect him from what his choice will do. I can't protect him from whatever Mike has planned for him. I'm powerless, yeah?"

Soul Siphon

"Then just be there for him. If you can do nothing more than just be his cause to fight. If he is to get through this, he is going to need an anchor."

"An anchor?" Mary asked.

"Something to bring him back if he goes too far, sort of a hand to pull him back from the ledge if you will. It is the reason that all of the other siphons failed. They did not have anything strong enough to come back to. Corban does. He was strong-willed enough to fight off Adramelech, which gives him a better chance than the others. He also has you… if you will stop being stubborn and talk to him!"

Mary closed her eyes and released a long, frustrated, sigh from her lungs, "You have an irritating knack for being right, yeah?"

"I prefer to think of it as one of my more endearing qualities," Lihua retorted.

"You would."

Lihua laughed, "Look, it is getting late. I am turning in."

She got up and began to leave, but stopped at the doorway, "For what it is worth, I am happy for both of you. No one deserves a shot at happiness more than you. I just hope you realize that you have got a good thing going before you mess it up too badly."

"Will you please just leave?"

"As you wish."

/

"Corban, you're not focusing… all right, let's try something else."

Corban's eyes narrowed, "What are you doing?"

"Scaling back a little."

Corban watched as a large red circle that was at least five feet in diameter appeared in front of where Mike had touched the ground. It glowed as odd

Soul Siphon

lettering appeared on it. A second later, a dark creature appeared in the middle.

Corban took a step back shocked by what he saw. The creature was about two feet in height. Its skin was black but when the sun hit it, the surface became green. The creature's red eyes burned with insanity which accented its long silver teeth and hideous grin. It was an odd creature that almost appeared to not really be there. It was as though the creature were trapped between the mortal realm and its own world.

"What the hell is this?" Corban asked.

"Iblis" Mike replied. "I caught the little prick trying to break out and come up here to wreak havoc."

"A demon?"

"Yes, but only a minor demon. He can't really even inflict his terror on humans."

"What do you want me to do?"

"I want you to kill it."

Corban looked down at the creature. It stood on its hind haunches rubbing its hands together like a mischievous child that had just created chaos. It was a menacing little-winged imp that didn't even seem to know where it was.

Corban stepped into the ring. He crouched down and slowly crept up on the little creature, trying hard to not be heard. At that moment, the creature spun around and smacked him in the face, "Surprise, motherfucker!"

Corban fell backward as the creature took flight. Mike chuckled under his breath as Corban got to his feet, "Fly!"

Corban immediately took off after the creature and gave chase up into the clouds, "No you don't, you're not getting away!"

The insane laughter of the little imp echoed in his ears as he quickly began to catch up. Within moments, he was right on the creature's tail. He reached out with all the strength he had available and grabbed the creature, "Gotcha you son of a bitch!"

Realizing that it had been caught, the creature reached out and scratched the air as though trying to avoid being dragged to the ground. Corban fought back and managed to return to the roof of the hideout. It was a fight, but at least he had the creature on the ground.

Mike smiled when Corban pinned it down, "Good, now kill it before it escapes again!"

Corban unleashed his energy. The black and green creature screamed as it began to glow blue. Corban had to focus even harder as Iblis wasn't entirely in his world and was clearly trying to escape back to his own, "Release me you son of a whore!"

"Not going to happen!"

Little by little, the imp faded from existence. It became a cloud of energy that was slowly absorbed into Corban's hands. He felt a sudden rush of energy as black electric bolts traveled up and down his arms, "Oh man... this is new."

"It should be. You've never absorbed a Celestial being. His powers are compatible with your own, so it should be more familiar to you."

Corban looked over at Mike as the power merged with his own. He grinned as demon's darkness slowly began to taint his soul, "Hee hee hee, such power!"

Mike frowned, "Okay, this is it. You're getting a taste of what you will be going against."

"Yes, I can feel it. It's so intense. I feel like I could do anything! It's like a sudden caffeine rush!"

"Now Corban, release it!"

Corban frowned as a sense of desperation filled his heart, "No, I can control it!"

Soul Siphon

"I know you can, but it's not time for that yet! You need to learn how to be strong enough to know when you can't keep something. Do as I said, release it!"

Corban sighed and pushed hard against the imp. He thrust his hands forward and unleashed a dark beam of energy that parted the clouds above them. The release drained Corban, causing him to collapse.

Mike caught him before he hit the ground, "Well done. You're doing very well."

"Mike, is that what I have to take on?"

"Infinitely more powerful."

"How could I expect to win?"

"We'll work on it. We'll keep working with a stronger force as time goes on. For now, you're done for the day. Go rest up for tomorrow."

Corban nodded and slowly limped toward the elevator. He made his way back to his room and stripped out of his clothes. He wanted to take a shower but decided that he wasn't in the mood. A shower would have to wait until later.

Corban stripped out of his sweat-covered clothes and threw on a clean pair of boxers and a shirt. He then went into the bathroom and wiped down his face and arms before returning to the bedroom. He knew that he would need to take a nap soon before he passed out.

Refreshed, he sat down on the bed, leaned against the wall and closed his eyes. His attempt to relax was thwarted when a knock came at his door. His eyes opened and he slowly got to his feet. *Oh, you have got to be kidding me! What is it now? Isn't Mike done with me?*

He unlocked the door and opened it. To his surprise, Mary was on the other side. Her eyes were red and it looked like she'd been crying, though he was sure that she'd never admit to it. She had an apologetic look on her face, "I was hoping maybe we could go for a night out, yeah?"

"Really? You stormed out and said that you needed space," Corban replied.

"I know," Mary said, trying to maintain a strong voice. "I'm sorry. I was angry. It gets the better of me sometimes, yeah?"

"So I've seen."

Mary bit her lip, "I came to see if you wanted to come with me to clear our heads, but if not I can leave you alone."

Corban studied her expression for a few moments. She didn't give him a chance to respond and quickly turned away, "Right, I'll go then, yeah?"

Before she could get far, Corban grabbed her arm and gave her a gentle pull to turn her around. She looked into his eyes for a moment before he quickly pressed his lips against hers. Her heart skipped a beat and her eyes closed. She touched his cheek and waited for him to release her.

Corban savored the moment. When he finally released her, his eyes opened right into hers, "I'm glad you came back?"

"Where else would I go?"

Corban shrugged as Mary lowered her eyes and looked at his hip, "Corban… can I ask you something weird?"

"Uh sure?" He replied.

"Can I see your left hip?"

"Why?"

"I thought I saw something there the other day when you were training."

Corban looked down and lifted his shirt, "Oh you mean my birthmark?"

Soul Siphon

He turned to his side with his shirt raised to let her inspect it, "It's the oddest thing. Everyone always says that it looks like a tattoo of some weird language."

Mary eyed it suspiciously, "Yeah, that's exactly what it looks like."

"Something wrong?"

Mary looked up and smiled, "No, not at all. So… What are you in the mood for?"

"You're not going to tell me what's going on, are you?"

"Nope."

"All right… shall we just find a nice pub? I could go for a burger."

"Sounds good."

XII

Thud!

Corban hit the ground after being thrown across the roof again. He'd been training all day, his shoulder was pulsing, and his hand was in pain. He stood back up and stumbled towards Johnny. Mike stood off to the side, trying to give Corban advice with a detectable level of frustration in his voice, "Focus your mind again! Draw upon your strength."

Johnny looked up at Corban with a dismal expression on his face, "Yes please take my powers. I don't want them, they're yours."

Mike rolled his eyes, "Your sarcasm is noted. You won't be permanently damaged by this. It's only a temporary drain. Whatever he takes, we'll put back."

"How comforting…"

Again Corban grabbed Johnny and focused his mind. Johnny's body reacted by sending electric shocks back through Corban as a defense mechanism. Corban ignored it and pressed harder, trying to draw from Johnny's power. He forced his own energy to counteract the shock flowing into him and began to draw energy.

Mike smiled when he saw that Corban was finally making progress, "Yes, that's it, keep focused. You got him!"

Corban clenched his jaw, "Come on..."

His skin turned red as he worked. Johnny's memories of pain entered his mind. Corban looked down at his hands, but they weren't his. He was seeing the world through Johnny's eyes. His stomach was in intense pain and his fingers looked like they were that of a skeleton. The room he was in was dark, damp, and filthy with only a single dim lamp that allowed him to

Soul Siphon

see anything. This was where Johnny had spent the last days of his life.

Corban's eyes teared up as he worked, "Johnny, I'm sorry…"

Mary watched from the other side. She could see that he was struggling and looked over at Mike, "He's in pain, end this!"

"As I told you before," Mike replied, "evil is not convenient. It won't wait because you're in bad shape."

Mary clenched her jaw, "We had an agreement, Mike."

"I am aware of that, but we've been at this for over a month now! Don't you remember what I said about no pain, no gain?"

"This is different, yeah?"

"I don't think so."

Mary shook her head, clearly frustrated that Mike wasn't living up to his end. She turned to Corban and yelled, "Corban, let him go!"

Corban was incapable of hearing her while he worked. He was in Johnny's world and completely unaware of what anyone around him was saying. The pain continued to mount and was becoming almost intolerable. He felt like he was about to pass out when he suddenly felt a soft hand on his shoulder.

"What are you doing?" A disembodied voice asked.

The pain slowly went away, making it possible for Corban to continue. *I can do this... I can feel it.*

Corban pushed with every ounce of strength that he had left. He was determined to get it right this time. As he pushed, something changed. Johnny's memories were being replaced with images of Mary. He couldn't understand what he was seeing. Why was Mary in Johnny's mind, or was she?

Soul Siphon

What the...? Corban thought to himself. *What is this? Mary? Why are you here?*

"I'm here because you need to let go." Another disembodied voice replied.

Corban gasped. Mary was trying to get between him and Johnny in an attempt to break the link. He wasn't feeling the pain anymore because she was blocking it. *Mary... oh God...*

Corban knew the only way Mary could be blocking out the pain was by taking it on to herself. He couldn't allow that to continue. Without warning or any slowdown, he immediately cut himself off and severed the drain.

Once again, Corban was sent flying, this time landing on the other shoulder. Mike sighed as Mary ran over to help him up, "You must learn to focus. You can't let your mind wander, you can't even think about focusing. You just have to focus on the task at hand. If you don't, you'll never be able to draw energy out of anything other than a mortal."

He then turned to Mary, "Are you going to fight his battles for him too, or are you going to let him grow and learn?"

"I'm doing my best," Corban replied as Mary helped him to his feet.

"I know you are," Mike said in a comforting tone, "but that creature isn't going to care about your best. If you can't do it, then most likely it will inflict even more damage on you. I can..."

"Mike, we've been at this for a month now and it hasn't gotten much easier. Maybe we need to wait until I have a little more power before we try this again? I don't think I can master this ability on what I currently have. The immortal barrier is simply too strong."

"Very well," Mike replied. "Take the rest of the night. We'll start bright and early tomorrow."

"All right," Corban replied, annoyed that they'd have to start over from scratch.

"Sure why not... no need to let me have any say," Johnny snapped.

Mary took Corban by the arm and led him back to his room, "You okay?"

"A little banged up, otherwise fine."

"Tough guy, yeah?"

"I wish."

Mary sat Corban down against the wall. He leaned back as she turned on the television, "You okay?"

"Fine, why?"

"I know what you did," Corban replied. "I know how much it hurt, so I can't imagine that you weren't in pain as well."

"I've had worse," Mary replied with little hint of emotion. "Don't worry about me. You're the one we need to focus on right now."

Corban nodded as he quickly changed the subject, "So any progress?"

Mary looked at him oddly, "Huh?"

"You've been looking up what my birthmark means."

Mary's skin turned white. It was true that she had suspected his birthmark of being more than it appeared, but she was trying to keep a low profile, "What the... how the fuck did you know?"

"You've been acting weird ever since the first time you saw it. You took a picture of it when you thought I was sleeping, you ran an image search on Google, and you contacted a professor at Oxford University for help. Next time, clear your internet search history."

Soul Siphon

Mary frowned, "I don't appreciate you spying on me like that!"

"You didn't seem to mind doing it to me when I first joined."

"You knew?"

"Of course, I'm not stupid. So did you find anything?"

"Yes…" Mary replied hesitantly. "It's Punic, one of the ancient Phoenician languages."

Corban's eyes widened, "What, really?"

Mary nodded, "I'm afraid so…it roughly translates out to the word 'host,' and definitely not in a positive way."

All these years, Corban had thought that it was nothing more than a simple odd-looking birthmark. To find out that there was more to it, was unsettling, "What do you think it means?"

"I don't know… but I plan to find out."

Mary smiled and placed a comforting hand on his leg, "Relax, I'll get to the bottom of this."

Corban was about to respond when Mike's alarm sounded. Mary sighed, "We never can get a break, can we?"

Corban got up and followed Mary down to the living room. Mike was standing in the dead center of the room with his back turned, "Mike, what the hell, I thought we had the night off?"

Mike was about to respond when his face went pale and his head jerked to the side. His jaw dropped open and he looked as though he'd just seen something horrific, "We've got another one… Oh, God…"

Johnny entered the room from the staircase at the same time as Corban, "Bad?"

A picture of a blonde woman appeared in his hand, "Tanya Noble... This one has been on the books for a while now. I've been keeping tabs on her to see if

Soul Siphon

she would turn her life around. I thought the woman had repented, but apparently, I was mistaken. Such a shame…"

Mary leaned back on the wall where the elevator shaft was, "Mistaken? Not like you to make a mistake, yeah?"

"No, it's not," Mike admitted. "I guess you could say that I was holding out a fools hope that she'd straighten out. I'd been keeping a close eye on this woman for years."

"Why the interest in her?"

"Let's just say she has a history and it seems that she's been unable to beat the sickness growing within her mind."

"Oh?"

Mike lowered his eyes, "Her uncle molested her as a child. Psychologically, she never recovered from it."

Mary clenched her jaw as a shocked look appeared on Johnny's face. "And we're going after her? We don't usually go after people with outstanding mental issues like this. What's her deal?"

"She's inflicting the same pain that she was put through," Mike replied. "She's a married teacher out in Oakland, California. She uses her authority over her students to get sexual favors from a select few. When she went to counseling on her own, I was willing to look the other way in the hopes that she'd recover, but now… she's gone too far."

"How old?" Corban asked.

"Up until now, it's been sixteen and seventeen-year-olds," Mike said. "However it seems that recently she's gone for younger students. She seems to favor one, in particular, that is only fourteen. I can't let this slide anymore. Too much damage is being done."

Soul Siphon

He looked up at Mary, who looked ready to explode, "Take Corban and Johnny and correct this before she hurts anyone else. Use whatever means necessary."

"Oh don't you worry," Mary replied, "we'll take care of this, yeah?"

"What about Vlad and Lihua?" Johnny asked.

Mike shook his head, "You don't need a sniper for this one. Besides, he's currently out getting some supplies. I'll have him get a good meal ready when he gets back."

"And Lihua?"

"Lihua is busy with another mission that I sent her on. You shouldn't need her help. This time it's just you three."

"Oh great..," Johnny said as a disgusted look came over his features. "Give us a workout and then poison us with Vlad's cooking!"

Corban laughed, "Oh come on, it's not that bad."

"Try eating it consistently for a few months and then tell me it's not a problem."

Corban turned to Mary, "This one should be easy, are we ready to go?"

"I've already got my blades, but maybe you guys should get your guns, yeah?"

Corban turned his leg to the side, showing the Smith and Wesson on his hip. Johnny shrugged, "This sounds like a quick one. I think we'll be fine. Besides, carrying too many guns around in view of the public could cause other problems. We've got one. That should be okay."

All three of them pulled up the hoods on their shirts and secured them in place as Mary stepped forward, "All right, I'll see you guys there."

The group headed outside into the cool air. Mary disappeared into the distance as Corban knelt down, "Hop on, Johnny."

Johnny rolled his eyes, "So this is what I'm reduced to... piggyback rides. –Do not say a word, Corban!"

Johnny grabbed onto Corban's back as Corban stood up. Corban steadied himself as he turned to Mike, "See you when we get back."

"Good luck, –and Mary, let Corban have the final kill on this one, he needs the energy."

"No problem."

Corban focused on the image of the blonde woman and began levitating. Within seconds, he was floating over the city of Oakland. He touched down outside a four-floor apartment complex and looked around.

Johnny's eyes were wide, "Holy shit that was fast!"

Mary was already there waiting for them as they touched down, "Beat you again, yeah?"

"Next time you carry Johnny!"

Johnny hopped off Corban's back, "Come on guys, keep it quiet. Let's get this done before the sun goes down all the way."

Corban sighed, "Right..."

The building was a rectangular brick structure with a white trim. There was a small parking lot, enough for about ten cars off to the side. It was fairly typical of low-end apartments and didn't look like a building that would be difficult to gain access to.

Corban reached for the handle on the door and tried to pull it open. His arm met with resistance as the white door made a metallic clanking sound. It was locked and would not open without considerably more force. He noticed a small card reader off to the side.

Soul Siphon

Apparently, this was the only way to open without drawing attention.

Corban shrugged and turned to Johnny, "Should we try to see if there's a back way in or...?"

His sentence was interrupted by the sound of shattering glass. He turned to see Mary lower her leg and reach through the broken window on the door to unlock it. She smiled as the door opened.

Corban sighed, "Yeah that's not going to draw attention to us at all. Do you ever do anything gently?"

Mary lowered her chin slightly with a faint smile and looked him in the eye, daring him to keep talking. Corban rolled his eyes, "Never mind, don't answer that."

"Do you see anyone else around?" Mary asked.

"Whatever, let's just get this over with."

They moved into the foyer and checked the mailboxes. They were small metal compartments that were just big enough for letters and not much else. There were four on each floor with a lock in the middle to allow the mailman to open them from the top to insert the mail.

"Let's see... Noble... Noble..," Corban said softly as he looked at the names. "Ah, here we go, third floor! This should be easy, nowhere to run."

Johnny took up the lead, "I don't know about this, guys. This doesn't feel right somehow, going after a woman with issues like this."

"I know," Corban replied. "It's just too much gray area. I don't know about this..."

"Who's more important," Mary asked in a hostile voice, "her or the children she's hurting? Who still has a chance?"

"Were you a child at 16?" Johnny demanded.

"Different time."

"I don't think so."

Soul Siphon

Corban rolled his eyes as he looked at them, "Look, I understand both sides here, but we're not talking about a sixteen-year-old anymore. Mike said that she's gone after younger kids. That makes her a predator, mental issues or not. From what I've seen in the news, insanity defenses and random mental illnesses rarely spare someone the death penalty or a life sentence. Normally, I would agree with you Johnny, but as far as I'm concerned, she's condemned herself."

Defeated, Johnny sighed, "I suppose so. At the very least, we can't allow this to continue."

With their differences momentarily settled, the group slowly proceeded up two flights of stairs until they arrived on the third floor. Immediately, they could hear the sound of moaning coming from the room closest to the outside. They opened the door to the stairwell and made their way into the nearest hallway.

A disgusted look appeared on Mary's face, "Sounds like she's taken yet another victim... still think we're not doing the right thing?"

"Point taken," Johnny admitted hesitantly.

Johnny pulled out a small pick he'd fashioned out of old silverware and began to toy with the lock on the metal door. He pushed the metal pick in and jerked it around a few times, trying to trick the mechanism. Mary leaned against the wall while he worked, "We'd be in there already if Lihua had come with us."

"Maybe we could just go with your method and kick the door!" Johnny shot back. "That should solve everything, right!"

"We'd be in now though, yeah?"

"Just a sec!"

The moment he finished talking, the door lock clicked and the door opened with a faint creak. "There, see? No problem."

"Yet," Mary replied.

The group immediately rushed into the apartment. Johnny dropped to his hands and knees, crawled into the living room, and glanced around quickly. To his relief, the room was empty. He quietly whispered back to his companions, "Clear!"

Mary and Corban followed Johnny into the room. Mary closed the door behind them and kept up the rear. The apartment was no more than a thousand square feet. It was a one-bedroom that looked fairly well furnished. Corban noted the pictures of her and her students that she kept on the mantle and wondered if they were former conquests, though he could not be certain.

The sounds appeared to be emanating from the bedroom. Corban turned to Mary and pointed to the left side of the door. Mary pressed herself against the wall on the left side. Johnny took the other side and nodded to Corban that he was ready.

Corban stood in front of the door and whispered softly, "Okay, here we go... 1... 2... 3!"

Mary gave the door a solid kick, forcing it open. Corban proceeded inside the dark room where Tanya and her partner were lying in bed. Tanya screamed when she saw them, "Who are you, get out of here!"

To Johnny's surprise, Tanya was actually very attractive. She was athletically built with long blonde hair and clearly took care of herself. This was not the person he'd pictured as being a child molester.

Corban looked in disgust at the guy she was sleeping with. He couldn't have been more than fourteen years old. It made Corban sick just thinking about it. His eyes began to glow red as he looked at the

Soul Siphon

boy. He spoke in an inhuman voice that even made the blood of his teammates run cold, "Leave now, and don't do something this stupid again or you will face judgment for it!"

The boy refused to move, trying to defend his teacher, "What are you going to do?"

Johnny pulled the gun off of Corban's belt and pointed it at him, "Let's go for a walk."

The boy raised his hands when he saw the gun and looked at Johnny oddly, "Is that thing real?"

Annoyed, Johnny cocked the gun and caught the first round as it popped out before pointing the gun at the boy again, "You want to find out?"

The boy raised his hands, "All right... please, all right!"

He grabbed his shirt and pants as he climbed off the bed, "I'm going, all right?"

As the boy was led out of the room, Tanya did the best she could to cover her womanhood with a blanket. She then cringed against the headboard, "Please don't hurt him..."

"He's an innocent here. We have no intention of hurting him," Corban growled. "You need to be more worried about yourself right now."

"Who are you, do you work for my husband? Look whatever he's paying you..."

"We don't work for anyone that concerns you," Mary interrupted as she stood next to Corban. "We're here stop you from hurting anyone else."

"Hurting anyone?" Tanya asked. "We were just having a little fun! It was consensual! I never made him do anything he didn't want to."

"Not with a fourteen-year-old!" Corban shot back. "There is no consensual. You don't know what kind of damage you're doing!"

Soul Siphon

As he took a menacing step forward, the red fire in his eyes intensified. Tanya pushed herself back harder against the headboard of her bed, "Please... no, don't hurt me! I won't do it again, you have my word! Please! I'll do anything you ask, I..."

Corban grabbed her by the neck, "You had your chance. You've been watched for a long time. This has to end and obviously, you're not the one to do it. We can't risk any more innocents getting hurt."

Before Tanya could say another word or cry out, Corban's eyes began to glow. Tanya's spirit energy flowed from her body into Corban's hand. He released her neck, revealing a white orb in his hand which he crushed.

A moment later, Johnny reappeared in the room, "The kids gone. He's heading home, but I don't know if he plans on calling the police or not, so we shouldn't stay here long."

Mary was relieved to see that this mission was almost over, "All right, well do your thing and get rid of the body."

Johnny rubbed his hands together and placed them on Tanya's lifeless corpse, "Here we go."

Instantly, her body began to wither until it became brittle bone. He continued to keep a firm grasp on it until the bone itself turned to dust. The remains exploded into a white cloud that was spread about the room.

Johnny wiped his hands as he turned to his friends, "We're good no evidence."

"All right let's get going..," Mary replied.

Corban felt his stomach churn. Something wasn't right. His eyes were glassy and his skin was far more pale than usual. He had destroyed the orb, but something was happening that hadn't previously with any of his other victims. Tanya's memories and

Soul Siphon

experiences flowed into Corban's mind and seeded themselves. He'd prepared himself for the memories that he'd absorb, but nothing could prepare him for the flood of sorrow that invaded his thoughts.

Mary grabbed him by the shoulders, "Corban, what is it, what's wrong?"

"I can feel her," Corban replied. "All her pain... her depravity... Everything that she went through... it's all here."

Multiple images flew through Corban's mind. First the boys Tanya had slept with appeared, and then he experienced the hardships of her marriage and what that had done to her self-esteem. She'd been cheated on more than once and it made her feel completely worthless. This was the final straw that broke the camel's back and led her down the path of darkness.

Finally, the images of her childhood appeared in his mind. He saw her uncle. He saw what the man had done to her and how he used to touch her. He saw her run and hide whenever the man came for a visit in a futile effort to get away. He then saw how violent and threatening the man could get if she tried to refuse him.

Corban dropped to his knees and vomited on the floor. Tears fell from his eyes as he breathed heavily, "No!"

"Aw shit, Mary..," Johnny said as he looked at Corban's face, "He's gone pale. He looks like he just caught death."

"We need to get him out of here," Mary replied. "We don't have time for this. —Corban, snap out of it! We need you!"

"No!" Corban shouted as he broke out of Mary's grasp and stood up. He lurched forward and stumbled to the door as fast as his legs would take him. His breathing increased rapidly as he staggered down the stairs and out the broken front door. He was off balance and looked like he was going to fall over more than once.

Mary and Johnny gave chase, worried about him and what he was planning. Mary called out as he slowly increased his distance, "Corban wait, where the hell are you going?"

No response.

"Corban, we'll come with you!"

Corban closed his eyes and focused his energy. He pictured Tanya's uncle in his mind and immediately took flight, ignoring his friends. He was completely deaf to the things going on around him, "Fly."

His body rocketed off into the skies considerably faster than usual. He punctured a hole in the first cloud he passed through and kept going. The wind struck his skin like a whiplash, but he barely even felt it. His mind was elsewhere and nothing was going to keep him from his new target.

Mary and Johnny got outside in time to see him disappear into the sky. By the time Mary spotted him, he looked like a jet at high altitude, leaving a trail of white smoke behind. Johnny couldn't believe how fast he was going, "Where is he off to in such a hurry?"

"I don't know," Mary replied.

Corban touched down outside of a house in Sacramento. He landed on one knee and looked up at the small dwelling. It was a quaint little house, yellow with light blue trim and a small white fence around the property. It looked like one of the many cottages he'd seen down at Cape Cod when he was younger. No one would ever guess about the monster that dwelled within.

Soul Siphon

Corban got to his feet and marched up to the door. The moment he was close enough, he performed a spin kick which destroyed the door's latch, causing it to fly open. A chubby man in his mid-sixties sat in an armchair on the far end of the living room. He looked up startled when he saw the door come flying in with a loud boom.

As Corban appeared in the doorway, the man grabbed a pistol out of the box next to his chair, "Who the fuck are you, asshole?"

Corban stepped inside and glared at him, "Patrick Noble?"

"Who wants to know?"

"I see no reason to introduce myself to someone who is about to die!" Corban said in a dark voice as tears filled his eyes.

Patrick pointed his gun at Corban, "Get out of here. This is your only warning. I'm not afraid to use this!"

Corban stepped forward, ignoring his warning. Patrick quickly took a nervous step back and fired two shots from his revolver. The first shot pierced Corban's shoulder and made his left side jerk back slightly. Blood dripped from the wound, but he ignored it. The second one pierced Corban's hip, causing him to again jerk backward a little bit, but he was still coming. Corban was functioning on pure adrenaline. He was focused on his target and nothing was going to get in his way.

It was unclear if Corban wasn't feeling the shots because of his power or the adrenaline rush, but nothing appeared to be capable of stopping him. He continued to move forward as though he hadn't been hit. He was a raging freight train and nothing was going to keep him from his target.

Soul Siphon

Before Patrick could fire off a third round, Corban's right fist connected with his face. Patrick fell to the floor and winced in pain, "Who are you... why are you doing this?"

"I'm here speaking for Tanya!" Corban replied. "She's waiting for you in Hell!"

Corban didn't give Patrick the chance to say another word. He wasn't interested in any denials, justifications, or pleas for mercy. There was no point.

Corban struck him again, this time with his left fist as he wound up with his right for another strike. The beating was relentless as each fist hit its target. The red in Corban's eyes burned even brighter with every hit. All of the sadness, rage, illness, and depravity that Patrick had inflicted on Tanya over the years was now being unleashed on him in one fell swoop.

/

Mary and Johnny arrived on the scene within moments, having followed Corban's trail. Mary's eyes narrowed when she saw the door. Johnny surveyed their surroundings, "Oh this is not gonna be good."

Their hoods were still up, so no one could make out their faces, but even that couldn't conceal Mary's concern, "We have to hurry, yeah? Someone would have seen this!"

Mary barged into the house, followed closely by Johnny. Mary had seen a lot during her long life and was ready for anything, or so she thought. Her legs became frozen when she saw Corban. He was covered in blood and viciously beating what she could only guess was a corpse. The grunts coming from him sounded almost like a rabid animal as he continued the vicious beating.

Mary looked at the blood that was spattered everywhere. She hadn't seen anything like this since her days in Whitechapel, "Corban..."

"What are we going to do, Ripper?" Johnny asked.

"I'll get Corban. You destroy the body. We've gotta clean this up!"

Mary stepped forward and grabbed Corban while Johnny went to work. She braced herself for the fight that she knew was coming. He was not about to stop, not even for her. She tried to grab his arms, but he was too strong. He was fixated on causing this man pain, even though he was already dead.

Chills ran down Mary's spine, "We don't have time for this. We need to get out of here before someone realizes what's going on. –I'm sorry for this..."

She quickly unsheathed her dagger and smacked Corban on the back of his head with the butt of the handle. Corban went limp and fell on top of the body. Mary breathed a sigh of relief as she pulled Corban off and got under his arm. Blood from the body smeared all over the both of them.

Johnny withered the mystery body until it was dust then looked up at Mary, "Now what?"

"Burn the place down," Mary replied. "I don't know what happened here, but better safe than sorry. We don't know what taint is on this house. Whatever it is, it drove Corban insane."

"I agree, plus there's too much evidence for us to clean up," Johnny replied as he ran to the kitchen and turned on the gas stove.

Mary carried Corban out front and waited for Johnny. Corban was breathing irregularly, even while he was unconscious. Whatever was tormenting him, was affecting his autonomic system in addition to his mental state.

A few seconds later, Johnny came running out the front door, "5... 4... 3... 2... 1... and?"

A thundering boom woke up the whole neighborhood and rocked window panes for miles in either direction. The windows blew out and the house was engulfed in flames. Several car alarms nearby went off in response to the blast and cried out in unison that there was trouble.

Mary's eyes narrowed, "What in the name of hell did you do?"

Johnny shrugged, "Lots of flammable shit in that house. It was bound to happen sooner or later. Pretty believable if you ask me."

"Believable, but a little on the bombastic side, yeah?"

"It got the job done, didn't it?"

"All right," Mary replied. "Let's go."

XIII

Mike was waiting for them in the main hall when the group returned. He was anxious to hear about how their mission had gone. Corban's altered state had somehow blocked him from being able to get a full read on what was happening. He knew that something had gone terribly wrong, but wasn't sure what. Nevertheless, he was irate and looked like he was gearing up to kill someone when the group returned.

Mary burst through the door, carrying Corban's unconscious body. They were covered in blood and looked like they had just been through a war. Johnny followed close behind, trying to help keep Corban steady. The tension in the air was high as they moved quickly to help their friend. They ignored Mike and moved towards the elevator.

Mike glared at the group as they rushed by, "Mary, what the hell happened out there? All I was able to detect was complete chaos!"

At that moment, Vlad came out of the kitchen and saw what was going on, "Chjort!"

"Mike," Mary replied, "I'll explain when I can, but right now we need to get Corban somewhere safe and contained before he wakes up. I won't risk him flying off on me again. Come with us if you want answers that badly."

Mary and Johnny got into the elevator the moment the doors opened. Mike quickly squeezed in behind them. The moment the doors opened on the dorm floor, Mary ran out and opened the door to Corban's room. Thankfully, he had left it unlocked. She dropped him on the bed and let out a deep sigh as she leaned back against the wall and briefly closed her eyes.

Soul Siphon

Mike was becoming impatient, "Okay, he's safe. Now, what the hell happened out there? Why is Corban in such bad shape? This is serious!"

Mary stood up and went to the door, "Outside, let him rest."

Mike followed Mary out into the hallway as she tried to wipe some of the blood off her face with her right sleeve. The moment that they were out of Corban's room, she turned to him with a worried look on her face, "Mike, I don't know what happened out there, honestly. We completed our mission, Corban took her soul just like you said, and everything was going fine... but after that, he just went pale, got sick, and then went nuts. He took off running like nothing I've ever seen, yeah?"

"Took off running to where? What happened then?"

"He wouldn't talk to me or Johnny. It was like his mind had become wired to complete a task and nothing could pull him away from it. Mike... what the hell was up with that woman? Did it have something to do with her memory or was she possessed?"

"She wasn't possessed," Mike replied. "Though she did have a very sordid past, I didn't think that it was anything worse than what he'd already absorbed."

Mike looked deep in thought. At that moment, Mary looked like she was choking on something. Her eyes looked almost glossed over and her breathing increased rapidly. A hint of desperation appeared in her voice, "Mike, I know he killed an innocent, but it wasn't him. I swear to you. He wouldn't... he must have been influenced by some outside source. Please, you have to believe me..."

"Calm down Mary," Mike replied gently, "the man wasn't an innocent by any stretch of the imagination."

Soul Siphon

"What?"

"Do you remember what I told you about Tanya? Do you remember what I told you about her uncle?"

"The man was a monster, yeah? Why do you ask?"

"Because that's who Corban killed."

"Her uncle was still alive?" Mary asked, shocked. "What the fuck? Why the hell weren't we going after him then? He deserved it as much as she did!"

"Two reasons," Mike replied. "First, he only had a few years of life left. He was going to die of cancer and it wouldn't have been a pleasant end. That was to be his punishment. Second, his crimes were restricted to Tanya. He never hurt anyone else. As far as we were concerned, he was no longer a threat."

Mary rubbed her forehead as a slight sense of relief came over her, "That's messed up."

"I know, but these decisions are never simple."

"So what are we going to do?"

"We need to figure out what happened to Corban," Mike replied. "I don't want a repeat of this, so we need to find out what happened and then prevent it from happening again. Stay with him."

"No problem, yeah? But what about what he did?"

Mike looked out the window at the end of the hallway. His gaze was directed upwards at the clouds. Mary nervously stepped forward, "I'll take responsibility for his actions. I should have been more alert."

"Noble Mary, but unnecessary. I have been given broad discretion to deal with what goes on down here. I think we can consider this a non-issue. It wasn't part of the plan, but I'll smooth things over with the people upstairs."

Mary released the tension in her body and sighed as relief poured over her. Mike patted her on the right shoulder, "You can relax. You're not going to lose him over this."

"Am I really being that obvious?"

"Just a little," Mike replied, "but it's okay. I'm glad you two are getting along so well. I don't like the idea of any of you being alone all the time. It's not healthy."

"Thanks, Mike."

Mary left Mike in the hallway and went back to Corban's room. Johnny stood up from the chair next to the bed, "He's okay, but it looks like whatever happened, drained him pretty bad. He may be off of his feet for a while… poor bastard."

"His powers are still in their infancy, yeah? We don't know about everything that he can do yet. Maybe he's not just a siphon, like we thought."

"At this point, I'd definitely say he's not."

Mary sat down on the bed next to Corban, "I'll look after him. You should go get some food and unwind. It's been a stressful night."

"I know right, but I wouldn't call Vlad's cooking unwinding."

"Oh just get lost!"

"Fine, fine, I'll leave you two alone. Good luck Ripper, give him a kiss for me."

"Why don't you just fuck off, yeah?"

Johnny winked as he closed the door behind himself and disappeared down the hallway. Mary shook her head as she looked at Corban. They were both covered in blood. Mary stripped off her sweatshirt, leaving her in a thin white undershirt

Soul Siphon

before she went to work on Corban. She pulled him out of his sweatshirt and rested him back on the bed. His pants weren't in bad shape, so she left them on, but the shoes needed to come off as well.

There was a laundry chute in the bathroom for clothes that needed to be incinerated. She tossed the shirts in and then looked in the mirror. There were small smudges of blood on her face and in her hair from carrying Corban. She needed to shower, that much was obvious.

Mary walked back out into the bedroom and looked at Corban, "You've been through hell, yeah? I'm so sorry. I should have been more careful."

She checked to see if there was any sign that he was going to wake up, but he didn't respond to her touch. She shrugged, grabbed a shirt out of his drawer and went into the bathroom. She stripped off her remaining clothes, saw that they were also stained, and threw them down the laundry chute as well. Only her underwear had been completely spared.

She quickly hopped in the shower, washed the blood off, and got back out within minutes. She knew that Corban could spring to life at any moment and kept the door open to make sure that she heard him if he did. However, it appeared that he was still unconscious. She slipped Corban's shirt over her head and pulled it down before looking at herself in the mirror.

Thanks to Corban's height, his shirt reached down to her knees and became an acceptable nightgown. Her hair would need a brush, but it would suffice for now. She could live with it curling into a puffy mess. There were more important things to deal with.

A knock came at Corban's door, startling Mary. Instinctively, she grabbed one of her daggers and

Soul Siphon

pointed it at the door. Her heart was racing as she stood ready for attack.

A quick glance at the mirror nearby calmed her down. She was standing with her sword drawn in attack mode with no pants on. *Calm down, girl. You're starting to lose it here.*

She regained her composure as a second knock came at the door and immediately went to answer it. On the other side, Lihua had a worried look on her face. Mary poked her head out to see what was going on, "Lihua, where have you been?"

"Dealing with a target. It regrettably took a lot longer than I thought it would."

"Sorry to hear that."

"Johnny brought me up to speed on what happened. How is our rookie?"

"I don't know. He's still unconscious. I don't even know what happened, yeah? He just went nuts and went after the non-target."

"Well, I can definitely understand why. I heard about what that man did to your target."

"I know..."

A sudden rustling noise behind her made Mary look back into the room. A looked of panic washed over her face as she quickly turned back to Lihua, "I have to go. It looks like he may be waking up. I'll need to be ready for whatever's going to come. I have a bad feeling about this."

"Are you sure you can handle him after what happened."

"I'm sure."

"All right, but call me if you need help. I will be in my room."

"I will, I promise."

"Good luck."

"I'll need it, yeah? Thanks."

Soul Siphon

The moment the door was closed, Mary grabbed a clean face cloth, ran it under some hot water, and brought it out to Corban, who had stopped tossing and turning for the moment. She sat down on the bed next to him and gently began to run the cloth over his face, cleaning the blood away. It wasn't much and she knew that he'd need to take a shower to get it out of his white hair, but she did what she could.

For her, this was a moment of tranquility. The situation had been defused for a brief time and she was caring for Corban as best she could. It was peaceful and under control. She continued to dab the cloth on his face as she finished cleaning up the blood.

Once his face was completely clean, his head began to move. His body shook as it quickly came to life. Mary's eyes widened as Corban shot up to a sitting position and screamed, "No!"

He got out of bed and charged to the door, barely giving Mary a chance to react. She jumped into action and grabbed him by the arms before he was able to open the door, "No you don't, you're not going anywhere like this, yeah?"

"Let me go, damn it!"

"No, not until you calm down! You can't go out there and wreak any more havoc!"

Corban fought as hard as he could, but Mary wouldn't let go. Corban was physically stronger than her, but she was persistent and more experienced. She remained strong and held on as tight as she could, "I can't be here. I need to get out... fucking sick piece of shit!"

"Corban, stop! You killed that maggot. It's over now."

He tried for the door again, but she wrestled him away from it. He put up a fight, but she turned him around and wrapped her arms around him, pressing her body against his and holding on tight.

Realizing that he couldn't get away without seriously injuring Mary, Corban gave up. His heart sank and tears streamed out of his eyes, "I did it..."

Mary hugged him tightly and hid his face in her shoulder, "Calm down, shhh, it's over now. We got the people we went after."

"No... no... I killed someone who didn't deserve it. God fucking damn it... I killed..."

"No you didn't," Mary replied. "The guy you killed was marked for death. He was our target's uncle. You knew that when you went there, yeah? He deserved what he got."

"Not him."

"Then who?" Mary asked.

Corban sobbed as he struggled to answer, "Her."

"Tanya?"

"Yeah..."

Mary shook her head, "Corban she was no innocent either. You saw what she was doing when we got there. That boy was fourteen."

"I saw her thoughts when I killed her," Corban replied. "She couldn't help what she was doing. She was mentally disturbed. She needed help, not to be killed. It shouldn't have been..."

"Yes, and she knew that!" Mary insisted, cutting him off. "She knew she needed help but stopped going to the counselor. Instead, her treatment became young teenage boys. At some point, she needed to take responsibility for her actions and she failed to do so, yeah? Think about it, how many of those boys are going to grow up to do the exact same thing she and her uncle did or have a very lax moral compass? If you saw her thoughts, then you saw the damage that was done because she decided to take the easy way out. Did you want that to continue?"

"No, that's sick."

"I know. What happened to Tanya was a crime, but that's no excuse for her to perpetuate it further! We did what we were supposed to do. We prevented it from going any further. Kill the pathogen to prevent the disease from spreading."

Mary got the feeling that her words weren't getting through to him, he still looked anguished. She could feel his heart race as though it were trying to beat its way out of his chest. She clasped her hands on the sides of his face and brought his eyes level with hers, "She could not be saved. You hear me, yeah? She was beyond help. If there were any other way, Mike would have told us! He had already tried to give her the benefit of the doubt."

The pain in Corban's eyes subsided slightly as he struggled to relax. Mary's heart sank as she watched him suffer. She gently laid him down on the bed so that his body rested on its side and rubbed his back, "What in the world made you go after him? What happened to you back there?"

Corban did the best he could to reconstruct the events in his mind, "I don't know. I was flooded with her memories... and was filled with an overwhelming sense of sorrow and rage... and an intense need for satisfaction. It was awful. He hurt her, badly... and I don't mean just in the physical sense. The things he did... He ripped into her... he... he..."

"Shh, enough. I know."

Corban's breathing became less and less labored as she rubbed his back, "How do we handle things like this, Mary? In cases where it's not clear that the person needs to die, how do we deal with it?"

Soul Siphon

"We trust that we're doing the right thing, yeah?"

"And if we're wrong?"

"Then we wouldn't be here right now, would we?"

"I just don't know anymore. I don't think I have that kind of faith."

Mary leaned down and kissed Corban's back, "Trust me, we haven't killed anyone who has not caused another person to suffer. That is a fact and it's the God's honest truth. I've been doing this for a hundred years and can say that with absolute certainty."

Corban nodded that he understood. Mary leaned over and rested her head on his back. She lay on her side and wrapped her arms around him, "Get some rest, you need it."

Corban's breathing slowed as she continued to hold him tight, "Calm down... rest, I'm here with you. I'm not going anywhere."

Vlad and Johnny were sitting down to watch a few Two and a Half Men reruns when Lihua came down. She shook her head as she watched them eat down their food on the couch, "You know, you two are supposed to be at the dining room table. Why you insist on eating in front of the TV when no one else is around, remains a mystery to me. You always make a mess. I might consider equating you to pigs if this keeps up!"

Johnny waved at her to be quiet, "Shh, keep it down, the Pats are taking a beating!"

Vlad laughed, "I tell Johnny, Pats not going to beat Broncos! Broncos too good!"

"Ugh... they are getting lucky with Brady being out!"

Soul Siphon

"One more touchdown for Broncos!" Vlad laughed. "Nail in coffin?"

"Shut up!"

Vlad laughed as he turned back to Lihua, "How's the lovebirds?"

"You know Ripper would cut your head off for calling them that," Lihua laughed.

"Mary threatens you for calling her Ripper, yet ve're still standing."

"True, but that is a little different."

Vlad chuckled, "I'm not vorried."

"So I noticed," Lihua replied. "They are doing okay I guess, Corban is out cold and Mary is keeping a vigil over him just in case. I think she is afraid to leave him alone."

"Can you blame her?" Johnny asked. "Holy shit..."

"I suppose not. He is the first real connection she has had in many years. She has never opened up to any of us... that much. Unfortunately, her choice seems somewhat questionable, given the baggage that will come with Corban."

Lihua was interrupted by Vlad unleashing an obnoxiously loud burp after drinking down part of a beer. "Though now that I think about it, her choice not to open up to us makes sense in some cases... and he has been having a tough time since he was raised."

"Corban be fine, he is good and strong boy."

"I hope you are right. I really do."

At that moment, Mike appeared in front of the TV. Johnny frowned, "Oh come on man, the game was just getting good! The Patriots were staging a comeback!"

Mike rolled his eyes, "The Pats will come back and then blow it right at the end of the 4th. They lose by 7."

Soul Siphon

Johnny scoffed and threw the remote on the table, "Thanks a lot!"

"Relax, it wasn't that good of a game anyway."

"Vat Mike need?" Vlad asked.

"We have another one that I've scouted out."

"Anything good?" Lihua asked.

"Small fry," Mike replied. "However, he's been terrorizing the streets of Mattapan for a while now. He's physically assaulted two women, sent his ex-wife to the hospital... three separate times, his child is in foster care for a multitude of reasons and he has at least three restraining orders against him. Rumor has it that he plans on killing his wife tonight."

Johnny stood up, "Great, so when do we leave?"

"Now," Mike replied. "Get out there, save the wife if you can, but above all, do not get spotted."

"No problem," Johnny replied. "Shall we head out then?"

"Wait..," Lihua said, stopping Vlad and Johnny in their tracks as they got up from the couch, "What about Corban and Ripper?"

Mike looked over at the elevator, "Corban needs to piece together what happened and come to terms with everything. Right now, his sanity is in pieces. If we don't give him his space, we could lose him. I don't want to risk him deciding to return to his grave, though that may be inevitable."

"And Ripper?"

"You're welcome to try to pull Mary away from him if you want to. Good luck to you succeeding and even more luck to the possibility of you walking away with all limbs attached."

Vlad laughed, "I pay money to see zat. I sink is probably best to let Ripper take care of Corban, yes?"

Soul Siphon

"I agree," Johnny replied. "He needs her more than we do at this point. This guy doesn't sound like he'll be too difficult to deal with."

"Good," Mike said. "To be honest, I wasn't looking forward to seeing you try it anyway. Just remember to be careful out there. Do your jobs and then get back here quickly. I don't want to risk anything happening to any of you."

"Do you suspect that something will happen?" Lihua asked suspiciously.

"No," Mike said calmly, "but given recent events, I'd rather not chance anything."

Without another word, he vanished into thin air. Lihua turned and headed back to the armory, "All right boys, you heard the man. Let us get going. We have got a wife beater and neighborhood terrorist to take out."

Johnny grabbed a pair of pistols out of the armory. Vlad could always be counted on to go with what he always went with. He grabbed his old Mosin Nagant and strapped it to his back. Lihua was always an eclectic fighter. She chose a variety of weapons including small pistols that could easily be concealed, throwing knives, and an old sword. She smiled as she looked at the other two. *So sad... they just do not understand the art of the blade.*

Johnny had often quipped that she usually doubled her weight in the weapons she carried. Lihua wasn't certain if he said that because she carried a lot of weapons or because she was so small. Either way, she usually smacked him for it.

Finally, she turned around and faced Johnny and Vlad, "Are we ready?"

"As we'll ever be," Johnny replied.

"All right, let us go."

Soul Siphon

Lihua put one hand on each of their shoulders and focused on the streets of Mattapan. The world quickly faded out and within minutes, the group found themselves on a dark, unlit road. There were small stores on either side of the street and many of the buildings were either decrepit or painted in graffiti. The area didn't look that friendly at all but was definitely where they wanted to be.

The sound of shattering glass broke the silence. Lihua turned to a small house at the end of the block, "All right, you guys know the routine. Spread out two points and take positions around the house. Wait for him to come out and if you see him first, you take him down. Quick and easy, just the way we enjoy it."

Vlad and Johnny looked at each other. Johnny beckoned towards the house, "So which side you want?"

"I'm higher on kill count. I let Johnny decide!"

"What?" Johnny scoffed, "Since when?"

"Since mob hit."

Johnny sighed, "Vlad, you got ten of those fucks, same as me. Because no way did that bullet pass through three of them!"

Lihua rolled her eyes, "Guys!"

They both looked over at her and then back at each other. Johnny spoke up first, "Okay, I'll take the front, wise ass!"

"Is better challenge in the back anyway, much darker and more trees. Better sniping position."

Johnny hid near the front door as Vlad headed around back and hid in the shadows next to a tall tree. Lihua patrolled the surroundings to make sure that nothing came at them unexpectedly. They lay in wait for their prey like a flock of hungry vultures, unseen by the eyes of mortals.

Soul Siphon

Another sound of shattering glass came from the house, as well as the sound of intense shouting. There were one male and one female voice going back and forth. The voices elevated every few minutes and what words could be heard were filled with profanity.

"You ain't getting another dime bitch! You're done!"

"Get the fuck out!"

"I'm going, better than staying with your fat ass any longer than I have to."

Lihua lowered her eyes. The anger in their voices reminded her too much of her father's reaction to finding out that she was pregnant and her mother's pleas to not throw her out. It was more than she could handle and she attempted to cover her ears and block the sound out.

Her pain was mercifully ended when the sound of gunfire broke the terrible mood. Lihua saw a tall man with a shaved head running from the back of the house, holding his arm. The gunshot was followed by Russian cussing, letting both Johnny and Lihua know that Vlad had somehow missed his target and was now struggling to try to hit him a third time.

Johnny lunged out of the darkness and gave chase, "Dumbass… he just made this so much more difficult!"

Johnny's legs weren't nearly as long as their prey, but he had the element of surprise and was lighter on his feet. He chased the man down two blocks past trees and a ripped up parking lot until he caught up. The man tripped on a crack in the pavement in fell to the ground.

Johnny took a flying leap and landed right on top of him. "Not getting away this time asshole!"

The man tried to put up a fight, but Johnny put his hands right on the man's face, paralyzing him in

Soul Siphon

place while Johnny sucked the life from his body, "Like tormenting women and children? Then this should be a fitting end for you! Your reign of terror ends now!"

Too many movies… Lihua thought to herself as Johnny continued his theatrics.

After a few moments of struggle, the life light left the man's eyes and he lay still, getting thinner and thinner with each moment. Lihua and Vlad arrived just in time to see the man turn to dust and be swept away by the wind. "Mission accomplished."

Johnny got up and brushed himself off, "Well that was fun. One less bit of vermin to terrorize the people of this neighborhood."

Silence.

He looked up at Vlad and Lihua, surprised when no clever retort came his way as they so often did, "Guys, what…?"

They were both pale as though they'd just seen a ghost. Johnny slowly turned around to see what they were looking at, "Oh shit…"

At the creature's first step, Lihua instantly came to life. She grabbed a knife off of her belt and hurled it at the oncoming assailant. Using inhuman reflexes, the creature slapped the knife away with its bare hand.

Vlad fired three shots from his Mosin while Johnny pulled his Glocks from their holsters and unloaded both clips. The creature continued to walk towards them, unaffected by their attacks. Johnny took a step back as he turned as white as his friends, "We're fucked… Where the hell is Mike?"

The creature stopped a few feet away from them and opened its hands, showing that it was unarmed, "Such a pathetic fight you put up. Where is the one with red hair, at least she offered a decent challenge, albeit with mortal weapons."

Soul Siphon

"What do you want?" Lihua demanded. "It seems pretty obvious that you did not come here to fight."

"Very true…" The creature replied. "I came to deliver a message. Tell your master to return to the world he came from. If he continues to trouble this world, I will hunt him down and destroy him once and for all."

"You don't scare us," Johnny said, in a futile attempt to make himself look bigger than he actually was.

"I'm not concerned with your fear or your opinion." The creature replied. "If you're that foolish, that's your problem. I'm simply delivering a message. Heed my warning, creatures of darkness, or you will fall! This is a courtesy, and the only one that I will offer."

Without another word, the creature disappeared into a cloud of smoke just as it had the previous time. The dark feeling of cold disappeared with it. It was as though the whole scene had never happened.

Johnny kept his eyes locked on the spot where the creature had been, "Did that thing actually call us the creatures of darkness? Isn't that the pot calling the kettle black? What the fuck, it's not like that thing should be talking!"

Lihua shook her head, "The most evil of beings never think that they are actually evil. If they did, that would suggest that they have a conscience. Demons and supernatural beings from the underworld never do. You know this."

"True," Johnny replied. "I just find a sort of sick irony to it."

"Come," Lihua said. "We need to report in and let Mike know what has happened here. He will need to sort this out. That's all we can do for now."

Soul Siphon

"All right," Vlad replied. "Let's go."

Soul Siphon

Concept Image

Soul Siphon

XIV

Hours had passed and Corban had just barely calmed down. Mary tried hard, but could not find a way to bring him out of it. He was suffering and she was ill-equipped to help. She knew that he'd never get better as long as Tanya's memories continued to haunt him.

She lay against him and rubbed his back as his heart pounded, "If there's anything I can do… please let me know. I mean it, anything."

Corban winced in pain as he spoke, "I don't want this… I don't want it at all. I killed her."

"Enough," Mary replied. "I've already told you, it had to be done. I don't know what else I can say!"

"No…" Corban said softly.

"All right, tell me then. I don't know what to do or how to help you! Just tell me!"

"Tell you what?"

"Tell me what you're seeing. What's hurting you this much?"

Corban struggled to respond as words were no longer coming easyily to him, "It's too much. I have to keep reliving what her uncle did to her as a child. I feel her pain and her sadness."

"Can you describe it?"

"Why?"

"Sometimes talking things out helps, yeah?"

Corban sucked down a deep breath before he began describing it, "We've been over this before... It's just the worst scenes from her life, the molestation, the mental issues, the betrayal by her husband, and the feelings of worthlessness replaying over and over again in my mind. Compared to this, reliving my failed exorcism would be a breeze."

Mary lowered her eyes, "Corban, I..."

Soul Siphon

"Could you imagine? Picture living through your death over and over, remembering all the fear and pain. That's what this is.

"I couldn't imagine," Mary admitted. "That would most likely drive me mad. You're going to need to find a way to let this go. Take some comfort in the fact that it's over now. You ended that pain."

The only response she got was more sobbing.

Mary could feel the tension building up inside of Corban. She knew that an explosion was coming and braced for it. After a few moments of silence, Mary could feel his muscles tense up. Corban couldn't deal with it any longer, "I can't do this! Get off of me!"

Mary hit the bed as Corban stood up and held his throbbing head, "These memories... I can't stand them echoing through my head. Get... out... Get out!"

Mary watched him as he pressed his hands against his temples, clearly in pain, "Get out! Get the fuck out!"

"That's it," Mary said. "I'm fed up with this now. You want them out, yeah? Then let's go get some air!"

Mary stood up, grabbed Corban's right hand, and led him up the stairwell to the roof. She brought him out away from the doorway and stood in front of him with an angry look on her face, "Release it."

"What do you mean?"

"Release the spirit, yeah? Just like you did before. It's the only way to get it out," Mary replied. "You have to let it go."

"What will happen?"

Mary shrugged, "In the past, when a soul siphon released the spirit energy they'd acquired, they lost some of their power as a result. Most likely you'll feel drained after, but it should be a relief."

Soul Siphon

Corban frowned and his heart sank in defeat. He felt like a failure. It was his job to accumulate power, but only now did he realize what the price was for that power; his own sanity. It was a price that he doubted he'd be able to pay.

Mary touched his arm in a futile effort to comfort him, "It's okay, yeah? You'll get it back later. We'll find you a baddie to take on that isn't as strong and we'll build you up little by little."

"I guess..."

"Good, so let it go then, yeah?"

Corban focused his mind in an attempt to center himself. He tried to force all of the pain and anguish to the surface and focus it into one powerful beam. His skin broke out in sweat as he focused harder and harder. His whole body ached as she finally thrust his hand upward, "Get out!"

Nothing happened.

Corban tried, but couldn't get it out. He extended his hand and spread his fingers, but again nothing happened. He strained as hard as he could, but only succeeded at giving himself a headache.

Mary decided to intervene as he struggled. She stiffened her lower lip and slapped him across the face with her left hand, "What's wrong with you? Are you enjoying this?"

"What the fuck was that for?"

"You, look at you. You're weak!" Mary shouted.

Corban frowned, "Gee thanks... is this your idea of being supportive?"

A sharp pain entered Corban's left cheek as her right hand connected with his face, "I've been supportive of you all along, but I'm tired of it. You've been impossible the entire time you've been with us. I've put up with you bitching me out, having to sew

Soul Siphon

your hand back together, and being your emotional punching bag, but I can only do so much."

"Mary…"

"Don't 'Mary' me! You're too weak for me. I let you in and you've been a complete disappointment and a burden. I should have just let you jump off the roof instead of talking to you."

Anger flowed through Corban. All of the sympathy, sadness, and withdrawal were gone and replaced with anger. He clenched his fists at his side. Mary nodded, "That's it, charge your power! Hit me!"

She backed away and opened her arms, making herself a clean target. She raised her chin and closed her eyes, preparing to be blasted off her feet, "I'm here, I hit you and I'll do it again! Hit me, you weakling!"

"No…"

"Hit me!"

"No!"

"Hit me, you fuck!"

Corban couldn't take it any longer. His body erupted with power. A massive pylon of energy shot up into the sky, "No!"

Mary backed away, startled as the ground shook beneath them. Clearly, she didn't expect that much energy to be released. The soul he had absorbed was intensely powerful. "My God… I didn't know it would be this bad! Corban… I'm sorry!"

At that moment, a white outline of a human sprung forth from Corban's body and floated in front of Mary. It looked at her appreciatively, "Thank you… from the bottom of my heart, thank you. I didn't want to hurt him or anyone else anymore."

"You're welcome… Tanya?"

The spirit vanished without another word. The pylon also faded as quickly as it had appeared. Corban

Soul Siphon

stood silently for a moment with steam pouring off his skin and then collapsed on the ground.

Mary raced over to Corban and caught him before his head hit the solid concrete, "Corban, I'm sorry... I'm so sorry. I didn't mean what I said. You know that, yeah? I just didn't see any other way to help."

Corban looked up at Mary and smiled, "I always thought a slap from you would hurt a lot more than that. Did you go limp-wristed on purpose?"

Tears fell from Mary's eyes, "I know... I only did it... Wait, what? You asshole!"

Corban chuckled as he rubbed his face, "Still that'll probably leave a mark."

"Yeah, look I'm sorry. I wouldn't have done it if..."

"I know," Corban replied. "You did it to light a fire under me so that I'd release the energy. You gave me enough of a boost to pull it off."

"Her spirit was too powerful for you as you are right now. You need more time."

"I don't get it. How was her spirit so powerful...? What made her so special? She was just a mortal."

Mary shrugged, "I've heard that people who experience traumatic events and live to tell the tale often have strong spiritual ties. Sorrow is a very strong emotion and that's part of what spirits are built off of, so it kind of makes sense."

Corban touched her face, "Why does it seem like you're always saving my ass?"

"You needed it," Mary replied. "You're still a fledgling here with a lot to learn, but you're a cute fledgling. So lucky you! We've got eternity for you to repay the favor, yeah?"

Soul Siphon

Corban sat up and kissed her. Their lips parted long enough for a smile to appear on her face before they reconnected. Corban wrapped his arms around her and squeezed tightly, removing any possibility of her escaping his grasp.

Their levity was unfortunately short-lived when an angry voice appeared out of the darkness, "What the hell happened? What have you done? I sensed a massive explosion of spirit energy and now it seems that your power has been greatly weakened. Explain this!"

Mary got to her feet and helped Corban up, "Mike, that soul was too powerful for Corban to handle. I saw it with my own eyes. He wasn't ready for this."

Mike did not look pleased as he spoke, "Mary, he's not going to do us much good with the power he has now! He needs more if he is to take on that creature. I understand that you're trying to help him, but you're holding him back by doing this and putting him at risk."

"I am not going to let you use him like this," Mary replied. "He's a person, not a weapon. We'll build his power, but it has to be done gradually or he'll be too damaged to do us any good."

Mike looked at Mary and Corban. She stood between the two of them as though she were protecting Corban in his weakened state, "I'm not letting you do it. You'll have to put me back in my grave first!"

Mike shrugged and looked at his newest student, "Well Corban, it would appear that Mary is calling the shots now. It looks like she's become quite protective of you, my compliments."

Mary didn't move. Her fists were clenched at her sides and she would not budge nor allow either Corban or Mike past her. Mike lowered his eyes,

Soul Siphon

"Corban, I apologize. You are absolutely right. We're pushing you too hard. If it wasn't obvious before, it is now."

He stepped up to Mary and looked past her, respecting Mary's foothold, "Corban, how are you? Are you feeling better now?"

"My cheek is a bit sore, but other than that, I'm fine," Corban replied. "Mike, I know I let you down."

"You didn't," Mike replied. "I let you down, and I'm sorry. We'll try a new approach to help you realize your power, something less grueling. I'll come up with a plan and we can go over it later on. How does that sound?"

"Okay Mike," Corban said confidently. "That sounds good."

"It won't be too soon either." A voice chimed in from behind.

Lihua, Johnny, and Vlad appeared on the roof. Lihua had a frightened look on her face, "We encountered the creature again."

A worried look appeared on Mike's face, "Are you all right? No injuries?"

"We are fine," Lihua said softly, "it did not attack us. It just gave us an ultimatum and disappeared."

"And that ultimatum was?"

"It told us to stop what we were doing," Lihua replied. "It told us to tell you to return to the place where you came from, and if you did not heed its warning, it would hunt you down."

Her words didn't seem to bother Mike, which gave the group some comfort, "All right, well you all should get some rest. I'm going to try to figure out where this creature dwells. Consider this an order to stand down for a while and relax. You've all earned it."

Soul Siphon

Mary turned back to Corban, "Sounds good to me."

Corban stepped by and headed to his room, "I need some ice."

Mary lowered her eyes and didn't move. Corban stopped and saw that she was just standing still as everyone else made their way back to the dorms. She apparently wasn't certain that she was still welcome with him after what happened.

Corban reached out his hand to her, "Are you coming?"

Mary's face brightened up as she took his hand, "Really?"

"Uh... of course?"

"Hey Ripper, you might want to get dressed next time before coming outside, sexy as that is!" Johnny called back as he went to the elevator.

Corban turned away to hide the smirk on his face as Mary looked down and realized that she was only wearing one of Corban's shirts. As she walked, the shirt rode slightly up her thigh. She quickly yanked the shirt down before it rode up too high and stuck her left middle finger up at Johnny, "Thanks, Johnny! Thanks a lot, asshole. You try dealing with everything I am and see if you're always able to control how you look!"

"I don't care as much about how I look," Johnny replied. "Beware the man who has no shame."

"Forget him. Beware the woman willing to dismember him with very little cause, yeah?"

The doors closed as the rest of the team took the elevator down. Mary walked side by side with Corban, clasping his hand tightly as they proceeded back to his room. The door opened to the corridor that Corban had finally begun to recognize as his home. It had taken some time, but he was happy there now.

Soul Siphon

Corban guided Mary back to his room to get some rest. He sat on the bed and turned the TV in the corner on. The channels flashed by as he flicked through them for a few moments trying to find a decent movie. Fox 25 was currently doing the news, as was Channel 5 and some of the cable channels were on the fritz. He finally found a movie channel, but it was on commercial. He shrugged and put the clicker down. He wasn't really planning on watching whatever was going to be coming on anyway.

Mary went into his medicine cabinet and grabbed an ice pack for Corban's cheek. She squeezed it until it began to get cold and brought it out to Corban. After sitting down next to him on the bed, she gently touched the pack to his cheek, "How does that feel?"

"Better."

Corban's cheek was red from where she'd struck him and his eye was fluttering. Despite being under his constant gaze, she refused to make eye contact with him. Every time he tried, she looked away without a word.

"Will you stop?" Corban demanded.

"Stop what?"

"You know damn well what," Corban replied, feigning annoyance. "I already said that I knew what you were doing. It's okay, I'm not mad. Just put it out of your head, all right?"

"Okay..."

"You're not going to, are you?"

"Nope."

Corban sat back against the wall opposite the TV and relaxed his body as he flicked through the channels. Mary sat in front of him, between his legs, and leaned back into his chest. Her head relaxed over

Soul Siphon

his heart, which prompted him to put his arms around her as he flicked the channels.

"Nothing good on, yeah?"

Corban shrugged, "Well... there are some reruns, but nothing I haven't seen a million times. I noticed we have Netflix, so maybe a movie?"

Mary shrugged, "Whatever you want. I doubt that I'm going to be awake much longer anyway. You're too warm."

"Sorry?"

"You should be."

Mary relaxed against him for a few moments as he put on some random action movie that she'd never seen before. She turned over and looked at Corban's cheek. The redness looked like it was going to eventually turn into a bruise, "Not going to watch the movie?"

"My life would make a far better movie than this shit, yeah?"

"Probably."

Mary pulled the ice away and gently kissed the red area. Corban placed a hand on her back and rubbed her gently. Her skin broke out in goosebumps under his touch and an odd sensation entered her chest. She felt warm as though she had dipped into a hot tub and allowed the water to slowly course over her.

Mary's skin glistened as it began to break out in sweat. She looked deep into Corban's eyes. His stare caused her to break out in goosebumps, making her wonder if he could sense what she was thinking. A small level of apprehension entered her mind as she lay with him.

Throwing caution to the wind, she leaned in and kissed his cheek again and again before moving down to his neck and then to his chin. She then turned over and straddled him as their lips connected once again in

Soul Siphon

a kiss that sucked the air out of Mary's lungs. Her body began to shudder uncontrollably.

At that moment, she felt a pair of hands run up her thighs and over her butt. She pulled back slightly and bit her lower lip as she looked into Corban's eyes. Any doubt about whether or not he knew what she wanted was completely gone.

Corban looked into Mary's eyes as his hands ran past her butt and up under the shirt. He fully expected her to make good on her threat to rip his hand off, but instead, she sat back on her legs. With a mixed look of nervousness and euphoria, she bit her lower lip and closed her eyes. She crossed her arms in front of her, grabbed the bottom of her shirt and without warning, pulled it off.

Corban's eyes dilated as he looked at Mary. Chills ran down his spine as his eyes traced over her figure. Light freckles covered her neck, shoulders, and arms, but gave way to the milky white skin on her breasts and stomach. He reached up and gently cupped her breasts in his hands, giving them a slight squeeze. They were average size for a woman of her height and build, but they were extremely firm. In his eyes, she was perfect.

Mary's whole body quivered uncontrollably under his touch and her lower extremities began to tingle. *Oh my God girl, is this really happening?*

Corban let go of her breasts and ran his hands over her shoulders and down her arms. The goosebumps followed his fingers as they traced down her arms and then proceeded back up her sides. She responded by slowly grinding against him with her hips, trying to release some of the intense feelings that had overtaken her. It wasn't working.

The anticipation was creating tension within her body and she was having a hard time tolerating it.

Soul Siphon

Frustrated, she leaned in and grabbed Corban by the jaw before kissing him repeatedly. This was a new side of her that he was certain no one had seen in over a hundred years. Though she had been kind to him, her very appearance made the idea of her being sensual a foreign notion.

Corban ran his hands down her back, stopping right on her hips. He grabbed her on either side as she continued to grind against him and slowly began to rub her hips. His hands guided her as she moved.

That was it; there was no going back now. She was completely exposed, but she did not care. Corban had earned her affection and regardless of what happened tomorrow, tonight, he was hers and she was his. Nothing else mattered.

Mary stared deep into Corban's eyes as he looked at her bare figure. He finally caught a glimpse of the tattoo on the outside of her right thigh. He had been too bent out of shape to notice it before, but now his mind was able to process it. The tattoo was a single word, written in very fancy text and adorned with flowers,

"Hope."

Corban now understood why she kept it covered up. This was something completely out of character for her, but it warmed him to know that she still believed in it. It was one shard of humanity that she had managed to hold on to.

As his eyes finally met hers once more, she nodded and forced out a whisper, "I'm ready..."

"Mary... I..."

"Shh it's okay, you won't hurt me... I'm ready for this."

"Are you sure?"

Soul Siphon

"I just said so, didn't I? Don't make me repeat myself."

Corban kept his eyes on Mary as he also slowly began to disrobe. She leaned in and kissed him before straddling his waist again. His eyes were locked into hers as she moved. It was like they were having a conversation without the use of words. He wanted to be absolutely certain that she was ready for this after so much time alone and her eyes tried to assure him that she was.

Mary tensed up her leg muscles as she held her position for a few moments and kissed Corban again. Then, when she was ready, she slowly shifted her thighs downward and sat back on his hips. Her eyes squeezed shut as she felt her body begin to stretch around him. Her breathing became labored as he slowly entered her. *Oh, God... I'd forgotten...*

She sank down a little further until their hips pressed against each other. They were both breathing heavily and covered in sweat as Mary began to sway her hips. Wave upon wave of intense pleasure poured over her and the only way she could absorb it was by biting down on her lower lip.

As the moment passed and Mary regained some control, she looked down at Corban with glossy eyes. Her sapphires sparkled and a thin smile appeared on her lips. She looked like she wanted to say something, but couldn't find the words.

"What is it?" Corban asked.

"It's nothing... I know it sounds weird, but I really feel like I'm alive again. That's not something that I've been able to say for a while."

Mike and Lihua sat down on at the table where they normally ate their meals while Vlad and Johnny resumed their normal routine of doing nothing but watching TV at night. Lihua usually scolded them for this, but tonight, she was preoccupied with more serious matters. She grabbed a water bottle out of the fridge and sipped it slowly as she joined Mike, "You look worried."

"Shouldn't I be?" Mike asked. "There's a creature out there that I seem to be unable to detect. It appears to have the power to cause you all great harm, and our only hope of defeating it is currently too weak to take it on. It's maddening…"

Mike sighed as he sat back, "I'm worried. I don't like the idea of sending you out there, not knowing if you'll come back. You're supposed to be immortal."

"We have dealt with supernatural beings before and always came out on top."

"I know, but they didn't seem to have this one's abilities. I just hope we can get Corban ready for what's yet to come."

Lihua smiled, "I do not think you have much to worry about there. He has Ripper to light a fire under him when he needs it. That is a major advantage if ever there was one."

"For all the good that's done us so far..."

The smile disappeared from Lihua's face and was replaced by an expression of annoyance, "Give our team a little more credit, Michael. Do not forget, Corban was torn apart by what he experienced from that woman's memories. I do not even want to think about what would have happened had Mary not intervened. You may see her as interfering, but I do not. To me, she is just being protective. Perhaps you should step back and see how much of an advantage you have with her keeping tabs on him."

"I know. Of course you're right. I just hate to see him take a step forward and then take three steps backward. I don't know how much time we have before that creature interferes again… or attacks us head-on."

"Have you informed the people above?"

"Yes, believe me, they know... but the decree of my superiors remains in effect. I can't interfere in any way with that creature unless asked to, and even then everything I do has to be passive. It's maddening."

A faint smile appeared on her face, "What if we asked you for help?"

"You know better than that," Mike replied. "You are not technically amongst the living so the rules don't apply to you. That's how you get away with so much."

"Well, you gave us those collars. Maybe we can devise a strategy to defeat the creature if we can get one on its neck."

"Possibly..," Mike said thoughtfully. "That might make it weak enough for Corban to be able to drain it."

"We are of like mind."

Lihua's thoughts were suddenly interrupted. On the couch, Vlad and Johnny sat watching Two and a Half Men. Vlad's heavy laughter thundered throughout the hall. Johnny was about the only one who was ever willing to put up with it. Lihua had observed that they could find virtually anything to fight about and tonight would be no exception.

As the show went to commercial, Johnny looked over at Vlad, "Think Corban is going to stick around after all of this?"

"Hope so."

"You're not sure?"

Vlad sighed, "Corban has been through much, too much for von person. Ze expectations Corban has to meet, zey are vey too high. Ve've seen zis before

Soul Siphon

vith others using same powers. Zey each have to live up to more zan ze rest of us."

"Yeah, but Corban has a few things they didn't."

"Yes... he's actually managed to stop a demon in its tracks, so vat? That doesn't make him any more likely to stick around if things get tough. Mike took big risk on him, no?"

Johnny pulled a cigar out of the box next to him and lit it up, "I was actually referring to Ripper."

"Vat?"

"Oh come on," Johnny replied. "Just because you're a relic left over frcm World War 2 doesn't mean you don't notice people."

"Vat are you going on about?"

Johnny sighed, "Tough or not, would YOU go back to your grave if you had someone that looked like Mary to keep you warm at night?"

"Ripper is too scary for me."

"Oh I know," Johnny replied. "I try to stay off her bad side too, but Corban doesn't seem to have that problem."

"... I sink Corban vill be sticking around."

Johnny laughed, "For once, I agree."

Soul Siphon

XV

The next night rolled around fairly quickly. Corban had slept most of the day with Mary keeping a quiet vigil over him. She spent several hours completely wrapped up in his arms, but even after adjusting to make herself more comfortable, she never left his side. He was both surprised and grateful for how patient she was. He woke up at various points throughout the day to see her flicking through TV channels or reading something, but she never left his side. Things had been fairly quiet.

Finally, Corban decided that he'd taken enough of her time and concern, "I can't do this. We've wasted enough time. I'm getting up."

Mary moved to the side and let him move. When he had himself balanced, she sat up behind him, put her arms over his shoulders, and gently kissed his neck, "How do you feel?"

"Better, thanks to you," Corban replied softly.

"Glad I could help."

"Seriously, you made all the difference."

"All right, all right, don't get all sappy on me, yeah?"

They both chuckled as Mary kissed his cheek and got out of bed, revealing that she had remained naked as he slept. Corban looked her over as she stretched, "Cute butt."

"You certainly thought so last night, yeah?"

"Yeah... hard to believe you're a hundred years out of practice."

"Oh shut up. Some things you never forget, yeah?"

"I'm glad to hear that."

Soul Siphon

"I know, I vas zere!" Vlad yelled as black and white images appeared on the TV screen.

"I don't care if you shook Stalin's hand yourself! There is no way the Soviet Union could have beaten back the Nazis without help!"

"Ve'd held out zat long, it vas not that unlikely at ve could have beaten zem back!"

"The Nazi war machine was too well-equipped. They were working on an atomic bomb. You guys couldn't even properly equip all of your soldiers!"

"Ze Nazis knocked out von of our biggest arsenals early on, yes?"

"That's because you let them trick you into a non-aggression pact!"

Lihua tip-toed around the kitchen, hoping not to get dragged into their argument when the elevator opened. Mary and Corban had finally awoken and decided to make an appearance. Corban stepped out first, "Hi Lihua, how's everything down here?"

"Shh!"

Corban looked at her oddly, about to ask why he was shushed when he heard the escalating argument in the living room. It almost sounded as though the two friends were about ready to come to blows. They were so focused on their debate that they hadn't even noticed the additional company.

"How long?" Mary asked.

"Let me think," Lihua replied as she went through the last couple of hours. "Today is World War 2 day on the history channel… I would say at least three hours?"

Their voices carried from the other side of the room as Mary shook her head, "No Vlad, without the allied advance from the West, the Soviet counter-attack wouldn't have been anywhere near as fast or successful. You would have destroyed each other!"

Soul Siphon

"I saw comrades hold the line. Weather was on Soviet side. Nazis couldn't beat us!"

Johnny sighed, refusing to say anything else to Vlad. The doors to the elevator slid open behind him, "Hey look who's finally up. How you feeling, Corban?"

"Better... well enough to kick some ass if the situation calls for it."

"You'll get your chance," Mike replied as he appeared in front of the group. "We've got one that's ripe for the picking."

"You look excited, Mike," Mary said in a high spirited voice.

"And you look happy for once, Ripper," Mike shot back. "I thought Hell would freeze over before that happened."

Mary twisted her lips into a scowl as the rest of the group joined them. Lihua looked at her oddly for a moment, "You have an unusual glow about you, Ripper. I take it that after the incident on the roof, the night improved? I hope nothing too strenuous went on."

Mary's eyes widened and she felt her face heat up, "Lihua!"

A shocked look came over Lihua's face as Corban closed his eyes and rubbed his forehead with his right hand. A sly smile instantly appeared on her face, "Whoa... I was only joking but look at you, Ripper. I have never seen your face get that red. It could almost blend in with your hair. Last night was that good, huh?"

Mary bit her lip and turned away, "I'm going to fucking kill you later."

Mike, Johnny, and Vlad all exchanged glances with each other before looking at Corban. They remained quiet. The closest Corban got to a reaction was Johnny making some crude gestures in his direction and a wink that was carefully timed so that Mary wouldn't see it.

Corban ignored him as Lihua turned to Mike, "So who's the target?"

"His name is Pan Wei," Mike replied.

Lihua's eyes widened as a sick feeling came over her, "I know that name... he is a Chinese businessman... one of my countrymen."

"Exactly. The man is guilty of several atrocities, not only in his own country but also abroad in many of the smaller Indonesian areas where such things would not be so easily televised. Murder, rape, prostitution, sweatshops, and more. The list could go on for a very long time."

"That's a pretty high profile target, yeah?" Mary exclaimed. "Are you sure we're up for this?"

"Yes. I've wanted to bring him down for a very long time. This will most likely be our only opportunity. He's constantly in the public eye and very rarely takes any kind of vacation. He'll be on his million-dollar yacht, sailing off the coast of Hainan. You get in there, kill him, and get out."

"What about the crew?" Corban asked.

"There are a few innocents amongst them," Mike replied, "so I will ask you to spare them. It will be easier than trying to sort out the innocents in the group. Sink the boat if you must, but make sure that the crew gets off."

"Sounds easy enough," Mary said as she pulled out one of her blades.

"When do we leave?" Lihua asked in barely a whisper.

"The ship leaves port at 8 PM sharp. That will give you good cover. So, I'd leave here at about 10

Soul Siphon

AM to make it over there. Until then, you can all relax."

"Now those are the kinds of orders I can get used to!" Johnny exclaimed.

Vlad and Johnny returned to their worn out leather couch and flicked through the channels. Lihua frowned and turned away. She disappeared up the stairs to the dorms. Mary beckoned to Corban to join him getting her knives ready, but Corban kept his eyes fixed on the doorway, "Did you see Lihua? She had the look of death on her face. Something's wrong…"

Mary shrugged, "She always kind of looks like that, yeah?"

"No," Corban replied. "More than usual."

"How so?"

"She was pale. I've seen that look once before when I looked in the mirror and saw Adramelech staring back at me."

"All right," Mary said in a slightly worried tone. "You want to go talk to her, let's go talk to her."

"Wait, really?"

"Yeah… what you think you're the only one with friends around here?"

"Well..."

A look came over Mary's face as though she were daring him to say something that would give her a reason to kill him. Corban saw it, straightened up, and shook his head, "No, no I don't."

"Good, then let's go."

Mary followed Corban to the elevator. As they got in, Mary pushed the button for the roof. Corban's eyes narrowed, "Not the dorms?"

"No, she likes going up to the roof too, yeah? Usually, we take opposite sides and we don't bother each other when we're up there. We know to respect each other's space."

Soul Siphon

"... I never got that courtesy!"

"Where would you be if you did?"

"Fair enough."

The doors to the elevator slid opened and the two of them walked out onto the roof. Mary was right. Lihua had hidden from prying eyes and was sitting cross-legged staring at the city.

Mary leaned against one of the nearby ventilation ducts while beckoning Corban forward, "Go for it, this was your idea, yeah?"

Corban shrugged and left Mary's side. Lihua seemed not to notice as he knelt down next to her, "You looked like you were ready to collapse downstairs. Something is eating away at you, isn't it?"

"Your perception is accurate," Lihua replied.

"Do you want to talk about it?"

"Pan Wei is a name that I have tried very hard to forget. He is actually my age... though he looks a lot older now."

"Okay?"

"You really wish to hear this?"

"Yes."

"You are a good friend, Corban. Well all right... His father pretty much ran the village where we lived. They were a very powerful family even then."

"You knew him?"

"Yes. In fact, he was trying to arrange a marriage for his son... with me."

The concern on Corban's face intensified as he listened to her, "What happened?"

"I did not want to marry Pan... he was a disgusting pig, even when we were kids. He abused his status and was a completely dishonorable maggot."

"How so?"

"You must know the type. He was a selfish, entitled brat who was able to get away with anything

Soul Siphon

because the authorities tiptoed around him. If not for his family name, he would have been in a Chinese prison long ago. I told my father over and over, but he did not care. He forbade me from doing anything that would dishonor the family. I thought if I spoke to Pan Wei and explained things to him, he would have his father call the whole thing off. I was young and naïve then. I did not understand my own circumstances."

"I take it that didn't work out very well, did it?"

Lihua lowered her eyes, "No... He was with a group of his thug friends when I approached him. My first mistake was going to him alone. They barely let me say anything before they attacked me."

Corban's face went pale, "Was he one of the ones...?"

"Yes..."

"Lihua... I...."

"I got the rest of them. They died slowly. I made them all suffer, but he always seemed to be able to escape me. When he realized the pattern of his friends being killed, he fled our village. That is when I found out that my father knew about everything that had happened... everything. In my heart, the man was evil, but he was still my father. Had he just refused to acknowledge me, that would have been one thing, but to find out that he knew... and covered it up... He sealed his fate. My father was to be my last kill, but Pan Wei escaped, making it impossible for me to get to him. So my father died in dishonor, begging for his life. I will spare you the details, but just know that he died very slowly."

Lihua clenched a fist at her side, "No more, not this time. Mike owes me this kill and I am going to take it."

She looked Corban straight in his eyes. The flame of anger and hate burned brightly in her, "I

Soul Siphon

know that Mike wants you to have first shot at any kill to build up your powers, but not this time. Please do not get in my way. Do what you must when we arrive, but know that it will be my hand that drives a blade through his black heart... even if I have to drive it through someone else's first."

Corban placed his hand on her shoulder, "Don't worry, you'll get your chance. He won't get away this time. We'll make this right."

"Thank you, Corban," Lihua replied as she calmed down. "Both for caring enough to come up here and for understanding. You are truly a good friend."

"I try."

Lihua smiled and looked behind him, "And despite your best efforts, so are you, Ripper!"

The only response was a faint grumbling from the shadows. Lihua chuckled as she turned back to her meditation, "Would you mind giving me some time? I need to center myself before facing him if I am to remain stable. I have waited a long time for this day."

"Stable?"

"Right now, I feel... nervous, sick, and disoriented. If I do not center myself, my powers will not work."

"Oh... of course," Corban replied as he stood up and turned to join Mary in the shadows. "Are you sure you're going to be okay?"

"I will be fine...I promise. I will be a lot better once he is dead."

"Then we'll do everything we can to make sure that monster never sees the light of day."

"Yes... I believe we will."

As Mary and Corban made their way to the elevator, Mary noticed how concerned Corban was and turned to confront him, "What's wrong?"

"Huh?"

"You look like something's bothering you."

"It's nothing."

"I know you well enough to know when you're lying."

"How could you possibly know that? We've known each other for a few months!"

Mary shrugged, "It's not as difficult when you spend a lot of your time watching people."

Corban remained silent, hoping that Mary wouldn't press him.

"Are you going to tell me what's going on, or shall I beat it out of you?"

"Fine... did you see the look on Lihua's face?"

"Yeah so?"

"It was a look of death like she'll go all the way to get him... to the point of not coming back. That's the kind of look you usually only see in the movies..."

"You worry too much. I've known Lihua a long time. She's got a level head on her shoulders. She'll be fine."

"I wish I was as confident as you are, but I'm worried. This could end badly."

Mary and Corban spent some time alone sharpening a few blades while Vlad and Johnny did their typical nothing. Mary shook her head, "Must be nice using a gun that you can neglect and somehow it will still shoot."

Corban looked over at Vlad, "The Mosin? I know right?"

Mary sighed as she looked at the guns, "It's so pointless. He's really the only one who uses them that much."

"Why don't you like guns?"

Soul Siphon

Mary shrugged, "I don't know, there's a sort of art form to using blades. It's a level of elegance that you don't typically get from a gun."

"I suppose," Corban replied, "but if I want to end a fight quickly, the gun still has value."

"You're still new, give it time. You'll see my way.

Mike appeared in the armory where Mary and Corban were working, "How's everyone doing?"

Mary looked at Corban for a moment before Corban turned to him, "We're fine Mike, we're ready to do our part and get this son of a bitch... but..."

Mary closed her eyes and braced for the bad news as Corban hesitated, looking for the right words. Mike picked up on the tension, "I'm worried about Lihua."

"Worried about her, why?"

Corban released his breath slowly as he continued, "She seems like she's at the breaking point and..."

"I will be fine, Corban," Lihua said as she appeared at the door. "Please do not worry about me. I can handle it."

"I'm sure you believe that," Corban replied, "but..."

Lihua looked at him sternly, "Corban!"

Corban lowered his eyes, "Sorry."

Mary stood up and smiled, "Corban's just being a good friend Mike. There's no issue here."

"Thank you, Ripper."

"All I needed to hear," Mike replied. "Just keep an eye on each other out there."

As Lihua went to her corner to work on her own weapons and Mike went back out to the living room, Corban glared at Mary, "Why?"

"What?"

Soul Siphon

"Do you really believe that?"

"Does it matter?"

"It should!"

"Lihua has been waiting for this for a long time. Regardless of whether or not I'm certain that she can handle this, it's her right. I know she'd support me if I had the chance to go back and finish on Jack the Ripper myself, so I'm supporting her here. No amount of huff or puff from you is going to change that."

"Mary..."

"Lihua was right; you are a good friend, yeah? But trust me, she needs this one. It's been eating away at her for too long."

Corban sighed, knowing that he wasn't going to win this one, "All right…"

Mary and Corban finished their work sharpening the last of the blades and reloading all the guns that needed it. Vlad and Johnny joined them in the arsenal when it neared 9 AM. Lihua went through her normal tradition of loading herself down with weapons. This time though, she was not alone. Everyone was grabbing any weapon that they could fit on their belts. Even Vlad, who normally refused to carry any weapon other than his Mosin Nagant, grabbed a couple of revolvers to fit in his belt.

Mary looked over at Corban as she attached her daggers, "This is a big one, you ready for this?"

"I've been ready," Corban said confidently.

"Good. We're going to need you out there, yeah? This guy is big business."

"Doesn't matter. We're going to kick some ass out there today."

Corban remembered to grab the collars as well. He took one and handed another to Mary. She looked at it for a moment and nodded that she understood his concern, "You think we'll run into it?"

Soul Siphon

"I have a bad feeling."

"All right, then we should definitely keep these close. Can't let that thing have the jump on us."

"Yeah..."

As they finished up prepping their armaments, Mike appeared in the room again, "Hello kids, everyone ready?"

"We're gonna kick some ass, yeah?" Mary replied as she brandished her daggers.

"Good to hear. –Everyone circle around."

The group secured their weapons and then stood in a perfect circle around Mike. He took a moment and looked each one in the eye, "No matter what happens out there tonight, know that I'm proud of all of you. Everything you've done has helped make the world a better place."

Vlad shrugged, "Ve've faced vorse zan zis, vy ze long face?"

"You've got a newer guy with you tonight and you're going into an extremely foreign area."

Mike looked at the group like a father sending his children off the college. Corban had never seen him like this before, "Everything okay, Mike?"

Mike nodded, "Yes, but let's bow our heads and say a prayer for one another. I want you all to come back safely. Not a single one of you is expendable."

The group observed a moment of silence. Corban said a prayer for all of his new friends while Mary did the same, except that her prayer focused on Corban more than anyone else. She feared for him above all, not only because of how she felt but also because of his inexperience and what happened during their last mission. His powers put him at risk and in battle. She might not be able to keep a close eye on him.

Soul Siphon

Whispers could be heard from everyone as they each named someone in the individual prayers they said to themselves. Everyone got one from each member of the group. If nothing else, it was a nice sentiment.

Finally, Mike beckoned them to depart, "All right, get yourselves out there! Good luck and good hunting!"

Mary fist pumped to her side and turned to watch Lihua. She stepped between Johnny and Vlad and smiled, "Ready?"

Neither one got the chance to answer before Lihua tapped them on the shoulder. Mary watched as her three teammates slowly vanished in front of her. There was no turning back now.

Mary turned to Corban, "Can I fly with you?"

Corban looked at her in surprise, "No race?"

"No," Mary replied. "If you're okay with it, I'd like to see what you experience. I didn't really get to enjoy it last time and I've never really flown before that. I've kind of always wanted to..."

"All right, outside."

Corban took Mary by the hand and led her out front. They were greeted by the morning light as the side road they lived on was not lit by any street lamps. It was slightly chilly and sent goosebumps down Mary's spine, but she ignored it.

Corban opened his arms and bent them to pick her up, "Ready?"

Mary looked at the way he was gesturing and realized what he was trying to do, "That way?"

"You know a better way?"

"Piggyback?"

"And risk getting choked? I don't think so."

"Really, you're going to make me look like a damsel in distress here?"

Soul Siphon

"Yes, and you'll do it if you want to fly with me. Now come on, we need to go."

"Fine…" Mary replied as she leaned back into Corban's arm.

Corban tensed his muscles as Mary shifted her weight from her feet to his arms. A moment later, she was being carried. Mary looked at him with a smirk, "No bride across the threshold jokes if you want to remain standing, yeah?"

"I wouldn't dream of it," Corban replied, "but damn, where did I get such a violent girlfriend?"

"Is that what I am now? Funny, I don't remember agreeing to that," Mary replied with a sly look on your face.

"Well if you don't want to fly there…"

"No, no, I'm good, point taken!" She said in a semi-sarcastic tone. "Sweep me away… lover. Do I seriously have to call you that?"

Corban laughed, "No."

"Sounds good, but you do know that I'm way too old for you, yeah?"

"You had to go and make it weird... That didn't seem to bother you the other night!"

Mary shrugged as her face began to turn red again, "Just shut up and go!"

Corban pictured Pan and his massive yacht, "All right, take my hand and hold on for the ride of your life."

As before, they began flying straight upward. Mary panicked and grabbed onto Corban's chest. He smirked at how strong her grip was. She began to breathe heavily as she looked down, "Corban… Corban… not so high, yeah?"

Corban chuckled, "Don't tell me that the tough girl they call 'Ripper' is afraid of heights."

Soul Siphon

"First of all, if you're my boyfriend, I'm not tolerating you calling me Ripper, got it?" Mary shot back. "Secondly, no I'm not afraid of heights… I'm afraid of being dropped from heights!"

Corban burst out laughing as they shot forward towards their target. Mary watched hundreds of miles pass by in mere seconds. Even though the world was almost a complete blur, she savored it. She would never admit it, but she partially enjoyed being held by Corban. It didn't fit well with her tough exterior, but it had its moments.

The world slowly came back into view after mere minutes of flying. Corban was slowing down as they approached Hainan. The night sky failed to illuminate the water which looked like a black void.

Corban's eyes narrowed. They should have been brought directly to the ship, but it was nowhere in sight, "Do you see anything?"

"No, it's too dark," Mary replied.

"We should be able to see it by now."

"Aren't they supposed to have some kind of running lights on at all times?"

"Probably… maybe they're trying something illegal?"

"Or Vlad and Johnny have already started trouble."

"More likely, yeah?"

"I hope not…"

At that moment, Mary heard the sound of gunshots coming from right below them. The guns were on full auto and the firing was almost continuous. She looked directly down, "Corban, they're literally right under us!"

"Sounds like they've already found trouble!" Corban replied in an annoyed tone.

Soul Siphon

"No kidding!" Mary replied. "Let's get down there, wouldn't want to miss it, yeah?"

Corban lowered them to the stern deck, away from the shooting. The moment they touched down, Mary hopped out of Corban's arms, drew her blades, and crouched down as she ran towards the battle, "Stay with me. Pan may be Lihua's, but that doesn't mean that we can't get a few kills along the way."

Corban pulled out the trusty M&P45 that he had carried with him since day one, "I agree."

They ran towards the gunfire, hopping over dead bodies and piles of ash that were no doubt left behind by Johnny. A disgusted look appeared on Mary's face, "If they clean house without letting me get a single kill... I swear..."

The yacht was about 250 feet long with a black hull and a white superstructure. It was clearly a newer model with a very sleek design. It had about five decks on it and wood planking on the main one. It was an impressive boat if ever there was one, but Corban would not have expected any less from their target.

Sensing that he was missing something important, Corban began to run to the bow of the ship. He ran through the superstructure and arrived to witness the scene that was unfolding at the stern. Vlad and Johnny were hiding behind an overturned table, Lihua was a deck above them trying to provide some cover, and Pan's men were laying down a ton of fire with fully automatic weapons.

Corban joined them, but there was no sign of Mary. Despite telling Corban that they should stick together, she had disappeared, "What's the matter Vlad, your Mosin not a match for a pair of Automatic Kalashnikovs?"

Soul Siphon

"I never too proud to admit ven he's beat, but if it is to be so, at least is at the hands of Russian weapons!"

Johnny turned and fired three more shots before he ducked down behind the metal table again, "I'm out... damn it!"

"Corban, vere's Mary?"

Corban looked around, "I don't know... where the hell did she go? She told me to stay close..."

As though answering them, the sound of a metallic object cutting soft flesh and choking sounds entered their ears. Corban looked over the table to see both of Pan's bodyguards collapse lifelessly on the deck. Their blood spattered all over the luxurious furniture.

Pan stood up and raised his hands. Corban heard him began to cry out in Chinese, *"I surrender, I give up! Spare me!"*

Lihua jumped down from the upper deck and walked towards him, *"I know you know how to speak English, Pan. Now cut the shit and speak so that my friends can understand you!"*

Pan's eyes narrowed, "That voice... I know you, don't I?"

"I would think that you would remember me... murderer."

"Murderer... I don't know what you're talking about!"

"No?" Lihua asked. "Does the name Lihua Lin mean anything to you at all?"

Pan backed away, "Lihua Lin? No... no, it can't be! How is this possible? You're... you haven't..."

Corban looked over at Mary, "How does he recognize Lihua? I thought that wasn't supposed to be possible?"

Soul Siphon

Mary shrugged, "She's a skilled manipulator… maybe she's letting him see her, or maybe he's taking her word for it?"

"Aged? No, I have not," Lihua replied. "I exist beyond what is considered living now. It is all thanks to you!"

"How?" Pan asked.

Lihua clenched her jaw. It seemed like every word out of his mouth was a knife to her back. She was unable to maintain her composure and looked like she was ready to explode.

Corban saw the tension building up in her eyes and stepped forward, "We're here with you, do whatever you need to."

Lihua gave Corban an appreciative glance before she turned back to Pan with her eyes burning, "You raped me. You left me for dead… carrying your bastard child. My father cast me out of his home when he found out! He covered for you. After everything, he cared more about status than his own family. Everything was completely laid to waste. My world was destroyed… because of you!"

"You… you were pregnant? I… didn't know."

"You did not care!" Lihua said as her voice became enraged. "You would not have cared even if you had known!"

Corban took a step backward, almost expecting Lihua to explode. The rage in her voice was crystal clear. There was nothing he could say or do now. He would need to let the scene play out.

Lihua had always been even-tempered. Now it was as though every single repressed feeling of rage was coming back to haunt her. This was her first and only outlet and she was clearly taking advantage of it.

Lihua began to hyperventilate as she faced down the man who ruined her life, "I was young then…

Soul Siphon

innocent… I did not deserve what happened to me. I lost everything… Everything!"

"Wait... are you responsible for the series of murders in our town, including your own father?"

"I am, and I enjoyed every minute of it."

"They couldn't even identify your father's remains. I... had I known."

"He was no father to me."

Pan squirmed under Lihua's menacing gaze, "I… Lihua, I'm sorry… please spare my life!"

"Spare you?" Lihua asked in a shocked tone. "Spare you... how many times did I cry out for mercy when you held me down? How much did I beg you to let me go? You just laughed at me… you laughed."

Corban stepped back next to Mary and whispered, "She's on the edge. Another step and she'll have a complete meltdown. I don't know if we should let this continue."

"Shh!" Mary replied as watched. "We all went through this, don't interfere. This is her closure."

Corban watched Lihua's eyes glow red as she looked straight into Pan's and screamed, "You fucking laughed!"

Lihua shook as she stepped towards him. She wiped her eyes, refusing to give Pan the pleasure of seeing any weakness from her, "How dare you beg for mercy… how dare you! I lay on the ground, bleeding after what you did. I was barely alive!"

Pan looked down to see blood dripping from his gut. Lihua had run him through with her sword. She slowly withdrew the blade as he looked up at her, "Lihua… please…"

Lihua clenched her jaw as she withdrew the sword and struck him a second time, severing his arm. Pan's screams appeared to excite her, "Should I

Soul Siphon

continue? Shall I leave you alive but deaf, dumb, and blind with no limbs?"

"Lihua... please..."

"No Pan," Lihua replied. "No, I am not that evil. I'll make this quick. You can make your peace with the devil."

Lihua brought the sword around again, decapitating her victim. As the lifeless body fell to the ground, Lihua spit at it, "Burn in hell..."

Lihua stood motionless for several minutes, breathing heavily. Corban couldn't stand seeing her like this and decided to risk trying to help. He stepped forward and tapped her shoulder, "Lihua, are you all right?"

"Yes... I am now," Lihua replied as she calmed down. "That monster will no longer haunt me."

"Monster?" A voice repeated. "I see a monster here, but it wasn't the sinner that you just murdered... it's you and your team."

All five of the friends turned their weapons towards the sound of the voice. Their eyes panned the darkness, hoping to see something. The lights on the yacht were still out and the boat was shrouded in complete darkness.

Corban stood up with his gun still fully loaded and stepped forward, "Come on out!"

The creature stepped forward glaring at them. Miraculously, the lights on the yacht came on as she stepped out of the darkness, illuminating the mess that they'd made on the deck. The creature, dressed all in black, stepped forward again, "Run into some trouble, did we?"

Lihua stepped forward, "We did not anticipate them being so heavily armed."

"Doesn't matter." The creature replied. "You've caused one hell of a mess and you will be punished for it. Unsanctioned killings, murdering a man who was pleading for his life, denying repentance… this is going to be a lot to explain."

Corban looked at the creature in surprise. Why would a demon care so much about people getting killed? Something didn't add up, "Who the hell are you?"

The creature stopped walking, "Who am I? Who do you...?"

Before the creature could finish its sentence, Mary appeared behind it with an iron collar in her hands. She grabbed the creature and locked the collar around its neck. The creature gasped as the Enochian letters on the collar glowed red. It dropped to its knees and tugged at the collar, desperately trying to get it off, "What have you done to me?"

Mary nodded to Corban, "Kill it quickly!"

Corban walked over to the creature and began to draw energy into his hands. The creature's face was covered by a mask, but he could hear its breathing quiver as he closed his eyes and placed his hand on its shoulder. He felt an intense flow of energy through his being. As more and more energy flowed into him, his eyes shot open in shock and he released the creature.

Mary looked at him oddly, "What is it?"

"I can't."

"What?"

"This creature doesn't have an evil aura."

"What are you talking about?"

"I can't explain it," Corban replied, "but I don't think this creature is a demon… Not even close…"

"Demon?" The creature shouted in an angry voice. "I am no demon! How dare you compare me to such a filthy creature? How sickening…"

Whatever this creature was, it's heightened voice had just revealed that it was female. Corban and

Soul Siphon

Mary exchanged glances before Corban reached down and ripped the hood and mask off. No one was prepared for what they saw underneath.

A woman with pale skin, piercing blue eyes, and jet black hair that flowed past its shoulders, glared at them. Her eyes burned with malice as she stood still as a statue, clearly waiting for them to make the next move. Her jaw was still and she held her chin up in an almost defiant manner.

Corban had never seen this level of arrogance before. She was trapped but still seemed to be fearless. His thoughts were interrupted as Mary tapped his shoulder, "What do you make of this?"

"I... I don't know. There's power here... more than we thought. This could be bad."

This spoke with an accent that he had never heard before, "I demand that you release me, creatures of darkness."

Corban stepped in front of her, "Answer our questions and we'll consider it."

A confused look came over Mary's face, "Corban?"

"It's okay," Corban replied calmly. "Trust me."

"I do not owe you any answers!"

"Then you can die."

The woman scoffed, "You do not possess the power to kill me!"

"No?" Corban asked. "Your powers have been weakened by the collar, even I can feel it. Shall we test your theory?"

The woman let out a defeated sigh, "Very well... What do you wish to know?"

"Well... who are you, for one?"

The creature closed her eyes as though about to reveal a terrible secret, "My name is Xaphine... General Xaphine."

Soul Siphon

"General?" Vlad asked. "General of vat army?"

"… of the Legions of Angels and the armies of the Celestial World. I am an archangel in command of the finest warriors in existence."

"No, that is not possible!" Lihua shouted. "Saint Michael is the commander of those forces. He leads the angels!"

"I am Saint Michael!" Xaphine growled. "Or rather the one you refer to as such!"

"Lies," Mary hissed. "Mike is our mentor. He's been with us for decades!"

Xaphine looked away, "I don't care if you believe me. You maggots have no idea how much damage you've done! Did you seriously believe that you could meddle with the order of the Universe and suffer no consequences?"

Mary grimaced and looked up at Corban, "Kill her, do it now, yeah?"

Xaphine looked up Corban, waiting for him to drain her, "Go ahead, slay me if you can. There are thousands more that will follow."

Corban thought about it for a moment and backed away, "I can't… I don't sense evil from her. There is much anger and aggression here. I even feel some darkness, but no malicious intent. I need more information before I do anything. Too much doesn't add up."

"If I answer your questions, will you let me go?" Xaphine asked.

"If I'm convinced you're being honest," Corban replied. "Now let's get to the bottom of this. If you are who you claim, why are you here now? Angels aren't supposed to directly interfere in the works of the world according to Mike."

Xaphine lowered her eyes, "Let me start at the beginning. I am the leader of the Angels. My part was

Soul Siphon

rewritten and cast for a male angel when I appeared amongst your kind. Apparently, the authors of your scripture didn't like the idea of a female being the leader of the angels. So first I became an androgynous creature, then I became male."

She scoffed at the thought as she continued, "I've been called many things over the eons... but to answer your question, I'm here because I have... unique experience dealing with humans. I've spent more time among you than any other angel. I was sent down here to investigate a series of murders that have taken place all over the world. We haven't been able to trace who is responsible... and we're missing a few spirits that are overdue to have judgment passed on them. Some are older than others."

She studied at each of them carefully, "And I'd be willing to bet my wings that you are those five... Corban McConnell, Lihua Lin, Johnny Tremane, Vladimir Pietrov, and the oldest... Mary Jane Kelly."

Johnny shuddered at the sound of his full name and looked up at Corban, "How the hell does she know all of this?"

"She is a demon!" Lihua replied. "Lies and deceit are how they function. Mike has warned us about this from the beginning."

"Yeah, but none of the others knew us by name!"

Xaphine sighed, "The demon is most likely the one you're working for."

"That's a lie!" Mary shot back. "Why should we take your word over that of the man who has looked after us all this time? Why should we listen to you instead of the man who gave us these abilities?"

Xaphine grabbed the collar around her neck and lifted her chin, "Look at this thing! What infernal writing is on it?"

Soul Siphon

Mary's eyes narrowed, "Mike said it was Enochian, the language of the angels."

"Language of the angels…" Xaphine scoffed. "We communicate with each other in ways your feeble minds could not begin comprehend. We have no use for a written language of our own. What needs to be recorded is done so in murals. Enochian is a language concocted by occultist heretics. It has since been used in an attempt by fools to control angels and demons by summoning them, trapping them, and bending them to their summoner's will. The fools never realize the damage they're doing or the danger they put their own souls in by partaking in such ridiculousness! That's how many possessions happen in the first place!"

Xaphine turned to Corban, "No angel would have given this to you, ever. No angel would do this… not even to a demon. It is a vulgar display of power and beyond cruel to our kind."

Mary shook her head, "You have no way to prove that!"

"Look it up, the information is easy enough to find!"

"I intend to after we finish with you!"

Xaphine shook her head. She was finished attempting to reason with Mary and turned to Corban who had fallen silent as he contemplated their situation, "I sense doubt in your mind. You are more open to the possibility of my words being true. You haven't spent as much time with this pretender as the others have."

Mary looked up at him, "Corban, it's Mike we're talking about. I know you don't fully trust him, but I've known him for years. He couldn't possibly…"

"Prove it," Corban replied to Xaphine, cutting Mary off.

Soul Siphon

"Very well..," Xaphine hissed. "Release me, destroy this profane device and I'll show you."

Vlad raised his gun, "Is a trick! Do not listen. This creature does not fool me!"

Corban didn't look convinced, "I'm suddenly not so sure it is."

Lihua stepped forward and looked into Corban's eyes, "Perhaps it would help us to know exactly what you are thinking. What makes you think that this creature is telling the truth?"

"I can't explain it," Corban replied. "When I touched this creature and attempted to drain its power, I felt something. I accessed memories, feelings... even love. I don't sense evil from this creature, darkness, but not evil. I think at the very least, she's telling the truth that she's not a demon."

"What do you intend to do?"

"Find out."

Lihua shook her head, "Corban, I cannot let you do that. We have fought too hard to get here."

"You have to trust me."

"I do, but..."

"If I'm wrong, I'll accept the punishment and return to my grave."

Lihua went pale as a look of disbelief appeared in her eyes. "You are really that certain that she is telling the truth?"

"Yes."

Lihua closed her eyes, "I cannot believe that I am agreeing to this. Do whatever you have to. I hope you are right... for your sake."

Lihua stood aside as Corban helped Xaphine to her feet and placed a hand on her shoulder, "I'm going to remove this collar so you can show me, but make any aggressive moves, and I'll rip the powers from you before you have a chance to use them."

Soul Siphon

Xaphine gave him a smug look, "You aren't capable of handling the powers of an angel, you'd kill us both."

"Then let us die together."

Xaphine stared at Corban for a few moments, studying his face, "I sense something in you... you're not suicidal. No... you seek to protect... her."

Xaphine turned and looked at Mary, "And I sense the same thing from you."

Her eyes darted back and forth for a few moments as she appeared to be studying the team, "You're not at all what I expected... Could you really all just be innocent puppets in this whole thing? Can it really be that simple?"

She turned back to Corban and raised her chin so he could get to the collar, "Well.... let's find out."

Corban reached for her restraints, but before releasing it, he quickly glared into Xaphine's eyes, "I mean it. Try anything and I will kill you."

Xaphine released a tension-filled sigh as the collar was released. She closed her eyes and breathed in deeply. It took a moment for her to settle herself before turning to look at Corban. The group was ready and waiting to see if Xaphine would try to make a move.

"You may relax your weapons. I have no intention of causing any of you harm... yet."

"Show me!" Corban demanded.

Xaphine looked at him with scorn, "To have lived so long and now to have to obey the orders of a human, how far I've fallen."

Xaphine remained perfectly still and kept her gaze on Corban as she concentrated. A pair of wings flashed and suddenly appeared on Xaphine's back. They were large, white, eagle's wings that seemed to shimmer when hit by light.

Soul Siphon

Corban took a step back and looked on in awe as Xaphine spread her wings to their full magnificence. She then folded them behind her back and waited for one of them to comment, "Convinced yet?"

"No," Lihua replied. "The devil was an angel at one time, and it is said that he appears as a beautiful woman. This proves nothing."

Xaphine rolled her eyes and turned to Corban, "Oh very well... may I?"

Corban wasn't sure what she was going to do and backed away slightly. Xaphine spoke in as reassuring a tone as she could, "Trust me, you are in no danger at the moment."

Mary clenched her fist as Xaphine touched Corban's cheek. Xaphine closed her eyes and focused, "Feel my thoughts as only you can... see what I know."

Corban closed his eyes as he focused his mind. There was a brief silence that was uncomfortable for everyone watching. No one knew what to expect as Xaphine provided her evidence to Corban.

Corban's eyes shot open and he backed away. Mary stepped up next to him and rubbed his arm, "Are you all right? What did you see?"

Tears filled Corban's eyes as he processed the information that Xaphine had given him, "Oh man... you've been through a lot."

Xaphine's face tightened up, "I'm not interested in your sympathy. Not every existence is easy and mine experiences made me strong. You have my information, do you believe me now?"

Corban lowered his eyes, "I believe..."

Mary grabbed his shoulder, "Come on Corban, say it, yeah? What's going on? Is she an angel or a demon?"

"She's an angel. I'm certain of it."

Soul Siphon

"That still does not prove anything," Lihua replied. "Angel or not, we have no reason to trust her. Mike gave us a second chance at life. He has been our mentor and nothing you say can change that!"

Lihua's eyes narrowed as she looked at Corban, "You have not been around as long as I have. You may not have reason to trust Mike, but I do."

"And I have been around longer than you, yeah?" Mary said. "Mike's been acting weird for a while now. He's become obsessed with bringing a soul siphon onto the team and he's been unreasonably hard on Corban. I'd like to know why. –Corban, is there anything else you can tell us?"

"Yes..," Corban replied hesitantly. "She's right; there is no Saint Michael... I was able to get a glimpse of her world."

An angry look appeared on Lihua's face, "This is not possible. You are being deceived by a skilled creature. Mike restored us and gave us what we needed to survive. Why would he do that if he were not one of us? This is not enough evidence to prove that she is anything more than a deceptor!"

"I agree," Corban said. "–Xaphine, do you have any explanation for any of this? If Mike isn't Saint Michael, who is he?"

"That's what I was sent to find out."

The wings disappeared from Xaphine's back, returning her to human form, "It's why I've been traveling like this. I can't risk being exposed any more than I am already. We can't track you or your mentor and that worries us greatly. The only reason I was able to catch you is because of the killings that we weren't prepared for."

"Wait," Johnny interrupted. "There is one major thing that I don't get... if what you're telling us is true, why couldn't your boss just put a stop to it? Surely that's within his power."

Xaphine let out a deep sigh as though she were releasing a pressure valve, "You people... when are you going to grow up and learn that it doesn't work like that? I grow weary of hearing that tired only question over and over. The answer isn't that difficult to figure out, even for such a feeble-minded species. 'My boss' gave you free will and the ability to make decisions on your own. The rules that have been made are ones that even angels are bound by. If they are broken, it invalidates them, and that's when existence begins to unravel."

Corban shrugged, "What are we supposed to do? You've given me some compelling evidence and certainly a lot to sift through, but you haven't been able to answer some of the most basic questions."

"If you believe me now that Mike isn't Saint Michael, then you know that you're being manipulated and you're most likely in danger. Whatever Michael is, he clearly has his own agenda. Can you really just ignore that?"

Xaphine turned and beckoned to Mary, "Are you really willing to risk what you have?"

Mary's mouth fell open as she tried to respond, but could not find the words to, "I..."

Corban leaned back against the nearest wall. He wasn't sure what to make of any of this. He had reached an intellectual stalemate with Xaphine. She had not answered all of his questions, but she had planted the seed of doubt about Mike's intentions. He needed to know more, "If I believe you, and you have given me no reason to, all I have is a gut feeling that you're not evil. That isn't a lot to go on."

"All I can do is tell you what I know. You must make the choice," Xaphine replied.

Soul Siphon

Corban turned to his friends, "Thoughts?"

Mary looked like she had a headache, "This whole thing is fucked up, yeah? A creature that attacks and tries to kill us reveals itself to be an angel. You believe it, despite a lack of evidence, and now we're here debating our own purpose. One thing that I find highly suspect is the fact that it's defending these evil people... It knows what they've done, yet still condemns our actions. I'd like to know why?"

"Ordinarily I wouldn't," Xaphine replied. "Scum like Pan Wei earned his fate many times over... however you've killed others that could have become penitent souls. Forgiveness is one of the greatest gifts that your kind has been given and you've denied them that gift and condemned them to Hell without even giving them a chance. Life is meant to be a proving ground for paradise. Who are you to deny someone the chance at repentance? By what right do you feel that this behavior is justified?"

"We were working under Mike's guidance," Corban protested. "We were doing here what angels are unable to do! It's not our fault if the universe is that poorly run!"

"It is for that reason alone that I'm here talking to you. If I thought for a moment that you were acting on your own, you'd be on a one way trip to Hell right now."

Lihua shook her head, "I do not believe you. Mike has looked out for us, kept us fed, protected us, and worked hard to rid the world of evil. No demon would do that. –Not to mention, Corban, that this is the same creature that severed your wrist! This is nonsense, plain and simple."

She turned back to her friends, "I got to reap the vengeance that I have been after. That alone is enough justification for me to remain loyal to Mike."

Soul Siphon

"Is it?" Xaphine asked. "Do you feel any better? Does the pain of what happened to you feel more manageable? Does your father's rejection no longer bother you? Has it really helped you heal?"

"Silence you!" Lihua shouted as she drew a dagger and pointed it at Xaphine. "I am not buying into your trickery!"

"I don't know what I can say that would convince you that I'm being genuine."

"All right, I will give you that chance. Tell me, if Mike is not who he claims to be, then why does he have us hunting evil souls? Assuming that you believe that he is a demon, why would he do that?"

Xaphine lowered her eyes, "That I don't know. I'm not saying that he is definitively a demon, just that he is not Saint Michael. In which case, I can think of any number of reasons for having you fight evil. I was sent here to put a stop to your actions and find the truth, nothing more."

"Yet you attacked us."

"To be fair, I didn't raise my weapons until you threatened me."

"You interfered in our mission, what were we supposed to think?"

Xaphine remained silent. She lowered her head as though acknowledging that Lihua had a point. Lihua sneered, capitalizing on Xaphine's lack of response, "I did not think so. I am done listening to you. Nothing you have told me is conclusive in any way. I am going back. Who is with me?"

Corban lowered his eyes, "I'm not turning on Mike, but I want to know more. Something about this whole thing is out of place. Not all of the pieces fit together the way they should. —Mary, you told me that you've dealt with soul siphons before. Tell me again, what happened to them?"

Soul Siphon

"They became too powerful. Absorbing souls, and thus, more power corrupted them and they plotted to take over the world. They became so demented that they actually sought to become Gods. The worst part is that they all thought that they were doing it for the right reasons. I was scared the same would happen to you. I still am, yeah?"

"Yet knowing that Mike continued reviving people who could wind up having that power... why? Why was he allowed to put all of existence at risk? You would think that someone would step in and stop him."

"He did that to combat demons," Johnny insisted. "When confronted with one, none of us possessed the ability to eliminate it. We were forced to watch possession victims die."

"But there are other powers out there that can combat demons just as well... and there are fewer risks involved," Mary replied. "Soul reavers, soul crusher, and others like them. They don't absorb souls, but Corban does, and he does it well. Mike chose him because of his sheer force of will. He thought that Corban could resist the lure of the demon's power."

Vlad frowned, "Mike didn't know Corban vould have zis power."

"But he didn't put him back in his grave when he did. He's been fixated on Corban's powers just like he was with the other soul siphons" Mary replied.

"What does that tell us?" Johnny asked. "Nothing."

"Nothing," Corban replied, "unless I was possessed again."

Mary's eyes narrowed, "What?"

"I overheard one of the people who helped with my exorcism say that if someone is possessed and survives, some of their mental fortitudes can be broken."

"Meaning that you could be easier to repossess," Mary said, finishing his sentence.

Her face went pale as she connected the dots that Corban had laid out, "And with your newfound powers, a demon could wreak havoc on the world... my God..."

"So Corban and Mary are saying zat Mike is a demon?" Vlad asked. "Can you really believe that?"

Corban looked over at Xaphine, "Adramelech?"

Xaphine shrugged, "Possibly. He's been looking for a way to regain some of the power he lost during his fight with you. What better way to redeem himself than by winning that fight a second time around? He's also not the only one in the Netherworld that is looking to gain an edge in the balance of power."

"It makes sense," Corban replied. "This is something we should definitely look into before taking any more orders from anyone."

Lihua sighed, "Then we need to decide what we are doing and who is going where... I'm going back. I have been offered nothing to convince me that Mike is anything other than a benevolent soul. I have certainly not heard anything that would convince me that he is not who he says he is. Even if he is not an angel, you have no proof that he is evil."

She turned to Corban, "Are you with us or against us? Make your choice."

Corban looked at Xaphine. Her expression was blank. She didn't know what anyone was going to do, no help there. He then looked at Mary. She was going pale and had a look of doom in her eyes, no help there either.

What could Corban do? Both sides had points, all he had was a gut feeling, and a lot of what Xaphine was saying was making sense. He couldn't make a decision, not on the information he had. He needed more, but something told him that following Mike would not get him the answers he required.

Xaphine spoke up, breaking his concentration, "If you help me unravel this mystery, you have my word that no harm will come to Mike until we're certain that we know what he is. If you help me, we may be able to absolve you of your past crimes."

Corban's mind was a mass of twisted thoughts. He knew that what he was about to say was going to upset his friends, "Yeah I... can't leave, not yet. I'm not taking sides... but I can't go back until I sort this out. Right now, I'm not sure who to trust. I just have a feeling that this is where I need to be."

He then turned to Xaphine, "I'll help you try to figure this out, but nothing more. I'm not working for you and I don't trust you, I just want answers. So don't try to order me to destroy or kill anything. I won't do it until I know that what you're telling me is the truth. For now, consider this a temporary ceasefire."

"I could expect no more," Xaphine replied satisfactorily.

Lihua shook her head, "I cannot believe this. Are you really prepared to cross this line? Are you ready to turn on the man who took you under his wing?"

"Absolutely not," Corban replied. "However at the moment, I'm on the sidelines. I'm not going to do any more of Mike's dirty work until I have my answers."

Lihua clenched her fists, "Then you are not my ally."

She turned to the rest of the group, "Who is coming with me and who is staying here?"

Soul Siphon

Johnny and Vlad looked at each other. Vlad shrugged, "I'm going. Mike has been friend for long time. I have seen no valid reason to turn on him now."

Corban nodded as Johnny looked at him apologetically, "I'm sorry man, I understand why you're doing this, but we've been around Mike for much longer. I know he hasn't earned your loyalty, so go figure out what you need to and then come home, all right? I know he'll understand."

"Thanks, Johnny," Corban replied.

Lihua nodded as Vlad and Johnny stood with her and then turned to Mary, "Ripper, what about you? Are you with us, or them?"

Mary looked at Lihua and the over at Corban. After listening to both sides, her mind was conflicted. Her loyalties were being torn and both sides had a point. She closed her eyes, knowing that her response was going to further complicate things for everyone, no matter which way she went. Her choice now was between a mentor and someone she cared deeply for and answering some critical questions that may change the game. She opened her eyes and looked at Corban, "I've been in your corner this long. Tell me honestly that you believe she's telling the truth. Tell me that you're convinced enough to believe her."

Corban nodded, "At least part of what she says is true, I know that much."

"Then..." *Here we go...* "I'll stand with you... for now. At the very least to make sure that this… angel doesn't stab you in the back."

A shocked expression appeared on Lihua's face, "You are going with them? After everything we have been through together?"

"This isn't us versus them, yeah?" Mary shot back. "This is us trying to investigate a few things that are out of place. If we're wrong, we'll return and face the music from Mike, but if we're right, we may have been causing a lot of damage that we may never be able to atone for. I have a doubt, and that is enough for me. If that turns out to be unfounded, we'll be back before you know it."

She turned to Corban, "Right?"

"Yes," Corban replied. "Absolutely we will, we'll have to be."

Lihua looked like she was going to explode. She was furious. Corban stepped in front of Mary and extended his open right hand to Lihua, "I am not turning on you. I hope you know that. We are on the same side. We are friends, even if not allies."

Lihua calmed herself and looked at his hand for a moment. She thought about what she should do and then looked back into Corban's eyes. The temptation to slice his hand off was alluring, but she knew that she couldn't do it. She didn't trust Xaphine, but she did trust Corban. If he said that they were on the same side, she believed him.

She reached out and took his hand, "You are my friend, Corban. I trust you, but do not think for one moment that I am a fool. We will leave you to figure this out. Please let me know of your progress when you can and I will pass on any information that I discover, but do not think that I will not cut you down if you interfere with our missions. Stay out of our way and we will stay out of yours until you come home. That is all that I can promise."

Corban nodded, "I understand."

"Good luck, Corban."

"You also."

Lihua turned back and placed her hands Vlad and Johnny's shoulders, "See you soon."

As they began to vanish, Corban quickly called out, "Lihua, just be careful, okay?"

Soul Siphon

"I will... you do the same."

Without another word, they instantly vanished off of the boat, leaving Mary and Corban to question whether or not they made the right decision. It was an eerie feeling, but one that they would need to come to terms with. They had made their decision and it was now time to face the reality of their situation.

Mary bit her lip and turned to Corban, "Okay... so here we are, yeah? Now what?"

Corban turned to Xaphine, "Do you have a plan to solve this?"

Xaphine nodded, "Well for starters, we need a place to hide. Right now, too many people know where we are. That makes us vulnerable."

"I agree."

"Wait!" Mary exclaimed. "Mike has kept tabs on us in the past, wouldn't he already know what's happened here?"

"No," Xaphine replied. "I took care of that. He can no more see what I'm doing than I can see his plans. I made sure of that when I first got here."

"So where do we go then?" Corban asked.

Xaphine looked around at the yacht in approval, "This would serve as a pretty nice base of operations. It's large and mobile."

Mary shook her head, "It's also a high profile boat that people are going to be looking for."

"Not for long," Xaphine replied as she snapped her fingers.

There was a blast of cold wind as the boat suddenly began to move. Corban could have only described it as the ship going to warp speed. He watched as the blood and human remains disappeared from the deck and the exterior of the ship began to change color.

Soul Siphon

Mary closed her eyes to keep from getting dizzy as the ship moved, "This is insane, yeah?"

A second later, the ship touched down in clearer seas. The sun was out and the boat could be seen a lot more clearly. There was a small island not far off of their port side. Wherever they were, it was warm and humid, almost tropical.

Corban looked around confused, "Where have you taken us?"

"Welcome to Clipperton Island," Xaphine said with a smile. "This ship is yours now. We'll use it until we get everything figured out. I've changed its appearance, name, and registration so that no one will think twice about it. However, that is the most I can do. Anything further would be a violation of our mandate here on Earth. I won't risk further alterations."

"So now we need to figure out who Mike is and what his plan was for us," Corban replied. "Where do you suggest we start?"

"We need to catch a demon," Xaphine replied. "If Mike is one of them, we need someone to confirm that and one of his brethren would be a good place to start."

"Okay, sounds good," Corban replied as he looked over the ship. "So I take it we're going to be looking for a possession victim?"

"Right... which unfortunately may take a while for us to find."

Corban turned his gaze back to Xaphine in surprise, "How so, Mike told us that there have been a lot of exorcisms in recent years."

An annoyed look came over Xaphine's face, "Yes but how many of those do you think were real exorcisms and how many were nothing more than the machinations of dysfunctional minds? There is a

Soul Siphon

reason that so many religious leaders are cautious to properly vet these cases."

"Fair enough."

"Take the next day or so and relax," Xaphine ordered. "I need to make a few house calls and see if I can find a legitimate case. I will let you know as soon as I have any news."

"All right," Corban agreed as he turned to Mary, "we could use a break anyway.

"Fine," Mary said as she pushed her red hair back behind her ears. "I'm going inside. This is too warm for me."

XVI

Lihua returned to Boston with Vlad and Johnny in tow. She could not believe what had just happened. Her heart was filled with both confusion and anger as she opened the door. A feeling of betrayal entered her heart and festered the more she thought about her friends siding with Xaphine.

It did not help matters when she saw Mike standing in the living room waiting for her to get back. She realized that she would now have to give him the bad news, but what would she tell him? Should she tell him that they were traitors or should she let him know that they were chasing the truth and keeping an eye on Xaphine? She just did not know.

Mike smiled, "Took you long enough to get back. I take it that Pan Wei is dead?"

"Yes..."

"Good," Mike replied. "I take it Corban is flying Mary home?"

"No."

"What?"

"They're... not coming back..."

A confused look appeared on Mike's face, "Why?"

"The creature appeared to us."

"What?" Mike shouted. "Tell me Corban is okay!"

"Corban is fine..," Lihua replied. "So is Mary, just so you know."

"Of course. I was going to ask about Mary as well. Now tell me what happened. Spare no details!"

"We caught the creature and found out that it's the angel Xaphine."

Mike's face went pale, "Xaphine... no… wicked creature."

Soul Siphon

He looked deep into Lihua's eyes, "What did she say to you?"

"She told us that she was the general in command of the Choirs of Angels... she told us that you are an imposter. She said that she was sent here to investigate the people we've killed."

"And Corban bought it?"

This was it. Lihua paused as she bit her lower lip. If she told the truth Corban and Mary would be finished, "Corban... has Xaphine in custody. He's using her to find Adramelech. She agreed to turn the demon over to him if he let her go. He's suspicious of her, but at this point, it seems like his best option."

Johnny and Vlad kept quiet but exchanged worried glances. Lihua could tell that they were nervous about lying to Mike. Even she wasn't sure that she was doing the right thing. Only time would tell with this decision.

Mike lowered his eyes, "Let me paint you another picture... Xaphine's true name was Xaphan. She uses the moniker 'Xaphine' when she's in human form because that's what she called herself when she worked for the devil as a spy in our world."

"What?" Lihua asked as her chest clenched in shock.

Vlad's face twisted as he processed the information, "So zis Xaphan is demon?"

"No, not exactly," Mike replied. "She's an angel, and unlike the devil, she has a sense of honor and loyalty, but she is not on our side and not to be trusted. Xaphan is one of the devil's angels who were banished to Earth for her crimes."

Mike sat down in one of the chairs near the TV as he continued, "I don't know how, but she managed to find a way to shield herself from detection. Since then, she's been a constant thorn in my side. I had hoped that she'd given up and gone away, but obviously, that's not the case."

"Then we must warn Corban and Mary, immediately!" Lihua insisted. "They do not have this information. They think they are holding a minor demon captive."

"We will," Mike replied. "Eventually, but for now, we need to figure out what her plans are. If she intends to move against the Celestial World again, I need to know about it."

Lihua immediately went into panic mode, "Mike, our friends are at risk! We cannot afford to..."

"I am aware of that, but this may be our chance to take her down. I won't waste it."

"So what do we do?" Johnny asked.

"We need to figure out what she's up to," Mike replied. "This could be a serious problem if she and the devil have resolved their differences. Did Mary and Corban say where they were going?"

"No," Lihua replied. "Truth be told, I do not think that even they knew what they were doing. Corban was just determined to get answers."

"That sounds like Corban," Mike said with a chuckle. "Well as long as he accomplishes his mission and comes back, I'm fine with him pursuing his own vendetta against a demon. I just worry that he's not ready for it."

"He did absorb some energy from Xaphine," Lihua said.

Mike nodded, "Well I hope it was enough, because if he fails... or if by luck he doesn't fail and he absorbs too much from Adramelech before he's ready..."

"We will have to kill him," Lihua said as she slouched back in her chair.

"Yes," Mike admitted, "yes I believe so."

Soul Siphon

"Then we need to find them," Lihua replied. "I get the feeling that Mary will protect him no matter what so she may be in even more danger."

Lihua fought the urge to just let go and completely unburden herself. Mike's story was believable, but she didn't expect such a lack of concern for her friends' well being. Something was out of place in her mind, making her more suspicious of Mike's true identity.

"I'll look into it," Mike replied. "For now, I have another mission for you. You'll head out after sundown tonight. Compared to what you already faced, this should be nothing to worry about."

"Zis is good," Vlad replied. "I vould appreciate an easier kill zis time."

"Yeah after you botched the last one by missing?" Johnny snapped.

"Vill see Johnny, vill see."

"Have you lost your mind, hero?" Mary demanded.

Corban lay back in the middle of the bed in the owner's suite that was way too big for a ship. They had spent too much time arguing, but still had not resolved their situation, and now Mary was getting restless. He sighed as he looked at her, "Look, will you stop calling me 'hero?' Do you want me calling you Ripper?"

"All right, fine!"

"Having a change of heart?"

"Oh come on Corban, of course not," Mary said with a disgusted look on her face. "I'm not blind. I can see as plainly as you can that something is out of place here. If you tell me you believe that she's an angel, then I believe you. Still... I've followed Mike for 127

Soul Siphon

years, yeah? You can't expect me to not be somewhat concerned."

"I know Mary... you have a knack for pointing out things I already know. Look I don't like this any more than you do, but I can't go back just yet. We're in this too deeply now."

Mary sat down next to Corban, "I trust you, Corban. You know that, but you need to tell me what you saw when she touched you. If for no other reason than just so I can keep my sanity, yeah?"

"All right," Corban agreed. "I saw her memories, just like I saw Tanya's memories when I consumed her. I saw everything. She fought a war that lasted for eons against the devil and she's been fighting him ever since our creation."

"So you think that our Michael is a fake?"

"He's not Saint Michael," Corban replied. "That much I'm certain of. The rest... let's just say we've cast our lot with the person who's been the most honest with us thus far, even though I'm still not convinced that she's on our side. However, just because Mike isn't who he said he is, doesn't make him a demon. There may be an explanation for this... maybe."

Mary sighed as she lay back next to Corban and rested her head on his shoulder, "You don't believe that, yeah? Great, we're being lied to by a friend, our enemy is telling us the truth, and we're caught in the middle with no idea of who the moral right is."

Corban looked at her as she lay back. Her shirt rode up slightly, exposing her stomach. Like many ginger women, her skin was a milky white where there were no freckles and it was incredibly smooth. She looked like a majestic lioness in full stride. It was hard for him to imagine that this was the same woman as the horribly mangled mass that he'd seen in the crime scene photos from Jack the Ripper's time.

Mary noticed him watching and made her hips wiggle a little to tease him, "See something you like?"

"Not sure yet, turn over."

Mary grabbed a pillow and whacked him with it as hard as she could, "Keep that up and you'll never get a piece of it again!"

"I'm fine with that," Corban replied.

"You are?"

"Yup, as long as I get another part," Corban replied as he placed his hand on her chest."

Even without pressing, he could feel her heart racing, "You're an idiot, yeah?"

"Maybe."

Mary sat up and looked at Corban, "So what happens if Xaphine turns out to be the bad guy?"

Corban shrugged, "Then we go with our original plan. We'll destroy her."

"I see..."

Corban could plainly see that something was bothering her and it wasn't just their current state of affairs. He put his arm around her and looked into her eyes, "What is it?"

"I keep thinking about what happened to you when you took Tanya's soul. You remember how bad you got, yeah? It wore you down pretty good."

"I know."

There was sincere worry in Mary's eyes. He hadn't seen anything like it before. It was like looking at a pair of bright sapphires and then putting something dark behind them, "I'm scared for you. She was just a normal human being who had a terrible past. This is a powerful angel. It could rip you apart."

Corban nodded, "So what should we do then?"

Soul Siphon

"Well… you remember what Mike said, yeah? Keep your wits about you. Focus on what matters most…" Mary said with a wink.

"You want me to think about Vlad?" Corban asked feigning surprise.

Mary burst out laughing and grabbed the pillow to swat Corban again as he continued, "Because I don't think that'll help. If anything that might make me explode even more."

Mary stopped laughing and wiped her eyes, "No seriously though… I mean it, please try to remember this when everything starts to look insignificant. Do the best you can to maintain control if it comes to that."

"I will," Corban replied. "Let's try to make sure that it doesn't come to that."

"Yeah... I was thinking about that and I may have a way to help you."

"Oh?"

"Mike was talking about having you look into one of our past. Essentially we'd act as a guide for you."

"What good would that do?"

"You'd be exposed to our horrors, but we'd work with you gradually on it."

"In other words, you'd desensitize me to the pain."

"Basically, yes. We'd allow you to see only what your senses could handle and then a little bit more. We'd gradually push you until you were used to what you were seeing and your mind could handle it."

"All right, but how would that work exactly? I mean how would you prevent me from seeing too much at once?"

Mary bit her lower lip, "Well... we do have defense mechanisms. Normally someone would block

Soul Siphon

you from the get-go, but if I let you in and have you steal my powers, I can control what memories I allow you to see. You'll see more if you push harder, but if you don't put up a fight, then my barriers should hold."

"Are there any risks?"

"Yes..," Mary said hesitantly. "One, when you drain my power, you have to put it back. If you don't you might damage my immunity to the passage of time."

Corban nodded, "Anything else?"

"And two... I'd have to relive the memories you do as if I were going through it for the first time."

"Absolutely not!" Corban shouted.

"Corban..."

"No. I'm not making you suffer through what happened again. I won't do that. I know what Jack the Ripper did to you."

"But it was a long time ago. I've accepted what's happened."

"Maybe, but you still have open wounds from it."

"Huh?"

Corban sighed, "Not all wounds are on the surface, some are deep within. I know you're still fighting off demons as well."

Mary lowered her eyes, "Corban, how bad do you think the demons will get if anything happens to you?"

Corban saw the earnest look in her eyes as she spoke, "I'm willing to endure this. I'd rather go through a pain that I know is coming than risk suffering a whole new one later. I'm offering you my help. Please accept it."

Corban lowered his eyes, "Mary... I just don't know..."

Soul Siphon

Mary turned on her side and rubbed his cheek with her left hand, "You said that you trusted me... well trust me now."

Corban squeezed his eyes closed and nodded, though he appeared to be in pain as he did, "Fine, but if I think something's wrong, I'm pulling the plug."

"All right."

Corban sat up and looked down at Mary, "So when do we start?"

"Right now. I want to get this over with. The sooner you're safe and I've got my past out of the way, the happier I'll be... if you're ready."

"As I'll ever be."

Mary sat up and looked deep into his eyes, "Focus your mind. I won't resist you. When you're ready, take what you can."

Corban sucked down a deep breath and nodded, "Are you sure about this... this is very personal..."

"Anything you'll see I've either already told you or don't mind you seeing."

"All right..."

Corban centered himself and slowly touched Mary's cheek with his right hand. His left hand wrapped around the back of Mary's neck and held her in place, "I'll be as gentle as possible."

"I know you will."

Corban focused on Mary and invaded her being. Mary's eyes widened and she gasped at the shock as she felt Corban drain her energy. Her heart rate increased and her breathing became more labored. It was as though she were in the middle of a tough workout.

Corban's eyes snapped shut as he was taken back in time to Limerick, Ireland. A sense of jealousy came over him as he saw her marriage play out before his eyes. He moved on past it and found himself in 19th Century London.

The sun was choked out by tall brick buildings that were virtually built on top of each other. There was a putrid odor of rotten food and sewage in the air and the crowded streets were wet with mist. Everything was dirty and many of the people looked sickly as they walked by. This was Mary's home.

Corban was transported a few blocks away to a large brick building. The name on the door had all but been worn away and was illegible. He was led inside where he saw women dressed in fairly stylish, albeit revealing, dresses and men in very fancy suits. The building looked old and worn, but it was clean and well-lit.

A flash of red hair caught Corban's eye. It took him a moment to recognize the girl it was attached to as Mary. Her hair was done up in large curls, she wore a red dress that was very low cut in the chest, and her face was completely caked in makeup. She was a little more portly back then, which made her a little harder to recognize, but her face was unmistakable. His heart sank as he watched men pull at her, some violently. He marched over to her and tried to intervene, but his hand passed right through the man who had grabbed her.

Corban remembered that what he was watching was an illusion and backed away. His heart raced and he began to sweat as he saw Mary down a few more drinks before draping herself over the nearest man. He couldn't stand it, but he knew that he had no choice.

This scene repeated itself with a different dress, different makeup, and a different man each night. He then watched her make her way home at night. She often had to avoid being roughed up by street thugs or run over by a passing coach. Each time, he felt an odd

Soul Siphon

sensation. It was a combination of intense sadness and loneliness. This was her lot in life and there was little that she could do to escape it.

Corban broke the link. He was covered in beads of sweat as tears formed in his eyes. He was brought back to reality where he saw tears dripping down Mary's cheeks. She was reliving everything he had seen and it pained him to know that he was the cause of this. He kept a tight grip on Mary as he forced her energy out of his body and back into hers.

The moment that he was certain that he'd returned everything that was taken, he released her and leaned back. She opened her eyes and looked at him sadly. It almost seemed like she was waiting for him to pass judgment on her for everything that he'd seen.

Corban immediately sat up, wiped her tears dry and kissed her cheek, "You poor girl... I am so sorry... That was your life?"

Mary nodded, "Like I said, it wasn't always that bad. I just let you see what you needed to."

Corban wrapped his arms around her and squeezed. She closed her eyes and released her breath. She knew what he was trying to do, but comfort wouldn't help at that moment. She'd had to relive times that she'd have rather forgotten and it wasn't over yet.

Corban's eyes blinked several times as he tried to focus. She watched him sift through the memories that she'd given him. "Are you all right?"

Corban nodded as his eyes watered, "I'm fine... what else you got?"

"Are you sure you're ready?"

"Yes, let's do this."

"All right."

Mary allowed Corban back into her soul. He again pulled the energy from her body and was

Soul Siphon

confronted with 19th Century London. This time, he found himself in a large open field with several stones protruding from the ground. The sign on the gate read 'Manor Park Cemetery.' Feelings of deep remorse and fear entered Corban's heart as he watched a cheap looking wooden box being lowered into the ground. A small plaque on the cover revealed the grave's soon-to-be occupant; Annie Chapman.

The intense feelings overtook him as he once again released the energy back into Mary and collapsed backward as the memories and intense sorrow overtook his mind. He pressed his hands against his temples and focused, trying to get a handle on the pain that he was feeling.

When Corban finally opened his eyes, he saw that Mary was finally surrendering to the pain. Tears streamed down her cheeks and she no longer bothered trying to hide it. Her lips quivered as she struggled to speak, "Are you okay?"

Corban nodded as he leaned forward once again. This time, he grabbed Mary and guided her back down onto the bed. She rested her head on his shoulder.

Mary sucked down a deep breath before trying to speak again, "Can we take a break, please?"

"Yes," Corban replied. "I think that's enough for a while."

Mary rolled onto her side and pressed herself against Corban as she sorted out the memories in her mind. She took a few deep breaths as she slowly calmed down, "Thank you..."

Mary relaxed as they rested comfortably on the bed. When she had finally regained enough strength to function, she looked at Corban, "Did that help? I know it was painful, but did that do any good?"

"Yeah, a little. I've seen memories that were as strong as those already, but it's definitely a step in the right direction."

"Good," Mary replied. "You should have enough now to be able to stave off at least some of the memory flood, but not all of it. We'll keep working until you're there, I promise."

Corban didn't respond. He just gently rubbed Mary's back as they rested in silence. There was nothing he could say that would take the pain away or change what he'd seen.

The sound of wings flapping broke the quietness, causing them to look at the ceiling where the noise had come from. The sound of wings was then replaced with light feet moving across the deck. They were little more than soft thumps, but it was enough to alert Corban.

Being cautious, Mary grabbed her two favorite daggers and went to the door. Corban grabbed his gun and stood at the ready. Mary stood on one side of the door with Corban on the other. Mary gave the door a good kick, causing it to fly open. Corban pointed his gun out while Mary pressed herself against his back, ready to take on anything that came at them.

They crept around the corner and jumped into view, brandishing their weapons. Xaphine found herself facing the working end of a pistol and a pair of blades. She looked at them and rolled her eyes, "Let me ask you something; what were you planning on doing with those?"

Corban lowered his gun, "We were being cautious."

"If an angel or demon were to attack, your only defense would be Corban's power. Choosing those weapons as your first line of defense is foolishness. You would have one chance to take the creature down

Soul Siphon

and using these would only steal that chance from you."

Xaphine looked at Corban's handgun with disgust, "Lose the weapons while on this boat. They won't save you against anything that could attack us here."

Corban lowered the gun with an annoyed look on his face, "Fine..."

Mary gave Xaphine a nasty look as she sheathed her daggers, turned, and headed to the upper deck in anger. It was obvious to Corban that she didn't like Xaphine and didn't appreciate her smug superior attitude. Xaphine's expression remained unchanged. Either she hadn't noticed Mary's scorn or, more likely, didn't care.

Corban leaned on the railing overlooking the port side. The ocean was beautiful to watch as the sun slowly came up over the horizon. Xaphine leaned next to him, her wings were once again gone, "Sights like this are better shared. I wish I had that luxury right now."

Corban lowered his eyes, "I know the feeling."

"How long have you and Mary known each other? Just the time you've been like this?"

"Yeah... just a few months."

There was a brief silence before Corban spoke again, "It's time we cleared a few things up."

Xaphine nodded, "It does seem inevitable..."

"Why is it that demons can interfere in the mortal world, but Angels cannot? I don't understand."

"I don't expect that you should," Xaphine replied. "You live in the mortal realm, a physical world. Your world functions on different rules than mine. Certain rules do not apply to you."

Corban rubbed his forehead, "Can you explain it?"

Xaphine sighed, "I'll try. Your world functions on a different plain from mine. A natural rule of your world is that you need certain elements to survive. Imagine if someone found a way to remove one of those elements. Imagine what would happen if any of those rules became invalidated. What would happen?"

"We'd die."

Xaphine pointed at Corban, "Exactly you would cease to exist and your reality would be irreparably damaged. The same thing would happen in our world. Our world isn't held together by logic or things that can be explained scientifically. It is held together by supernatural law. If those laws are broken, our world would cease to exist."

Corban nodded, "All right, that makes sense, but how do the rules of your world apply to ours?"

"Our worlds are bound together. If you violate the rules of one... if you destroy one, you destroy both. Our world is the secondary world, the base. Think of us as the backstage. If we collapse, nothing will hold the main stage together. There is a balance that must be maintained. Undoing the rules at work here and not holding to the decrees are how an angel could do that damage. These workings are like a tapestry, if you pull one loose, the whole thing could come undone. My job is to enforce that balance at any cost."

Corban twisted his lips as he listened to Xaphine speak, "To answer your other question about demons getting away with interfering... well... It's a bit more complicated. Demons are not of the Celestial World and thus are not bound by them. Unfortunately, this allows them to run amok in your world. It's something we didn't foresee happening when we cast them into the pit."

"I see," Corban replied.

Soul Siphon

He turned back and watched Mary pace around the upper deck, "So what's the plan? I assume you came back for a reason."

"You're correct," Xaphine replied. "I found us a possession victim. She's out in Florence Italy… of all places…"

Corban nodded, "When do we leave?"

"… We're going to leave soon. Whenever you're ready."

The look on Xaphine's face was one of unease. Something was clearly bothering her and Corban needed to know what before they left, "Everything okay?"

"Yeah… I was just hoping that there'd be one somewhere else… anywhere else."

"Why?"

"Let's just say that Florence and I have a bit of a history. A lot of the time that I spent on Earth and the things I did… it all went down there. We're leaving it at that."

There was more to the story. Corban was sure of it. Something about Florence made Xaphine very uncomfortable, but she clearly didn't want to talk about it and Corban doubted that he'd get anywhere trying to force the issue.

Having no other choice, he shrugged, "Fair enough."

Mary came down from the upper decks, "I'm ready now. Let's get this over with, yeah?"

"Okay," Xaphine replied. "You guys need help or…"

"No that's okay," Corban replied. "Where in Florence?"

"Piazza del Duomo. Look for the Caffe' Duomo when you get there. The building it's in is pretty old so you shouldn't be able to miss it. The girl would be on

Soul Siphon

the third floor. Wait for me to get there before you try approaching her."

Corban nodded, "Sounds good."

"Before you go… you'll need better clothes."

Xaphine guided Mary and Corban up to the deck where she initially landed. There was a black suitcase waiting for them with metallic edges resting on the deck. The latches were not locked.

Mary threw the case open and found some black and white clothing. She looked up at Xaphine with an annoyed stare, "What the hell is this?"

Mary pulled out a jumper that was her size, a button down undershirt, stockings and uniform shoes, "There is no way in hell that I'm donning the school girl look, yeah?"

"Oh, nice!" Corban said with a lustful grin.

"Shut up!"

Xaphine gave them both an annoyed look, "It's not a school girl uniform. It's an initiate's outfit."

"Initiate for what?"

"Becoming a nun?"

Mary rolled her eyes and lowered the outfit back into the box as Corban burst out laughing. The very thought of it was hysterical. The annoyed expression did not leave her space as she looked at Corban, "Yeah yeah, I know, I'm no saint! I get it! Now shut up and see what's in there for you, yeah?"

Corban grabbed the suitcase and pulled out a pair of black pants, a black top, black shoes and a white strap. His eyes narrowed as he looked everything over, "This is a clerical collar."

Xaphine nodded, "Yes."

"I'm posing as a priest?"

"Not just any priest, an exorcist."

Corban looked up, surprised, "But won't there be one there?"

Soul Siphon

Xaphine shook her head, "Let's just say I have an understanding with the church in Florence. They won't interfere until we're done."

"All right, I hope not...," Corban replied.

Corban picked up the case and carried it into the owner's suite. Mary followed him in to get changed. The moment the door was closed, Mary stripped off her shirt.

Corban couldn't help but watch as she disrobed. She caught him staring and smiled. He instinctively looked away the moment her eyes met his. A hurt look came over Mary's face, "You don't have to turn away, yeah? You've already seen me."

"I know..."

"What's wrong?"

"It's nothing... I'm just being stupid..."

Mary wasn't buying it. She was too concerned for him to buy him trying to once again weasel out of talking, "I don't think so. Tell me..."

Corban's eyes looked back up at her, "I guess I just can't get over the look you had on your face when that guy was groping you."

"In my memories?"

"Yeah."

Mary sighed, "I was afraid this would happen... look, working at that brothel was hard sometimes and always downright demeaning, but it kept me fed."

Corban nodded as she continued, "That was a long time ago and that's not what you did with me that night. Those men were interested in something completely different from what you are... right?"

"Yeah of course!"

"I mean you did label me as your girlfriend, yeah? So I assume you were looking for something a little more intimate."

"Okay good point."

Soul Siphon

Corban stripped out of his clothes and threw on the priest outfit as quickly as he could. He straightened out the black clothes and then went to work brushing his hair back. Convinced that he looked presentable, he turned to see how Mary was faring. She had her white blouse on and was quickly trying to pull the dress over it. A deep sigh escaped her lips as she then went about straightening her hair.

Mary went into the bathroom and found an unused hairbrush. She worked it through her long hair to make the get up as convincing as possible. The brush pulled on her red hair and she forced it back into a ponytail, something she hadn't done in many years.

Corban watched her fix her hair. For the most part, she kept in either partially up in braids or done on the back of her head, but now that it was completely down, he could see that it was a bit longer than he'd originally thought. It was a shiny orangey-red color that complimented her pale skin very well.

For Corban, it was strange. He'd never really gone for redheads before, tending more to favor blonde women. Now he'd found a kindred spirit in a girl with the fieriest red hair that he'd ever seen.

She took one more swipe through her hair and tied it back in a ponytail. Once it was up, she took a moment to glance in the mirror and came out to Corban, "Okay… do I look bland enough?"

"It would take a lot more than a conservative outfit to make you look bland."

"You know, you can be quite nauseating sometimes...."

"I try."

Corban opened the door and led Mary back out on the deck. Xaphine was waiting patiently for them. The moment they appeared, she shook her head,

Soul Siphon

"Well… you'll pass I guess. If that's the best we can do, we'll make it work."

"Gee thanks!" Mary replied. "You know there is no place for us to hide any weapons in these outfits, yeah? How do you figure we'll defend ourselves?"

"That's true," Corban added. "We're going out there blind, unarmed, and possibly with some uninvited guests waiting in the wings!"

"That's what I'm here for," Xaphine said confidently. "You don't have to worry. They are no match for me should they attack."

"All right," Corban said, showing only partial confidence.

"See you in Florence then."

Xaphine's wings appeared on her back as she turned towards the railing. With one mighty thrust, she pulled away from the deck and disappeared into the clouds. It almost looked like she vanished as she passed a nearby cloud.

Corban looked over at Mary, waiting to see what she wanted to do. Mary returned his look, rolled his eyes and leaned backward into him so that he could pick her up. The weight shifted from her legs to his arms just as before, "I'm not running in these heels. I've had more than enough pain in my life, thanks!"

As Mary lay back, she grabbed on to Corban's chest, reached up, and kissed him on the cheek, "See you in Florence, yeah?"

Corban nodded and lifted off of the deck of their yacht. He climbed into the clouds as quickly as he could and quickly headed west. The air got cooler as he climbed higher and higher.

Mary looked down for a brief second as, without warning, Corban began to move forward and picked up speed. The world quickly blurred out of view. They were now traveling at Mach speeds, trying to get to Italy as quickly as possible.

XVII

Lihua was on the roof of the Boston hideout. More than anything, she wanted to be left alone as she stared out at the city. Her feelings were a conflicted mix of confusion and betrayal. Mike didn't even seem concerned about his long-time assassin. Did he even care or was Mary more of a thorn in his side?

Lihua knew that Mary could be difficult to live with, but she was a powerful and skilled fighter, and a good friend. She was as far from expendable as any of them could be. If anything happened to her, she would leave behind shoes that would be impossible to fill. So why wasn't he more concerned about her? Was it possible that she was thinking too much into Mike's reaction?

Lihua understood that Corban was a prodigy and perhaps the answer to defeating any demons that they might face, but he was still new and that didn't make lying to Mike any easier. It was true that Corban had become a good friend in the short time he'd been there, but he still had a lot to learn. This decision to go rogue, was extremely questionable.

"Hey Lihua, busy?"

Lihua grimaced and turned to see Johnny standing behind her with a lit cigar hanging from his lips, "I really wish you would not smoke those up here. The smell is intolerable"

Johnny smirked, "Yeah Mary said the same thing... sort of. She actually threatened to rip off something resembling a cigar if I didn't stop, but where else am I going to do it? If I do it inside, you'll have to smell it all the time."

"Fine," Lihua replied. "Well I was deep in thought, but I suppose I could use a break. What is on your mind?"

Soul Siphon

"I'm starting to wonder if we did the right thing leaving them behind."

"How so?"

"Well... I mean we're talking about Corban and Mary here. Corban didn't just wander in off the streets. Mike brought him here and Mary's been around longer than any of us. We just left them at the mercy of a fallen angel."

"Your point?"

"They wouldn't just abandon us. Corban must have seen something that convinced him of what he needed to do. I'm certain that this wasn't just a whim on his part. He's not that stupid."

"And Mary?"

Johnny shrugged, "I don't know... Ripper has been kind of acting like a starry eyed school girl since Corban came around. I mean if they're together, she'd probably support him no matter what... So maybe that's why she chose to stay..."

"I do not believe that, and neither do you," Lihua interrupted. "We have known Mary for a very long time. We both know her better than that. Maybe she did believe Corban, but that would not have been cause for her to leave. There has to be more to it."

"Like what?"

"I do not know yet... but she has been around longer than the rest of us. Perhaps she has been noticing a pattern that has disillusioned her to the cause? She did say that Mike was oddly fixated on Corban's power."

"You're not convinced that Corban's wrong either, are you?" Johnny said in surprise. "That's why you lied about what Corban is up to!"

"I never said that I was convinced either way, but I am not about to sell my loyalty to the man who brought me back to life and gave me the ability to stop

Soul Siphon

crimes like the ones I was subjected to, at least not without more proof than what we have been given. Corban may have seen enough to convince him, but since he cannot share that with us... all we have is the word of that creature... Xaphine. Corban's word would normally be enough, but I cannot be certain that she was not manipulating him."

"She was a weird one... I'm surprised Corban is willing to trust her after she severed his hand."

"I am not certain he that does. I do not think Mary trusts her either. I think they have taken a 'wait and see' approach to this whole thing, which may have been a wise move on their part."

"You think maybe we should have done that?"

Lihua considered the events surrounding the creature, Corban being brought onboard, and everything else that they had been through recently. Anyone of those events by themselves would have seemed like normal business to Lihua, but when connected together, something about the whole chain of events was eating away at the back of her mind and it would soon drive her insane, "I think it is time that we started looking into this ourselves."

"Oh good," Johnny replied in a relieved tone. "I don't like the idea of sitting on the sidelines and just waiting for something to happen. Where do we begin?"

"That is a good question," Lihua admitted. "It is usually best to start at the beginning and go from there."

An annoyed look appeared on Johnny's face, "Oh for fuck sake... spare me the condescending philosophy, will you? It's getting old."

"Very well, Johnny. Then we should probably start with the four months that Mike was gone. During that time, the only communications we received from

Soul Siphon

him were notes containing our targets. Other than that, we were left to fend for ourselves. I want to know why."

"You think it's connected to this?"

"Does it not make sense? When I asked Mike about it, he pretty much brushed me off. He said that he was monitoring Corban's possession to make sure that he was the right person."

"Yeah so, that makes sense..."

"Maybe... but he has never done that before. It is plausible that he was right where he said he was, but why do that for him and none of the other possession victims that we tried to enlist? Also, did he really need to monitor him continuously with all of his attention? We have seen Mike deal with multiple situations at once previously, why did this one take all of his time and energy?"

Johnny frowned, "I don't know about this. I think we're barking up the wrong tree here. Every question you've asked has a plausible answer. Maybe he'd learned his lesson from other possession victims? He needed someone who could resist a demon, so no ordinary possession victim would work."

"I agree," Lihua replied. "Every single one of my questions has a plausible answer. Plausible... but not definite... and that we have not been offered any answers is highly suspect. By themselves, any of these events and mysteries would seem pretty benign but put together, they form a dangerous puzzle."

"Then what do we intend to do about it?"

Lihua sighed, "For now... what can we do? We will lie low for the time being and I will continue to press Mike for more information. I would love to be able to exonerate him and get this team back to its purpose."

"Do you need me to do anything?"

Soul Siphon

"Keep your eyes open and your mouth closed. Inform Vlad of what we are looking into, but do not give Mike any cause for concern. I will not confront him until I have more solid evidence of what is going on around us."

"You got it."

"Thanks, Johnny."

Corban touched down just outside of the Caffe' Duomo, out of view of the public. It was the middle of the afternoon and people were bustling about. Mary jumped out of his arms and looked around. The buildings were old and worn. Many of them had been there since medieval times or even earlier. The shutters on the windows were a stark contrast as they were definitely newer. The walkway was an old gray stone tile that also looked like it had absorbed the footsteps of many millions of people over the years.

Mary grimaced at the sight of the walkway, "Great, and I'm in these God damned tight shoes… Xaphine did this on purpose!"

Corban chuckled, "Sorry!"

Mary closed her eyes and took a deep breath, "Florence, Italy... tell me we'll have time to look around when this is over, yeah?"

"Maybe," Corban replied as he eyes the building where the Cafe stood.

"Maybe? You are no fun at all. It's actually refreshing to be around buildings that are actually older than I am!"

Corban shrugged, "I don't like making promises that I can't keep. I don't know what's going to happen once this exorcism is over. I wish I could say that we'll have time, but I don't know that we will."

"All right, fine," Mary pouted. "Can you at least promise me that we'll come back here later and see the sights?"

Corban nodded, "Once this is over, I'll take you where ever you want to go."

"You better mean it," Mary replied with an evil look. "I'll gut you if you don't!"

Corban looked at Mary nervously, "I'm... not sure if you're joking or not... I guess I know now why they call you Ripper!"

"Corban..," Mary growled in a low voice.

Corban took a defense step back, "All right, all right, no more Ripper. I promise."

"Thanks."

Another voice appeared behind them, "Welcome to Florence!"

Both Mary and Corban turned quickly to see who had spoken. Xaphine was standing behind them with a solemn look on her face. Her black dress now flowed down to her ankles and had sleeves on it. Her wings were once again gone and she had taken on a human persona. She joined them in front of the building, "Let's get this over with..."

Mary looked at her oddly, "You don't look happy to be here."

"This place has a lot of memories for me... not all of them good. It's amazing how little this city has changed in 400 years."

"Say no more," Mary replied with disinterest. "Please."

"I had no intention to."

Corban rolled his eyes. This was going to be a very short trip if Mary and Xaphine came to blows. Too much was at stake for them to be at odds with each other.

Soul Siphon

Attempting to break the tension, Corban focused on the task ahead, "All right we're here, Xaphine, so where are we going?"

She pointed to the entrance, "There is a small bedroom up on the third floor. The family paid to keep their daughter there, close to the church. We need to get to her and confront the demon within."

"Any idea who we're dealing with?"

"No," Xaphine replied. "Whoever it is, has at least some power about them. It takes at least a mid-level demon's abilities to hide their identity."

Corban looked at the doorway to the café, "This isn't going to be easy... I don't exactly speak Italian..."

"Leave that to me."

The trio entered the cafe where they were greeted by the aroma of various types of Italian cuisine. Corban could hear Mary's stomach rumbling, as they walked. She hadn't eaten in a while and he knew it. Hopefully, they'd be okay for a few more hours without getting too hungry.

The walls on the inside matched the outside; a sort of yellowish, off-white tone accented by dark wooden furniture. A beautiful painting of the river that separated the city hung on the wall off to the side. The back counter had shelves with various drinks and food that was available for purchase.

A young waitress was standing behind the counter wearing a collared, striped shirt that was white at the top but faded down to black. The word 'Firenze' ran across the chest. Her eyes widened when she saw them, "Padre, Padre, grazie a Dio!"

She ran out and kissed Corban on the cheek. Xaphine stepped forward, "Buongiorno, siamo qui per vedere la ragazza."

The waitress nodded, "Si certamente. Da questa parte!"

Soul Siphon

Corban looked back at Xaphine with an inquisitive expression. Xaphine nodded, "She'll take us to her."

The young waitress led them back behind the counter to the hallway and the stairwell to the second and third floor, "La prima porta alla fine... Non voglio andare oltre."

Xaphine nodded and turned to Corban, "She said it's the first door after the stairs. She won't come with us any further. I can't say that I blame her."

The stairs were old and narrow. Mary had a hard time with the shoes she was wearing. They pinched her feet terribly and almost made her fall more than once. After the first flight, she bent over and ripped them off, "Fuck it, I don't care if it makes me look less 'churchy' I'm not wearing these anymore."

"As you wish," Xaphine replied.

The group was alerted to the sound of moaning as they reached the third floor. Mary reached down instinctively to grab her blades but grimaced when she realized that they weren't there. She was defenseless and there was nothing she could do about it.

"I told you, no weapons," Xaphine said sternly. "We don't want to attract attention."

"Yeah whatever..," Mary grumbled. "Be worth attracting a little attention if it means we're better protected..."

She glared at Xaphine, "... against enemies and people who claim to be allies."

Xaphine ignored what she viewed as childish posturing as she continued, "Sure..."

A man sat at the door to the room. Judging by the lines on his face, it was fairly evident that he had not slept in a while. He was struggling just to keep himself from falling over as he kept a quiet vigil. His

Soul Siphon

hair was a dark gray and his eyes had massive bags under them.

Corban looked over at Xaphine for guidance. Xaphine nodded and walked over to the man who perked up slightly when he saw them coming, "Padre, grazie a Dio! Mia figlia..."

Xaphine put her hand on his shoulder with a sympathetic look on her face. She quietly spoke in a soothing voice, "Shh... ripcso..."

The man lay back in his chair, unconscious. Xaphine looked up at Corban and Mary, "Her father, poor man."

They entered the room and beheld the dark scene that unfolded in front of them. It was a small chamber with a bed that had clearly seen better days in the middle. The room had been stripped of furniture except for a single chair and a bed. There were scars on the walls that resembled scratch marks as well as blood stains where the blue wallpaper had been torn.

In the bed, slept a young girl with brown hair and fairly tanned skin. She was covered by a white blanket up to her waist. Her shirt was torn so that one sleeve no longer covered her arm. Her hands were tied to the bed with tight straps.

Corban likened this scene to several horror movies that he'd seen over the years. He took a step back when he remembered that things didn't always go so well for the priests in those films, "What do we do now?"

"Abriana, sverliare!" Xaphine said in a stern voice.

Abriana's eyes opened and a soft cackle exited her lips. Her eyes widened and her skin went pale when she saw who was watching here, "You... I know you Xaphine... I know you well. That disguise suits you. I'd hoped to be able to rip your wings off myself someday, but I'll settle for this... for now."

Xaphine smiled maliciously, "Baal, it's been too long, old friend."

"So you say."

Xaphine walked around to the side of the bed and sat down next to the possessed child, "I need information."

"I have none to offer you," Baal replied as he spit in Xaphine's eye.

Xaphine grimaced as she wiped the saliva from her face, "You know what I can do to you if you don't answer me. Cooperate and I won't destroy you."

The demon grumbled. The look on its face was a good indication that it knew full well what Xaphine was capable of, "What do you want to know?"

"Who's here?"

Baal cackled again, "The five of us!"

Xaphine grabbed the girl by the throat. Her hands began to glow as they trembled, "I'm in no mood for games, Baal. I need to know who is currently residing in the mortal world."

There was a brief silence. Xaphine's eyes turned red and she threw Baal back against the bedpost, "Answer me!"

Corban was feeling increasingly uncomfortable. No doubt Baal deserved whatever he got. Corban was well aware of what demons did to people, but he was concerned that Xaphine was hurting the little girl who was an innocent in all this.

Baal hissed as it finally gave up the information, "There are a few of us... Caim, Gremory, Orias, Phenex..."

"Small fry," Xaphine replied. "Who else?"

"Beleth... Barbatos, Adramelech..."

Corban's eyes widened as Mary shuddered. Xaphine's expression remained unchanged, "Now that is interesting. Barbatos hasn't left the pit in a very long time and Adramelech... I didn't think he'd back be for a while yet. I understood that he was weakened after a failed possession."

"He never left," Baal replied.

Xaphine nodded, "I see... do you know where they are?"

"I cannot say."

Xaphine's eyes flared up again and she was about to strike when the creature protested, "I swear I don't know! Even if I did, I fear their wrath more than yours, angel. Kill me if you must."

Xaphine sighed and stood up, "We have what we need, let's go."

Corban tried to protest, "But we still don't know which..."

"He won't tell us," Xaphine interrupted. "I know him well enough to tell you that. If this Mike is being manipulated by a demon... or is a demon himself, it's one of those three. They're the only ones that have the power to do what's been done to you. We just need to figure out which one we're up against before we make a move. It'll be easier now."

Xaphine turned and headed for the door. The creature spat at them one more time, "You'll never defeat them. You're in way over your heads."

Xaphine ignored it and walked past Corban and Mary, "Come on."

Corban didn't move, "Wait a minute, what about the girl... Abriana?"

"It's not our problem," Xaphine replied. "If we do anything here, we risk tipping our hand."

"That's a risk I'm willing to take," Corban replied.

Soul Siphon

Mary leaned back against the wall next to Corban, "I'd do what he says, or you can forget about our help. You'd be surprised how stubborn he can be."

Xaphine sighed as she turned back, "Actually I probably wouldn't be. I'm familiar with how stubborn humans are, believe me."

She turned back and looked at Baal who still lay in the bed, cackling. She raised her right hand and thrust it towards the creature, effortlessly creating a yellow beam that struck Abriana in the chest. The force knocked her back against the wall again.

Baal cried out in pain. Little by little, his voice was replaced by the natural voice of a young girl. It appeared that whatever Xaphine was doing was working. The demon's power was quickly beginning to disappear as the girl regained control.

Their hope was shattered when the beam disappeared and Baal began laughing hysterically. Xaphine looked at her right hand in confusion. Anger spread across her face as she looked up at the ceiling, "Really, even now you view what I'm doing as interfering? This is too short of a leash for us!"

The menacing grin on the girl's face became even more hideous as Baal spoke, "You can't throw me out, that's against your rules!"

Baal's relentless taunting enraged Corban. He could feel his face heat up as he remembered what Adramelech had done to him. The taunting was so similar that it was unbearable. He clenched his jaw as he stepped in front of Xaphine, "She can't... I can!"

"Corban, no!" Mary screamed in panic.

"It'll be okay," Corban replied, "just be ready to grab me if I fall."

"Count on it."

Corban took a few more steps forward and grabbed the girl by the neck. The demon's cackling stopped as he realized what was going on, "You... the master's host?"

Corban ignored him and spoke in a demonic voice, "Your powers... give them to me, demon!"

A pained look appeared on the girl's face as red energy flowed from her body into Corban. His jaw ached as he continued to draw as much as he could. The demon once again cried out in pain as Corban worked, "You can kill me... but it will only make my master stronger... you will see!"

"I'll take my chances," Corban replied.

The demonic taint was slowly being erased. The girl began screaming and crying out for her parents. She was herself once again. The last of the demon's essence flowed out of her, leaving her soul intact.

Corban lurched backward as his body absorbed the demon's energy. His hands and arms glowed for a few seconds before fading. He leaned forward with his hands on his knees as though he was ready to throw up.

Mary moved quickly and grabbed his shoulder, "Corban, are you all right?"

The sound of heavy breathing was her only response.

"Corban!"

"I'm... still here," Corban replied. "Just give me a moment."

Mary nodded as he focused his mind on the task at hand. He fought through the madness that Baal had tried to inflict on his victim. His breathing became labored as he struggled to bring the energy under his control.

Mary looked up at Xaphine, "Can you do anything?"

Soul Siphon

"No," Xaphine replied. "He has to wage this war alone. If I interfere, I could wind up doing more damage than good."

"How so?"

"The demon's energy has become entwined with his soul. Only he can remove it. If I try, I could damage him."

"That won't be necessary," Corban replied as he stood up. "It's okay I got it."

Mary watched Corban carefully as he stood up, "Are you sure?"

Corban nodded, "Yeah... I think what you and I did, worked. The energy was a lot easier to control this time."

"That's great," Mary said in a relieved tone, "but I'm still going to keep an eye on you just in case."

"No problem."

Xaphine looked at him, "Did you get anything from him?"

"No..," Corban replied. "He was telling to truth. He doesn't know.

"Very well."

Xaphine turned and left the room without saying a word. Corban and Mary moved quickly to keep pace. As they exited, Xaphine put her hand on Abriana's father's shoulder, "Your daughter needs you."

The man's eyes opened and widened when he heard his daughter's cries, "Abriana, Abriana!"

Once they were out of sight, Xaphine turned and looked back at Corban, "Satisfied?"

Corban nodded, "Completely. Thank you."

"Keep an eye on those powers. You've clearly improved, but that's demonic energy."

"I will."

/

Soul Siphon

In Boston, Lihua, Johnny, and Vlad sat down for breakfast. Mike had joined them in the room. The mood was extremely somber as Mike spoke up, "So still no news from Corban or Mary..."

Lihua frowned, "I know... I wonder if they are okay."

"They've done a very good job of staying off the radar."

"Mary is no fool."

"Yes, this I know."

The way Mike was talking made Lihua uncomfortable. It was almost like he knew she wasn't telling him the truth but was trying to make her break and admit it herself. The air around her seemed to chill as her neck stiffened up. She looked across the table at Johnny who had a cautionary expression on his face as well, "Neither is Corban. I am sure they are doing what they think is best."

Mike nodded, "Yes, I'm sure they..."

Mike's words trailed off. Lihua watched as his face went pale and he looked like he was about to get sick. Before she could do anything, he turned away from the group and hid his face, which suddenly flickered brown. He grunted quietly as his face slowly twisted and changed. It was no longer a human's face, but that of a rabid animal.

Mike turned away just in time to keep the team from seeing it. Lihua looked at him oddly, "Mike, are you all right, what is wrong?"

"Nothing... I'm fine, just stay back."

Mike stumbled out of the chair and dropped to his knees. Johnny and Vlad stood up as Lihua came around the table, "Mike...?"

"I said stay back!"

His voice was no longer human. It sounded demonic, "Baal..."

Soul Siphon

Something was wrong. Lihua had a feeling that they were in trouble. She reached behind her and pulled a small pistol from her belt, "Mike... what is going on?"

Before anyone could react, Mike turned and grabbed her by the throat. His eyes looked more like a horses eyes, his nose had disappeared and was replaced by two large nostrils on his face, and his teeth were sharp, "You should really learn to listen when people tell you things! You might have lived a little longer!"

Lihua struggled under his grip, "Corban... was right..."

"Yes," Mike replied. "Corban was right. Did you think I didn't know what you were planning? Do you think I'm that easily deceived? Had you discovered anything, you never would have gotten the chance to report it to him... you still won't!"

Johnny and Vlad jumped up from their seats and tried to get to Lihua, but were thrown back against the far wall by an unforeseen force. Johnny got to his feet and screamed, "Lihua!"

As Mike tightened his grip, Lihua could feel her life force draining from her body. She quickly turned to Vlad and Johnny, "Ack... get out... of here, run!"

Lihua was choking to the point of passing out and forced out one more sentence, "You... ugh... You are no match for him! Run!"

Johnny shook his head, "Fuck no!"

He pulled a small pistol from under his shirt and fired three shots at Mike while Vlad grabbed a nearby knife and tried again to run to her. The bullets dissolved before getting anywhere near their target and Vlad was once again thrown backward.

Mike lowered Lihua to the ground and turned his attention to Johnny and Vlad, "Pathetic!"

Soul Siphon

Using her last ounce of strength, she jumped on Mike and attempted to use her powers to distract him. Her eyes glowed red as she focused her mind. She was desperate to distract Mike long enough to give them a chance.

It worked. Lihua's mind tricks gave Mike enough irritation to turn his attention back to her. Deep lines began to appear on her face as her red eyes met his yellow ones, "It is useless. You cannot save me... I am already dead. Go while you can... Find Corban... ack... tell him he was right... Go, please, save the world... save yourselves..."

Vlad grabbed Johnny and threw him over his shoulder, "Is time to go Johnny!"

Johnny fought back, "Let me go! We have to help Lihua!"

"Ve can't," Vlad replied. "Feel creature's power. Is too much for us."

Vlad disappeared out the door with Johnny kicking and screaming on his shoulder, "Let me go! We can still save her! There has to be a way, please Vlad... Let me go!"

Lihua always liked Johnny, even when he annoyed her. A warm feeling entered her heart as they escaped, knowing that they would not suffer her fate. They would survive to fight another day and hopefully avenge her death.

As her body collapsed around her, she turned back and looked at Mike with menacing eyes as her powers gave out, "My death here is irrelevant. My life ended long ago. I have been prepared for this for a very long time. I hope you are as prepared when Corban and Mary come for you!"

Mike focused even harder, draining the last of her energy. Her flesh turned to dust and her bones fell to the ground. Mike looked smugly at her remains,

Soul Siphon

"Such an honorable death... truly a shame that it was wasted."

Outside, Johnny and Vlad jumped in the dodge charger and sped away from the warehouse. Johnny had tears in his eyes as he looked back to make sure that they were not being followed. He felt a sharp pain in his abdomen and leaned forward as it spread throughout his body. It was as though he was experiencing painful cramps, but he knew what they were.

Vlad also experienced the pain but maintained his composure in order to continue driving. A tear fell down his cheek as he also knew what the pain meant, "Lihua has fallen..."

"Why..," Johnny demanded. "Why didn't you let us stay? We should have helped her! What does running accomplish? We lost…"

Vlad gripped the wheel tightly as he veered around the nearest corner. He was trying to maintain control of the powerful car while at the same time not draw attention to himself from the local law enforcement, "Ve tried. Me and Johnny vere no match for Mike. Did Johnny vish to suffer Lihua's fate? Lihua gave life to save Johnny. Lihua cared enough to do that."

"It's not right, damn it!"

"No is not... but is what happened. Ve need to find shelter."

Johnny shrugged, "Where can we go? He'll know where we are at all times."

"I do not sink zat Mike views Johnny and me as threat. Ve'd be dead if he did."

"We still need to hide."

"Ve need to find Corban and Mary... zey vere right all along. Ve have to warn zem!"

Soul Siphon

"But we have no idea where they are or even where to begin looking! If we don't find them soon, we could both be picked off fairly easily."

"Zen ve vill hide in public. Mike not attack us in view of mortals. Draw too much attention I sink..."

"That's a pretty big gamble."

"Is all ve have."

"What is he anyway? Who is he? He's clearly not the person we thought he was and that cannot be an angel."

"Is demon," Vlad replied. "No doubt about it. Question is vich demon?"

"Could he be the one that Corban's been hunting?"

"Is possible."

"What happened in there, it's like he suddenly lost control of his own power..."

"Maybe somesing Corban and Mary did?"

"You think they're on to this?"

"Hope so... zey must have felt Lihua's death as well."

"Then we don't have much time. We need to figure out a way to find them and warn them about this."

XVIII

Corban and Mary had returned to the yacht after the exorcism. They had more information now, but nothing was conclusive. They still didn't really know the true identity of the people that they had been working for or their intentions. Too many questions stood in the way of them finally being able to confront their friends.

They hadn't even had a chance to begin talking when an intense feeling of pain overcame Mary and Corban. It was more than Corban had experienced previously and he was unable to cope with it.

Mary caught him as he fell backward, but she too was clearly in pain. He could feel her arms shaking under the strain of trying to hold him up. She helped him sit down before her own legs gave out under her.

Xaphine's eyes narrowed in confusion, "What is it? What's happened?"

"I don't know… It's like a piece of me was just ripped away," Mary replied. "Something terrible has happened. I can feel it."

As the pain subsided, Mary got to her feet and adjusted the daggers on her belt, "I need to get to Boston. If something's happened, our friends will know about it... and who knows, maybe they've uncovered more info."

"Do you really think that's wise?" Xaphine asked.

Mary glared at Xaphine, "They're my friends... my family... Just because they chose not to follow us, doesn't mean that I don't still care about them, yeah? I need to make sure that they're all right!"

"Okay, I'll go with you," Corban said.

"No, Corban," Mary replied. "You stay put for now."

Soul Siphon

Corban stood up with an adamant stare, "Hell no, you don't know what you're walking into up there. This whole thing could be a trap!"

"I agree," Xaphine replied, "which is why only one of you should go. If you both go and are both caught, our cause is lost. Whatever you have to face there, you will do so alone. I've gone as far as I can here."

"I don't give a shit about some ancient decree," Mary replied. "All I'm concerned with is keeping my friends alive. I'm going."

"Let me go," Corban insisted. "I can..."

"You can what?" Mary asked. "I have stealth. I can sneak into the hideout if I need to and quickly get out again."

"Mike would pick up on you in a second! I can actually fight a demon!"

"A minor demon. We still haven't refined your powers. If Mike is what we think he is, your powers won't work against him. I'm the logical choice, yeah?"

"Logical or not... I... I don't want you going."

Mary kissed Corban on the cheek as a smile spread into her left cheek, "You're really sweet when you wanna be, yeah? I promise I'll be back before you know it."

Mary then turned to Xaphine, "Do not let him leave the ship."

Xaphine watched silently as Mary ran outside and jumped overboard. Xaphine then turned back to Corban, "Quite the imposing woman you've gotten yourself entangled with."

"Not another one like her in the world," Corban replied. "Now get out of my way."

"Not going to happen," Xaphine replied.

Corban allowed his hands to begin glowing, as his eyes almost bore a hole in Xaphine's chest. An annoyed look appeared on Xaphine's face as the sword she'd used to cut Corban's hand off appeared in her hand and began emanating bright flames, "Please..."

Corban sighed as he released his powers, "You better hope that she makes it back in one piece."

Mary quickly swam to the nearby shore and then built up speed running to get herself back to Boston as quickly as possible. The world blurred around her as she exceeded any humanly possible speed. She was determined to get to Boston as quickly as possible to make sure that nothing bad had happened to the people she cared about. She held out hope that this was nothing more than a fluke, but reality had never been kind to her.

The wind passing over her skin acted like the dryer at a car wash and quickly blew all the moisture from her clothes and hair. This made it easier for her to run even faster without any water weighing her down. *Sweet relief...*

Mary arrived in Boston within minutes of her run. She slowed herself down as she approached Southie and made her way over to Faye Street. She came around the corner and was shocked to see that both the front and garage doors were wide open. There were no lights on, and what looked like tire streak marks leading away from the building. Something had definitely gone wrong and Mary needed to know what it was. She waited another few minutes and surveyed the surroundings, but her fear was too much to keep in check.

Mary drew her daggers and looked around to make sure that no one was present who could see what was going on. Confident that there were no witnesses, she steeled her nerves and slowly made her way to the door. The area was eerily deserted for a mid-morning weekend day in the city. Her heart raced as she clenched her daggers and held them close to her sides. Her mental fortitude was barely holding on.

She approached the warehouse door from the side, careful to keep out of sight of anyone who might be waiting to strike. Her back was pressed against the wall while her eyes remained fixed on the door, waiting for someone, or something, to appear. Every moment she waited and watched felt like an hour.

After she decided that no one was coming out, Mary brandished her daggers in front of her and jumped through the doorway. She peered inside to see what had happened. A black void stared back at her.

Inside was nothing but darkness. Even the lights from the window were choked out by whatever was creating it. Every bone in Mary's body screamed at her to get out of there, but she needed answers. If anything had happened to her friends, she needed to know or she'd never be able to live with herself later.

Mary had never been afraid of anything. She had already experienced a horrible death, but something was different this time. Her thoughts dwelled back to the boy waiting for her on the yacht. They caused her to be filled with a sense of dread as she stepped into the darkness. It was not her death that she feared, but the prospect of not seeing Corban again. The new fear annoyed her, but there was nothing that she could do about it at that point.

The void was cold as ice. It choked all the light out of the room as though a black veil had been thrown over the window. Mary kept her blades close, but maintained a defensive stance, fully expecting an attack. She knew that she would have very little reaction time if something appeared out of the darkness, but even so, she had no intention of being caught off guard.

Soul Siphon

Mary's thoughts were interrupted when the door slammed shut behind her. The only visible exit had been cut off and she was now at the mercy of whatever was in the room with her. Goosebumps appeared on her arms and her breathing became labored. Her eyes darted left to right in a vain effort to try to see something in the darkness.

Her ears slowly picked up the sound of heavy breathing that caused a snorting sound. It wasn't human lungs that drew breath like this. Another sound followed the breathing. It was a thundering impact on the concrete floor, followed by another and another. *It sounds like someone let a horse in here!*

Whatever this creature was, it was huge. Each breath sounded like the low growl of a lion, while each breath out sounded more like a horse's snort. She gripped her daggers even harder when she realized that whatever was making that sound was coming closer.

Mary stiffened her jaw to prevent it from quivering. She was tired of waiting and was pretty certain that whatever was waiting in the darkness was trying to break her and topple her inner strength. She was not about to allow that to happen and called out in a demanding tone, "I know you're there. Show yourself!"

No response.

"You're not scaring me. Whatever you are, I'll take you down, yeah?"

It was a lie; she was very scared, not just for herself, but also for the people that were supposed to be there. She was slowly becoming convinced that at least some of her friends had not made it out alive. The tire tracks out front were pretty good evidence that someone had, but who?

A few more seconds of silence went by before she finally received a response. A pair of red eyes

Soul Siphon

appeared in the void. It was as though someone had just dipped a pair of golf balls in gasoline and lit them on fire, "Your words are brave, Mary. It's too bad the tone of your voice is unconvincing."

Mary's eyes narrowed, "Who are you?"

Again, no response.

Mary was about to say something when the light above her came on. The void didn't block it out but instead allowed it to act like a spotlight. The small beam of light hit the floor, revealing a small area of the main hall right in front of her.

Mary looked down and gasped. A skeleton lay in front of her, dressed in a leather outfit and clenching a pistol in its hand. The pistol was small and had Asian characters carved into the barrel.

Mary dropped to her knees and rested the neck of the skeleton on her arm. Dust fell out onto the floor as she carefully moved it, "No! Lihua... no!"

All the strength that she had mustered and every nerve that she had calmed had instantly unraveled. She cradled the skeleton in her arms as, for the first time in a very long time, tears streamed down her cheeks uncontrollably, "Why...?"

Mary clenched her teeth again and looked at the burning eyes, "Why, damn it? She was no threat to anyone! She was a good person! Why do this?"

"Even a sweet person can be dangerous, she learned too much and was about to get in the way. I could not allow that."

At that moment, Mary realized who she was speaking to, "Mike, is that you?"

"Not anymore... there is no longer a point to that disguise! You helped kill my friend and in doing so, weakened the power of the pit. You've forced my hand and sealed your friend's fate."

Soul Siphon

Mary carefully rested Lihua's remains on the ground before shooting to her feet, "What about Vlad and Johnny, did you kill them too?"

"I never had the chance. They ran like cowards at the first sign of trouble."

Mary looked down at Lihua's remains and shook her head, "Lihua, I'm sorry..."

Mary's blue eyes burned almost as brightly as those of the creature that was standing in the darkness, "Though we didn't always see eye to eye, Lihua was still my friend. Creature... you're going to pay for her death!"

The creature cackled, "She died long ago. I gave her life again and it was mine to take away. It was not hers to claim as her own."

A large tentacle-like energy stream appeared out of the darkness and wrapped around Mary's neck. Once firmly in place, it sent her flying back against the wall. The impact stunned her for a moment before she recovered and sliced the stream with her right blade, freeing herself.

Mary dropped to one knee and kept her left blade out in front of her for protection, though she was sure that it wouldn't do much, "If you want to kill me, you're going to need to do better than that!"

"As you wish..."

Three more tentacle-like energy streams shot at her from the darkness. Mary dodged the first one and twirled around the second, but couldn't get out of the way of the third. It struck her with incredible force and pinned her against the wall.

The first stream reappeared. This time, the end of it was a solid, sharp tip. It plunged into Mary's left shoulder before she could react. She screamed out in pain as the tip pierced her shoulder like a lance hitting

Soul Siphon

its target. The sharp tip drcve all the way through her shoulder into the wall.

Two more beams shot at her, one stabbing her in the right hip, and the other in the left arm. Blood gushed from the wounds as Mary stood pinned against the wall. She had been forced to drop the blade in her left hand because of the injury, but she still had the one on the right. The wounds were painful, but not fatal.

The creature laughed with a hint of disappointment, "I spent over a century training you and this is the best you can do? Have you really been spoiled this badly by your relationship with our master's host?"

Mary's eyes narrowed, "Master's host? I've heard that before... What the hell are you talking about, what does it mean?"

"Nothing that concerns you. I grow tired of this little game. You've lived long enough."

Two more streams shot at her, one towards her head and the other towards her heart. This time, Mary saw them coming and brought the dagger in her right hand around. She knocked away the two kill shots while simultaneously cutting away the ones that she had been stabbed with, "I don't think so! This life may not be mine, but I'm not done with it!"

Retracing her steps, Mary was able to map out exactly where she was in the main hall. She began picking up speed and ran to her guestimated location of the nearest window. The wound on her hip stung badly as she ran, but slowing now would come at too high a price. She had to keep going.

Mary counted a few steps and then dove forward. Her estimation was perfect. Her body crashed through the window and out into the sunlight where the creature could not follow in its current form. She

Soul Siphon

landed on the sidewalk with cuts all over her face and hands from the glass.

Covered in blood, Mary looked back up at the window where the burning eyes stared back at her. The level of malice was almost tangible, "Run little girl, tell the others of what you saw here today. It will do you little good."

Mary spit blood from her lips as she struggled to get up, "I'll be seeing you again..."

The creature scoffed as Mary regained her balance and limped away, "Soon enough, my girl... soon enough..."

Corban had been pacing back and forth for over an hour waiting for any sign of Mary. Xaphine sat down in one of the lounge chairs that were out on the deck and watched him fidget, "If you keep that up, you'll wear a hole in the hull and we'll sink."

"Something's wrong... she should be back by now. Something happened to her."

"You don't know that. Give her a little more time."

Corban couldn't shake the sense of dread in his heart, "Why did I ever let her go alone? Why didn't you help me stop her?"

Xaphine smiled, "You'll learn as quickly as... well you'll learn quickly that strong-willed women do what they want regardless of what anyone else says. Mary is no exception to that. If you plan on having a long relationship with her, you may want to get used to that fact now."

Corban groaned and turned toward the bar just off the deck in the superstructure, "I need a drink... I wonder what kind of booze our Chinese friends have stocked here."

"Just take it easy with whatever you choose."

Soul Siphon

"Yes, mom!"

Xaphine didn't respond as Corban left the deck. Like the rest of the yacht, everything on the inside was wood paneled. Corban ducked down behind the bar to see what was available. The usual arrangement of various hard liquors including scotch, rum, and vodka greeted him. There were also a few cases of beer in the fridge behind him.

Corban was about to give up and just grab the scotch when he heard a loud thud on the deck. He popped his head out from behind the bar and saw Xaphine looking down at the aft-most deck below her. She turned back to Corban with an intense look of concern, "Corban, you better get down there!"

Corban jumped out from behind the bar and took the nearby stairs down to the main deck as Xaphine jumped down. His jaw dropped open when the horrific scene revealed itself to him. Mary was on her hands and knees, soaked and covered in blood that was clearly her own.

Corban ran to her side, "Mary, oh shit!"

Mary looked up at Corban weakly, "You were right... you were right about everything..."

Corban held on to her arm, trying to give her some support, "What happened?"

"Mike is a demon... no doubt about it," Mary replied.

Corban picked her up and brought her into the main suite where he was joined by Xaphine. Mary had her eyes closed and was clenching her jaw from the pain, "Xaphine... I'm sorry... you were right, yeah? Mike... I can't believe it... he killed her."

Corban rested Mary on the bed and looked at her injuries, "Killed who?"

Soul Siphon

"Lihua," Mary replied. "That bastard... He sucked the life right out of her. All that was left was a dirty skeleton and a pile of dust."

Corban froze in place, "No..."

"What about the others... Johnny and Vlad?" Xaphine asked.

"He said he didn't get to them. He said that they ran," Mary replied.

Corban looked over at Xaphine, "But he will... we need to find them first, we'll need their help."

"I agree, but your place is here right now. She needs you. Those injuries were inflicted by a demon. They may take longer to heal. I'll find your friends and bring them back, don't worry. I'm willing to bet they're trying to find us right now."

"All right," Corban replied as Xaphine backed out of the suite.

The wings appeared on her back the moment she was outside. She took off with one powerful thrust of her wings and disappeared into the clouds. In her heart, she'd hoped that she would be wrong about all of this, but there was no denying it now. The legions of Hell were on the move once again and she was once again the one standing between them and victory with a bunch of unlikely allies.

Mary looked as though she was in extreme pain. She had holes in her left shoulder, arm, and her right hip. He hoped they would heal but only time would tell. She also had several small gashes all over her that would need to be tended to as well. A mortal human would have bled to death.

Corban frantically searched the room for something he could use to tend her injuries. He went through drawer after drawer in the dresser. Luck was with him as there was an advanced and fully stocked

first aid kit in the bottom drawer with plenty of
bandages and gauze. He pulled it up on the bed and
began to tend to Mary's wounds. It took him a moment
to decide where to begin as there were so many, but
the one on her hip looked like it was the worst.

Corban looked at her apologetically, "The pants
need to come off. I need to get to this wound."

"You've already been in my pants once, what do
I care?"

Corban rolled his eyes as he unbuttoned the
waist and pulled them off. The black bikini bottoms
that she had on underneath had been on her hip right
where the wound was. They had been torn and were
now being held up by the other side. Corban quickly
pushed the torn straps out of the way and began
dabbing the wound with a hydrogen-peroxide-soaked
piece of gauze.

Mary winced in pain as Corban went to work.
He cleaned the cut and saw that it was already
beginning to heal, though a lot slower than it should
have. He quickly tugged her briefs down off of her
hip, just low enough that he could wrap her wound in
gauze. She flashed him a dirty look, "Hey there!"

"They're in the way. I need to wrap this if it's
going to heal right." He said as he worked.

"I know…" Mary replied as her voice cracked
with the pain. "Ah… I'm just giving you a hard time,
yeah?"

Corban scoffed, "Funny that you can joke at a
time like this."

As he finished up, he gently pulled them back
into place. He then pulled up her shirt on the left side
and guided her arm out before gently lowering the bra
strap to get it out of the way of where he needed to
wrap. With each movement, Mary let out a breath of
pain, he could see that she was trying not to let the

Soul Siphon

pain get to her too much but it wasn't working, "Wow... you're getting a good show today, yeah?"

"What...? I don't know what you're talking about," Corban replied.

"Then why are you turning red?"

Corban touched his cheeks as he gave Mary an annoyed look. Mary laughed, "I'm just teasing."

"Well stop it. I'm trying to help you here."

"Sorry... I know this is serious... it's just better than the alternative..."

Corban looked up at her eyes. Though she tried to feign a happy, playful look, her eyes were filled with pain. Seeing the tears build up, he realized what she meant. He frowned as he continued to work, "No, I'm sorry. You're right; I know this must be hard for you. Losing Lihua sucks..."

He quickly repeated his treatment of cleaning her wound the same way he had for the one on her hip. He then helped her sit up while he bandaged the injury. He was careful as he wrapped it, trying not to hurt her.

While he worked, Mary pulled the shirt off the rest of the way, "It felt awkward the way it was."

"No problem."

Mary felt a tight tug on her shoulder as Corban finished up, "There we go... the bleeding should stop now."

Mary watched as Corban picked up another piece of gauze and poured more peroxide on it. He then dabbed it on her face as the cuts she'd received from the glass slowly began to recede. He knew that they weren't serious, but didn't want to risk her face being scarred.

Mary looked into Corban's eyes as he cleaned her face. There was an almost overwhelming sense of worry about him. She was very touched by his

Soul Siphon

concern, even if it was unnecessary, "I'm okay, Corban."

"I know you are, you're tough. The wounds are healing... but Lihua..."

"I wish I'd gotten there sooner."

"You don't know that it would have made any difference," Corban replied. "Most likely he would have killed you too. I doubt there was anything that you could have done to prevent this."

Mary continued to stare into Corban's eyes and said nothing else. He lowered the piece of gauze that he'd been using and was about to grab another when Mary got in the way, "Christ Mary, where would we be right now if that had happened? I can't do this on my own, you know that."

Before Corban could say anything else, she grabbed his neck and pulled him close. Their lips touched for a brief moment. Corban tried to pull away, but Mary wouldn't let him. A few seconds of levity was all she wanted, "Shh... it's okay, the pain is going away."

Corban gently laid her back and held on to her the same way that she had done for him when he'd lost his hand. Her wounds were not as severe, so she wasn't in nearly as much pain, but he still felt the need to keep an eye on her, "Corban... thank you."

"For what?" He asked.

"Just thank you."

"Okay..."

Corban raised his head slightly and looked at her, "What happened in Boston?"

Mary rested her head on the pillow, "It was there, lying in wait for me. The damn thing knew that someone would eventually come, so it waited..."

"What was it?"

Soul Siphon

"I don't know... a demon of some kind, but I've never seen one that powerful before. It choked all the light out the room. Even sunlight couldn't penetrate the void. I can't say for certain, but I get the feeling that it can't tolerate powerful lights in its demon form."

"We may be able to use that to our advantage in the fight."

"Maybe."

"Did you get a good look at it? Did it have the head of a horse or a mule?" Corban asked.

Mary shook her head, "I didn't see much... just a pair of burning red eyes and what sounded like an animal breathing."

"Round eyes, like a horses eyes?"

"Maybe... I'm sorry Corban... I don't know... they could have been horse eyes, I suppose. I really wasn't focused on it much. Too many other things going on, yeah?"

"Don't be sorry," Corban replied. "I shouldn't push. I'm just worried..."

"I'm worried too..."

"About?"

"You. He said the person that I have a relationship with is the master's host. That has to be you he was talking about."

Corban's lips twisted thoughtfully, "Could he mean the devil? Or Adramelech... I did host him for a while if you remember."

"But you think Mike is Adramelech."

"Yeah, I definitely think he could be."

"Then we may be facing off against the devil himself... He would be Adramelech's master!"

"It does sound like it," Corban admitted.

Terror entered Mary's heart, "Corban... I'm honestly scared for you."

Soul Siphon

"I know... but it'll be okay, don't worry. We don't know for certain what's going on yet. Let's worry about it when we know."

"I can't help it."

"Just relax and heal up," Corban replied.

Mary rested her head on the pillow and closed her eyes. Corban tried to go to sleep as well, but his mind was filled with too many questions. Who was Mike, how could Adramelech possibly have returned so quickly, and more importantly what was this about Corban being his master's host?

No matter how Corban traced the pattern, the answer was a dangerous one that had frightening consequences if they failed. He felt sick like someone had punched him in the stomach. He needed answers and was not going to get them there, but Mary needed him more than he needed those answers. They'd have to wait until she was better.

Corban closed his eyes and tried again to relax, "Mary?"

"Mm?"

"What do you think we'll do after all of this is over?"

"What do you mean?"

Corban turned on his side and spoke to her, "I mean that our powers were given to us by a demonic entity, our lives were returned to us in an unholy manner, and we're trying to kill the one who did this to us. Once that's over and done with, I don't think we'll even have a reason to exist."

"So?"

"So, do you think we'll be able to keep our powers... or our lives after this?"

Corban closed his eyes as he continued, "Do you even think we'll be able to remain together, or will we be ripped apart to go face whatever destiny has in store?"

A relaxed look came over Mary's face, "I don't know what the future holds, but damn if I'm going to let anyone rip you away from me, yeah?"

"Yeah," Corban agreed. "We'll find a way."

A perplexed look came over Mary's face, "You know, something doesn't add up here."

"What's that?"

"Well up until recently, we thought Mike was Saint Michael, yeah?"

"Yes."

"Then when we figured out the truth, we figured that Mike was some kind of benevolent spirit."

Corban looked at her oddly, "What's your point?"

"Well… now that we know he's a demon, it raises a pretty big question."

"What would that be?"

"Why he had us going around killing bad people. You would think that would be hurting his cause."

Corban shrugged, "Maybe he thought that the angels would overlook it? Maybe it made a good cover to get us to work for him, given how we all died?"

"Couldn't he have just said that they were bad people? It's not like we'd have known the difference."

"I would have, the moment I pulled away their soul."

"Maybe… "

"I have a feeling that this whole thing was a ruse to get a soul siphon that would wield the powers that he absorbed."

"Yeah, but why? What does he need all that extra power for?"

"The devil."

Soul Siphon

"What?"

"The devil... when I looked into Xaphine's memories, I saw that the devil had been stripped of much of his power when he was thrown into the pit. If he can possess a soul siphon with enough power, he can regain much of what was lost. Then he could attempt to retake the spirit world."

"Which would explain why you were referred to as his host... Oh, fuck..."

Corban sighed, "Look, we can't do anything about that now. Maybe we can ask him before we kill him. Either way, he's not going to get what he wants."

"I hope you're right."

Soul Siphon

XIX

Corban and Mary were roused by loud thuds and shouting on the deck. Mary pulled her pants back on, but her shirt was too damaged. She went through some of the drawers and found a few shirts for women. There was a spaghetti strap top that was black with lace trim. She carefully pulled it on as Corban sat up.

As she went to work on her hair, he turned her face towards him with his right index finger, "Let me look at you."

Corban quickly checked her injuries. The ones on her face and arms had healed up without a trace, but the larger ones were still pulling themselves back together. He sighed as he quickly replaced the bandages, "Xaphine was right, you're not healing as fast as I thought you would."

Mary shrugged, "Demonic attacks… At least the wounds are healing."

Her words didn't assuage Corban's worry. The paleness of his face was a clean giveaway, so she tried rubbing his arm gently, "I'm okay, really. I've looked a lot worse. This isn't the first time I've been injured by a demon."

"All right," Corban replied.

Mary stood up and walked towards the door with a slight limp. The wound on her hip was the worst off and still hurt, but she did her best to ignore, "Come on let's see what's going on."

Corban followed Mary out onto the deck. Vlad and Johnny were yelling at each other with Xaphine trying to calm them down. Their voices were filled with rage as they still hadn't sorted out their situation.

Vlad was on the defensive, "Been over zis before! Ve could not save Lihua!"

Soul Siphon

"We still should have tried! She's gone now... and we're on the run!"

"Zat is not my fault. Zer is nosing I could have done! If zer vas, I vould have. Lihua was little sister to me! But ve're here now."

Xaphine shook her head and turned to Mary, "I'm leaving them to you."

Vlad and Johnny were so heated that they didn't even notice Mary standing in front of them. After a few more minutes of arguing Mary finally had enough, "Both of you, shut up, yeah?"

Mary's harsh words startled Johnny as he turned to respond, "Mary! What the fuck happened to you?"

"I went looking for you..."

Johnny went pale, "You... went to the hideout?"

"I did, Mike got the jump on me. Cut me up real good, yeah?"

"Mary looks to be on the mend though," Vlad observed in a relieved tone.

"I am."

"Did you see Lihua?" Johnny asked.

"Yes, what's left."

Johnny shook his head, "Now what the fuck are we going to do? Lihua's gone and Mike isn't who we thought he was. What's worse, he gave us our lives and our powers... and proved that he can take them away if he so chooses. He taught us all we know... and now we're on the run from him!"

"We're still alive though," Corban replied. "We still have our powers and we now know where we stand. The days of us being manipulated are over."

"Are they?" Johnny asked, beckoning at Xaphine.

Corban's eye's narrowed, "We've worked with her so far and she hasn't given us reason to question her."

Soul Siphon

"Yeah, neither did Mike up until now."

"Look, this is stupid, yeah?" Mary stepped in. "We need to go after the people we know are bad guys instead of attacking each other. We also need to know which demon we're dealing with here."

"Any leads?" Johnny asked.

"We have three possibilities," Xaphine said, "Beleth, Barbatos, and Adramelech."

"Adramelech?" Vlad sounded shocked. "Does Corban sink...?"

Corban shrugged, "It's possible, but it doesn't seem like anyone got a good look at him! Mary only saw the eyes."

"I saw Mike's face," Vlad said darkly, "dark eyes and large stubbed nose with nostrils out to side."

Corban rubbed his forehead with his right hand, "Adramelech... no doubt about it."

Mary looked at Corban oddly, "Okay, I can stand it anymore. How do you know what he looks like?"

"I saw him..."

"When?" Mary asked.

The look in Corban's eyes became dark as he began to speak, "He came to me in my sleep. I saw his face as he entered my mind. When he restrained my spirit and ripped it away from my body, I saw him. When he took over and spoke to the people I loved or ripped me apart, I saw his hideous face in my mind. I know what he looks like and, make no mistake, I'll never forget it... not as long as I live. A part of him will always be there."

The dark look in Corban's eyes was a pretty good indicator that Adramelech may not have entirely cleared out when Corban pulled the plug, "I understand. We'll get him. Just remember your promise to me..."

Soul Siphon

"I never forgot."

"Good. I owe him some payback now too, yeah? Don't worry; he's not getting away with this. I don't like being used as a pawn."

Johnny looked out on the ocean, "So we know who we're dealing with, we know what he's capable of... now, how do we kill him?"

Xaphine stood next to him, "That is not an easy question to answer. Like angels, demons are almost omnipotent and are immortal. It would be nearly impossible for a mere mortal to do it... unless..."

"Unless vat?"

Xaphine shook her head, "My sword of flame will only banish the demon back to hell. It won't kill them."

"Well, then what other options do we have?" Mary asked.

Xaphine turned to Corban, "Your powers. You have the ability to rip souls from mortals. Those powers also allow you to steal the powers of immortals... which you tried to use on me."

Corban lowered his eyes, "You've seen firsthand how that goes. I've never been able to use that ability against anything as strong as Adramelech. Whenever I try to, the end result is always the same. Either I wind up being flung across the room with a burnt hand, or I'm flooded with memories that I do not want."

"But you can expel those memories. I've seen you do it."

"Yes...."

A sympathetic look came over Xaphine's face. Mary could tell what was coming and really didn't want to hear it. She knew that Corban was already well aware of their limited options, but that didn't make things any easier on them.

Soul Siphon

Corban rolled his eyes as Xaphine spoke, "I know you don't want to do this and I understand your reasoning, but you can remove the taint on your soul after."

Mary stepped between them and placed her hand on Corban's abdomen, "He is not ready for that. Taint or no taint, there is still the chance that he could be corrupted by the sheer amount of power that he would be stealing. How are you any different from Mike? He wanted to use Corban as a tool and now so do you. You say he can remove the taint later, but how many times are we going to make him do this before he damages his soul permanently or actually hurts himself. It's the same song and dance, yeah?"

"You're right," Xaphine conceded.

"Yeah... wait, what?"

"You're right; it's no different, other than our motives. –Corban, no one can force you to do this... it has to be your decision."

Mary turned and looked at Corban, shaking her head as a means of telling him that she didn't like the idea, "There has to be another way. This is how other soul siphons like Corban have been destroyed. I really don't think that this is a good idea at all."

An irritated look appeared on Xaphine's face, letting Mary know that she was done being nice, "Corban?"

Corban hesitantly agreed, "If it's the only way... then it's what we have to do."

A feeling of shock and anger came over Mary, "Corban, but you promised!"

"And I've kept that promise," Corban replied. "I haven't gone hunting Adramelech, just like I said, but we're not hunting him, he's apparently hunting us. I don't know what his issue is with me, but this will be our second encounter. I can't let him roam free. We

Soul Siphon

can run and hide all we want, but eventually, he'll find us. The only way we'll ever be safe is if he's dead. Please try to understand that."

At that moment, Mary was reminded of a little girl she'd known many years before when the team was still fairly new. The last time Mike tried to acquire a soul siphon. She remembered everything about the ordeal and it made her sick to her stomach. She went pale and her eyes began to water, "I think I need to be alone... do what you want, just call me when you're ready."

Without another word to anyone, Mary stormed off the deck into the owner's suite. Her wounds were still healing and she was still worn out. She lay back and released the tension from her chest. *History is about to repeat itself, just like it did before.*

Corban once again watched her disappear. The same feeling of frustration overtook him as he stood alone with Xaphine, "I'm sorry?"

Xaphine looked up at the Sun, "It's getting late. You can't attack the demon at night he's too powerful. You have to wait until daylight to even stand a chance. All of you, rest. We'll talk more tomorrow."

"All right!" Johnny replied. "Come on Vlad, I thought I saw a bar one deck up."

"Hopefully is not just Johnny's imagination again."

"We'll see..."

Xaphine shook her head and turned to Corban, "May I make a suggestion?"

"Sure," Corban replied.

"Go talk to her."

Corban looked over at the cabin, "She looked like she was ready to take someone's head off... I really don't want to be in her path when she's like this."

"Just because a girl storms off, it doesn't mean she doesn't want you to follow her. You're her strength and clearly, she's yours. You won't stand a chance against Adramelech if you're divided, believe me I know. He'll capitalize on any advantage that he can get and he will work you against each other if you are not unified."

"All right."

Corban immediately left Xaphine to her thoughts while he went and tended to his own problems. Xaphine turned back and looked up at the sky as the sun began to set. She kept her eyes closed as the wind blew by.

Corban cautiously opened the door to the suite and stepped inside. Mary was lying on the bed, looking up at the ceiling. Corban's presence didn't give her cause to move or change the mood of their environment. She was too angry, frustrated, and worried to be bothered by it.

Corban sat down next to her and placed his hand on hers. She immediately tugged her hand and turned away from him. Corban sighed, "Can we talk?"

"No."

"Okay… will you at least listen?"

"I listened to you once, Corban. I believed you when you said that your priorities had changed. I truly thought that you were being honest."

"I was being honest!" Corban shot back. "I meant it when I said that my priorities had changed. I'm not hunting Adramelech. He's the one coming after us!"

"I don't want you anywhere near him… I don't want to see you corrupted by him. It's cruel… I had to kill the last one… please don't make me do that again."

"What?"

Mary immediately sat up and placed her hands on his cheeks, "Take my memories."

"Why?"

"Just fucking do it, please!"

"All right fine!"

Corban immediately focused his mind, and carefully began to drain Mary's energy. Mary gasped slightly as she felt part of her energy being drained. It was more painful than last time, but she held her ground as Corban was transported several years back in time where he watched a scene from Mary's memory unfold.

Mary watched as Lisa pulled the last of Astaroth's energy from his form. It was an incredible strain on her life force, but she pulled as hard as she could. Mary could not have been certain, but it seemed like Lisa was smiling as she worked. She reached into the depths of the demonic being and pulled her hand back with a red orb in it. She held it up in triumph as the battle seemed to be over.

Astaroth screamed out in agony as he dissolved into dust. The sound of his voice was near deafening as it was slowly choked out by his own corrosion. As he decomposed, the wind picked up and carried his remains away. The group took it as an omen that all the damage he had caused would soon be similarly whisked away. It may have been a philosophical pipe dream, but there was always hope.

Lisa crushed the orb in her hand and watched as the power was slowly absorbed into her body. The familiar sound of glass shattering filled the air. Lihua raised her hand as she moved closer to Lisa, "Remember, my friend… focus. This is no ordinary soul. You may not be able to control it as easily. Please be careful."

Lisa was the newest member of the team. She had lost her life at the age of thirteen after a minor demon had torn her apart from the inside. Since then, she'd longed for the day that she would be able to get revenge. She breathed in deeply as the power entered her being, "It's time to end this once and for all. I can feel the power flowing through me... it's so intense. I feel like I can do anything. I can use this power... I can control it. "

"Lisa..."

"This is intense! I can take it and lay waste to the underworld. I can pay the devil back for what his minions did to me! I've transcended beyond all of them!"

A nervous look came over Johnny's face, "Lisa, you don't sound like yourself. Maybe you should release some of it before it's too late?"

"Release it?" Lisa scoffed. "Oh, Johnny... why? The power here is so intense. Just think of what I can do with it. I can stop evil... pain... and anything bad. Wouldn't it be better to use it and complete our mission? I could create a new world and base it on a strict code of law and justice."

"Whose justice?" Lihua snapped. "Yours? Do you truly believe that you are the person to make those decisions for everyone?"

"Why not? If people can't choose to do right, if the draw of evil is so strong, then they should have their choice revoked in favor of someone more enlightened. Otherwise, this vicious cycle will continue and more will suffer the same fate that we did."

"Lisa does not sound like Lisa. Zis is not good!" Vlad said in a worried tone.

Soul Siphon

"Where should I start? Perhaps I should begin with exterminating the murderers, then move my way down to rapists, abusers, adulterers, druggies, thugs… It would not take much."

Mary went pale and felt like she was going to get sick, "Lisa, stop! You're allowing that power to corrupt your soul! You think you're doing good, but it's pushing you to madness, yeah? Let it go, now! There are other ways to fight the good fight! This isn't worth it!"

"Not worth it, Mary?" Lisa scoffed as her eyes turned red. "Not worth it? Wouldn't you like to prevent another tragedy like the one you suffered? Think about it. In a world where people submit to the collective good, crime would be eliminated. No one would have to worry about getting hacked to death in a dingy back room!"

Then an idea popped into Lisa's head, "What if I could send you back in time to prevent it? Think of it… you could have your boyfriend back and the lives of the others could be saved. History would never know the name 'Jack the Ripper.' With this power, it could be possible!"

Mary clenched her fists as Lihua stepped forward, "No one person should ever have that kind of power. One person cannot determine what is best for everyone. It is simply impossible!"

Lisa shook her head, "You don't understand… you couldn't possibly comprehend the power I have been granted. I am transcending beyond your limited reasoning of power and morality, I… am no longer human. I am a…"

"Enough!" Mary shouted. "Lisa, you fucking release that power, now! Do you hear me?"

Soul Siphon

Lisa's head jerked so that she was looking directly at Mary. Her eyes glowed red and she thrust her arm forward, "Silence!"

Mary was hit by an unseen force and went flying backward. There was a loud thud as Mary's back struck the wall of the dilapidated building they had battled the demon in. She struggled back to her feet with a desperate look on her face, "Lisa… I took you under my wing, yeah? I taught you how to fight! You have to…"

Johnny ran at Lisa, only to be thrown back at against the wall in a similar fashion to Mary. Lihua shook her head, "No good… Mary, we're not getting through to her."

"Give her a chance…"

"… It's not happening. If we allow her powers to manifest much longer, she'll become so powerful that she herself could become a God! It has to be done, Mary. Quickly before it's too late!"

Mary squeezed her eyes closed as her face turned red, "Damn it Lihua, she's just a kid…!"

"You know what you have to do."

"Fuck you… no… no, I won't!"

"Mary!"

Mary didn't move. She didn't want to do it. Lisa wasn't evil, she needed help. Mary wanted to try again, but even she could feel the increase of energy that was coming from Lisa. It blazed off of her like light from the sun.

It was quickly becoming obvious that there was no way around it. Mary desperately tried one last time to reason with her friend, "Lisa, fucking listen to me… release the energy!"

Lisa wasn't listening anymore. Her eyes began to glow brighter than before and her skin was now emanating a bright yellow glow. Steam began to fly

Soul Siphon

from her body as the energy overtook her. She unleashed one more blast, blowing her friends back.

As Lisa became completely entranced, Mary got back to her feet, "Lisa... damn you... listen to me..."

Silence.

"Damn it, girl. Don't make me do this... Please!"

A white-hot energy pylon appeared above Lisa and stretched into the heavens. It would be the only answer that Mary would get. She knew that it was over.

Realizing that she had little other choice now, Mary stealthily moved behind Lisa, doing the best she could to not be noticed as Lisa focused on her new power. She slowly pulled one of her daggers from her belt. Her heart ached as she looked down at it, knowing what she was about to do. She focused her energy into the blade, making it lethal to even her own comrades. Her head began to spin as she struggled to put all thoughts out of her head and quickly ran the blade across Lisa's neck.

Tears flowed from Mary's eyes as she squeezed them shut. Her muscles tensed as she dug the blade into Lisa's skin. Lisa's neck cut like butter, releasing blood to flow everywhere. Within moments, her chest was stained crimson red.

Lisa tried to fight back, but it was too late. She dropped to her knees as she pressed her hands against the wound, trying to hold it closed. She gurgled as she tried to speak, but was unable to form words as blood poured over her fingers.

Mary knew that she couldn't take any chances and drove the blade into the young girl's back, pulled it out, and drove it in again. She had to make sure that Lisa was dead. If she was able to survive, she could heal herself and then be free to wreak havoc.

Soul Siphon

After the fourth stab, Lisa fell to the side. The energy that she had acquired flowed from her body and exploded in a mass of energy. Mary's face was covered with Lisa's blood. One final tear escaped her eye as she pulled the blade out. She had done what was necessary, but that provided her no comfort at all. She looked at the blade and debated driving it into her own chest in the hopes that it would end her suffering as well.

"Mary…"

Mary looked down and dropped to her knees. Lisa looked up at her weakly as her blood pooled on the ground, "Thank you…"

Corban gasped as he released Mary's energy and returned it to her. His heart ached and tears began flowing down his cheeks as he lowered his arms. Everything he had seen was taking its toll on him, "So that's why you were so bent out of shape about all of this... Lisa was your friend."

Mary fought through her own tears as she struggled to respond, "Yes, I'm the main assassin in the group. I was the only one who could get close enough to do the job and I hated it."

Corban lowered his eyes as it started to become clearer why Mary wanted him to stay away from Adramelech, "I'm sorry… it must have been…"

"You have no idea what it must have been like!" Mary shot back in a harsh voice. "She was a little girl. We had just taken down Astaroth. She had taken his power and his soul for herself…"

"I never used that fucking knife again… ever. I kept it in my room as a reminder of an evil that I could never forgive myself for. She was my friend and I killed her, just like that. She was just a kid."

Soul Siphon

Corban kept his eyes on Mary as she struggled to clear her mind. Maintaining her composure was an impossible task as each detail had returned and she was forced to relive it. This was the missing piece of the puzzle. This was why Mary was so cold to him when he first joined the group. His heart ached as he realized just how scared of the possibility of history repeating itself she was.

As her breathing finally calmed down, Corban rubbed her arm gently. She pulled away and shook her head, "If you go… if you do this, it will poison your soul beyond repair. Each soul siphon we brought on board was the same thing. It happened over and over again and in the end, I had to kill them myself. They were innocents and… Lisa looked up to me. I never understood why and I pushed her away as much as possible, but it never made any difference. She kept coming back…"

"Mary I…"

Mary lowered her eyes, "I'm a fool, yeah? I knew that this was inevitable and still let my guard down. I let myself fall for you, knowing what was to come. It's my own fault."

"I'm sorry, I didn't know," Corban replied as he carefully inched his way closer to her.

Mary closed her eyes and rubbed her forehead, "I don't know what to do here. My head is pulling me in one direction, telling me to separate myself from you… while my heart tells me not to… that you may be the one to overcome the corruption of power and even if you don't, the brief time I spent with you is worth more than the years I spent isolating myself. I've never been this bent out of shape. It's so stupid and it's maddening!"

"Okay Mary, you win."

"What?"

Soul Siphon

"What do you want me to do?"

Mary was surprised by his question. For the first time in a very long time, she wasn't sure how to respond, "What do you mean?"

"Do you want to run?" Corban asked. "We can run if that's what you want. I'm sure Xaphine can get a handle on things without us, she seems capable enough. We can go where ever you want."

Mary didn't respond at first. It appeared as though she was carefully considering his offer. A few moments passed as a pained expression appeared on her face. Her response was hesitant, "You have no idea how tempting that is. More than anything, I wish we could just run off somewhere safe… if such a place existed. Maybe we could finally live in peace, yeah? But it's just a fantasy… no… we can't. In my heart, I'd love to, yeah? But we can't. We'd never be free or safe. I know that."

"So then you'll have to trust me to be strong enough to overcome the draw and temptation of power."

"You talk like it's easy, yeah? It's not. I've heard these words before."

"I never said it was, but I don't have another choice, it seems. What else can I do?"

"Corban this isn't just like ridding yourself of something you don't want. The energy will test you. It will make you face your true self... and in the end, what kind of person you are will determine if you can release the powers are not. Honestly just being a good guy won't be enough. If you have the desire for power, even just the desire to use it for good, you will fall."

Mary felt a gentle touch on her right hand. She looked down to see Corban's fingers gently stroked hers, "Trust me?"

Soul Siphon

Mary pulled her fingers away and ran them over his cheek, "I… trust you. Believe me; I absolutely trust that you'll try. I guess I just wanted to hear you say that you'd run with me if I asked. Stupid, yeah?"

"No not stupid at all."

Neither of them said another word about it. Nothing either of them could say was going to change anything. Corban guided Mary's head back to the pillow and lay down next to her. He knew that they both desperately needed to relax.

Mary's eyes fluttered, but she appeared to be fighting sleep, "It's not fair… We have so little time together, yeah?"

Corban sighed as he looked at her, "Mary, I'll still be here when you wake up. Get some rest. You need to be healed up before this fight."

"I'm fine."

"Please?" Corban asked.

No reply.

"For me?"

Mary turned and looked into Corban's eyes. Finally, she sighed and relaxed, "Fine, for you…"

"Thanks."

Mary rolled over and placed her hand on Corban's chest. She stopped fighting and relaxed her body. A few slow breaths in and out were all it took for the tenseness of her muscles to slowly fade away. She slowly drifted out of consciousness, feeling Corban's heartbeat.

Corban watched her finally relax. He gently stroked her hair, desperately trying to get her to go to sleep. Mary had always been a very stoic person, so he had no clue just how high strung she could get. He was relieved when her blue sapphires disappeared behind her eyelids and she released one last deep breath.

Soul Siphon

With Mary finally attended to, Corban turned on his back to stare at the ceiling. He had put on a strong face, but even he knew of the dangers that came with confronting Adramelech. He was an ancient demon with immense power.

Corban had defeated him once before, but it was at the cost of his own life. Now he was being asked to take the creature on in full force yet again. He was barely twenty-two years old with powers that he'd yet to harness, how could he be expected to win? Could he even do it? He began to question how any of them were going to be able to walk away from this one, especially if he had found a way to take physical form.

Every scenario Corban pushed through his head spelled doom for the team. They were a man short, leaderless, and their guide was a dark angel that had so far proven to be extremely abrasive herself. The team didn't trust her and with the exception of a few memories, he wasn't sure that he should be either.

The ceiling proved to be poor company and offered no solutions to him. He continued to stare at it for a few more minutes before shaking his head. *What the hell am I doing?*

He turned and looked at Mary, who looked uncharacteristically peaceful as she slept. He gently touched her cheek and rubbed gently until it was cupped in his hand. Though asleep, she instinctively grabbed his hand and held it on her face.

Corban sighed as he watched her. *I am no martyr. There has to be another way!*

XX

The fight had been tough, but they had finally brought Adramelech to his knees. Everything came down to this pivotal moment. Mary watched as Corban extracted the last of the demon's energy. The strain on Corban's spirit was intense. Beads of sweat formed on his brow as the demon fought back. It was a futile effort, given how badly he'd been weakened, but it was obvious that Corban was not going to get his power without a fight.

Relief finally came when a red orb appeared in his hand. He held it up in triumph as the battle seemed to be over. All that remained now was for Corban to absorb the energy and banish Adramelech into oblivion.

Adramelech screamed out in agony as he dissolved into dust. The inhuman roar echoed across the land as he slowly vanished. The wind picked up and carried his remains away to be spread across the land and forgotten. The group took it as an omen that all the damage he had caused would soon be similarly whisked away.

Corban smiled gleefully as he crushed the orb in his hand and watched as the power slowly swirled around his arm. It parted into two bolts that swirled around him until eventually disappearing into his body. Johnny raised his hand as he moved closer to Corban, "Remember buddy... focus. That's no ordinary soul. If things get to be too much, release some of the energy. You don't want to let it get out of control..."

Corban looked over at Johnny to reassure him that he still had control, "I know... I got this... It's time to end it. I can feel the power flowing through me... it's intense. I feel like I can do anything. I could restore us to the lives we lost! I could go back and change everything!"

A nervous look came over Vlad's face, "Maybe Corban should release some power now? Like right now maybe?"

"Release it?" Corban scoffed. "Why would I do that? I can control this. The power here is so intense. Just think of what I can do with it. I can stop evil… pain… and anything bad. I could create a new world and base it on a strict code of law and justice."

"Fuck man, whose justice?" Johnny asked. "Yours?"

"Why not? If people can't choose to do right, if the draw of evil is so strong, then they should have their choice revoked in favor of someone more enlightened. Think of it, no war, no pain, no murder, no rape, no betrayal, nothing!"

"You got control over nothing!"

Mary realized what was happening. This was Lisa's fall all over again, except now Corban had replaced her. Terror filled her heart as she realized what was about to happen. The hair stood up on the back of her neck as she quickly stepped forward to confront Corban, "Listen to me Corban, please hear my words. You can't do this! You need our help. Please…"

It was like he didn't even hear her, "Where should I start?"

"Corban?"

"Perhaps I should begin with exterminating the murderers, then move my way down to rapists, abusers, adulterers, druggies, thugs…"

"Corban, you listen to me right now, yeah?"

"It would not take much."

Mary went pale and looked like she was going to get sick, "Corban, this is happening just like I told you it would. It's exactly the same as what I showed you, how can you not understand? You're allowing Adramelech's power to corrupt your soul! You think you're doing the just thing, but it's pushing you to madness, yeah? Let it go, please! You're smarter than this!"

Mary fought back tears, refusing to show weakness, even though her voice was slowly betraying her, "I know you mean well, but it won't work, trust me! We've been through this before, more than once!"

"Won't work, Mary?" Corban scoffed as her eyes turned red. "How do you won't work? Wouldn't you like to prevent another tragedy like the one you suffered? Think about it. In a world where people submit to the collective good, crime would be eliminated."

Mary lowered her eyes, "I've heard this all before Corban, more than once. Too many false promises have been made, yeah? Too many friends have died because they thought that they could handle this. Well, they couldn't and neither can you! Release it while you still can!"

A disappointed look appeared on Corban's face, "You just don't understand… you couldn't possibly comprehend the power that I have been granted. I am transcending beyond your limited reasoning of power and morality, I…"

"Enough!" Mary shouted. "Corban, you made me a promise! Now keep it and release the power. Focus on me and release them, please! Remember…"

Corban's eyes glowed red and he thrust his arm forward, "Silence!"

Mary went flying backward and struck the wall of the dilapidated building they had battled the demon in. She struggled back to her feet with a desperate look on her face, "Corban please… I… I lo…"

Soul Siphon

Johnny ran at Corban before Mary could finish her sentence, only to be thrown back at against the wall in similar fashion. There was no getting around the reality of the situation. They had lost Corban just like they had lost the others.

Vlad sighed as he turned to Mary, "Is no good… ve're not getting through to Corban."

"Give him a chance…" Mary pleaded

"Mary… is not happening. If ve allow Corban's powers to manifest much longer, Corban will become so powerful that he will become unstoppable!"

Mary squeezed her eyes closed as they teared up, "Vlad, please don't make me do it. I can't… not him… please…"

Johnny struggled back to his feet, "You have to. You're the only one who can! I'm sorry Mary… but there's no way around it."

Mary didn't move. She didn't want to do it. Her chest felt like a gaping maw. If she killed Corban, she'd be killing herself. He was the first true connection she'd had in many years and losing it now would be the last nail in the coffin for her humanity, "No… no… I can't do it. I won't! There has to be another way."

"Mary please, you have to."

"No!"

"Mary, zis is our only chance!" Vlad insisted.

There was no way around it; even Mary was beginning to accept that. She desperately tried one last time to reach the boy, "Corban, please… release the energy! Don't make me kill you. Please…"

Corban wasn't listening anymore. His eyes began to glow brighter than before and his skin was now emanating a bright yellow glow. Steam began to fly from his body as the energy overtook him. Corban unleashed one more blast, blowing his friends back.

Soul Siphon

As Corban became completely entranced, Mary got back to her feet, "Corban… forgive me… I'm so sorry…"

No response.

"Goodbye…"

A white-hot energy pylon appeared above Corban and stretched into the heavens. The clouds around the pylon began to twist and turn, creating a vortex around the light. It was as though he was reshaping the sky with his power.

Realizing that she had little other choice now, Mary stealthily moved behind Corban, doing the best she could not to be noticed as he focused his new power. Mary slowly pulled one of her daggers from her belt. Her heart ached as she looked down at it, knowing what she had to do. She charged the blade with her own energy, making it capable of killing Corban. Her heart ached as she struggled to put all thoughts out of her head and quickly ran the blade across Corban's neck.

Tears poured from Mary's eyes and she let out a loud, painful grunt as she tugged on her blade. His skin cut like butter, releasing blood to flow everywhere. Corban realized what was happening and tried to fight back, but it was too late. The damage had been done and there was no way to stop it.

Corban dropped to his knees as he pressed his hands against the wound, trying to hold it closed. Mary couldn't take any chances and drove the blade into his back, pulled it out, and drove it in again. She had to make sure that Corban was dead. Tears fell from her eyes as she plunged the dagger in again and again. With each stab, her own spark of life began to vanish.

After countless stab wounds, Corban fell to the side. The energy flowed from his body and mixed with the pools of his blood on the ground. Mary was left standing in front of Corban's near lifeless body. Tears dripped down her cheeks. She had done what was necessary, but that provided her no comfort at all. She looked at the blade and debated driving it into her own chest in the hopes that it would end her suffering. She had already ripped out her own heart. No physical pain could possibly be worse. Her eye ran across the sharp edge of the blade as her hand began to shake.

"Mary…"

Mary looked down and dropped to her knees, "Corban?"

Corban looked up at her weakly as his blood pooled on the ground, "I thought we had something… I thought you…"

"No…"

The light left Corban's eyes before Mary could say anything else. The scene around her faded to black in sync with the loss of life. Mary found herself alone in a black void, "No!"

Mary gasped as her eyes opened. She shot up in a cold sweat and covered her eyes with her hands. After a few minutes of coming to terms with what she'd seen, she looked back down at the bed. Corban was sleeping soundly and actually looked like he was at peace. It was a small miracle that her abrupt awakening had not disturbed him.

Mary's heart ached as she looked at him. She realized that there was no way she could do it. If Corban's fate followed Lisa's path, there was no way that she could bring herself to kill him. She knew it meant that the world would most likely be destroyed, but there was no way that she could kill Corban. Asking her to do so would have been nothing short of asking her to cut off a limb. There had to be another way and fortunately for her, the answer was on the aft deck.

Soul Siphon

Mary carefully got out of bed, straightened up
the straps on her shirt, and crept to the door. She
looked back as she opened it to make sure that Corban
had not been disturbed. She didn't want him knowing
what she was doing. Fortunately, he appeared to be
fast asleep. Unwilling to waste another minute, she
slipped out quietly and made her way out on deck,
closing the door behind herself.

Xaphine was near the aft railing, leaning over
the side. She seemed focused on something, but it was
not immediately clear what. Anyone else might have
stopped to question it, but Mary could not have cared
less. She had a mission and nothing was going to deter
her from it. *Perfect, no one will hear us.*

Mary stepped out a few more feet until she was
standing directly behind Xaphine. The angel either
didn't sense her presence or simply didn't care that she
was standing there. Mary was hardly a threat to her, so
why should she be concerned?

Mary took another step, at which point Xaphine
spoke up, "I know why you're here. You want
something from me."

"Yes," Mary replied.

"You're willing to make a trade for that precious
item, correct?"

"Yes."

Xaphine sighed, "Mary, I can't save Corban.
That's beyond my power."

"I don't care how you do it," Mary insisted. "Go
before your boss, the devil, Adramelech, I don't
fucking care! I'll trade my soul for his life. It's of far
more value to me."

A surprised look came over Xaphine's face,
"You have only known him for a mere few months!
Why is this so important to you?"

Soul Siphon

Mary closed her eyes and turned away, "I've lived a long time… a long time. I've spent twenty-five years in some of the worst conditions imaginable and then a hundred years alone. We may have only been together for a short time, but we've grown so close. I wouldn't trade that time for anything and I… I…"

Mary's face went red. She was frustrated and her inability to put into words how she felt only made things worse. She turned and began to walk away, "Oh fuck it! You wouldn't understand!"

"You're wrong…" Xaphine replied as she looked back up at her star. "I actually do understand, more than you know."

Mary froze in place, turned around, and looked at Xaphine oddly. The angel had a sympathetic look on her face, "I too have lived a long time… and I have been blessed with experiences that most other angels never have… but I can't help you. 'My boss' won't allow me to interfere in this world."

"Then don't go to him!" Mary insisted. "I know you have contacts on the other side! Corban told me everything. I'm offering myself as payment, yeah?"

Xaphine shook her head, "I can't. I won't make a deal with the demons. That could turn a bad situation even worse and it would be considered treason. How do you think Corban will react when he finds out what you've done?"

"I don't care," Mary replied.

"You should… he'll search the world for you and follow you into the depths of Hell to retrieve you from the devil. When someone cares that much, no force in Heaven or Hell can keep them apart, believe me I know. I won't allow something like that to happen. It causes too much damage and way too much hurt on people who don't deserve it. That is absolutely out of the question."

Soul Siphon

"Please…" Mary pleaded. "I'll do whatever you ask. Why won't you save him?"

"Mary, I want to help you, I really do, but my hands are tied. I can't take on Adramelech here as he is now and I can't interfere in the fight to come. Whenever we do, bad things happen. No matter how good our intentions are."

At that moment, Mary pulled a knife that she'd had hidden behind her back, grabbed Xaphine, and held the knife to her throat, "I asked nicely, yeah? Now I'm not going to be so nice! For the love of God, help us!"

Xaphine smiled and pressed her neck against the blade, "Go ahead."

A surprised look came over Mary's face, "What?"

"Go for it, you clearly think you can. So go ahead and try."

"You have a death wish, yeah? You know I'll do it!"

"Yes, I believe you will."

Mary closed her eyes, "All right bitch. If this is the way you want it..."

Mary braced herself and began tensing her muscles to pull the blade across Xaphine's throat. As she prepared to finish Xaphine off, her arms tensed. She was not certain that she could do it. She had been a vicious killer for many years, but never a monster. Killing Xaphine could push her to that level.

Mary's moment of hesitation was all that Xaphine needed. She knocked the blade away and hit Mary in the face with the back of her head. The force of Xaphine's blow knocked Mary across the deck. Within seconds, she found herself on her back with the same knife to her own throat. The tides had been completely turned.

Soul Siphon

Xaphine's eyes were glowing red as she looked down at Mary, "Bold… I am the general of the finest armies in existence and you thought you could take me down… with a sharp piece of metal? The arrogance!"

Mary clenched her teeth and raised her chin, further exposing her neck, "If you won't help me, then I have little to lose, do it!"

"Stop!" An angered voice called out from across the deck.

Xaphine looked up in time to see a blast of energy strike her in the chest. She was thrown against the railing, releasing Mary from her grip. It took her a moment to recover, but when she did, the red in her eyes was gone, "I apologize… sometimes my dark side gets the better of me… it's not always the easiest thing to control."

Corban knelt down next to Mary, "Are you all right?"

"Yes… but don't be mad at Xaphine. I attacked her. She defended herself."

"Why, what the hell's going on here?"

Xaphine pushed herself back to her feet, "She wanted me to put a stop to this, as if I had that kind of power."

"Mary?"

Mary shook her head, "I don't care what you say… I've heard it before, all of it. Too many times before I've had to take the lives of people who arrogantly thought that they could resist the temptation of that level of power. It always ends up the same way."

She looked up Corban, "They were my friends. You're much more than that, yeah? I can't allow that to happen this time… I won't."

Soul Siphon

Xaphine eyed them both for a moment before responding, "Corban, you're aware of her feelings for you?"

"Of course I am."

"And you share those feelings?"

"... yes, completely."

"Then that is your best chance for survival."

"Just hope it'll be enough," Mary snapped.

Corban placed his hand in Mary's, "Faith?"

Mary finally gave in, "All right Corban, you win. I believe in you, I'll do my best to keep the faith."

"I have a hard time believing that after what I just saw. We've already been over this."

Mary was taken aback and angered by his words, "That's your problem, Corban. I trust you, I believe in you, but if there is any way to avoid putting you to the test, I would rather do that. Your life is worth too much to take this risk!"

Corban sighed, "Mary... I wish I could say something that would ease your concerns, but I wouldn't know where to start. All I can do is ask you to trust me. When the time comes for me to face this down, I'm going to need you to be strong."

"I know that... I know... Corban, I trust you, but I'm staying close to you."

"Good enough thanks," Corban agreed.

"Vell, since ve are all friends again, does some von vant to tell me ze plan?"

Johnny and Vlad appeared out of the darkness. Apparently, the commotion on deck had stirred them. Xaphine nodded to them, "I think the best bet would be to mount a final assault at sunrise. If he's still at your old base, we can flush him out quickly."

"Sounds good," Johnny said. "How long do we have?"

Xaphine turned as the first light began to peak over the horizon, "We should head out soon... very soon."

The next morning, as the Sun came up over the horizon, the group prepared to depart for Boston. They were each armed with what weapons they'd gotten away with. Mary only had one of her twin kodachi blades, having lost the other one during her first encounter with Adramelech. Johnny and Vlad were forced to use the guns they found on the yacht. Johnny grabbed a pair of pistols while Vlad, favoring long guns, was forced to grab an SMG that was about as close as he was going to get to his old gun.

Armed as well as they could be, the group set off for Boston. Xaphine flew by herself while Mary helped Vlad and Corban carried Johnny. They regrouped at the end of Faye Street, which was eerily deserted.

Corban stepped out in front of the group. Unlike the others, he kept his weapons holstered and sheathed. He knew better; the weapons weren't going to save them against Adramelech. This wasn't the average bad guy that they'd faced down before. He knew that Mary understood it as well, but even so, he knew that she'd never give up her dagger. For some reason, the dagger appeared to comfort her, so he didn't question it.

The doors were still open on the warehouse. Nothing had changed since Mary had been there. It was quite ominous to look at. They crouched down, single file, and crept by the windows to the door.

Mary used her speed to push herself to the other side of the door without being seen. She knelt down on the other side of the door and looked at Corban, signaling that she was ready to go. He had a feeling that this was useless posturing as the creature most likely already knew that they were there, but she played along.

Corban looked back at the rest of the team. Vlad and Johnny hunched over right behind Corban while Xaphine, whose wings had once again disappeared, remained behind them. As far as the team was to be concerned, she was a non-combatant in this fight. It was a fact that appeared to annoy Xaphine greatly and Corban could certainly understand why. Being a warrior in her own right, having to hold back while a group of humans went in would be a major insult. Unfortunately, there was no way that she could interfere.

Mary blew Corban a kiss before she sprung forward and charged into the building. Corban followed closely behind as she twirled her wrist, bringing her sword to bear, "Adramelech!"

The room was empty. There was no voice, no darkness, and even Lihua's remains were gone. Corban took a quick look around, scouting out any potential ambush sights that Adramelech could be hiding in, "Adramelech!"

He turned back to Xaphine, "Anything?"

Xaphine shook her head, "If he's here, he's managed to shroud himself."

"Is that even possible?" Johnny asked.

"For most... no, but Adramelech has existed for many ages. It's impossible to measure how far his powers have grown during his time in the pit."

Vlad and Johnny split off and headed to the back of the room, "We'll take the basement. You guys should probably check the back rooms up here."

"Be careful," Corban replied.

"I vill, but Corban never know vith Johnny."

Soul Siphon

Johnny rolled his eyes as he led Vlad to the lower level. It was only one flight of stairs, but the way was pitch black and it didn't appear as though the lights were working. No matter how much their eyes adjusted, they could not penetrate it. The atmosphere got cooler with each step they took. Each step created a hostile, ominous feeling in both of them. Could the creature have made its way into the basement?

Johnny proceeded forward with Vlad close on his heels. The look on Johnny's face as he relied on his memory to guide him through the darkness was one that was completely absent of emotion. He wasn't afraid, fear was a waste of time and he didn't have any to spare. He kept going forward as, little by little, he disappeared from view.

Vlad began talking to himself in annoyance, "Take ze basement, Johnny says... Why does Johnny's mouth alvays seem to get me into trouble?"

"Shh!" Johnny replied sternly out of the darkness. "I think I hear something."

Johnny took a few more steps forward but did not see anything and whatever noise he had heard was completely gone. A chill went down his spine, "The thought occurs to me... if we were to find Adramelech down here, what are we going to do about it?"

Vlad shrugged, "This Johnny's idea. Not a very good one, but ve do vat ve can."

"Of course," Johnny replied. "Whenever it's a good idea, 'is Johnny and Vlad's idea zat ve both came up vith,' but when it's a bad idea, you separate yourself from it as fast as humanly possible! Why is that?"

"I not know vat Johnny's talking about."

"No, of course not."

Johnny rounded the next corner into one of the rooms they used for interrogation. He tried the switch on the wall, fully expecting that it would not work. There was a slight click as the switch went into the 'on' position, but nothing happened. They were still completely encased in darkness.

"Perhaps ve should try ze circuit breakers?"

"Good idea, why don't you try that, since this time it's your idea? I'll cover you."

Vlad grumbled as he walked quietly to the next room with Johnny following him this time. Vlad quietly whispered to himself as they moved, "I need to learn to keep big mouth clcsed. I get in less trouble zat vay..."

Johnny turned back and listened behind them one last time. As far as they could tell, there was nothing following them. He followed closely behind Vlad, fairly confident that if anything was planning on attacking them, it would have done so by then. Vlad and Johnny had no real way of defending themselves in the darkness, so they would have made easy targets. Even so, Johnny kept his guard up.

Vlad felt his way around the next hall until he came to the end and felt the large metal box that was bolted to the wall. He slid it opened and found the small flashlight that had been left inside in case of emergencies. Thankfully, it still worked. The inside of the box lit up, revealing the black switches for each room on the inside.

Johnny stayed at the corner of the hallway in case anyone showed up. He watched as Vlad flicked each switch from top to bottom, hoping that it was making some difference in those areas of the hideout and if there was a demon prasent, it would soon be revealed. There were two left before the basement lights. He flicked the nearest one and waited to see if anything would happen. There was a slight humming sound which got louder as he moved to the next one.

Soul Sphon

Finally, he was on the basement switch. He suddenly felt intense hesitation about turning the last switch. It was a suspenseful feeling like the times he had watched an action movie where the hero had to choose whether to cut the blue or red wire. He sighed as his finger hovered over the switch. He found himself unable to press the button. His finger shook as he looked at it.

"Hey asshole, what are you doing over there? Find some Vodka or something? Come on move it!"

Vlad's hesitation was quickly replaced with frustration. He applied a slight pressure to the switch and flipped it. There was a slight metal clanking sound as the switch flipped into the on position.

Nothing.

The lights didn't come on at all. No electricity flowed as the two friends stood there waiting. The low hum continued for a few moments, but it appeared as though nothing further was going to happen.

"Did you check the circuit breakers, yet?"

"Yes, zere not vorking! Now shut your mouth!"

"Great… well, might as well make our way back upstairs then. This is giving me the creeps."

Vlad shrugged and began to turn away when a flash of energy flickered through the box. The hair stood up on the back of Vlad's neck as he turned to see what was happening. Before he had a chance to react, the box exploded in a rainstorm of sparks. Vlad blocked his eyes as the room was momentarily lit up as bright as day.

The moment Johnny and Vlad disappeared, Corban waved his arm, beckoning the remaining team to the kitchen and dining room. Mary followed close, but Xaphine stayed behind. She stood between the couches and refused to move any further. Corban

Soul Siphon

looked at her for a moment, trying to figure out what was going on, "Not coming?"

She returned Corban's gaze. The look on her face was completely emotionless as was the tone of her voice, "This is as far as I dare go. I can't risk upsetting the balance any more than I already have. I will monitor your progress from here."

Mary grimaced in annoyance as she turned to follow Corban. No doubt she felt that Xaphine's refusal was nothing short of cowardice. However, challenging the angel was pointless; he'd seen how easily she took Mary down.

The hallway forked in two different directions, to the right was the kitchen and the dining areas while to the left were the holding cells and the armory. Both hallways were illuminated by the light which shined through the windows, indicating that the void which had surrounded Adramelech was not there. At least for the moment, it appeared that they were safe.

"Take the armory. I'll check the kitchen and the dining room," Corban said, keeping his eyes forward.

"All right… be careful," Mary replied. "I'm beginning to think that we're not going to find anything. Even so, don't take any chances. This isn't something you can take on alone. Call me immediately if anything looks suspicious."

"You know I will."

Corban proceeded down his hallway and quickly entered the dining room. Except for the lights being off, it looked like it normally did. The table and chairs were all as they should be. It was like the team had never left. There was no demon to be found there.

He moved to the kitchen where he was greeted by an unwelcoming aroma. The pungent stench of filthy dishes and utensils hit him the moment he entered the room. Corban's eyes watered and he felt like he was going to vomit. He covered his mouth and nose with his arm and took a few more steps forward. *Oh dear God...*

A small amount of light bled through the square window in the corner, appearing like a spotlight on the tiled floor of the galley kitchen. The buzz of a fly that was no doubt in a state of euphoria over the mess, could be heard somewhere in the room. *Ugh... this is actually worse than how this place smell after Vlad cooks!*

Corban's eyes glanced around quickly, making sure that there was nothing threatening nearby. When his nose finally couldn't stand the smell anymore, he stepped out into the dining room. The air was much clearer and gave Corban some relief as he took a couple deep breaths, "Kitchen is secure!"

"Armory is also secure!" A voice responded from down the hall.

Corban left the kitchen and was relieved by the scent of fresher air as he moved back through the dining room to the hallway. He stepped outside where he was met by a dark black figure at the end of the hall, "Mary?"

"Yeah, I'm here."

Corban breathed a sigh of relief as he walked towards her. She looked at him oddly as his features became more visible, "Thought I was a demon, yeah?"

Corban smiled, "The thought has crossed my mind a few times since the day I met you."

Mary gave Corban annoyed look, "So it looks like he's not here... at least not on this floor."

"I wonder where he would have gone off to. If he were still in the building, we would have seen him the moment we came through the door. I hope we would have, anyway."

"We had to check... so what's next?"

Soul Siphon

"Well we've got Vlad and Johnny downstairs, should we head up to the dorms? I get the feeling that we'd know by now if something were down there."

"All right."

Mary and Corban headed out past Xaphine who was now sitting on one of the couches. She appeared to be in a trance-like state. It was almost as though she were completely unaware that they were nearby.

Mary looked at her oddly and waved a hand in front of her face. When she didn't respond, Corban spoke up, "Xaphine, are you okay?"

Xaphine didn't move and didn't open her eyes. The only response they got was a low growl that uttered only one word, "Dormitories."

"He's there?"

Xaphine fell quiet.

Corban looked over at Mary in alarm, "We'd better get up there!"

Corban turned to the elevator, but noticed that Mary hadn't moved, "Mary?"

Her breathing became erratic as she took a step forward, "Corban... maybe this isn't such a good idea? If he's up there... you're going to have to fight him..."

Corban nodded, "Yeah, that's been the plan all along."

"Corban... I don't know."

"Relax," Corban said in a comforting tone. "It'll be okay."

"I hope so."

The power was still out, so the elevator would not work. Even if it did, Corban decided that it probably wasn't the best idea. Being trapped like rats in an enclosed space that dangled from a cable was not a situation that they wanted to be in with an aggressive demon on the loose. Instead, Corban led Mary to the stairwell a few feet over to the side.

Soul Siphon

Mary stood on to the left side of the door, while Corban took the right. They looked at each other for a few seconds before Corban inched forward, "All right, my turn…"

Corban threw the door open and stepped inside. He charged his powers and kept his hands open at his sides, ready to absorb anything or anyone that came at him. Just like almost everywhere else in the building that was not illuminated by sunlight, the stairwell was dark to the point of blindness. They would have to rely on their memory in order to find their way to the dormitories.

Corban extended his hand and probed the darkness for the handrail that would lead him to the next floor. He then reached behind himself to find Mary. A warm feeling ran through his fingers as her hand grabbed his. She stayed close, not wanting to lose him in the darkness and give the demon a chance to separate and attack them individually. Though it was unlikely that she could do much, two bodies were better than one, even against a demon.

Their footsteps echoed on the dark staircase as they slowly made their way up the first flight of stairs. Each echoing step made Mary flinch. Corban could feel her press against his back. Her right hand was clenching her dagger, and her eyes continued to dart around the room in a panic.

Corban reached out and touched her hand, trying to calm her. She flinched and let out a faint yelp before she realized what it was. He smiled, "Calm down, I don't think he's still here."

Mary sighed in disgust, "I'm sorry... he's not what I'm afraid of."

"I know."

The goosebumps that had broken out on her arms subsided. Her breathing slowed as Corban

Soul Siphon

rubbed her arm. She shook her head and smiled, "I guess maybe I'm still on edge from last time, yeah?"

They arrived at the first foyer. No attack came. Perhaps none would. Maybe he wasn't there at all, but even if that was the case, they had to be certain.

Yeah right. Corban thought to himself. *We haven't been that lucky. Xaphine saw something up there, she had to have and now we're walking right into whatever it is.*

The steps they took continued to echo, they were faint, but Corban was certain that if the demon was not already aware of their presence the sound would have made it obvious. He held his breath as they reached the next foyer. The door was closed and there wasn't enough room for someone to stand on the other side of it.

Corban put his hand back and pressed it against Mary's side, directing her to stand against the wall. She immediately turned and pressed her back against the cold concrete as Corban slowly reached for the handle. The two exchanged glances for a brief moment.

Mary sucked in a deep breath and appeared to be holding it as beads of sweat appeared on her forehead, soaking strands of her red hair. Corban's fingers wrapped around the old brass latch and slowly pushed down on it. There was a faint click as the door released from its hinge.

This was it, whatever horrors awaited them on the other side of the door were about to be revealed. Corban sucked down one more deep breath, pushed the handle down and forced the door open. He then dove through with Mary close on his back. Fists raised, he quickly scanned his new surroundings. It was completely dark in the next room and almost impossible to see anything ahead of them.

Soul Siphon

At that moment, the lights flickered on. They were dim but more than enough to see what had become of their home. What Corban had stepped into could only be described as chaos. The walls had massive scars running the length of the hallway, as though they had been gashed open by a massive animal. The whole place was reinforced concrete; it should not have been possible to leave such marks. What's worse, there was blood everywhere. It covered the ground, the walls, and even the lights, making the room glow in a malicious crimson hue. It was sickening, but who's blood was it?

Corban looked back at Mary, "Is this Lihua's blood?"

"It can't be," Mary replied. "Except for her bones and clothing, Lihua's remains turned to dust. No, this isn't her."

"Would Adramelech really kill someone else to do this?"

"You tell me."

The lights flickered every few moments as Mary and Corban proceeded cautiously down the hall. The window at the other end had been covered over thickly with blood and was not emanating any light. Corban kept his hands out in front of him, fully expecting to be attacked while Mary brandished her blade.

The hollow sound of a faint breeze made things even worse. Corban suspected that one of the gashes in the wall was deep enough to expose it to the outside air, but he couldn't be certain. They moved very cautiously, step by step.

The sound made Corban uneasy to the point where he was desperate to drown it out. He thought back to another song he learned when he was younger and quietly began singing. He wasn't even sure where he knew this song from, but it seemed appropriate somehow,

"In that merry month of May, From my home I started,
Left the girls of Tuam, Nearly broken hearted,
Saluted father dear, Kissed my darlin' mother,
Drank a pint of beer, My grief and tears to smother,
Then off to reap the corn, And leave where I was born,
I cut a stout blackthorn, To banish ghost and goblin,
In a brand new pair of brogues, I rattled o'er the bogs,
And frightened all the dogs, On the rocky road to
Dublin."

Corban was about to start the chorus when he heard Mary's voice next to him,

"One, two, three, four five,
Hunt the hare and turn her
Down the rocky road
And all the ways to Dublin,
Whack-fol-lol-de-ra."

They kept close as they moved past the first set of doors. These were Johnny and Vlad's rooms. The windows were completely black and it was impossible to see anything. Corban's breathing increased as he reached for the handle to Johnny's door, "You want to check Vlad's?"

"No, I'll stand guard here while you check Johnny's then you can do the same when I check Vlad's. We definitely shouldn't separate, yeah?"

"Okay," Corban replied as he twisted the handle and opened the door.

Mary turned her back on Corban and stood facing the hall as Corban made his way into the room.

Soul Siphon

He put all fear out of his head and focused on Mary'
voice as she continued singing,

"In Mullingar that night, I rested limbs so weary,
Started by daylight, Next mornin' light and airy,
Took a drop of the pure, To keep my heart from
sinkin',
That's an Irishman's cure, Whene'er he's on for
drinking.
To see the lasses smile, laughing all the while,
At my curious style, 'Twould set your heart a-bubblin'.
They ax'd if I was hired, the wages I required,
Till I was almost tired, of the rocky road to Dublin."

Corban took comfort from listening to Mary as
he entered Johnny's room. As long as she was singing,
he knew that she was okay. The room was dark, but it
was otherwise normal. Johnny had magazines and
posters strewn about, as well as empty bottles of beer
littering the floor. He grimaced as his eyes scanned the
room. Everything in there was pornographic in nature,
"Typical Johnny…"
Corban took a quick look in the bathroom before
coming back out. Mary had finished her verse, so
Corban picked up where she stopped,

"One, two, three, four five,
Hunt the hare and turn her
Down the rocky road
And all the ways to Dublin,
Whack-fol-lol-de-ra."

Mary closed the door behind him as they
proceeded across the hallway to the next room. Mary
opened the door and went in as Corban continued
singing,

Soul Siphon

"In Dublin next arrived, I thought it such a pity,
To be so soon deprived, A view of that fine city.
Then I took a stroll. All among the quality,
My bundle it was stole, In a neat locality;
Something crossed my mind, Then I looked behind;
No bundle could I find, Upon my stick a wobblin'.
Enquirin' for the rogue, they said my Connacht brogue,
Wasn't much in vogue, on the rocky road to Dublin."

From what Corban could see, Vlad's dorm was far more Spartan. He had pictures of his victims with red X's over their faces on one wall. The adjoining wall had pictures that didn't have a red X, but Corban was sure that they soon would if they all survived the fight with Adramelech.

Corban finished his verse, so Mary picked up again with the chorus and then started on her own verse,

"From there I got away, My spirits never failin'
Landed on the quay As the ship was sailin';
Captain at me roared, Said that no room had he,
When I jumped aboard. A cabin found for Paddy,
Down among the pigs I played some funny rigs,
Danced some hearty jigs, The water round me bubblin',
When off Holyhead, I wished myself was dead,
Or better far instead, On the rocky road to Dublin."

Vlad's room was secure. If the demon was in the building, it wasn't in that room. Mary moved back to the hallway and rejoined Corban in the hallway as she finished up her own verse. Then they sang the chorus line together,

Soul Siphon

"One, two, three, four five,
Hunt the hare and turn her
Down the rocky road
And all the ways to Dublin,
Whack-fol-lol-de-ra."

They were about to start on the next verse when Mary cut in, "I have a confession to make..."

"Oh?"

"I lied to you?"

"What about?"

"Julien Lestraude."

"What?"

"Jack the Ripper."

Corban's eyes widened, but he did not turn around, "That's who Jack the Ripper was?"

"Yeah... He was a French surgeon that had lost a lot of his status when he operated on a local noblewoman, resulting in her death. After his disgrace, he became resentful of women... The man moved to England to escape his reputation."

The look on Mary's face turned to a frown, "It didn't work. He was known here as Dr. Death and couldn't find employment. His mental state deteriorated and he took his frustrations out on street-walkers... He beat up a few of my friends from the brothel before he finally snapped."

"A French surgeon... didn't see that coming."

"He managed to stay out of the history books and off of the suspect list because Scotland Yard didn't know about him."

"Huh..."

Mary smiled, "Had your own theory, yeah? Who did you think it was?"

Corban shrugged, "I never really thought about it until I met you..."

Soul Siphon

"… but then you thought you'd try to find out who it was, yeah?" Mary asked, finishing his sentence.

"Yeah… actually… I thought finding out who it was and how they died might actually give you some closure."

"You're sweet Corban, but it wouldn't have done me any good. Besides, people have been trying to solve that one for a long time, and so far, no one's come close. So tell me, who did you think it was?"

"I thought maybe Charles Allen Lechmere?"

Mary laughed as they approached the next set of rooms, "The witness to Polly's killing? He wasn't even a suspect!"

"Yeah, but he was on the scene, he found her body first, and he may have faked info he gave to the police."

"True... it is suspicious, but it wasn't him."

Corban looked at her oddly, "Now wait… if you knew who he was, how come you didn't go after him?"

They continued walking towards the next two rooms. On the right side of the hall was the janitor's closet. The door was so badly damaged that it could not be used. The room on the other side was Lihua's.

"I lost my chance." She replied as she touched the handle. "He fled London when the investigations picked up. I tracked him all over Britain, but back then I was still learning how to use my powers, so I couldn't move as fast for as long and couldn't make trips over the water. Anyway, I thought I was going to catch him in Plymouth… I really had him, yeah?"

"What happened?" Corban asked as he opened the door and stepped into Lihua's room.

"I found out that he had booked passage on the SS Duke of Buccleuch out of England. I watched that horrible black ship disappear on the horizon and heard the deep bellow of its whistle, taunting me in the distance."

"Is that why you then went to Boston?"

Mary nodded, "I had a few people to take care of in London first. I'd promised myself that I would deal with the thugs who used to rough up my friends before moving on. When I was done, I made my way to the so-called new world."

"How come you didn't track him down when you got here?"

"I tried to. I made inquiries the moment I hit the shore."

"And?"

"The Duke of Buccleuch collided with another ship on her way over here. She went down with all hands. I missed my chance."

"Damn, I'm sorry."

"Ancient history, yeah? There's nothing I can do about it. I've taken my revenge by going after anyone who roughs up girls that walk the streets. Their lives are hard enough."

"I guess so."

"So why didn't you tell me before?"

"It's a sore subject that I don't like going into great detail about. I just felt like it was time I told you the full story."

"Well, I'm glad you did."

"Yeah, so am I."

Lihua's room was empty minus a few Buddhist artifacts. She was always somewhat of a minimalist, so this was not unexpected. There was also nothing of any outstanding significance in the bathroom. He gave up and rejoined Mary at the door, "Do you think we're on a wild goose chase?"

"Don't think Adramelech is here?"

Soul Siphon

Corban scanned that darkness one last time before responding, "No… he was, but I don't think he is anymore."

"But then why would Xaphine tell us to look up here?"

"I don't know."

"Well come on, we might as well check the rest of them, yeah?"

"Fine."

Mary took point with her dagger out front. She led him down the hall to the next set of rooms,

"One, two, three, four five,
Hunt the hare and turn her
Down the rocky road
And all the ways to Dublin,
Whack-fol-lol-de-ra."

The next set of rooms in the hallway was Corban's and Mary's rooms. Corban looked at his door hesitantly. He couldn't explain why, but these two rooms caused the hair to stand up on the back of his neck. Something was out of place here. It wasn't Adramelech, this was far more passive, "All right, I'll check my room, you go ahead and check yours."

"Sure."

Corban crept slowly into his room, not knowing what to expect. He quickly checked the closet, peaked into the bathroom, and checked under the bed. Nothing, just as with the other rooms. He wasn't there, nothing malicious was. Corban couldn't explain what he'd felt. What had Xaphine seen and what was the angry, ominous feeling he got from being there. Could it be residual energy from the demon or was there something there that he'd missed? He knew better than most what it was like to be caught in the demon's clutches, and what he was feeling was not that.

Corban opened the door to his room, checked the bathroom, and searched in every crevice to make sure that she was not missing anything. The light flickered for a moment as his eyes scanned the darkness. The light flickered again, but then immediately turned back off. *What's going on?*

An ominous feeling came over Corban. Something wasn't right. The mess in the dorms was bad enough, but he couldn't shake the feeling that something was out of place. Whatever it was, he had a feeling that the lights would soon reveal it

A loud thud came from downstairs, which somehow caused the light to come on strong. Corban's eyes quickly darted around the room. There was nothing. Everything was in its place and accounted for.

Relieved, Corban stood up straight and turned to head back to the hallway when he heard a blood-curdling scream, "No… No! Corban!"

Corban's head jerked at the shrill sound, "Mary?"

Oh dear God... what's happened? Corban quickly scrambled out of his room, dashed across the hall, and burst through the door into Mary's room. She was pale and looked like she'd just seen a ghost. Her teeth were clenched almost as hard as her hand was around its dagger.

Corban grabbed her by the arms and pulled her close, wrapping his own around her, "What is it, what's wrong?"

The rage in Mary's eyes almost turned them red. It seemed like the muscles in her jaw refused to unclench as she pointed a shaking right index finger to the opposite wall.

Soul Siphon

Corban followed her finger to the wall behind him. His body flinched as he saw the grotesque image that had made Mary go berserk. Bones covered in blood had been fixed to her wall, bent and shaped in a way that they spelled out a single word 'Carthage.'

Corban's eyes narrowed, "Carthage? What the hell… is that…?"

Mary looked like she was going to get sick. Seeing her friend's bones desecrated in such a manner was clearly too much for her to handle. Her teeth remained clenched as she spoke, "Yes… it's Lihua. He did this to torment me."

"What?"

"Mike… Adramelech, after everything we went through, he did this to torture me! He wanted me to see this first!"

"Why?"

"I don't know… perhaps he thinks that I'm your weak link?"

"And he's trying to make you misstep?"

"Maybe…"

Corban tried to turn her away from the wall, "Come on let's go talk to Xaphine. I think we're done here."

Mary fought out of his grip, "No."

"Mary…?"

"No!"

Mary reached under her bed and grabbed an old green bottle and an odd looking dagger. She ripped the cork out of the bottle with her teeth, spit it on the ground, and took a long drink of the bottle's contents. The color returned to her face and her breathing slowed slightly as she appeared to calm down.

Mary held the dagger up to her face, and showed it to Corban, "This is the dagger that I told you about."

"The one you used on Lisa?"

Soul Siphon

"The one I used on all of them." She corrected. "It's still stained with their blood. Mike upped the ante... now it's my turn, yeah? Driving this blade into his worthless hide will be payment for Lihua's death!"

"Mary... you know that won't kill him."

Mary's face turned bright red with rage, "Then at the very least, wound him enough so that you can finish the job!"

Before Corban could say anything, Mary drove her dagger into the sheets on her bed. She cut one thick strip free of the rest of the fabric and began stuffing it into the bottle. Her eyes looked almost entranced as she worked.

Corban saw what she was doing and was about to intervene when Mary turned to him with an angry look. Her eyes were black and the redness around them gave her an almost demonic look, "Get out."

Something about the way Mary spoke, made Corban nod and back out of the room without questioning her. He had a bad feeling about what she was going to do and didn't want to be the target of her rage. He knew better than to try to challenge her when she was like this. *This is going to be bad...*

Once Corban was gone, Mary pulled a box of matches from her dresser drawer, lit the ripped sheet, and gripped the bottle tightly for a moment. She looked at her friend's skull with tears in her eyes, "Be at peace now. No one deserves it more than you."

Mary sucked down a deep breath and held it as she threw the bottle against the wall with a loud grunt. The bottle shattered, spraying green shards of glass in every direction and causing the flame to spread like a puddle of water on the ground in a rainstorm. The crackle of the flame picked up and became louder as the fire spread.

Mary raised her chin in defiance as the intense light of the flame illuminated her face. Her eyes glowed in a way that made them look demonic and her skin appeared as though it were vibrating under the strain of her tense muscles. Her clenched teeth made her even more menacing as the flame burned away the desecration on her wall. The intense heat on her skin was almost unbearable, but she ignored it, "Mike, I'm coming for you!"

As the last of Lihua's remains burned away, Mary nodded and walked calmly out of the room as though nothing had happened. Her demonic expression disappeared and was replaced by bland, emotionless expression. She walked by Corban, barely even acknowledging his presence and headed for the elevator, "Let's go."

Corban didn't say anything. He just followed her down the stairs as they made their way to the main hall. The orange glow from the floor above lit the stairwell.

Xaphine was still sitting on the couch when they reappeared in the living room. Corban and Mary rushed over to Xaphine as Johnny and Vlad reappeared from the basement. Vlad's beard was singed and looked like it had been burnt off in a few places. There was a detectable level of annoyance in his eyes as he attempted to straighten out what was left.

Mary saw that Johnny was no better off. He looked as though his nerves had been completely shot and he had just been through hell. His shirt was singed and he had an agitated expression on his face. Though they had not found anything in the basement, his tolerance had clearly been stretched to its limit.

Mary looked her friends over as the two appeared in the doorway from the basement, "Vlad, what the hell happened to you two?"

Vlad was about to respond when the smoke detectors finally went off. The room echoed with the loud beeping noise that indicated danger. Xaphine immediately came to life and looked up in the direction that the alarm was coming from, "It's time to go, now."

XXI

An hour later, the group arrived back on their yacht. They took some time to watch their old hideout burn. They weren't so much standing in reverence of the base as much as bidding a final farewell to their fallen comrade.

As they arrived back on the yacht, Corban dropped Vlad on the deck walked over to Mary, "Are you all right?"

"I've been better."

"I'm sorry."

"We weren't all that close I guess… and she talked like a computer, yeah? But in her own way, she always had an annoying knack for getting under my skin. She was my friend."

Vlad was still trying to comb the soot out of his beard while cursing like no other, "Rotten machines! I said ve should replace long time ago, but did team listen? No!"

"Relax Vlad," Johnny replied. "It'll grow back."

"Is not ze point!"

Johnny uttered a faint chuckle as he slapped Vlad on the back, "Come on buddy, I'll buy you a drink. We'll toast our fallen comrades; Lihua and your beard."

He then turned to Mary and Corban, "Coming?"

"Maybe in a bit," Corban replied. "I need a few questions answered first."

Corban looked at Mary, "How about you?"

She looked like she'd calmed down since their encounter at the hideout. Her nerves were still tense and she definitely felt like drinking her problems away for a little while, "I'll be up in a few minutes. I want to hear what Corban's going to say."

Soul Siphon

"Man, you two are no fun anymore. Ever since you got all lovey, we barely see you. Come on and have a drink in a little while, okay?"

"You got it," Corban replied.

"I'll hold you to that!"

Johnny headed upstairs to the bar while Corban and Mary turned to Xaphine. The angel was staring up at the sky, not really paying attention to anything. She once again seemed almost entranced.

Corban approached her first, his mind filled with questions that needed answering, "Why did he write 'Carthage' on Mary's wall? What does it mean?"

Xaphine sighed, "Carthage doesn't mean anything. It's the name of a city, not an actual word."

"A city?" Corban asked. "Where?"

"I see someone wasn't paying attention during geography class, yeah?" Mary replied. "It's in Tunisia, North Africa."

Corban flashed Mary an annoyed look, "All right, so why then would Adramelech go to a Tunisian city? What's the connection I'm missing?"

"Carthage may be a mere Tunisian city today," Xaphine replied, "but at one time, it was the seat of a vast empire. The Carthaginian Empire, which spanned around half of the Mediterranean. They held their territory for almost seven hundred years and then experienced a slow decline until Rome attacked and wiped out the remaining stronghold city."

"Thanks for the history lesson," Mary replied sharply, "but it doesn't get us any closer to an answer, yeah? What does Carthage have to do with Adramelech?"

Xaphine sighed, "Well that is where things get a touch more complicated. Adramelech has been around a very long time. Like myself, he's gone by a few

Soul Siphon

different names, depending on who you speak to. One of his names was Moloch."

Mary shook her head, "Now Moloch I've heard of. He was a God that was worshipped in ancient North Africa."

"Where did you hear that?"

"The nuns I stayed with... always a doom and gloom bunch, yeah? They went on and on about demons. It was kind of creepy actually, but what makes you think he's one in the same?"

"Because I met him during my time in the pit," Xaphine replied. "People were influenced to worship them the same way... by sacrificing children. Countless children were brutally slaughtered to worship that profane demon who saw fit to call himself a God! It was a sickening thing he did."

"So he's gone home, yeah?"

"I'd say so. That is the logical conclusion from all of this."

"But why go there, what's the significance?" Corban asked.

"The ancient city still stands, albeit in ruins. Most of what can be seen is opened to tourists... what can't be seen however is far more malicious."

"What would that be?"

"Tunnels that led deep underground. There is a whole network of them that have been kept well-concealed even from the eyes of your modern technology."

"Where do they lead?"

"To an ancient necropolis. A city of the dead if you would. The living do not belong there, but it is a place that was desecrated for use to worship Moloch. His taint and that of what his followers did is still on that place. Think of it as a demonic battery, a window

Soul Siphon

that connects his world to ours. The fools who worshipped him unknowingly created it."

"Would that be how he was able to remain in our world?" Corban asked.

"It is possible I suppose, but we've never seen one so powerful that it could sustain a demon after they were driven from someone. Adramelech is not the only demon worshipped by profane rituals. Either way, he's there now recharging his power. We'll need to attack there and end him. I don't want to even consider the ramifications of allowing him to regain his power unchecked."

"All right, then we need to leave soon," Corban said adamantly.

"Are you sure you're ready for this? You haven't had enough time to fully explore your powers. Going after him does come with its own set of risks, even for someone who had fully realized their potential."

Mary placed her hand on Corban's shoulder, "I'll be with him. We'll get through it."

"Had a change of heart, I see?"

Mary shrugged, "I owe Adramelech a little payback... also, I've seen how Corban handles himself now. I should have had more faith in him all along. That's what he's been asking for, yeah?"

"Finally," Corban replied. "So when do we go?"

Loud belly laughs emanated from the deck above, as though answering Corban's question. Xaphine smiled, "In a few hours... Go be with your friends tonight. We still have time, just make sure they don't get too intoxicated."

"All right."

Corban and Mary left Xaphine to concentrate on their next objective. They headed upstairs to see what

Johnny and Vlad had gotten themselves into. Neither one spoke as they entered the bar on the second deck.

Much to their amusement, Vlad and Johnny were already deep into a bottle of vodka, singing the Soviet National Anthem. Mary almost had to cover her ears at the sound of Vlad's deep bellowing voice. He sang with such passion that anyone listening from the outside would have thought that the Cold War was still on.

They held the last line for a few moments and then looked over at Corban. Vlad had a huge grin on his face, "Corban and Mary, join us for a drink!"

Mary sat next to Vlad at the bar, "A full selection and you go for the cheap Russian swill… typical!"

Mary reached over and grabbed a red bottle from behind the counter. Corban looked at her oddly, surprised that she avoided the bottles of scotch. The bottle was dark with a white label and extremely fancy writing that he wasn't certain was in English.

Mary turned it over in her hand as Vlad gave her a scornful look, "Vat piss vould Mary have us drink zen?"

Her eyes scanned the bottle, "I would offer you a lot better than that…"

After reading the label, a surprised look came over her, "Domaine Leroy Echezeaux Grand Cru… 1955! Wow, talk about incredible vintage, yeah?"

She worked the cork out of the bottle and up-ended it for a few seconds. A few drops of red liquid dripped from her lips as she lowered the bottle. She had a wide smile on her face as she placed it back on the bar, "That may not be 'the creature,' but it would give the old bastard a run for his money!"

Corban took the bottle and sampled it for himself, "So this is what quality fine wine tastes like."

Soul Siphon

"Not just fine," Mary replied with an annoyed look as she grabbed the bottle back, "this is probably a two thousand dollar bottle."

Vlad looked over at Mary and Corban, "Odd occasion to open up such a rare bottle."

"Not really… we're attacking Adramelech at his home in Carthage. This will be his last stand. It's the perfect time to enjoy such a bottle. You want something red on such an occasion, yeah?"

"Ven?"

"Another few hours."

The look on Vlad's face softened, "Zen give me ze bottle!"

Mary reached out and handed Vlad the bottle of wine. Vlad tipped the bottle back and then handed it to Johnny, "To victory! May ve come back unscathed and vith stories to tell!"

"Hopefully we'll make it a day worthy of song, a day worthy to remember Lihua with..," Mary replied.

As the group enjoyed one last drink together before the sun went down, Corban watched Mary as she interacted with the group. *Mary… you try too hard to make yourself a loner. So much time wasted on the roof. This is where you should have been all along.*

Corban's thoughts drifted to the battle ahead. So many things could go wrong. Any of his friends could die, he could lose himself to the demon's power, or worse. The cards seemed completely stacked against them.

His thoughts were interrupted by a gentle knock to the side of his head, "Earth to Corban, you're in there, yeah?"

"Yeah," Corban replied as he looked up at Mary.

"So why the distant stare? You look like you got a lot flying through your head."

Soul Siphon

"Not really," Corban lied. "I was just wondering how I got such a hot girlfriend out of all of this. Things haven't been easy, but I think I'm finally getting used to all of this."

Mary laughed, "A hot girlfriend, yeah? Anyone I know?"

"I'm not sure," Corban replied. "She's a fiery redhead, who's nearly impossible to get along with sometimes, but a lot of fun when she's drunk and a beautiful singer."

A half smile appeared on her face, "Doesn't ring a bell, sorry."

Corban leaned over and kissed her. The smell of wine on her breath complemented her very well. She shook her head, "I'm so kicking your ass at some point, yeah?"

"I can't wait."

A few hours went by while the group relaxed. They took full advantage of what little time they had. Mary and Corban did the best they could to avoid too much booze, but Mary couldn't resist taking a few extra gulps of wine.

Corban eyed her suspiciously, "Something wrong?"

"I hope we're ready for this…"

"You don't think we can win?"

"I don't know..."

"I mean, we've trained hard for this and we've been put through hell. What's left for us to do?"

Mary fell silent. She didn't want to talk about what was going on in her mind, but she knew that he needed to face the last piece of his training. He had faced anger, sorrow, pain, joy, lust, and hate, but there was still one piece that he had not faced; death.

Soul Siphon

436

Corban looked at her oddly as he became impatient, "Mary?"

"Can we go lay down for a little while?"

"Yeah sure."

The two of them got up and headed from the lounge to the main suite. An inebriated Johnny hooted at them as they left, "Hey you two kids have fun now!"

"Fuck off Johnny."

Once they were behind closed doors in the main suite, Mary guided Corban over to the bed. He sat down and looked at Mary quizzically, "What's all this about?"

"I have one more memory that I need you to see before you try to take on Adramelech. You've managed to handle everything else that I've thrown your way, but this one is the worst of it. It's the memory that I've held back until I thought you could handle it."

"And you think I can?"

"I don't know," Mary admitted, "but at this point, it doesn't look like we have much choice, yeah?"

"I guess not."

Mary sat down next to him and leaned forward, "I'm not going to block you out at all now. Take as much energy as you need to find the pieces that I haven't shown you. Just remember to put it all back."

"I will, I promise and I'll make this as quick as possible."

Corban sucked down a deep breath and closed his eyes as he braced himself. He focused his powers and put himself into a transic state as he slowly raised his hands to Mary's cheeks. There was a sudden charge that felt like static between their skins as his hands connected.

Soul Siphon

In less than a second, Corban found himself back on the streets of 19th Century London. A rotten aroma filled his nostrils as he looked around. The darkness was so thick that it took his eyes a few minutes to adjust to the dim street lamps. The rain was coming down hard, but he didn't feel it.

At that moment, Corban heard the sound of hearty laughter. He turned to see Mary approaching from the opposite direction. She was clothed in a less fancy dress than what he'd seen her in before. It was fairly worn and looked frayed in a few places at the bottom. Only her white apron appeared to be clean.

She was accompanied by a man with a curled mustache. He was wearing a dark felt hat which he had pulled down enough to keep his eyes from being seen. His shoulders were covered by a long dark coat, trimmed in astrakhan. Around his neck was a white collar with a black necktie fixed in the middle with a horseshoe pin.

Mary was clearly intoxicated. Her speech was badly slurred as she spoke, "I've lost my handkerchief."

Without a word, the man handed her his red one, which she then uses to wipe her face clean or the rain as they walked. Corban stood under the light, but Mary didn't see him. She was either too preoccupied with the other man or incapable of seeing him. *You're seeing Mary's memories. I doubt you could do anything about them.*

As they walked by, Corban noticed a worn out sign on the opposite side of the street which had the words 'Miller's Court' written on it. He felt a sudden jolt as though electricity had struck him when he realized exactly where and when he was. In a panic, he turned to the couple, completely forgetting that she couldn't see him, "Mary, get away from him! That's Jack the Ripper, he's going to kill you!"

Mary continued to a small alley next to a filthy white building at the end of a covered passage which led to Dorset Street. She reached through the broken window of her room and unlocked the door. The couple proceeded inside with Corban in pursuit.

The worn out wooden door shut before Corban could reach them. Corban tried to get in, but the door was stuck tight. There was nothing he could do.

As Corban tried to figure out a way to break the door down, he was instantly flung from the night scene to about six in the morning. The door opened and the man stepped out in front of him. His clothes were crumpled as he appeared to have dressed in a hurry. He took a quick look around the neighborhood before disappearing around the block.

Corban slipped inside to see what she was doing. Her eyes were closed and she was motionless, but she was still alive. That was clearly not Jack the Ripper.

He pulled a chair up next to her bed and sat down. When the murderer arrived, he would be ready. Julien Lestraude would not claim another victim if Corban could find a way to stop him.

A few moments later, Mary's eyes shot open and she looked up at Corban, "You, what are you doing here? Get out!"

Corban tried to respond. He wanted to let Mary know that he was there to protect her, but his lips would not budge. He suddenly felt his arm move and to his horror, noticed that it was holding a small knife.

Mary screamed, "No, murder! What the fu…"

One quick thrust was all it took. Blood spattered from Mary's throat all over the bed and Corban's arm. At that moment, his world blurred. He came to, looking up at a man with a euphoric look on his face

Soul Siphon

that was covered in blood. He was now seeing everything from Mary's perspective.

A sharp pain entered his throat as mixed feelings of fear, confusion, sorrow, and anger entered his mind. He knew everything that Mary remembered from her death. It was a horror that he'd never known or understood.

Corban watched helplessly for as long as he could as Lestraude went to work carving her into pieces. Intense fear of the unknown took over as he was forced to embrace the void of death. Not knowing what was to come was a familiar feeling, but he had not feared his own death as much as she did her's.

The world went black and Corban was slowly transported back to reality. Corban's eyes burst open and he gasped for air. Mary's face had gone pale and thin lines where Jack the Ripper's knife had struck appeared on her cheeks, forehead, and nose.

Corban jerked backward and lay flat on the bed. His whole body began to tremble and foam appeared on the left corner of his lip. He made odd gurgling noises as his breathing became erratic.

"Corban, Corban, what's happening? Snap out of it!" Mary screamed in a panic.

Out on the deck, Xaphine was locked in a trance as she looked up at the stars. She'd be in communication with the Celestial World and as such, was oblivious to what was going on around her. Suddenly a gentle breeze touched her back. She turned around to look at the main suite, "No..."

She ran across the deck to the cabin and threw the door open. Inside was pure insanity; Mary looked like she had just fought off a ninja and Corban was having a seizure. She ran to Corban's side and looked at Mary, "What have you done?"

Soul Siphon

Mary looked up at her momentarily, "He needed to see it. He couldn't take on…"

"You showed him your death?" Xaphine demanded. "Fool… you've sent him into sensory overload!"

"It had to be done. He can't face Adramelech without a stronger defense! I didn't know this would happen, yeah?"

"He may not be able to fight at all if I can't bring him out of it!"

She immediately pushed Mary out of the way and put her hands on Corban's temples. Her eyes rolled over white and closed as she focused on repairing the damage, "Wake up Corban… I heal you…"

Corban's head jerked back out of her grip. He gasped for air as his eyes opened. A sense of relief appeared on Mary's face as Corban's eyes opened and he began to breathe normally.

She moved to Corban's side and grabbed his hand, "Corban… I'm so sorry! I didn't know this would happen!"

Corban took a few deep breaths and sat up. He looked at Mary and brought his hand up to her face. As though guiding his hand, Mary grabbed it as he touched her cheek.

Corban ran his fingers along her scars with a sympathetic look on his face, "I… I know these wounds… Mary…"

Tears flowed down Mary's cheeks, "I didn't mean to hurt you."

"You didn't," Corban replied. "You gave me strength… you are my strength. I'm ready now."

"I hope that's true."

"Only time will tell."

Soul Siphon

He then turned to Xaphine, "Thanks for the save."

"Anytime."

She then turned to Mary, "But I hope that's the last of it."

"That's all I had left that he hadn't seen."

"Good."

Xaphine backed out of the room quietly and returned to the deck. The door closed, leaving Corban and Mary to sort out what had just happened. It didn't seem like either of them was in a hurry to begin. Corban looked intrigued as he ran his fingers over the scars on Mary's face. There was no logic or pattern behind the slashes. Each one ran in a different direction than the one next to it.

Mary looked both ashamed and humiliated. She tried to hide her face to stop Corban from seeing the scars, "Please stop."

"What?"

"I... I never wanted you to see me like this."

"Mary, I've seen the crime scene photos."

"That's not the same thing, yeah?"

"I don't understand "

Mary let out a deep sigh as she turned back to him, "Did you recognize me when you saw me there?"

"Yes... well, kind of."

"Kind of?"

"You were different."

"Exactly... I looked different. I acted different... because I was different. I'm not that person anymore."

Corban was confused. He wasn't sure what that had to do with anything. Mary rolled her eyes as she tried to explain it more plainly, "Back then I called myself Marie Jeanette Kelly, even though that wasn't my birth name. I tried to reinvent myself after my time in France."

"So?"

"So Marie Jeanette Kelly is who was knifed to death on November 9ᵗʰ, 1888. Today I have about as much in common with her as you do with Adramelech."

Corban finally understood what she was saying, "I see, as far as you're concerned you're a different person with a different identity and a new life. Which means that those scars would connect you to her once again."

Mary fell silent and turned her head to the side, looking away from Corban. She rubbed her arms and huddled herself together slightly as though trying to make herself harder to see. Clearly, she didn't like airing her dirty laundry this way.

Corban placed his right hand on her shoulder, "Here, have your dignity back."

He forced the energy that she'd lost in the transfer back into her body. The scars quickly healed themselves and her skin turned back to its normal pigment. Despite the fact that she was back to normal, she still wouldn't speak to or look at him.

Corban gently caressed her cheek, "Can I let you in on a secret?"

"Sure."

He leaned over and whispered into her ear, "I like Mary a lot more than Marie."

A faint smile appeared on Mary's face, "Good to know, yeah?"

"We don't have to say anything else. At least now I understand a little better."

"Right."

He continued to rub her cheek and slowly ran his fingers down to her chin. Using the minimal force, he pushed her chin up so he could look at her, "This doesn't change anything. You're still the most awesome girl I've ever met."

Mary smiled as he looked at her, "You're full of shit, yeah? Still... thanks. It's nice to know that what you saw didn't drive you away."

It seemed like night would never fall over the western border of Mexico. There was a calm sense of serenity onboard the ship that day. However, it wouldn't last long and when the sun eventually did begin to set, Xaphine appeared, "It's time to go. Carthage awaits."

"She can always be counted on, yeah?" Mary asked.

Johnny smirked, "Yeah, like a hotter version of Mike."

Corban said nothing. He cleared his mind of all dark imagery and was doing the best he could to cut off his fear so that his friends wouldn't see it. He had faced off against Adramelech before and knew what lay ahead of them. His mind was now reinforced by Mary's strength. He at least thought that he had a chance, but this would be the greatest trial that he had ever faced even with all the training in the world, there was still the possibility that he would not survive.

Corban had put on a good show for Mary, but he knew deep down inside that his own inexperience could be his undoing and while her faith in him was a source of strength, it did not make up for his own lack of the same in himself. He barely believed his own words, but he knew that he had to try. Adramelech could not be allowed to harm another person the way he had been harmed. If he didn't face down the demon, he would most likely be forced to obey its whim. He couldn't live with that.

Soul Siphon

444

"All right, let's get ourselves geared up then," Johnny said as he began looking for a gun.

"No," Xaphine replied sternly. "Take only your powers and those collars that you used to ensnare me. Your weapons will be worthless there. Nothing that resides there, lives as normal humans do."

Mary stepped up in front of Xaphine so that they were face to face and looked into her eyes, "I'm not going anywhere defenseless. The others can leave their guns behind, but I'm taking my blades."

She held up the one that she'd taken from her room, "I have a debt to settle and I need this blade to settle it. No one is stopping me, yeah?"

Xaphine sighed, "I can't force you to listen to reason. It's up to you. Your weapons will just slow you down, but do as you will."

Mary ran her hand up one of the sheaths on her belt and shook her head, "I made myself a promise. The dagger comes."

Corban smiled, "I know."

Mary turned and looked at Vlad, "Not bringing your rifle?"

"Rifle is great weapon, but I don't sink it vork vell against demons."

"So you're going in defenseless? Kind of foolish, yeah?"

"Defenseless, no," Vlad said with a smile as he opened his shirt, revealing a set of throwing knives that were strapped to his chest. "I have zese blessed long ago for just such an occasion."

Mary grinned, "All right. –Corban, what about you?"

Corban looked down at his fists as they began to glow, "My powers will be my defense."

"Wise," Xaphine replied in approval.

Soul Siphon

"Or foolishly bold," Mary countered as she reached down and detached a sheath from her leg. "Take this, it's one of the twin kodachis. Since I'm bringing my other dagger, I won't need it."

Corban looked at her for a moment but made no move to take the blade. Mary shook it in front of him, insisting that he take it, "Look, put it on your belt and forget it it's there, yeah? Just do it for me, so that I know you have... something!"

Corban took the blade and attached it to his belt, "For you."

Mary turned back to Xaphine, "We're ready."

Xaphine closed her eyes and settled her thoughts as she prepared to move out, "All right then... let us depart."

As before, Xaphine touched Vlad and Johnny on the shoulder and transported them off the ship. Corban opened his hands to Mary. She gently fell backward into his arms, "Playing the hero again?"

"Always."

Mary closed her eyes and grabbed onto Corban's shirt with her right hand as he took flight, leaving the yacht deserted. Just like before, the world became a blur as they traveled above the clouds. A slight feeling of nausea came over her as the wind whipped over her skin. She kept her eyes closed and leaned into Corban, pressing her head into his chest, "How high can you go?"

"Let's find out!"

"What, um I didn't mean..."

Before Mary could finish her sentence, Corban skyrocketed upwards at amazing speeds. Mary's eyes shot open in time to see them pass through the clouds. She looked up and saw the night sky overhead, "Holy shit!"

A few more seconds went by before they stopped. The air was freezing cold, but it somehow didn't bother them. Mary looked down to see the clouds far below them in the distance. She immediately forgot all fear and the nausea seemed to disappear, "How far up are we?"

"As far as you can go without becoming an astronaut."

"We're at the edge of space?" Mary asked in amazement.

"Yup"

"Wow… how are we still breathing and not turning into popsicles?"

"No idea."

"Best not linger here, yeah? Don't want to find out that we can't do this forever."

Corban looked down at Earth, "Yeah good idea…"

"Just promise me we'll come back, yeah? This is beautiful."

"I promise."

Corban began his descent back to Earth. Mary closed her eyes again and stared into the void behind her eyelids. She breathed slowly and waited until the wind stopped blowing over her skin. As the seconds passed, the air became warm and stale. It was almost completely dry and there was no wind.

Mary opened her eyes and found herself in the middle of a dark ruin. She hopped out of Corban's arms and looked around. The sky was dark. It was a starless navy blue color that just barely lit up the ground. An orange harvest moon sat roughly two inches above the horizon from their perspective, "Is this it?"

"I think so," Corban replied cautiously.

"This can't be right…"

Soul Siphon

"Huh?"

Mary's head darted back and forth as she scanned the landscape. She took a step back as she smelled the air, "Something isn't right here... no... This whole area is just completely wrong."

Corban looked at her with concern in his eyes, "What are you talking about?"

Xaphine appeared with Johnny and Vlad. The moment she landed, a nauseated look appeared on her face. She appeared to be in pain and was having trouble remaining on her feet. She struggled to regain her composure as Mary responded, "I don't know... I... can't explain it, but something feels wrong here, very wrong. It's almost like this whole place doesn't make sense, like the laws and physics of nature somehow don't apply here. Something in the air just has me spooked. It's... wrong, yeah?"

"Okay... so something is wrong here," Corban replied in a disturbed tone.

"Shut up!" Mary said in an annoyed tone. "I know I'm not making much sense, but I don't need that condescending tone from you!"

"Sorry, I just don't know how you mean."

"Listen, do you hear any wind? Do you hear anything?"

"No."

"No... not even the sound of a faint breeze or open air. That's not natural. It's the same thing if you smell the air. There's no scent, no fragrance, nothing."

"So what do you suppose all of this means?"

"I... don't know..."

Corban's gaze didn't change after Mary fell silent. He continued to look her over, studying her distressed expression. He wanted to say something, anything, but he didn't even know where to begin.

Soul Siphon

Mary could tell that he had no idea what she was talking about, "Look I'm sorry, I know this sounds insane, but I can't shake the feeling that something is incredibly off here. Something is at work here that isn't natural."

"You're not wrong," Xaphine replied. "This land is twisted. Look…"

Xaphine pointed out across the crumbling stone buildings to the moon, "What is that to you?"

Corban shrugged, "A harvest moon?"

"But it's not," Xaphine replied. "That's the sun."

"That's not possible," Johnny replied. "If the sun were that high in the sky, it would be as bright as day out right now. There is no way…"

Xaphine pressed her right hand against her temple, "The land has been desecrated by the taint of Adramelech. It's the same taint that he put on this land thousands of years ago. He blocked out the sun and any light that could come to this place. It will not shine so long as he is here."

Corban looked out over the old ruins, "But there are other people nearby! No doubt they've noticed this too! That can only mean…"

"They likely have," Xaphine replied before Corban could finish his thought, "but not in the way you have. To them, everything would appear normal, but those who are sensitive to nature and more... aware of the things around them would know that something isn't right here. It would most likely feel like a cold chill, but would they see what you do? No."

"How is that possible?" Corban asked.

Mary's eyes continued to scan the darkness as she spoke, "Do you remember what we told you about how we exist outside of life and the living?"

"Yes…"

Soul Siphon

"This is what we meant. As creatures that aren't really alive, we can see things that normal humans can't. We see all of reality, not just what the mortals see, but also whatever is in the background. Spirits, demons, angels, and other celestial creatures will appear to us as plain as any human being."

That didn't make any sense to Corban, "So wait... then how come we haven't seen anything until now? With all the haunted houses and paranormal activity you hear about, you'd think we'd see ghosts everywhere!"

Mary rolled her eyes as Xaphine spoke up, "Corban... by now you should know that most of the stuff you see on TV is fake. Yes, some cases are legitimate, but all too often the spooks that you see on TV or read about in books and travel brochures are nothing more than a desperate bid to attract attention. Unseen monsters and horrors wreaking havoc on humanity would not go unnoticed and would be quickly dealt with. Most demonic interference is far more passive so that they can avoid detection until exposed by an exorcist. This is why I had such a hard time locating a legitimate possession victim. As for ghosts... you most likely have seen a few and just didn't know it."

"How so?"

Mary laughed, "What you think they walk around with sheets over their heads, making noises, and hovering above the ground?"

"Well... okay yeah, I guess that does sound kind of stupid," Corban admitted. "So all the uneasy feelings people get, the scratches and bruises on their skin, the random feelings of unease in certain areas, and being pushed down flights of stairs by unseen apparitions?"

Xaphine smirked, "Mind games, high EM fields, mental issues, wounds received while doing other work that went unnoticed, and people deliberately being deceptive to get attention. That's just all there is to it. For the most part, there is a scientific explanation for those encounters."

"I see... so that icy feeling, the sense that we're getting right now... even though no human can see it, someone can probably sense what's going on here?"

"Yes, what you're feeling and what you're sensing is what any human being with even the slightest sensory perception would. You know your environment and this isn't it. This is an environment that has been altered enough for a demon to exist. For a human, it's a mild nuisance, for an angel..."

Johnny placed his hand on Xaphine's shoulder as she rubbed her temples with both hands, "You okay?"

Xaphine shook her head, "All ready the taint of the demon's essence is pulling at me. It's so strong... so painful... I've never seen it this bad before..."

"Is there anything we can do to help you?"

Xaphine dropped to one knee, unable to shield herself from the dark lure of the area, "This... is as far as I dare go. You are neither angelic nor demonic creatures... So you should be protected from this madness. It doesn't appear to affect you as much."

She looked up at Corban with frustrated tears in her eyes, "I'm sorry... I'd go with you if I could... but this is overpowering..."

"You're an archangel, yeah?" Mary asked. "If it's too much for you, how can we expect to stand a chance?"

"Angels are able to fight in their own environments. This is like asking one of you to survive in outer space. It's just not possible. You were made to hunt down evil, but you are not amongst the living nor of the Celestial World. Whatever Adramelech's motives, that was your purpose, and it still is. Even if the evil you're hunting is your own creator. That is still what you are here for. –Corban, you defeated him once, you can do it again, I know you can."

"All right, why don't you head back to the yacht? See if you can get it to Boston. We could use a mobile hideout for when the one on Faye Street is too far away."

"I'll take care of it... I'll also see about cleaning up the mess on Faye Street," Xaphine replied as she quickly flapped her wings and took flight.

Vlad sighed as he watched her fly away, "No help from ze angels. Zis could not get much vorse."

"True that," Johnny agreed.

"Sure it could," Corban replied. "Trust me, it can always get worse... and it probably will before it's over. Saying that it can't, only invites more problems."

He then turned to Mary, "Where do you think we should go?"

"You're asking me?" Mary asked, surprised.

"You seem to be in tune with this place. I thought maybe you might feel something that could tell us where to go."

"No..."

Corban sighed, "All right then... perhaps we should head to one of the enclosed buildings that are still standing. One of them is bound to have a passage to the underground Necropolis."

"All right," Johnny replied. "There are a few of them, so maybe we should split up into two groups and start searching the area."

Mary shook her head, "Oh yeah, that's a brilliant idea! We're in an area tainted by demonic energy that is obviously hostile. The place is a fucking maze, most

Soul Siphon

of us are ineffective against demonic attacks, and you want us to split up? We'll get picked off one by one without much difficulty."

Corban took a quick look around. The buildings almost looked black against the sky. The crumbling ruins were built out of massive stone blocks that bent and twisted into a large labyrinth of ancient ruins.

Johnny glared at Mary, "All right then, general! Since you've apparently elected yourself our leader, what do you say we do, stay together and search?"

"Yes," Mary replied. "Strength in numbers if nothing else"

She looked over at Corban for approval, "Yeah?"

Corban thought for a moment, either choice presented its own set of problems. There was no way around it at that point, but Mary's plan seemed to be the safer of the two, "I… agree with Mary, strength in numbers is our best bet. Should anyone or anything attack us, we'll be better suited to defend ourselves. Just ask anyone who's ever been in a horror movie. – Vlad, what do you think?"

Vlad didn't answer.

"Vlad?"

Johnny looked at his buddy oddly. Vlad appeared to be focused on something in the distance. He wasn't responding to anything his friends said. It was very clear that he was not with them at that moment.

"Vlad!"

"Shhh!"

An irritated look came over Vlad's face as he focused harder and harder. He waved his hand, signaling for everyone to keep it down. After a few moments, his eyes shot open and he charged forward into the darkness.

Soul Siphon

Johnny's eyes widened as his friend quickly began to fade into the darkness, "Vlad!"

"Follow him!" Corban cried. "Quickly before we lose sight of him!"

Corban gave chase with the rest of the group not far behind him. Vlad moved faster than should have been humanly possible, but Corban was able to keep track of him. They approached the central district where Vlad had stopped. A circular structure with moss growing out of it stood in the center. He ran through one of the archways and stared into the middle of the structure.

Large scattered stones stood in the way of where it looked like Vlad wanted to go. He quickly went to work trying to clear the lighter ones before turning to his friends, "Help me."

Vlad turned back and grabbed one of the larger stones and began to push. Johnny got under Vlad and pushed while Corban stood next to them and added his weight. Mary tried to pull from the other side. Her arms shook as they strained under the heavy boulder.

The massive boulder ground against the earth as it fought back against the team's collective strength. Beads of sweat poured down Corban's face as he put all of his strength into moving it. The rock groaned as it finally began to give way. There was a crumbling sound as little by little, the rock moved aside. Dust kicked up around them as the rock finally gave way and crashed to their left.

The dust instantly disappeared as a large gaping maw appeared behind the rock. There was a massive gust of wind and a thick smell of must that rushed out of the hole in the ground. It was as though the ancient air was desperately escaping its prison and almost sounded like a low roar as it passed by their ears.

Soul Siphon

Corban covered his mouth with his hand as the thick smell of mildew blew past his nostrils. It was so strong that his eyes watered and he felt like he was about to choke. He was not looking forward to going in. The smell was only going to get stronger.

Johnny shook his head, "Of course this is where we're going right? We're in a cursed, demonic land and we're going into a tight dark passage that will lead us to some infernal trap. Yup, this is what I signed on for... fuck me!"

"I sink Johnny should probably stay put and stand guard. Is probably much safer up here, alone in dark of night."

The howl of an animal in the distance made Johnny jump in fright, "No... no, I don't think it'll be much safer at all. I actually think that it would be a lot safer if we all just left... but I suppose that isn't possible, is it?"

"Nope," Mary replied. "So you better be sure you want to do this, yeah? You coming with us or staying behind? It's your choice, just hurry the hell up and choose, will you?"

"All right, all right, you guys win. I'll go with you. Jeez, you all suck!"

Corban chuckled, "It's just a tunnel, I'm sure that it'll be fine."

Johnny sighed, "Yeah right... famous last words if ever there were any. Just keep your eyes open for fuck's sake. Who knows what could be waiting for us in there and if the passage is as narrow as the entrance, we're going to have problems."

"Johnny worry too much."

"Johnny know better than to get himself into trouble needlessly!" Johnny replied in a mocking voice. "Johnny live longer that way, he thinks! It's called being careful!"

Soul Siphon

Corban cut in before they could start arguing again, "I'll go first then if it will make everyone feel better. Cover my back and make sure that we're not followed."

"My job," Mary replied as she pressed one hand against Corban, intent on keeping it there when he slid into the tunnel.

Corban crouched down and jumped into the hole, head first, completely unconcerned about the darkness in front of him. He hoped that Adramelech wouldn't let him come to harm unless it was absolutely necessary. He was obviously valuable to the demon, thus it made sense for him to go first.

There was a brief scuffling sound as Corban disappeared into the darkness and then silence for a moment after that. He was encased in darkness that seemed to drown out all of his senses. After a moment, he heard a nervous voice call to him, "Corban?"

He turned back to the entrance, but didn't get far before Mary's voice broke the darkness again, "Corban, you answer me right now!"

There was a brief gust of wind that emanated from the hole. It carried Corban's voice, making it echo through the entrance, "Yes, I'm here, come on in. The tunnel widens as you go deeper into it. It's large enough to stand up in here."

Corban could hear Mary release the air that she had trapped in her lungs. A moment later, Mary appeared in front of him. She landed on her feet inside, in a pile of warm sand that made up the floor. Johnny and Vlad followed closely behind her. The moment that they were reunited on the inside, they proceeded down the dark corridor.

Soul Siphon

XXII

The tunnel, like the buildings outside, was old and decrepit though in slightly better shape. The smell of must and mildew filled their nostrils once more as they entered the small opening. There was no light in the passage and no sunlight could break through the stone. Their eyes adjusted as much as they could, but even then, it was impossible to see anything.

"Well this is great," Corban said with a frustrated sigh. "We're going straight into darkness. This really isn't a good idea. I didn't think we'd be going into this blind."

"We won't be."

Corban turned to see Mary staring into the darkness. Her eyes flared a bright red as she stepped in front of him. She appeared to be fixated on the path ahead, "Follow me, I can see where we need to go."

"Do you see anything ahead of us?"

"No, just an empty tunnel. I think we're safe for the moment."

Corban shrugged and stayed very close to Mary as they moved, "I didn't know you had the ability to do that."

"I move in the shadows," Mary replied. "How do you think I see when I'm stalking my prey?"

"I dunno, I just kinda assumed you got them drunk and had them sing folk songs!"

"That was just you, yeah? Though I may try that next time. It seemed to work pretty well."

"Nah I kinda like the idea that I'm the only one you used that on."

"You sure?"

"Yup."

"Well all right then."

Soul Siphon

As they proceeded further, Mary's foot accidentally kicked something on the ground. She stumbled forward and almost fell, but Corban was there to catch her, "You all right?"

"Yeah… I tripped over something that felt like a stick or something… wait…"

Mary's red eyes illuminated the ground where she had tripped. There was a skeleton propped up against the wall to the right. In its hand was an iron poll that appeared to have some kind of cloth wrapped around the top. She picked it up and carefully inspected the cloth, "Anyone got a light?"

Johnny reached into his pocket and pulled out a silver-plated zippo, "Always."

He flicked it open, causing the flame to appear. Mary held out the rod and placed the cloth end over the flame. It immediately ignited in an impressive burst of energy and coated the area around them in an orange hue. It only covered a small radius, but it was enough for them to proceed forward more comfortably.

Mary looked behind her and beckoned Vlad to come forward, "Vlad, you're our history buff. Take a look at this skeleton. Do you recognize his outfit?"

The old Russian looked him over carefully, "Roman… probably from ze Republican time period before ze began to expand zeir territory."

Mary looked at him oddly, "He predates the Empire?"

"By a hundred years, most likely," Vlad replied. "Probably from ze Punic Vars."

"Wonder how he wound up here."

"Stumbled onto somesing he shouldn't have, perhaps?"

"Like the Necropolis."

Soul Siphon

Corban sighed, "It's not like the Romans didn't have their own dark histories. They had their fair share of sadistic rituals as well."

"Zis is true," Vlad replied.

"A mystery for another time, yeah?" Mary asked.

"Yeah," Corban replied. "Let's keep moving."

He was about to move on when Vlad noticed something next to the skeleton, "Vait, vait!"

"What is it?"

Vlad grabbed the torch and brought it down to the area where he was looking in excitement. There appeared to be writing scrolled on the wall. Corban looked at it oddly, "It looks like Latin."

"It is," Vlad replied.

Mary examined the writing, "I don't recognize this writing. Can you read it?"

"I vill try…"

Vlad studied the writings carefully. His eyes focused as he worked. Seconds later, he turned to Corban and sucked down a deep breath, "Zis man vas an officer from ze Roman Legion. He condemns ze actions of his people during ze last days of ze var…"

Vlad sucked in a deep breath and began to read, "I vas in command of ze force zat attacked zis unholy place. Let no ill tidings befall my men on ze vay to ze afterlife. I and I alone bear ze full responsibility for my actions, and I alone shall burn for zem. Ve interrupted a ceremony vich ve believed vas a profane ritual by zos who vorship it, ven in fact it vas a ritual to bind ze evil spirit zat dwells here. Let my remains serve as a varning to any von who discovers zem. Leave, now. To pass any furzer vould spell doom to zose poor fools."

The warning made Corban uneasy. He released a short breath from his tense lungs and took a step back.

Soul Siphon

Mary shook her head, "Spooky, yeah? Nothing we haven't seen before though. Let's go."

"Yeah, the sooner the better," Corban replied. "Worrying about this won't solve anything."

Corban took the torch back from Vlad and raised it above them. Mary's eyes remained as red as her hair, even though Corban now carried a torch that should've been enough to light their way, but he had to be careful. The light from the torch was dim and unreliable as it flickered off the walls. One good gust of wind could easily extinguish it.

The group proceeded further into the tunnel. The further they went, the more Corban began to notice that its direction had become a slow decline. The ground was little more than sand that seemed to flow past their feet as they moved. It weighed on their knees as the path became steeper, causing them to slide every few steps.

Vlad began to huff as he balanced himself, "Zis is going to kill me."

"Then stop drinking so much," Mary replied. "You won't have as big of a problem with it if you actually take care of yourself, yeah?"

"I prefer drink. Is no fun othervise! Healthy living with no fun is not living!"

"Whatever."

The group kept going until they reached a flat surface and a doorway. Like the rest of the underground lair, the doorway was crumbling stone that had worn with the passage of time. The ground was still nothing more than sand beneath their feet.

Corban took a deep breath and stepped in front of Mary, "Here we go…"

Mary tried to push back, not wanting to give up point, "I should go first on this one."

"Not going to happen."

Soul Siphon

"Corban, you're the only one who can kill him. Your abilities aren't physical combat, mine are. I know you're trying to protect me, but right now that's my job, yeah? If we get attacked in there, I'll be better suited to deal with it. Now knock off the macho, chivalry, bullshit. Sometimes it suits you, but not right now."

Corban sighed and stood aside, allowing her to get past him. She smiled as she stepped forward, "You're all right, Corban. Next time, I'll let you protect me."

"You better."

Mary stepped out ahead of Corban, her eyes still burning red as she moved. The look on her face was completely stoic and fearless. This was comforting to Corban, knowing that she was that tough.

Mary stepped through the door, into the next room with Corban close behind her. There was a hollow sound in the next chamber, quiet and eerie. Just from the sound alone, Corban could tell that they were entering a large underground amphitheater. Their steps echoed off of the walls as they moved.

Corban grimaced as he entered the room. If felt as though someone had jabbed a sharp blade into his nostrils. The stench was overpowering, "Oh man... what is that smell?"

"I not know all of it. Zere is more zan one scent in here, but zere is definitely petroleum oil."

"Oil?" Mary asked.

Corban sniffed the air to figure out which direction the smell was coming from. His head turned to the side as his eyes focused on the wall behind him. Against this wall, was a small trough that seemed to run the length of the room and was filled with black liquid. The smell was even stronger as he looked on. He cautiously dipped his finger into the liquid and

Soul Siphon

inspected the murky liquid that came out, "Definitely oil."

Corban kept a safe distance as he lowered the lit end of the torch into the trough. There was a hissing sound as the flame grew from the torch and spread across the wall. It quickly surrounded the room in a line of flame.

Corban watched as the walls began to light up in an orange hue. The flame illuminated the massive chamber around them with a menacing glow. The room was dome-shaped with loose stones holding everything together. The walls were fairly smooth and the stones looked as though they had been carefully crafted. Whoever did this, took great care to get it right.

Corban was relieved to finally be able to see again, "Well that's better, at least now we should…"

Corban stopped and his eyes went wide as he looked up. Mary looked at him oddly as the red flame left her eyes, "Everything all right?"

Corban pointed to the middle of the room, "I think we've come to the right place…"

Mary slowly turned and followed his gaze until she saw exactly what he did. Her eyes also widened as she brandished both of her daggers, "I definitely think you're right…"

In the center of the room was a massive bronze statue. It was the effigy of a muscular man with the head of a bull. It was blackened, covered in soot.

Corban pointed to the base of the statue, "Looks like this thing was meant to be lit on fire. It almost seems like the base was meant to be an oven."

As the flame traveled around the room, it proceeded behind the massive statue and connected with a stream on the floor. The fire ran under the statue where it illuminated its furnace compartments and eyes. It was as though the effigy had suddenly come to life and was glaring at them.

Corban's eyes narrowed, "Did they use this to cook or something?"

"Cook?" Mary asked. "No… not cook… I've heard stories about this… thing. The nuns that I stayed with at the Providence Row Night Refuge sometimes spoke of pagan practices when trying to help us wayward souls avoid the devil."

Mary's voice became little more than a growl as she slowly approached the statue and touched its outstretched palms, "They have set their abominations to defile my house. They have built on the high places of Topheth, in the valley of the son of Hinnom, to burn their sons and their daughters in the fire; which I did not command, nor did it ever cross my mind. Jeremiah 7:33."

Johnny shivered as Mary continued, "This chamber was used as a sacrificial altar. This is where they worshipped Moloch… It was as horrific as it was profane. Disgusting…"

"Do I even want to know what exactly went on here?" Johnny asked.

"I doubt it, but I'll tell you anyway. Just so you know what we're up against."

She pointed to the hands with its palms facing up, "The statue would be set ablaze. Sacrificial offerings were placed in each compartment. It would usually be offerings of food, animals… and a child was placed in its hands."

Corban's stomach churned when he heard the last part. He thought that he'd be able to handle anything that could be thrown at him at this point, but this was far beyond what he expected, "What?"

A tear formed in Mary's eye as she continued, "It's said that when the sacrificial child screamed out

Soul Siphon

in pain, the priests beat a loud drum, so that no one, including the father, would hear its cry. They didn't want him trying to save it. One of the few things that the Romans did right was to slaughter these monsters."

Corban's face went red as a nauseous feeling overtook him, "That's the sickest thing I've ever heard."

"I know," Mary replied. "It was pretty horrific when you think about..."

"Stop talking," Corban demanded.

"Excuse me?"

"I don't want to hear any more about this. That's something that will haunt my dreams for years to come."

He looked into Mary's eyes, letting her know that the next few words from his mouth were extremely serious, "We don't leave here until this place is completely toppled. I'll kill Adramelech, but then I want his temple defiled."

"You mean cleansed?"

"Whatever."

"All right, we'll figure out a way to ground this place into dust, yeah?"

A loud growl interrupted the group as they looked around. Corban jumped as he turned and looked at the statue. Smoke poured out of the nostrils and the eyes now glowed a yellow color that was way too bright to be from the small flame below. More smoke poured from the statue, making a hissing noise as it was forced out.

Johnny raised his hands defensively and stepped back, "Oh man... did we just wake it up?"

"I sink it not like what Corban said."

Mary held ground with her blades close and backed up a little so that she was closer to Corban, "This is going to be bad... Corban, stay behind me."

Soul Siphon

Corban didn't react. He didn't even hear her. His mind blanked and he found himself unable to move. He was filled with a sense of dread as intense power overtook him. This was the exact same experience he suffered through when he was first possessed. It was a feeling that he'd hoped never to have to live through again.

Mary turned to him with an irritated look, "Hey are you even listening to me?"

Mary stopped dead in her tracks when her eyes met Corban's. She grabbed his shoulder and examined him more closely, "Corban…?"

Corban's vision blurred to the point where even Mary's face was obscured. The dark sound of whispering filled the air. He wasn't certain if the others could hear it or if it was just in his own head, "E tuo mio turnunen wesari… Asaditempari."

Corban's head began to spin. His head began to pound as the words flowed through his mind. Mary took a step closer to him, "Corban… speak to me, now!"

Corban shook his head violently, desperately trying to get the sound out of his head in any way he could, "I can hear him… just as before. His words… he's trying to attack me!"

"What, from where?"

"In my mind... I can feel him! Adramelech… Moloch… Egredimini de capite meo!"

"Corban!" Mary shouted. "Pull yourself together."

Corban stopped shaking and gave her a pained look, "I… I'm okay… I think…"

Mary appeared to calm down. She seemed cautiously optimistic that he was coming out of it, but was still worried, "Talk to me, what is it?"

Soul Siphon

Corban dropped to his knees and he looked up at the statue. He was no longer in control of his body. It was as though he was a mere, lifeless, shell of himself and there was nothing he could do about it, "They're here…"

A confused look came over Mary's face, "Corban wh…?"

Rerereak!

The high pitched screech from beneath the sand interrupted her. She clenched her daggers tightly and pointed them to either side, "This could be bad…"

"Vat ze hell vas zat!"

A hand appeared out of the sand. It slowly rose up until a body appeared underneath it. The creature was humanoid, but it was decrepit beyond any chance of looking like a person. It had thin patches of skin and some organs, but much of it had withered away. Its eyes glowed bright white and the gray lips formed a smile of broken teeth.

Mary shook her head, "Ugly bastard. It isn't friendly, yeah?"

She quickly whirled around, doing a 360-degree spin. Her dagger came around and connected with the creature's neck. The creature howled in pain as its head detached and fell into the sand. The blow did not kill the creature as Mary had hoped. Instead, it immediately turned and moved towards her.

Johnny jumped on it from behind and placed his bare hands on the creature's shoulders, "Oh no you don't!"

The creature's skin slowly turned from brown to white and it burst into dust. Johnny dropped to one knee as the creature disappeared from beneath him, "Well at least we know it wasn't immortal! That was almost too easy!"

Soul Siphon

Five more hands burst through the sands, followed by high-pitched screams. Three more followed after that. They slowly pulled themselves up out of the sand and flanked the group on either side. Johnny took a step back, "Aw shit… I had to say it. I knew better and I said it anyway!"

Mary stepped back, closer to her friends. Vlad and Johnny joined her while Corban remained on his knees, staring off into space in complete silence. The creatures spread out so that there was no way for the group to escape. They were completely surrounded. Their only chance was to fight their way out.

Mary clenched her jaw and decapitated another one of the creatures, sliced off its arms, legs, and then cut its torso in half. The creature's remains scampered about the floor and attempted to retake their form, but it was momentarily incapacitated.

Mary turned quickly enough to use her daggers to block another creature that was carrying an old sword. She was determined not to leave Corban's side, but he was in a precarious position that was quickly being overrun, "Johnny, I could use your help over here!"

Johnny had his hands on another one of the creatures, causing it to disintegrate, "I'm a little busy right now, do what you can! I'll get there as soon as I'm done over here."

Mary sighed as she continued to fight defensively, bringing her dagger around in front of her. She knew that it was a losing battle, but she'd hoped that she was just buying Corban enough time to wage whatever mental battle he had to. However, it was fairly obvious that he wouldn't have long. Between dodging these creatures' strikes, she could see that Vlad wasn't having any easier a time of it. He used his powers to draw the throwing knives from his vest and sent them spinning towards the creatures. He managed to cut down three of them, but they quickly repaired themselves, reattached severed limbs, and continued bearing down on the group.

Vlad stepped back closer to Mary, "Not good, Vlad not have the power to kill zese!"

Johnny placed his hands on the first creature that got within arms reach. He appeared to be enjoying himself as he drained the energy from it and watched it turn to dust, "Hey, what do you know? One down!"

His success drew the attention of two more creatures. They jumped on him from behind and quickly restrained his hands. Johnny fought back, but had already been neutralized, "Really guys? Attacking from behind? Dick move...!"

A second later, Vlad was also knocked over, losing control of his knives, "Damn cossacks!"

Mary tried to use her super speed to get around her attackers and free her friends, but the moment she began to run, one of the creatures caught her by the neck. The surprise and strain of the impact caused her to drop her blades. She began to gag as the creature lifted her off of the ground. She closed her eyes, believing that she'd lost, "Corban..."

The creature holding her let out a malice-filled laugh as it raised her higher off the ground. She tried to kick but was unable to connect with the creature's torso. Her arms were going numb and she was slowly slipping out of consciousness, "Corban... we need you..."

A shocked look came over the creature's face and it began to shake. Mary looked at it oddly as she was released from the harsh grip. The creature appeared to collapse in on itself as though being sucked into a tiny black hole. It disappeared into nothing, revealing Corban standing behind it. His hand

Soul Siphon

was outstretched as he absorbed its power. The look on his face was one of intense anger as tiny red bolts of energy flowed up his arms, "No hands are allowed on her unless they're mine."

Once the creature was gone, Mary dropped to her knees and began to cough. Corban ran to her side, but she shook her head, "No, help them… I'm… fine!"

Corban turned to the creatures holding down Johnny. He grabbed them and absorbed their powers as well. At that moment, his eyes began to glow white just like the creatures' had.

Johnny fought to get free as the creatures turned their attention from him to Corban. Once they were gone, Corban opened his hand to Johnny, "Ready?"

"Hell yes!"

Corban turned to deal with the two creatures who were trying to pin Vlad to the ground. Vlad was on his back, swearing loudly in his native tongue as Johnny's eyes widened at the sound of his voice, "Oh man is he pissed..."

Corban extended his fingers and allowed energy to flow from the tips. The two creatures disintegrated and their bodies were absorbed into the beam which then returned to Corban's form. Vlad was left lying on his back with a surprised look, "Vat?"

Corban's eyes began to glow even brighter than before. Mary had finally regained her composure and could feel the power that he had accumulated blazing off of him. She feared what might happen next as she turned to Johnny. He had just finished off another one of the creatures as Mary spoke, "Johnny, you take care of the other four! –Corban, that's enough!"

Corban smiled, "It's okay, I can control it."

The hair on the back of Mary's neck stood up and she began to experience Déjà vu. She spoke in a far more nervous tone, "Then control it and stop, now!"

The smile vanished from Corban's face. His eyes slowly began to fade back to their original color, "You're right, I'm sorry… I'm done. –Johnny, they're all yours."

Relief poured over Mary's features as Corban came back down to her, "Thank you."

Johnny touched two more of the creatures, causing them to decompose and vanish into dust. Vlad helped out as much as he could by pinning the creatures to the walls until Johnny could get to them. He shook his head as Johnny sucked the life out of these monsters, "I guess you vins zis round."

"Nah," Johnny replied, "no betting on the final battles. It's bad luck."

He turned and placed his hands on the head of the last creature. It screamed out in pain as he pulled at its energy. Johnny was clearly enjoying every minute of this, "Yeah you like that, don't you, mother fucker!"

As the creature exploded into dust, Johnny turned to the group and nodded. Corban smiled, "Good job everyone! We…"

He was about to say something when a gust of wind caught his attention. At the back of the chamber was a large doorway that appeared to lead into yet another black void. The eyes on the bull's head glowed even brighter as the voices returned. They were louder now and appeared to be taunting Corban.

"What, what is it?" Mary asked.

Corban placed his hands on his temples and squeezed his eyes shut. His jaw clenched as he struggled against the creature. He was going through agony, trying to fight back.

Soul Siphon

"Corban... What's wrong? Tell me how to help you, yeah?" Mary asked desperately.

"Adramelech... he's here... I can feel him..."

"Shut him out!"

Corban couldn't respond. He was too busy trying to put up mental barriers between himself and Adramelech's taint. It was a fight that he wasn't winning. Mary grabbed his shoulder and held him steady, "Corban, open your eyes and look at me!"

"Too... powerful... I can't."

"Yes, you can! Empty your mind and just focus on me!"

Corban slowed his breathing as he opened his eyes. The black orbs were bloodshot and wet as he struggled to keep them open, "Mary... I can feel him clawing at me."

"I know, I know... it's okay, he can't hurt you. Just focus on me, focus on my eyes and our memories. Focus on what we shared and forget everything else."

Corban peered into Mary's eyes. He once again saw the demons that she fought and all the pain that she had been through, but he also saw that happiness that dwelt within. He saw how far she'd come in such a short time and how much they had accomplished together. In the darkness of her eyes, there was also light.

Corban used that light as his source of strength. Suddenly, Adramelech's hold over him didn't seem as strong. He felt like he could actually resist the demon and win.

With his newfound strength, Corban focused harder and harder as he tried to fight the mental torment that Adramelech was levying against him, "No... you're not getting in my head again..."

An inhuman, yet familiar voice appeared in his mind, "Again? I never left... my boy!

Soul Siphon

"What the hell does that mean?"

Mary continued to stare at him as her eyes helped wage his terrible battle, "Focus Corban..."

Corban's eyes blinked and he growled, "Get out... get out..."

Finally he threw his head back and screamed, "Get the fuck out!"

At that moment, a black cloud shot out of Corban's head and flew like a comet around the room. It bounced off the walls as though it were looking for a way out of the room. It appeared to be flying completely blind. It bumped the walls two or three times before it appeared to regain control. It stopped for a moment as though deciding where to go and then flew towards Mary at incredible speeds.

Mary was unable to move in time and Corban couldn't jump in the way before it reached its target. It hit her in the stomach and vanished within her body. She fell backward and hit the ground hard. Her eyes closed and she went pale. She looked like a corpse.

Her lips began to move, but the voice was not her own, "*I should never have resurrected you, bitch!*"

Corban dropped to his knees next to her and grabbed her hand, "Mary.. talk to me... Mary? Come on..."

He placed his hand on her wrist, "Her heart's racing..."

Johnny and Vlad joined him at her side. Johnny checked her other wrist, "She's ice cold... what's happening?"

Corban carefully examined her face for any sign of life, "I don't know."

Corban struggled hard to bring Mary back to reality. He tapped on her cheek and tried to get her to respond, but nothing was working, "Mary come on, come out of it. We still need you! I still need you!"

Soul Siphon

At that moment, Mary's eyes opened widely and she looked at Corban. She had an extremely distressed look on her face as her teeth clenched together, "Corban... I can't hold him off for much longer... Please... kill me..."

Corban furrowed his brow as he looked at her, "Hell no, there has to be another way."

"Corban... please... I can't fight it!"

"No!"

A massive surge of energy ripped through Corban's body. He began to feel his powers flow through to his hand as his skin began to glow. An unseen force guided his hand into her chest. He focused harder than he ever had before and slowly closed his hand around something that had inhabited her soul. He wasn't sure what it was, but he was sure that he wasn't pulling at anything that was supposed to be there. This was something of evil that had to come out.

Corban crushed it with his fingers and pulled the darkness out of her body. As he withdrew his hand, the dark shadow came out with it. The shadow took on the form of a snake and gyrated in an attempt to free itself from his grip.

Corban did the best he could to hold onto it, but the spirit was too powerful. It seemed desperate to get away before Corban could absorb its power. After a brief struggle, it coiled itself back and jolted forward, causing Corban to lose his grip. The entity shot into the darkness and disappeared into the next room.

"Corban man, you did it!" Johnny shouted. "You've harnessed the power to rip demons from their hosts... Now we can fight possessions!"

Color slowly began to return to Mary's face, but she was still unconscious. He ran his fingers gently over her left cheek as he watched her lay motionless.

Soul Siphon

The look was one of sadness. He knew that she was out cold and probably not in control of her facial features, but it still angered him.

Vlad looked up at him, "Mary be all right."

Corban could feel the rage surge through his body. His faced heated up as he looked into the dark maw ahead of him and got to his feet, "Stay with her. –You too Johnny."

Johnny nodded that he understood, "Go get him, buddy!"

Corban aggressively charged forward into the next room. He couldn't see, but he didn't care. Nothing that could be residing there held any fear over him. He was far too angry for that.

The next room was damp and cold. There was no way to tell how big it was, but the echo of his feet made him feel like this was probably the necropolis. An icy feeling came over his skin as he entered the next chamber. It stung his skin as he moved.

Corban could hear what sounded like echoing in the distance. He stopped moving when he was quite certain that he was close to the edge. His eyes burned with rage as he looked out into the void, "Adramelech!"

He could hear his voice echo across the walls of the chamber, but there was no response. His eyes scanned the darkness, shifting from left to right as he waited for a response. The silence only served to anger Corban even more, "Adramelech!"

Again, no response. Corban could feel his whole body heating up. It spread throughout his body and then across his skin like warm goosebumps. He knew that the demon was there, so why was he not responding? "Adrameleeeeeech!"

"No need to shout! I'm right here!"

Soul Siphon

Corban turned and looked behind him. Vlad, Johnny, and Mary were gone, as was the doorway to the previous room. In their place was an almost mirror image of Corban, himself. The skin around its eyes was red and its smile was beyond hideous. It almost looked as though his face was about to transform into something demonic.

"Adramelech..."

The creature shook its head. Its lips curled into a hideous smile as it responded, "No... I'm you."

"What?"

"I'm what you are meant to become, everything that you can be. I'm you, fully realized."

"I... don't understand..."

"You are destined for something great. Your power will be greater than any mere mortal has ever experienced. Unlike the others that I tried to train, you have the ability to withstand its corruption. All you have to do is join with me. Allow me to finish my mission and you can accomplish anything!"

Corban shook his head, "No..."

"You understand what I'm saying." The facsimile said with a smile. "Deep down inside you knew that something was different about you. There was always something out of place since the day you were born... I have the answers you seek. I'd be happy to give them to you."

"I'm not interested."

"How can you not be even a little tempted?"

"Because I'm not evil. I've been given a second chance and I have friends that I care about. You're not tempting me..."

"Oh, I get it now..." The facsimile replied.

"...?"

"It's because of Mary, isn't it? If you accept my offer, you lose her."

Soul Siphon

Corban remained silent as the facsimile continued, "Yes I see the bond that you've created with her. I thought that such a bond would prove advantageous to me later on as it was something that I could use as leverage against you. Clearly, I underestimated the power that you two were able to create in such a short time, but no matter. You mustn't worry about that either. Joining me won't cause you to lose her. She can be yours forever, simply for the asking."

At that moment, the facsimile began to change shape. Its form began to shrink to a smaller size and take on a female form. It grew long red hair and smiled as its face became Mary's. It was an exact copy of her, or was it? Either way, she was now wearing different clothing. Her shirt had become a sweatshirt with a zipper and her pants were now tight slacks.

Corban took a step back and clenched his fists, "What the hell..."

"See?" Mary asked. "You wouldn't have to give me up. I can be here for you too... available... should you want me..."

A seductive look appeared on her face as she reached up to the collar of her sweatshirt and slowly unzipped it. To Corban's surprise, she wasn't wearing anything underneath. He sucked in a deep breath as Mary's shirt opened, revealing her pale freckled skin. She took a sultry step forward and reached under the open sweatshirt with her left hand, cupping her right breast so that Corban could see it, "That is what you wanted... isn't it?"

"It's not real."

"It can be as real as you want it to be."

"That's not the same thing."

"Does it matter?"

Soul Siphon

"It does to me."

Mary stepped closer to him and leaned on his chest, "Are you sure?"

Corban was disgusted, not only because of what the demon was doing but also because he was actually tempted by it. He quickly pushed her away, "Get back, you filth! That's not going to work, Adramelech! I know that this isn't Mary. You're not going to seduce me so stop being a coward and show yourself so that we can end this!"

Mary frowned as she re-zipped her shirt and stepped backward, "You have no idea what you just denied yourself."

"I'll live."

"No... you won't."

Corban found himself back in the chamber that he'd run into. He could see light from the room behind him and the pitch darkness in front of him. Johnny called out to him, "Corban, you all right?"

"Yeah, I'm fine. –That the best you can do, Adramelech?"

The sound of deep breathing filled the chamber in response. It grew louder with each passing second. The sound was similar to that of a lion that was trying to be quiet as it stalked its prey. This was it for him, regardless of whether he won or lost. That would be the end of it.

A flash of light ignited troughs of oil that lined the walls of this chamber just as it had in the previous one. Corban didn't bother watching what was happening, choosing instead to keep his eyes fixed forward. He wanted to be ready for Adramelech. Nothing was going to distract him and give the demon a chance to strike first.

The fire illuminated the massive chamber. There were winding staircases that twisted and turned around the wall in odd patterns. Each led to the same place; the pit at the bottom of the room which was occupied by a single stone altar. The ground was flat, but it led to a massive obelisk that stood in the center. The pillar was stone black with odd carvings all over it and what looked like ancient stains that had long since dried up. It stood about five stories tall from floor to ceiling. The walls around the cavern were all intricately carved with murals or doorways that led to possible tombs and other chambers. This was the necropolis and it was large enough to be a city.

Corban forced what energy he could into his hands. He was blazing with power from the creatures that he'd already absorbed and was anxious to unleash it on this demon. He had seen the evil and the depravity wrought by Adramelech. It had pushed him into a sick obsession that he was unable to escape. Adramelech had become his white whale.

Corban's eyes scanned the room. It was quiet, too quiet. Something was waiting in the winds, deciding if he could truly be a match for it, but it hid itself well. He would have to draw it out if he wanted to finally end the battle.

Corban was growing impatient as he stood on the back balcony of the chamber. He blood was boiling beyond tolerance and it caused his hands to shake, "Adramelech!"

The malicious hiss of an unnatural gust of wind blew past him as though responding to his demands. A sound flowed through the chambers that echoed in the empty room. It sounded like the echo of a person after they had finished chanting. Could this be the residual trace of those who had worshipped the demon so long ago?

The echo was then followed by a deep thundering voice, "Cor... ban... my friend..."

Soul Siphon

Corban's eyes flared up as the writing on the obelisk began to glow a hideous green color. The light grew to the point where it blinded Corban for a few moments. He blocked his eyes with his arm until it faded away.

When he realized it was safe, Corban lowered his arm and looked to see what was facing him. It took a moment for his eyes to focus, but it was something he considered merciful when he finally saw what he was up against. His eyes widened at the large creature standing at least four stories tall, bearing down on him.

Corban recognized this creature from his own nightmares. It had the head of a rancid mule, but the rest of its body was anything but a normal creature. It had wiry patches of hair, unlike the soft hair most donkeys and mules grew. It was also bipedal, standing on two hoofed hind legs, a skill that should not have been possible. Its arms were like those of a Tyrannosaurus Rex, short and skimpy. The tail stood out more than anything. It resembled that of a male peacock with long feathers which appeared to look like eyes. The look on its face was hideous, "Hello my old symbiont. How fair you now that I am gone?"

"Symbiont? You were a parasite and nothing more!" Corban replied. "You took everything from me. My family, my friends, Janine, my future, and my life!"

The creature scoffed, "What I took away from you was a fantasy! It was not your life to live and it never would have been. Everything that happened to you was predetermined years ago!"

Corban's eyes narrowed as he placed his hand on the birthmark on his hip. Adramelech cackled, "Yes... you're finally starting to get it, aren't you? Your name isn't even Corban. None of this is real and none of it was going to last forever."

Soul Siphon

"What the hell are you talking about?"

"How do you think that you were able to hold out against me? What made you so special that you were able to fend off a demon?"

Corban shrugged, "I had more control over my body."

"Exactly. You were given abilities that normal possession victims would not have had. You were given the chance to be stronger thanks to a dark blessing you were given at birth."

"How?"

"Dark rituals and rites that were performed over your mother before you were born."

Corban didn't believe it. "Bullshit! My mother wouldn't have let that happen. More likely you're just not as strong as you think you are."

Adramelech roared with laughter, "Have I existed this long to be taunted by an insignificant mortal?"

"For being so insignificant, you seem to be very interested in me."

"You have nothing that was not given to you by us. Your mother is not your true mother. The life you have lived was never yours to live! You were manufactured to serve a purpose."

"What?" Corban asked, surprised.

Adramelech took great pride in his words. He clearly enjoyed his attempts to destroy Corban's reality, "All of this, all of it, was preordained long ago. Your mother, your true mother, was a woman named Lilith Bonnaire. She was a beautiful woman with dark hair much like yours."

Corban ran his fingers through his hair and lowered his eyes as Adramelech continued, "She was devoted to my master and gave herself to the cause during a dark ritual that was conducted by a group of my servants. You were conceived that dark night."

Adramelech pointed to his hip, "You were given that mark as a sign of your purpose. You killed your mother when you were born. Fortunately, another mother had just given birth. Her child, Corban, was stillborn and rushed out of the room before she could even see him. A few members of the medical staff at that hospital, with some help from me, made the switch and placed you in Corban's incubation tube."

Corban could not believe what he was now being told, "No… that's not true… it can't be…"

Adramelech laughed, "Oh it's true, and you know it is. You noticed the differences between yourself and your mother long ago. You actually used to joke about being adopted. You had hoped that you simply resembled your father, but that's not the case either. You are a child of darkness, and in darkness is where you belong!"

"Corban!" A familiar voice cried out. "Don't listen to him. This is what demons do! They lie and deceive!"

"Lie?" Adramelech asked. "Yes demons certainly do, but why lie when the truth is far more fun?"

Corban lowered his eyes as Mary appeared in the room, followed by Vlad and Johnny. Several scenes from Corban's life flashed through his mind. Many unusual or unexplained moments were now making sense. It hurt to think about, but somehow, he knew that the demon wasn't lying. He wasn't who he thought he was and nothing was going to change that.

Mary clenched her jaw as she glared at the demon, "We're not buying it, Mike! You have been playing us for a very long time, and we're supposed to believe you now?"

Soul Siphon

Adramelech smirked, "Nope, just Corban."

"Well, he's not buying it! –Are you Corban?"

Corban's silence made Mary nervous, "Corban?"

"It's true…"

"What?"

Corban's heart sank as he came to terms with everything, "It all adds up. I was considered a miracle child for being able to survive a supposed still-birth. I look nothing like my mother and… I always thought that the birthmark on my hip was a tattoo."

The demon nodded, "Now you're catching on. You didn't even cry when it was cut into your skin."

"Corban, none of that proves anything," Mary insisted. "Just because you have some mark, doesn't mean that you are destined for evil. That's not the man that I've come to know! You control your own fate. Don't let him into your head again! He's just trying to mess with you."

Corban looked up at the demon, "Assuming that I believe you, why would you go through all of this trouble? Why this elaborate scheme? Why bring back a team to kill off bad people? It all seems unnecessary."

The demon revealed hideous yellow teeth from behind its loose gums as it spoke, "I suppose I should tell you since you know this much. You don't know how important you are to us. You are prized beyond all others."

Mary didn't like where this was going and tried to grab Corban by the arm, "Corban…"

"No, I want to hear this," Corban replied sternly.

Mary let go of his arm, but stayed in close proximity as the demon continued, "For many centuries, we've searched for someone who could wield the powers you have. I assembled this team to

Soul Siphon

aid in my search and then help train the siphon. Reaping vengeance against evil was just a cover for the truth and kept the angels from finding out. Our demons then went about possessing random people, hoping to find a suitable host."

Mary clenched her fist at her side as Adramelech continued, "After so many failed attempts, we realized that no mere mortal could wield celestial energies on their own. It took us some time, but we were able to pull together enough energy to perform a special rite that would give you the strength you needed. We knew you'd have siphoning abilities. We knew that eventually, you would overuse your abilities just as every single soul siphon that has come before you has. However, we also know that you have a much stronger will and that you would be able to control it longer than any other. You are perfect, strong-willed enough to maintain your faculties, but not strong enough to resist possession without sacrificing your life. You are exactly the host that my master was hoping for."

"The devil, I take it?" Corban asked in an unsurprised tone.

"Very good Corban, yes," Adramelech replied as though her were praising a dutiful child. "Now you understand. You see, a certain acquaintance of ours cost my master his powers long ago during the Celestial Wars. If you were to achieve enough power, he could infiltrate your mind, possess you, and take your powers for himself. He would instantly become all-powerful and thus have everything he needs to retake the Celestial World."

"All this time…" Corban said through clenched teeth. "All this effort to give the devil enough power to reclaim what he lost… that's what this is all about…?"

"Correct."

Soul Siphon

"All along… I've been a puppet… playing my part exactly as I was supposed to. There was no way around it. No matter which way I turned, it was the way you wanted me to turn…"

"Also correct," Adramelech replied gleefully.

Mary shook her head, "Corban, none of this matters!"

"How could it not?" Corban demanded as he turned to Mary, "My entire life has been engineered. All of this, everything I worked to achieve… it's all been for nothing… For fucking nothing!"

Mary grabbed Corban's hands and placed them over her heart with a hurt look on her face, "Nothing? You think this is nothing? My heart hasn't beat this hard in a very long time. Nothing has made me tense or worry... nothing until you came along. So parts of your life weren't what you thought they were. You're still you. The guy you are, they couldn't decide that for you! The decisions you made are still your own. You could have gone back to your grave. Instead you stayed on to help us fight. That was your choice, not theirs! Was it their choice that you and I got this close?"

"They certainly found a way to use it against us, didn't they?"

"Fuck them, who cares? We're still here, yeah? I'm still here and I'm not going anywhere. Why do you think Adramelech keeps trying to attack me?"

"…"

"No idea? Fine, I'll tell you. Since things didn't go as planned, our relationship has become a threat to him, plain and simple. I'm an obstacle he hasn't been able to overcome."

"Yet," Adramelech hissed.

"And you never will, asshole!"

Soul Siphon

Corban didn't know what to say. He was angry and frustrated at the same time. Mary's words were comforting, but nothing could have prepared him for this.

Mary's voice quivered as she continued, "Who you are may have been fixed, but it doesn't change what you are. You are an awesome guy… you have to be, you've held my attention for this long, yeah?"

Corban chuckled as she continued, "That is something they have no control over."

Corban looked up at Mary, "This doesn't bother you?"

"No, why would it? You can't help what others did to you as an infant. All you can do is cope with it, yeah? Do you want to be a puppet of theirs for the rest of your life?"

Corban peered deeply into Mary's eyes for a moment before smiling, "Hell no!"

He turned to Adramelech with a menacing look on his face, "Everything I had may not have been mine to claim, but you had no right taking it away from me. My life was still my own making! You will pay for what you've done!"

Adramelech threw back his head and roared as his peacock-like tail fully bloomed. Each eye on the tail shuddered and glowed. Corban could feel the energy that was accumulating in the creature's tail, giving it more power, "Everything I took from you, I replaced with something better. You lost a dying relationship and a non-existent family life. Look at what you've got in replacement; someone who actually wants to be with you and a family to call your own."

"And you killed one of them!"

"A regrettable loss, but a necessary one."

Soul Siphon

Corban clenched his jaw, "I don't think so...
you're done."

Mary pressed herself against Corban's side and
grinned at him, "So, no hands on me unless they're
yours?"

"Nope," Corban replied as though he were
laying down the law.

"Then let's kick this demon's ass. If we both
survive the day... I'll let you put your hands anywhere
you want."

"I'll hold you to that."

The moment was spoiled by a loud roar as
Adramelech's head came back down towards them.
The demon brought his eyes to bear and glared at
them. The menacing look on its face was enough to
make the bravest man's blood run cold.

"Oh, shit..."

"Mary watch out!" Corban screamed as a blue
blast emanated from Adramelech's eyes.

Mary maneuvered out of the way using her
inhuman speed but was barely able to avoid the
demon's attack. Corban clenched his fists at his sides,
"No, you're not going to take them from me too! You
took everything else, now it's my turn!"

Corban took a running leap off of the platform
and landed on Adramelech's chest. Mary screamed
when she saw what he was doing, "Corban no, he's
too powerful! It won't work!"

Her words went unheard. Corban latched on and
began channeling his siphoning abilities through his
hands. He closed his eyes and focused as his hands
began to glow.

Wave upon wave of intense energy entered his
body. The force was like being hit by a massive titles
wave that he was not prepared for. His head filled with
the screams of all of Adramelech's victims. The

Soul Siphon

screams of babies and the people he possessed echoed through Corban's mind like a pendulum swinging back and forth, striking the sides of his head. He closed his eyes, trying to absorb the energy, but it was too much for him. He screamed as waves and waves of pain overtook his mind.

Corban thought for certain that he was about to die as the pain became agonizing. The conditioning that Mary had put him through had not worked. He could not control the flood of energy that was entering his body. His eyes blurred out for a moment before he felt a hand grasp his arm while another one wrapped around his chest. There was a sudden pressure in both places as Corban felt himself being yanked away from Adramelech.

Corban's vision cleared. The wiry, patchy hair of Adramelech's chest was replaced by Mary's long red hair. She pulled him back to a safe distance and held on tight as she laid him down, "You idiot! What did you think you were going to accomplish? You think you can take him on all by yourself? You can't!"

Corban's breathing was labored. It was as though someone was lying on his chest as he tried to take in air. When he was finally able to take enough into his lungs he opened his eyes and forced out a few words, "The feathers… attack the feathers… he has to be weakened! The feathers conduct his energy!"

Mary nodded, "All right, I'll take care of it. You rest, yeah? You need your strength to finish him off."

Mary drew her daggers and looked at the one from her room. She quickly kissed the handle, "Lisa, Maggie, Tobias, Giovanni… Lihua, this one's for you!"

She dashed at the demon and attacked. Her powers allowed her to dodge around Adramelech's

Soul Siphon

blasts and make her way to his tail feathers. Using her impressive speed to her advantage, she severed three of the eye-like feathers in a matter of seconds before turning and retreating far enough away that she was out of his reach.

Vlad looked at her oddly, "Mary, vat are you doing?"

"Attack the feathers!" She replied. "We can weaken him that way!"

Adramelech laughed, "If you think I'm going to just let you destroy my mane, you're far more foolish than I thought. Back down and leave this place, and I may let you survive the coming apocalypse."

"No dice," Mary replied. "I don't really care much for the world, but I'm not letting you hurt my friends. This is it for you, Adramelech. I hope it's not too hot where you're going."

Corban looked on in fear as Johnny jumped from the platform and landed on Adramelech's head. While Mary and Vlad focused on the feathers, Johnny touched Adramelech's left eye. He focused his powers and waited to see what happened.

Adramelech tried to swat Johnny away, but its arms weren't long enough to reach his face. It tried blinking, but Johnny was able to dodge around the massive eyelashes as he worked. There was nothing the creature could do to rid itself of this pest. All it could do was try shaking it off violently by jerking its head to the side.

Adramelech let out a deafening roar as Johnny slowly withered his eye away, "Fool! My eye will be regenerated in seconds. What do you hope to accomplish? Your powers are too weak!"

Once the eye had been destroyed, Johnny jumped to the next one, narrowly missing Adramelech's enormous claws. His powers did the same thing to his right eye as they had to his left. This gave Mary and Vlad all the time they needed to slice away at the endless feathers.

Mary brought her blade around again, "Good Johnny, keep him blind!"

Corban clenched his head as he tried to sort out the voices in his mind. They were loud and unbearable, but Corban knew he needed to hold on to the energy. He needed to be able to hold out in case his friends needed help. The screams harbored powers that he could harness if only he could hold on to them, as well as his sanity, for a little while longer.

It was not easy. Corban managed to silence a scream or two within minutes, but the rest of them cried out in unison like a church choir. It was becoming impossible to handle.

Mary danced around another attack but was inadvertently hit by one of Adramelech's claws as he thrashed about, blinded by Johnny's attacks. She was thrown across the room and struck the back wall hard. Jagged rocks sliced her face open as her body slid to the ground. The impact stunned her to the point where she lay partially paralyzed on the ground in front of Adramelech. She struggled to pull herself away as the demon regained his sight. The scars on her face quickly disappeared as she looked up at it, "Aw shit…"

Adramelech looked down at her with a malice-filled grin, "Now you die!"

The demon lunged towards her with his mouth opened. Mary could feel the heat and smell the rancid fragrance of a thousand consumed souls on his breath. She closed her eyes, knowing that she was about to die.

Corban opened his eyes and saw what was happening. The screams were still agonizing, but he

Soul Siphon

knew that if he didn't do something, he'd lose the only friends he had left. As the screams once again combined into a choir, Corban pressed his hands to his temples and clenched every muscle he could, "For fuck's sake, be quiet!"

The voices instantly stopped, allowing him to focus on what was happening around him. His eyes began to glow as he thrust his hands forward. The glow spread to his fingers as they began to pulse with energy. He channeled all of his anger and frustration into his left hand and forced the energy from his body. A light blue beam shot from his hand and lit up the entire room as it blazed towards its target.

Adramelech didn't see it coming until it was too late to move out of the way. The beam struck its lower jaw, instantly vaporizing it. The creature screamed out in pain as it backed away from Mary and reached for its attacker.

Corban dodged the first attack and released a second beam with the other arm. This one struck the ceiling of the necropolis and bore a hole to the surface. A small ray of sunshine appeared as he continued to force more energy into the beam.

On the surface, the ground shook like an earthquake was beginning to make itself known. The ground at the center of the ruined city erupted in blue energy that shot straight up into the sky. The beam penetrated the dark veil that Adramelech had covered the area with and shattered it.

Sunlight poured into the cave and scorched Adramelech's skin. The demon let out another agonizing cry as it struggled to shield itself from the sunlight. It flailed its arms about, trying to cover it's more vital areas from being exposed.

Desperate to end the fight quickly, Adramelech turned and reached for Corban, "Now you die!"

Soul Siphon

Before Adramelech could lay a finger on Corban, Mary jumped in front of them and drove her sword into his wrist and ran the blade from one side to the other. His hand fell off and quickly turned to dust as it hit the floor.

Adramelech scoffed as another hand grew in to replace it. As his jaw and hand slowly regenerated, Mary dodged around Adramelech's hands to give Corban enough time to get away. Vlad continued to hurl his knives at the feathers while Johnny withered ones from the other side when he wasn't focused on the demon's eyes.

Vlad smiled, "We're getting zere! Keep up ze pressure!"

"Easy for you to say!" Johnny replied. "I have to keep dodging eyelashes the size of fucking whips here! We can't all just sit there and throw knives from the back row!"

"Less talk, Johnny! Ve're about half way zere! Not much longer!"

Johnny shook his head as Adramelech began shaking from the loss of power. The rage in its damaged eyes was more than apparent as they burned red. Corban watched as the team worked, "We're winning… but this isn't over yet…"

The demon's attacks became more and more vicious. It alternated between throwing fists in random directions to energy beams that shot out across the room. Adramelech apparently no longer cared if the necropolis collapsed. It seemed to be completely focused on eraticating Corban and his friends, at any costs.

Vlad took a step backward defensively as a massive fist landed near him, knocking over one of the stone pylons that help up the room, "Oh zis is no good."

Soul Siphon

Mary seized on the opportunity and took to the walls at high speed. She used her inertia to push against the wall until she was high enough to reach the demon's feathers. In one fell swoop, she sliced away the remaining feathers.

Adramelech fell to its knees, completely cut off from its powers. Its breathing became labored as it fought to regain some control. It looked exhausted as though it were carrying a large boulder on its back.

This was Mary's chance. Corban watched as her legs propelled her onto the back of its neck. She quickly climbed to the top of its head, dodging its attempts to grab her, and plunged her dagger into its skull right between the ears. Exhausted, Mary used her remaining energy to drive the dagger as deeply as possible. When the hilt reached its skin, she threw her left arm into the air and cheered, "Vengeance!"

Adramelech roared in pain as it turned to deal with Mary. She attempted to dodge away, but the demon was too fast for her worn out legs. Its massive hand impacted against her right side, sending her flying against the opposite wall.

Mary grunted as her body hit the wall a second time. The blow caught her off guard and knocked her senseless for a moment as she fell to the ground. Her head spun as she attempted to get back to her feet. Her legs gave out as she attempted to push herself up. Though her vision was blurred, she was able to see what was left of the blade that she had attacked with. Most of it had broken off in Adramelech's skull, where it would be impossible to draw out.

She let out a satisfied sigh as she rolled onto her back. *You have been avenged, my friends...*

Mary knew that the battle wasn't over. Adramelech had to be finished off or he would just regenerate. She quickly located Corban on the other

Soul Siphon

side of the room, "Now, kill the beast while it's vulnerable!"

Corban stepped forward, "My mother, Janine, Lihua, and my life. You've taken all of them from me, Adramelech! I'm taking them back!"

Corban clenched his jaw and charged forward. He could sense fear in the demon's eyes as it turned, too late, to try and block Corban's attack. The demon's fist missed their target by less than a foot as Corban took a flying leap onto the demon's chest and once again planted his hands on it.

"No!" Adramelech cried out.

It quickly used its right arm to bat Corban away. The blow reminded Corban of when he'd hit the side of the warehouse when he learned to fly. He landed a few feet back as Adramelech unleashed a yellow beam of energy on him. There was almost no time for him to dodge out of the way. Instead, he unleashed his own energy in a yellow beam.

Both combatants forced every shard of energy they had available into their hands to power their attacks. Adramelech no longer had access to its infinite powers, but it still had enough to take on Corban. It continued to force the energy beam at its opponent, intent on killing him this time.

There was nothing more anyone could do to help. The team had done all they could to weaken the demon for Corban, now it was his turn. He had his jaw clenched as he forced as much energy as he could into his beam, but it didn't look like he could hold out much longer. His skin began to look disheveled and his nose began dripping blood.

Mary got to her feet and held onto the wall behind her, still clearly stunned by the blow, "Find the strength within, Corban! You can do this!"

Soul Siphon

Corban heard her words of encouragement and pushed harder as Adramelech began to shrink. It appeared that the more energy the demon used, the smaller it got. It wouldn't be long before he was looking into its eyes at equal height.

Corban forced more energy into his arms as his muscles clenched. He had to end this quickly and he knew it. The first step forward was agonizing, but a sense of satisfaction filled his heart as he planted his right foot on the ground in front of him. Another step followed, and another, and another. Blood was now gushing from his nose as he stepped closer and closer to Adramelech. *One more step and I'll be close enough... just one more step.*

Adramelech was now barely a foot taller than Corban. This was his chance. He pushed as much as he could with his legs and lunged forward.

His efforts paid off when the palms of his hands impacted against those of Adramelech's. The beams of energy disappeared as Corban clasped his hands around the demon's fingers and held on as tightly as he could. *Gotcha!*

Corban's eyes glowed bright blue that quickly began to spread over his body. Adramelech's screaming just prompted Corban to force his hands harder onto the demon's palms. Just as Corban was beginning to glow blue, Adramelech's arms started glowing red. The hideous glow slowly spread over the demon's body. This was now a battle of spiritual auras.

Adramelech's red specter decreased in size as power was drawn from it into Corban's blue form. They glowed brightly as they hovered above the ground for a few moments. Corban's blue form became more and more luminescent with each passing second.

Soul Siphon

Time seemed to stand still as she watched the two glowing forms hovering motionless. It was a sight that would otherwise have been beautiful to her eyes, but right now it represented something horrible that could cost her the last connection she had to the human world. Fear of the impending doom that lay ahead of her gripped her heart as she watched.

Mary held out a hope that the fate that she feared most would pass Corban by. She hoped that somehow he would be able to fend off the temptations, considering he survived the demonic onslaught at all. Her hands shook and she had to resist the urge to interfere, knowing that it wouldn't do any good.

Her hope was all but crushed as the two entities began to spin around each other, slowly at first, then picking up speed as though locked in combat. The forms moved so quickly that the air around them was sent flying towards Corban's friends. It picked up sand and slowly took on the form of a wave as it traveled.

Johnny got behind Vlad as the Russian spread his feet apart and ducked down to prevent being knocked over by the wind. They did the best they could to take their eyes off the spiritual battle that was unfolding in front of them for as little time as possible, all afraid that if they lingered too long, Adramelech would win. They couldn't see much more than a multi-colored aura through the cloud of sand.

The two spirits swirled until they became one. The blue and red parts merged and became a dark purple. The formless mass pulsed three times before slowly taking human form. The mass grew arms, legs, and began to form a head.

Everyone waited to see what would happen. Would it be Corban returning to them, or Adramelech? The fate of this battle came down to whatever was about to happen.

Soul Siphon

Mary watched quietly. Her chest felt tight as though her heart had completely stopped beating. She knew that even if Corban came out, they would still have a ways to go before they could declare victory. If he had absorbed the demon's powers, he could be an even greater threat.

To the team's relief, the purple outline landed on the ground and transformed back into Corban. He dropped to one knee for a moment to regain his composure. Blood and sweat poured off his body as he stared at the ground.

Mary watched as Corban absorbed the last of Adramelech's energy into his body. The pulses continued every few moments. It was an incredible strain on Corban's own life force as he struggled to keep hold of his own energy while attempting to control Adramelech's.

On the outside, the battle seemed to be over. Corban had absorbed Adramelech and appeared to have killed him. The room was completely quiet as the group watched Corban nervously.

Mary reached out her right hand as she regained her footing and moved closer to Corban, "Corban... focus. This is no ordinary soul you've absorbed, yeah? Please don't let it corrupt you!"

"It's okay... I'm okay. I've got this..."

Mary wasn't certain that she believed him, "How do you feel?"

Corban closed his eyes and gently tensed his muscles. It was as though he was scanning his own mind for any issues. He smiled as he responded, "I think I can handle this... I have the reigns."

Mary breathed a sigh of relief as it appeared that her faith in Corban was justified. He was still at risk and even Mary could feel the energy blazing off of him, but for the moment, he appeared to still have control, "Maybe you should release some of the energy. You don't want to take any chances, yeah?"

"Yeah… no problem… I… I… sho…"

A red hue flickered through his pupils. He grabbed his stomach and leaned forward before dropping to his knees, "Urgh!"

"Corban, what is it?" Mary asked in alarm.

"I can feel him. Adramelech… this fight isn't over!"

Corban squeezed his eyes closed every few seconds as Vlad and Johnny appeared next to them in the dimly lit room. Johnny peered into his eyes and saw that they were alternating between black and red, "Not good… there's a fight going on in there. I've seen this before."

Mary began to panic, "Corban, release some of the power now while you still can!"

Her words came too late. Corban stopped wincing and stood up with a smile on his face, "I… can feel the power flowing through me. I can direct it anywhere and make it do anything. It's so intense. I feel like there is no limit to this. How much damage can I undo? How many of Adramelech's victims can I heal?"

"No!" Mary screamed as tears entered her eyes. "God, no... Please!"

A nervous look came over Johnny's face, "It's happening again."

Mary's mind immediately returned to that horrible day. The day that she had to kill Lisa. Her heart raced as the familiar feeling of dread came over her. The fear was amplified a hundred times in her heart. It felt as though someone had driven an ice spike through her chest and was trying to force it deeper. Her hands began a panic-induced quiver. She found it impossible to control the tremor in her voice as she

Soul Siphon

spoke, "Corban, you remember what we talked about, yeah? You can't hang onto it, you promised me! Let it go. Listen to what I'm saying to you and release this power before it corrupts you too much!"

"Mary, it's okay! I have control... I can wield it!"

"No!" Mary screamed. "No, you can't! You think you can, but it's not possible! Please, release it!"

"Release it?" Corban scoffed, barely even listening anymore. "Why, the power here is so intense. Just think of what we can do with it. Think of what we can accomplish together! I can stop evil, pain, suffering, depravity, and establish peace! Think about it we can eliminate evil altogether. With this power, I can create the perfect world... no more hatred, war, or killing!"

"It's a beautiful thought," Johnny admitted, "I'd be almost tempted to let you try, but the prospect is an illusion. You're not a demon or an angel, you can't control these powers because they weren't meant for you. They're not naturally yours and you don't have the physical ability to control them. They'll end up controlling you."

"How do you know? If I'm strong enough, I can handle it. Why not let me try?"

"Because it's not worth risking your life!" Mary insisted. "Or that of the entire planet. Please see reason! I... we can't afford to lose you!"

"Where should I start?" Corban asked. "Perhaps I should begin with exterminating the murderers, then move my way down to rapists, abusers, adulterers, druggies, thugs... It would not take much. A simple flick of the wrist and I could eliminate them all!"

Mary went pale and looked like she was going to get sick, "Corban... please, you're allowing that power to corrupt your soul! Let it go, please! Remember your promise! Remember me… remember us!"

"You think I've forgotten?" Corban scoffed as his eyes turned red. "Do you want to spend the rest of your days fighting and killing endlessly?"

"With you by my side? I could think of worse things, yeah?"

"Oh please..," Corban scoffed. "Wouldn't it be nice to not have to worry? Wouldn't you like to eventually live in peace? To be able to get back what we were robbed of?"

"I don't know that world anymore, Corban. I only know the one I live in, it's not perfect, but its mine, yeah? I'm fine with it."

Vlad stepped forward, "Corban knows better! Zere is no destroying all evil as long as people exist. Even if it vere possible, no von person should have zat kind of power! Ours is a job zat can never be complete."

It almost seemed like Corban barely even knew that his friends were there, "You don't understand… none of you do. You couldn't possibly comprehend the power that I have won. I am transcending beyond the limited understanding that humanity has of power and morality. I see the universe like none other. I…"

"Enough!" Mary shouted. "Corban, you promised! Focus on me! Look into my eyes! See what you have here! Release that power, now!"

Corban's eyes glowed red and he thrust his arm forward, "Silence!"

Mary went flying backward and hit the ground a few feet away. She hadn't fully recovered from the previous blow and had to hold on to the wall as she stood up again. Blood dripped from her lip, which she quickly wiped away as she clenched her jaw.

Soul Siphon

At that moment, Xaphine appeared on the scene. The look on her face was pure rage. She had seen what had happened and was now there to correct it. Upon seeing her, Vlad and Johnny backed away, fearing the immortal battle that was likely to unfold.

Corban had a gleeful look in his eyes, "Xaphine, we did it. We've won! Look what I've become! Now I can truly fight demons, just like we said."

Xaphine looked at Corban like someone would look at maggots in a rotten piece of fruit. Her lips curled into a sneer as she spoke, "Yes, look at you."

Xaphine's eyes began glowing red as she pointed to Mary. The volume of her voice increased to the point where she was yelling, "Look at what you've done! Look how you've treated the person who has been there for you since the beginning!"

Corban followed her hand and looked at Mary. A regretful expression appeared in his eyes. He'd hurt her. It was something that he never wanted to do, and it made his heartache. The redness in his eyes slowly began to shift to black, "I… I didn't mean to… I'm doing this for her!"

"You think this is an improvement? If you're capable of doing that, what else do you think you can do? This is the demonic taint that you have fought so hard to defeat and now you're welcoming it with open arms. That demon is billions of years older than you and you think that you can control his powers? The arrogance!"

Xaphine was fed up. She'd heard justifications like this before and to her, Corban's protests were no different, "Release the power, now!"

"I can't," Corban said, regretfully, almost seeming like he'd regained some of his humanity. "There is too much at stake… too much. It's for the greater good."

Soul Siphon

"Too many horrors have been committed for the greater good and you know it!" Xaphine hissed. "Too many people have died for the best of intentions... I cannot allow this to continue. I'm sorry, Corban ..."

Xaphine thrust her right hand forward, "... but if you won't listen to reason, then I have to take you down myself. I don't want to do this, but you've left me no other choice!"

"Xaphine, no!" Mary replied. "He's still in there!"

Xaphine lowered her eyes, acknowledging Mary, "I know he is, but he's buried too deep for us to get to him."

"Give him a chance..."

"I already have. I can't allow this to go any further. I am sorry."

White spectral beams emanated from Xaphine's fingers and shot towards Corban. The red in Corban's eyes suddenly flared as he faced down his former ally, "I don't think so!"

The moment the beam was close enough, Corban grabbed hold of it as though it were a rope and absorbed it into his right arm. He then thrust his left arm forward, emanating a dark energy beam at Xaphine.

The angel tried to block the beam with her wings, but it was too powerful. She was knocked on her back as black beam entered her chest and drained some of her energy. She was incapacitated from the energy loss.

Corban sighed in disgust, "Angels..."

The energy he'd stolen from Xaphine pushed him over the edge. His skin began glowing again. This time, he became a bright white entity with lighting-like pulses flowing all over the form.

Soul Siphon

Vlad took another step back, "Zis is no good... I can feel ze power flowing from Corban. If zis doesn't stop, Corban vill soon be beyond us!"

"Corban, please!" Mary replied, slowly embracing the horror that she wasn't getting through to him.

Johnny shook his head, "Mary... I'm sorry. It's not happening. If we allow his powers to manifest much longer there will be no way of stopping him. He can't control what's happening. I know it's not his fault, but we need to stop him while we still can!"

Mary squeezed her eyes closed as they teared up, "Johnny, no..."

"You know what you have to do. You're the only one who can. None of us could get close enough!"

Mary didn't move. She didn't want to do it. Corban, like the others, only had everyone's best intentions at heart. Mary wanted to try again, but even she could feel the increase of energy he was emanating.

There was no way around it, he had to be stopped. Mary desperately tried one last time, "Corban, please... release the energy! I... You have to, please!"

Corban wasn't listening anymore. His entire body began to glow brighter than before. He was even more powerful than Lisa or any of the others who had come before them.

Nothing Mary could say was going to change anything. She looked at him with anger in her eyes, "You lied to me."

Fire entered her eyes, turning them red enough to match her hair, "You promised me... I trusted you!"

An empowered look came over her face as she slowly stepped forward, "I know what I have to do."

Soul Siphon

She drew what was left of her dagger and shot herself behind Corban. The broken blade still had more than enough of a point to drive into him. A sense of determination entered Mary's soul as she took another step. She managed to get within a few inches of him and was lining up for the final blow.

At that moment, to Johnny and Vlad's horror, she threw her blade away. Before anyone could react, she jumped on Corban's back and wrapped her arms around him. Her eyes closed as she pressed her head into his back and whispered, "Please... hear me."

Corban's form spoke in an annoyed tone, "Why is this so important to you? Why can't we try? What does it matter to you what happens?"

Mary sighed as she closed her eyes and squeezed him tightly, "Because... I don't want to lose you. Because... I can't..."

"Why?"

"Shit, you're really going to make me say it?"

There was a slight tremor in Corban's powers. Xaphine felt it, bringing her back to consciousness. She sat up and looked at what was going on. She heard Corban and Mary's exchange and saw that she was somehow getting through to him. She clenched her fists as she looked at them. *Tell him, Mary. It's the only way you can save him. Find the strength to open up and tell him! It's your only chance!*

Corban looked back at Mary as she held on tight, "I asked you a question, why?"

Mary sucked down a deep breath and finally released the words she'd wanted to say for weeks, "Because... I love you!"

"What?" Corban demanded.

"You're deaf, yeah? I said I love you, you idiot!"

Soul Siphon

The words pierced through his heart, causing it to ache like never before. Mary might as well have stabbed him with her daggers. It might have actually been less painful. Corban clenched his eyes closed and pushed at the energy within his being. *What am I doing... what have I become...? Oh God, no!*

There was an extreme sensation that overtook him as the rush of energy flowed from his body. *I don't want it... I don't want it... I don't fucking want it!*

Corban threw back his head and screamed, "Get it out!"

The feeling was intense and quickly overwhelmed Corban's senses. A massive energy beam flowed out of his body and shot into the heavens. The beam penetrated the cloud above Carthage, obliterating it and then shot out into space.

Dust and debris fell from the ceiling of the cavern as the rush of energy caused an earthquake that rattled the ancient foundation. The debris was followed by massive blocks of stone and damaged columns.

Johnny jumped closer to Vlad and Xaphine, "This place is going to shake itself apart if this keeps up!"

"Is too heavily damaged from ze fight!"

At that moment, a column came crashing down on top of them, "Oh shit!"

Xaphine followed Johnny's gaze and saw the column coming down. She raised her arm, creating a force field that protected Johnny and Vlad from the falling stones. Xaphine then looked back at Corban, "He's almost drained... just a little bit more!"

Corban pushed hard, one last time. He was able to force the last of the tainted energy out of his soul and breathed a sigh of relief as the beam dissipated.

Soul Siphon

The energy drain was intense, causing him to collapse. Within seconds, his world faded to black.

Soul Siphon

XXIII

Corban opened his eyes and found himself in a black void. There was nothing nearby that was visible, just the ground underneath him. It reminded him of when he was possessed. This was the type of cage that Adramelech kept him in. The only difference was that he could hear what his body was doing. In this void, there was nothing but silence. *No… could it be happening all over again? Did Adramelech win?*

As though responding to his thoughts, a pair of red eyes appeared in the darkness, "So Corban, here we are again."

A sinking feeling entered Corban's stomach, he had lost and was once again a prisoner, "Adramelech… or should I call you Moloch? How about Mike?"

"Whatever you call me is irrelevant. You have my power now."

Corban couldn't believe what he was hearing. Was Adramelech admitting defeat? "Yeah, and?"

"If you force me out again, you'll give up on everything you hope to accomplish. Think about it, you'll be sacrificing your chance to rid the world of evil and finally be able to fight beings like me!"

Now Corban understood. The demon was trying to tempt him. As long as the creature's powers existed, it would continue to linger. "I understand."

Adramelech could feel itself slipping away, "You fool, stop!"

"Sorry, times up for you. You've had your fun, but all good things end. Time for you to go!"

"I have existed since the dawn of time. It means nothing to me."

Soul Siphon

"It will now, you've existed far too long. You're done. I cast you out now, not into the pit from whence you came but into oblivion where you belong!"

"All this for that red-headed whore? Is she really worth giving up everything these powers offer?"

"Worth it and more… but it's not just for her, it's for me as well. Besides, keeping those powers doesn't feel right. I don't particularly care for whom I'd have to thank for having god-like abilities."

Corban closed his eyes and pushed ever harder, "I won once again you son of a bitch!"

Adramelech cried out in pain as it quickly faded into nothingness, "No!"

Corban's eyes opened and he found himself back in the cavern where he belonged. He felt a massive orb of energy in his chest and thrust his hands upwards. He screamed as one last massive pylon of white energy flew from his body straight up into the heavens. This was more of Adramelech's power. He neither wanted nor needed it.

The beam dissipated, leaving Corban in his original form. Sunlight poured into the massive chamber from the surface as he breathed a sigh of relief and turned to Mary, who had finally let go of him, "It's over, we won!"

Horror overtook Corban's world when he saw what had happened. Mary was lying on her back looking at him. Her face had gone pale and her hair was fading to match. She was aging at an accelerated rate, "I know we did… you kept your promise."

"Mary, what happened?"

Mary smiled, "I don't know how, but the rush of energy drained me of the power Adramelech gave me. When you expelled all that power, it dragged my immortality with it."

"You saved me…"

Soul Siphon

"Least I could do, yeah?"

"No…"

Xaphine watched from afar as Johnny and Vlad ran over to her, "Mary, no… vat happened!"

Corban looked over at Vlad with tears in his eyes, "She's dying!"

Mary's red hair slowly turned white. She reached up to Corban and wiped away the tear that was making its way down his cheek, "No crying, yeah? You kept your promise to me. I couldn't ask for anymore."

Corban's breathing intensified as he channeled the energy to his hands again. Vlad looked at him oddly, "Vat are you doing?"

"My power stole her immortality, maybe I can give it back!"

Corban held his right hand over Mary's head and forced the energy from his hand, creating a force field around her. It flickered for a moment and then disappeared. He tried again with the same result.

Xaphine frowned, "It won't work."

"How so?" Corban demanded. "Adramelech's power gave her this immortality, it can do it again!"

Corban tried a third time, this time holding his power in check. This time, instead of a pulse, his energy formed a beam that shot from his hand and quickly engulfed Mary's body. It was far brighter than the previous attempts.

Mary lay back with a content look on her face. She was certain that his efforts wouldn't be enough to save her, but she was happy in that he cared enough to try. Being wanted was a feeling that she'd all but forgotten about.

Corban clenched every muscle in his body. He was in intense pain as the energy drained from his being. Beads of sweat formed on his skin as he

Soul Siphon

pushed. The pain quickly overwhelmed his senses and his hand began to tremble to the point where he was unable to direct the beam correctly. The field around Mary slowly faded away just as the others had.

Corban slammed his fist on the ground, "Damn it, no!"

Mary reached up and touched his face, "It's okay hero, you tried. It's okay."

"That's not good enough."

Mary's hair was almost completely white now. Corban leaned forward and kissed her deeply for as long as he could. When he finally pulled away to catch his breath, Mary could see that tears were pouring from his eyes. He knew that there was no way to save her, "I'm sorry..."

"You did everything you could."

Scars appeared on her face as she continued to age, "Corban... look away... remember me as I was. I don't want this to be your last image of me, please."

Corban held her close and closed his eyes. Mary looked over at Johnny, "Look after him for me, yeah?"

Johnny lowered his eyes but did not respond as Mary's skin ripped itself apart and she began to revert to how she looked after she had been murdered. She released her last breath as the skin on her face was peeled away and her wounds reopened. A second later, her body turned to dust. There was nothing left for Corban to hold on to.

Corban looked down at the small piles of dust on the ground around him, "I love you too..."

In the back of Corban's mind, he heard the sound of deep laughter. He wasn't certain if his mind was playing tricks on him, or if Adramelech was still in there. It taunted him to the point of rage. His whole body began to shake has his face turned red.

Soul Siphon

As though still possessed, Corban rose to his feet without using his hands. It looked like an invisible force had picked him up from behind. His eyes were still glowing red as they fixed on Xaphine.

An apologetic look appeared on Xaphine's face as she took a step forward, "Corban, I'm so sorry. I didn't think it would go this way."

Corban took a step forward but remained silent. Johnny looked at him oddly, "Corban what..."

It immediately became apparent that Corban hadn't given up all of Adramelech's power. It wasn't enough for the demon to manifest itself, but it was just enough for Corban to make himself more powerful than he had been previously. He clenched his jaw as his glare cut into Xaphine, "You give her back!"

Xaphine's eyes widened, she hadn't expected this reaction from him, "Corban, I can't. Angels can't undo the actions of a demon. That is outside of our scope. All we can do is try to help with the mending. I am sorry my friend, I..."

"Don't give me that!" Corban yelled in an almost inhuman voice. "I know what you can do and I know that it was within your power to save Mary! I saw your past and since when do you care so much about the rules?"

"Corban, I told you before... it doesn't work like that. I can't..."

"Give her back!"

"Corban..."

"Give her back!"

"See reason!"

"Fucking give her back!"

Xaphine snorted as her lips curled into a vicious frown, "No!"

Corban's fists glowed as he thrust them forward, sending a blast of dark energy in Xaphine's direction.

Soul Siphon

The hit impacted on her shoulder, causing a dark red burn. The redness disappeared quickly, but the pain lingered long enough to trigger an angry presence within Xaphine.

The angel drew on her own power and sent a white spectral beam at Corban in retaliation, "How dare you!"

The beam struck the left side of Corban's face, blowing it clear off. Part of his lower left jawbone was momentarily visible before the flesh regenerated around it. He clenched his muscles until the pain subsided.

The moment Corban was able, he wound up for another attack. Xaphine stood firm, ready to counter when Johnny quickly jumped between them, "Enough you two! This isn't going to solve anything. You can't kill each other, so knock it the fuck off! Mary would not want this!"

Xaphine lowered her hands, "He's right... I apologize."

Corban turned his back on her. He was done. After everything that had happened, he'd lost too much to tolerate the words of another immortal being.

Xaphine turned to Johnny, "You three have my eternal gratitude, as well as that of the entire celestial world."

"Fuck that," Corban replied, not listening. "Those are pretty hollow words for what's been done and what you refuse to undo."

Xaphine's eyes suddenly glowed white, "I speak now as the voice of the Celestial World. Because of your service, and the circumstances of your resurrection, we are prepared to make you an offer."

"Vats zat?" Vlad asked.

"I can take you on into the next life. You'll receive a reprieve for any wrongdoing that you may have done, though I doubt that there is any given who you'd been killing."

Xaphine sucked down a deep breath, "Or…"

"Or?" Johnny asked.

"You have two other options; you can be relieved of your powers and given a second chance at life, or you can continue the fight against evil."

That caught Johnny by surprise, "Continue the fight, but I thought you said that we'd caused a ton of damage? You really want us out there running amuck? How are we even supposed to know who the evil is without Mike's guidance?"

"You did cause damage," Xaphine replied, "but you'd be under my guidance from now on, and you'd mostly be focused on demons, rogue supernatural creatures, and the people that help them. You'd be surprised how many there are."

Vlad looked over at Corban as he considered his options, "Zen ve'd need Corban. He's ze only von vith powers to kill zese creatures!"

"Yes…" Xaphine said hesitantly.

Vlad, Johnny, and Xaphine all looked over at Corban as she continued, "That option is only valid if Corban agrees."

Corban turned back and glared at Xaphine. He extended his hand as though he were about to unleash another beam, but stopped at the last second. He'd regained his senses at the last possible second. He lowered his fist, but held his gaze, "Fuck you! You're not putting this on me!"

Xaphine stepped forward," Corban, I understand you're upset, but…"

"Where were all of you when Adramelech did all this to me?" Corban demanded. "Where were you when we were brought back and made to fight? Where

Soul Siphon

were you when Mary lost her powers? Hell, where were you when all of this started in the first place?"

Xaphine didn't respond, opting instead to let Corban vent. It was a privilege that he had earned after all of his suffering.

"You could have protected her…"

Xaphine lowered her eyes, "I'm sorry, it's just not that simple. As I already said, angels can't undo what's been done. That's not within our powers, but you can still help prevent future tragedies like this."

Corban didn't look convinced and turned his back on them again. He was done listening, "Send me back to my grave… don't send me up to the next life, just blink me out of existence. I can't believe that the universe is this poorly run. If it is, I don't want to be a part of it."

Xaphine stepped forward and placed her hand on his shoulder, "Corban, please, the world still needs you. There is still so much you can do here."

Corban fought out of her grip and looked straight into her eyes, "Then give Mary back to me!"

"Corban, I can't…"

"I know because you can't undo Adramelech's work. Well if that's the case, then you're useless to me and have nothing to offer. Since you can't undo his work, I want to talk to someone who can. Tell your superiors, that if they want my help, I'm willing to give it, but only if they're willing to return her."

"You really want me to tell them that?"

"Yes, that is my price."

Xaphine's eyes narrowed, "Am I to understand that you intend to extort us?"

"If that's how you want to look at it, that's your problem. You all stood by and let demons influence every aspect of my life. You did nothing to stop them and now here I stand before you, the result. This whole

Soul Siphon

ordeal is more than I can stomach. Every fiber of my being is telling me to leave this entire existence to its own devices, but that's not who I am. Still, I think I deserve some form of reparation, but you've refused... and then you come to me and ask for my help?"

"So you're justifying extortion because you've got a grudge?"

"Yup."

A mischievous smile appeared on her face, replacing the angry look, "Very good."

Johnny looked at Xaphine oddly, "What?"

"Let's just say that Corban's right. I never was big on following the rules."

Xaphine turned her head to the side as though looking at someone behind her. She closed her eyes for a few moments and focused. Everyone watched and waited as she remained completely still.

No one knew what she was doing. Was she talking with her boss or was she putting on a show for them? Finally, she opened her eyes, "I've sent the message to the boss. I'm sure he'll love this."

Before she could say anything else, her body froze. She closed her eyes again and listened intently to a voice that none of the others present could hear. She turned back to Corban, "Well it appears that he agrees to your terms. Since you exist outside of life on this planet, it would not violate his decree. You continue the fight against evil and Mary will be returned to you."

Vlad stepped forward, "Vait, vat about Lihua?"

Xaphine frowned, "She got what she wanted when she killed her rapist... I'm sorry my friend, but she doesn't want to come back."

"At least she's found peace."

Xaphine turned back to Corban, "Do we have a deal?"

Soul Siphon

Corban turned, looked Xaphine in the eye, "Done."

At that moment, Corban felt a hand on his shoulder. He whirled around to see Mary smiling at him. Before he could say anything, she yanked him close and pressed her lips against his.

Corban's heart fluttered as he felt her embrace. Her heart raced as her hands ran up his spine. For a brief moment, everything seemed right with the world. However, the feeling was quickly replaced by waves of pain emanating from Corban's stomach. A round, blunt, object entered his belly and completely knocked the wind out of him.

Corban pulled away and fell to his knees, wheezing. A devious grin appeared on Mary's face as she lowered her fist, "That's for making me practically beg you to keep your promise. From now on, you do what you said you'd do or I'll kick your ass, yeah?"

Corban managed to force one word out, "Noted…"

"Good," Mary replied as she grabbed Corban by his shirt and pulled him back up on his feet.

Corban looked deep into her eyes, "Did you mean what you said?"

A stoic look appeared on her face, "You'll just have to find out I guess, won't you?"

Corban reached her cheek with his right hand and ran his fingers over her jawline. He then clenched the back of her neck and peered into her eyes, "Well I love you too."

Mary smiled and bit down on her lower lip. She squeezed her legs together as she spoke, "Oh don't get all mushy on me, yeah?"

Before Mary could say anything else that would spoil the moment, Corban pulled her in for another kiss. Mary gave up and closed her eyes. *There will be no living with him after this, now that he thinks he has me wrapped around his finger... Oh well...*

With Adramelech gone, things settled down for a little while, giving the team some time to rebuild their Boston hideout. Following the fire, a futile investigation, and the building being condemned, the team was able to reacquire it with the help of a few forged documents.

The weather had turned cold as Corban stood out on the roof, looking over the city. Each breath from his mouth was like a small cloud that quickly disappeared into the air. The hideout was almost completely rebuilt. There was some concern about demons knowing where they lived, but Xaphine sanctified the property and made a good point that this would be an effective way to draw demons to them as opposed to searching the world for them. *Home field advantage.*

Corban was lost in his thoughts. They had won, but he'd lost so much in the process. It was a tough pill to swallow, but having Mary around made it easier. There was also still the issue of replacing Lihua that was lingering over their heads. Would Xaphine keep the team as is, or would she offer another murdered soul the chance at revenge?

Mary joined Corban on the roof and gently rubbed his back as he kept his gaze on the city. She smiled as she leaned down next to him, "Penny for your thoughts, mister?"

"Cute..." Corban replied, sarcastically. "I was just thinking about my life. There are so many questions that I need answers to."

"I understand the temptation, but be careful. Some mysteries are better left unsolved, yeah?"

Soul Siphon

"I know... that's true, and given who's responsible, I probably won't like what I discover, but I have to know... You know, who Lilith Bonnaire really was… who my father is, and how things could have gone differently."

"Could have gone differently?"

Corban noticed a momentary hurt look on Mary's face that she quickly hid away. He sighed as he turned to her, "Not that I would want my life to be any different. I just need to know."

"Adramelech may have been lying to you about all of that. Could be a waste of time."

"I don't think he was. I just have a gut feeling that he was being honest. Either way, it's something that I need to figure out or else I'll go insane."

"Thoughts for later on."

"Maybe, but I still want to find who my father was at least."

"You will, don't worry. I'll be there to help you find those answers."

Corban nodded, but the distant look in his eyes had not gone away. There was something else still there. He still had some concern that was eating away at him.

Mary noticed it and turned to face him, "That's not all that's bothering you, yeah?"

"No, it's not."

"What then?"

Corban sighed, "It's not over. Adramelech has been destroyed, but his actions and the ripples in reality that he created still flow over this existence. I'm still here, the devil's host. My powers have grown as the result of our battle… and I'm sure he'll want to collect them at some point."

"And ven devil comes, ve vill be here to give devil his dues!"

Soul Siphon

Vlad appeared from the elevator behind them. Johnny also stepped out of the darkness and joined them on the roof, "Damn fucking straight! You bet your ass we will."

"I just hope it will be enough," Corban replied.

"Have faith, my friend," Xaphine said as she appeared out of the darkness on the opposite side of the roof. "Remember, you have divine support now. Things will be different, but hopefully, it will be an improvement."

Corban stood up, surrounded by his friends, "Then where do we begin?"

Xaphine looked out onto the city, "Rumor has it that Tetragrammaton sensed the death of Adramelech, and he's not happy. Apparently, he's stirring up trouble in the Holy Land. He's a lesser demon when compared to Adramelech, but he's still very slippery. I'll need time to figure out exactly what he's up to, but be ready to go at a moment's notice."

"We will be."

Mary admired Corban's determination as an idea entered her mind, "You know, though we never said it, Lihua was always sort of our leader in the field. With her gone, someone should step up."

"You?" Corban asked.

Mary laughed, "You're joking, yeah? I'm too much of a lone wolf on the field. I think you're the person we want."

"Zis is true!"

"Absolutely."

"It would be wise."

Corban looked each of them in the eye before responding. He wasn't prepared for this. The idea of a leadership role wasn't something he planned on. Then again, none of this had been planned, but there they

Soul Siphon

were. What choice did Corban truly have? "All right…
if you're sure."

He then turned back and looked out onto the city
with his friends at his side. The lights slowly turned on
to take over illuminating the buildings as the sunset on
the horizon. It was a tranquil moment that Corban
interpreted as the calm before the storm. There was
more to come, much more, and he had to be ready for
it.

*Those who have ears and are willing, let them
hear. The only ones who need fear us are those in
possession of an evil soul, those wicked creatures that
would prey on the weak and the innocent. We invite
them to run and hide for as long as they can, but know
that they will be hunted down and returned into fires
of Hell from whence they came. That is our purpose,
and that is our place... Caretakers to the world of
light... judgment to the world of darkness. We are
vengeance.*

*We've each lost much that can never be
regained, but we take solace in the fact that we've
dealt a crippling blow to the forces of evil. We will
now take the offensive against them.*

*To those who would stand against us, or simply
not know of us, I say this;*

*Innocent souls need not fear us. To them, we are
but a shadow in the darkness. To those in possession
of an evil soul, those wicked creatures who would prey
on innocent lives, we know who you are and we invite
you to run and hide for as long as you can, but know
that no matter where you go, no matter where you
hide, we will be there to chase you down and return
you to the towering fires of the pit from whence you
came.*

*To the devil himself, I say this… I know what
you've done, I know your plan, and I know you intend*

to move against me. When you do, know that I am
here… I will be waiting… and I will not be alone.

Soul Siphon

James Harrington:

James Harrington was born and raised in Boston, Massachusetts. He holds a Bachelor's in History, but also studied religion and how it related to his chosen subject matter. It was from those studies that Divinity was born.

James has written several essays and short stories, but had never gotten a full-length novel published until his big breakthrough with *Magnifica, The Last Enchanter*. Following its success, two more titles were added to the *Magnifica* series.

James currently lives in Massachusetts with his wife and son.

For more info on James and his books, please visit his Facebook page:

The Creative Works of James Harrington.
https://www.facebook.com/JamesHarringtonsMagnifica

Or his Blog page:
http://jamesharringtoncreativeworks.wordpress.com/

Soul Siphon

<u>Check out James' other novels</u>:

Magnifica: The Last Enchanter

Magnifica: Tears of the Fallen

Magnifica: Gravestalker

Divinity

Damnation

Soul Siphon